COFFEE AND GHOSTS 4: THE GHOSTS YOU LEFT BEHIND

THE COMPLETE FOURTH SEASON

CHARITY TAHMASEB

COLLINS MARK BOOKS

COPYRIGHT

CONTENTS

THE GHOSTS YOU LEFT BEHIND

MISTY SANDBORNE AND THE VAMPIRE HUSBAND

THE NECROMANCER'S NEPHEW

For Darcy

THE GHOSTS YOU LEFT BEHIND

COFFEE AND GHOSTS SEASON FOUR, EPISODE 1

CHAPTER 1

My grandmother had a never-fail solution when it came to catching ghosts: brew some coffee. We always served twelve cups: three black, three with sugar, three with cream, and three extra sweet and extra light. Because my grandmother always said, "Even ghosts have a preference."

Until they don't.

Or rather, they have so many that I'm not sure I can keep track. Our never-fail solution is failing—rapidly.

The aromatic scent of Kona blend fills the lobby of K&M Ghost Eradication Specialists. It mixes with the heady perfume of lilacs floating in a crystal bowl on the coffee table. Someone—possibly my business partner, Malcolm Armand—has scattered fashion magazines across the table's scratched surface. Usually, our customers don't visit us. When they do? They're not looking to update their style.

Instead, we go to them. After all, we are K&M Ghost Eradication Specialists, and even the friendliest sprite needs encouragement to vacate the premises.

Right now, two dozen of those sprites, each in a tiny Tupperware container, are bouncing around the lobby with gentle thump, thump, thumps. They're everywhere—underfoot, under the coffee table, and under the velvet in our storefront display.

I snag a container and bring it to eye level. The sprite inside dances—as much as the small space will allow. I try to gauge its intentions, its personality. Sprites don't have much of either, but they love attention, which is why you'll find them playing pranks at three in the morning.

This one swirls under my scrutiny and adds a flourish—definitely an attention seeker. I shift my grip and search for something more, something familiar. I run my fingers around the seam of the lid, hoping for a clue.

Nothing, not even a whisper. I've never caught this one before.

Still, it's sweet and not much of a threat. I hand the Tupperware to Tara Davenport, our pre-teen summer intern. "What do you think? Gold star?"

Since the ghosts can't—or won't—stay in any one place, we've been using star stickers to keep track of the ones we've cataloged. Gold for good, silver for iffy, and red for an all-out troublemaker.

Tara nods, the beads in her hair jangling in a way that sets off the sprites around her. The beads are translucent, almost like little ghosts at the tip of each braid. I'm guessing the sprites approve of this fashion choice.

"Yes," she says and pulls a sticker from a sheet. With the utmost care, she places it on the side of the container. The sprite inside does a backflip.

"Does it have a name?"

Tara is only twelve. In some ways, she's more attuned to the supernatural than even the most experienced necromancer. The sprites see her as a compatriot, one of them, more so than all the adults trying to catch and catalog them.

"Unicorn." She rolls her eyes and bites her lip. "It says its name is Unicorn."

Laughter comes from the laptop on the receptionist's desk.

Malcolm and I have never had a receptionist—or much for them to do. Still, we have a desk, and today it's coming in handy.

On the laptop's screen, Malcolm's brother Nigel Armand taps away at his own keyboard. "Unicorn number nineteen, now logged."

I shut my eyes and sigh. I'd bet my stash of one hundred percent Kona that not one of these sprites is actually named Unicorn.

Nigel laughs again, and even Tara giggles.

"Not to worry," he says. "I've got other key identifiers for them."

I nod like I know what that means. Nigel is revamping our database. Since all these new ghosts came to town, we've struggled to keep track of them. This database will, in theory, help us catch them in the future. Nigel claims he can create a mobile app for our phones. Enter a few details, and up pops a ghostly candidate.

In theory.

Right now? We have a lobby full of sprites and not much else, which is why it's good he's working from home. Even though his addiction to swallowing ghosts is under control, there's no sense tempting him with an all-you-can-eat buffet.

On the screen, I catch sight of his grin and the shock of pure white hair, a legacy of his addiction.

"How does it take its coffee?" Nigel asks Tara.

She turns the container in her hands and tilts her head. The ghostly beads sing out a happy tune.

"Black with extra sugar." She pauses and raises her chin like she's tasting the air. "But it has to be organic raw sugar."

Of course it does.

If my grandmother caught ghosts with the equivalent of 1950s diner coffee (but excellent diner coffee, mind you), then we're now catching them with the equivalent of a Starbucks. Almond and soy milk. Flavored syrups. Cinnamon Dolce sprinkles. You name it, these ghosts want it.

Our business might be booming, but I'm out of my depth with these new ghosts.

I push aside the fashion magazines to clear a space where I can sit on the coffee table. Technically, they're not so much fashion magazines as *wedding* ones. They have names like *Bridal Best Bet* and *Your Dream Day*. There's even a *Martha Stewart Weddings* lurking somewhere in the stack.

I rub my hand, or more accurately, my left ring finger. The engagement ring Malcolm gave me sits there, the sensation still strange and wonderful even after all these months. The moonstone glimmers like the otherworldly. Sometimes I swear it glows in the dark. I love my ring. I love Malcolm. Technically, I've said yes. I cast a glance at the magazines.

Just not to the dress.

Sunlight glints on the bay windows of our storefront. The gold lettering of K&M Ghost Eradication Specialists sparkles. Somewhere out there, Malcolm is biking up and down the side streets of Springside, uncapping thermos after thermos of coffee in an attempt to lure and catch more sprites so we can catalog them.

He's been gone for hours. We're nearing the end of the last batch he caught, and he must be exhausted. I'm almost hoping he returns empty-handed. We'll call it quits, go get breakfast for dinner at Springside Pancake House, and ignore our pesky ghost problem for an evening.

I rub the ring on my finger one more time. Yes. We deserve that.

What I see instead is Malcolm careening down the center of Main Street. He's pumping his legs so hard that his feet slip from the bike's pedals. He swerves, the bike crashing into his cherry-red convertible before he bumps up and over the curb.

He doesn't stop, not to check for scratches or when six precision-made German thermoses scatter in his wake.

I jump up. My hand gropes for some Tupperware. Maybe

today's brew lured something more dangerous than a sprite. My fingers meet nothing but wedding magazines.

Tara tosses me a large container the moment the bell jangles over the door. Malcolm bursts inside, breath ragged, face flushed with exertion. He stumbles forward and crash-lands in the center of our sprite collection. Tiny containers skitter across the floor.

"Get it." His chest heaves with the words. "Get ... it."

Frantic, I glance around, my gaze keen. I'm expecting something fierce and unflinching—the sort of ghost that crawls inside your head and destroys dreams.

Instead, before the door closes, a nearly insubstantial sprite slips inside.

I'VE BEEN CHASING and catching ghosts since I was five. Sometimes, I think the sprites are the hardest to capture. They're small and slight, often barely there. Some people have sprites for years without realizing it. Some people don't mind, which is just as well, since once you have sprites, they're almost impossible to get rid of. Kind of like bedbugs.

Honestly? I'd rather have the sprites.

This particular sprite pings around the office, ricocheting off the front bay windows and arrowing straight into the conference room. It whirls around the space, gathering up steam, until, at last, it targets the coffee table.

The sprite plows through the stash of wedding magazines. One flies through the air and smacks me in the face. When the magazine lands on the floor, the spread inside urges me to *Go Vintage!*

Tara leaps into the air, Tupperware container clutched in her hands. She misses. Because this sprite?

This sprite does not want to be caught.

Malcolm is still prone on the floor, chest heaving. After each circuit of the room, the sprite dive-bombs and cuffs him on the back of the head.

"Ow." The word is barely a protest, and it takes all his effort to raise a hand to shoo the sprite away.

Nigel is shouting something that sounds a lot like, "Catch it!"

Like we're not trying. Well, Malcolm isn't. So maybe Nigel has a point.

The sprite whips around the room. For something so insubstantial, it's powerful enough to shake the walls. The other sprites in their containers are oddly quiet, a respectful sort of silence that has me wondering what this crazed thing is up to. It buzzes in tighter and tighter circles. Its target? Me. Even Tara must feel it, since she cries out.

"Katy, look out!"

A second later, the sprite smashes into my chest.

I land hard on the floor, the fall jolting my tailbone and sending a spike of pain up my spine. The sprite spins in front of me. This is no happy dance. Its moves are frantic, uncoordinated, and agitation flows off it and through me.

With that agitation comes a spark of recognition.

I know this one.

This is a Springside sprite.

Or rather, it's a sprite from before all these new ghosts came to town, before everything happened with Orson Yates, before I captured a powerful entity, before Malcolm conspired with all the ghosts of Springside to bring me back to this plane.

"Malcolm?" I'm so breathless that his name is little more than air.

He cranes his neck to peer at me.

"This is a Springside sprite." I hold up my hands, and the sprite swirls between my palms, still agitated but more content. "From before."

Nigel falls silent—at last—and Malcolm pushes to his knees. He reaches a tentative hand toward mine.

He's close enough now that the heat of his skin washes over me. The barest hint of his nutmeg and Ivory soap scent fills the pocket between us. It's warm and reassuring, and some of the tension leaves my shoulders.

"I've caught you before," I say to the mist between my palms.

"So have I," Malcolm says.

"Where do you think it came from?"

True, Malcolm did gather up every ghost in Springside last September, but that doesn't mean he *found* every last Springside ghost.

My question perturbs the sprite. It starts up again, pinging from me to Malcolm and back again. Clearly frustrated, it zooms across the room and knocks over Tara.

She sits for a minute, the sprite buzzing around her head. "Oh!" Her eyes brighten, and she nods. "Yes, I'll tell them."

The sprite careens off, but it shows no intention of leaving, so I don't chase it.

"It's been locked up," Tara tells us. "It escaped, but there are other Springside ghosts that also want to leave but can't."

"Who locked them up?" Malcolm asks.

She tips her head, left ear in the direction of the sprite. "A necromancer."

Well, obviously. We could probably run through a list of names, but at this point, I'm not sure that would help.

"Where?" I ask instead.

Tara considers the air for a moment. "A mall."

Springside doesn't have a mall. I glance toward the reception desk and the laptop sitting there.

"I'm on it," Nigel says. "Malls in what? Thirty-mile radius? Fifty?"

"Let's start small." I peer out the front bay window. Sunshine glints on the silver thermoses scattered in the gutter and along the sidewalk. "Maybe we can offer it some coffee?"

With my words, the contained sprites start thumping and

bouncing about the room. The Springside sprite whirls about Tara's head.

"Okay." I lean down and offer Malcolm a hand. "Maybe *everyone* can have some coffee."

DESPITE THE PROMISE OF COFFEE, it takes longer than I think it should to chase and corral all the sprites. Their containers slip from our grip, bounce beneath the reception desk, and invade the storefront display.

At last, we gather everyone in the conference room. I head for our newly remodeled kitchenette. The appliances gleam, everything silver, black, or red. The design itself is retro. In the place of honor, next to the filtered water, sits one of my grandmother's percolators.

We have a samovar, too, of course. The cupboards overflow with spices for Malcolm's tea. There's saffron and cardamom, concoctions that soothe, and others that bite. While Malcolm fills the percolator with water, I pull out the one hundred percent Kona.

Behind me, a cheer goes up. Tiny Tupperware containers clatter across the conference room table—someone's old dining room table. It's ancient but serviceable, just like my grandmother's truck. Our new kitchenette is efficient, and I love the way everything gleams.

Even so? It can be hard to let go of some things.

"Are you kidding me?" Nigel's voice comes from the laptop's speakers. He has a full view of what's going on. His tone is measured, as always, but his words are thick with chagrin. "I knew I should've come in today."

Well, no, he shouldn't have. Not with a conference room full of twenty-five sprites.

"I'll save you a thermos," I say.

As if on cue, Tara stumbles in, arms wrapped around six thermoses. They clang against each other when she dumps them into the stainless steel sink.

"Do you want me to scrub them out now?" She's ready to, bottle brush and soap in hand.

"Just one," I say. "So I can bring Nigel some coffee. Leave the rest for tomorrow."

She grins and gets to work.

Something about those words sounds so grown-up. Even now, I'm wary about all this good fortune—Malcolm as my partner and fiancé, K&M Ghost Eradication Specialists in the black, with enough to spare for remodeling and sponsoring Tara's Girl Scout troop. Sometimes I feel like I should close my eyes, hold my breath, and make a wish—all so I can keep things the way they are, right now.

I don't want to examine all of this too closely, jinx any of it, so I turn back to the percolator and do what I do best:

Brew a pot of coffee.

It doesn't take long to discover the lone sprite's preferred brew. Since it's a sprite, I start with extra sweet and extra light. I end there as well.

The thing lazes in the steam rising from the cup. The other sprites surround it as if they're curious and a bit perplexed about this choice. Then they, too, insist on their own cups.

"Power of suggestion?" Malcolm says.

"Maybe." I'm certain they'll go back to demanding coconut milk and vanilla syrup the next time we catch them. Sprites don't have much of an attention span.

The conference room settles into a post-coffee stupor. Everyone —ghost and human—has had their fill. Tara has gone home for the day. From the laptop comes the warm clatter of Sadie and Nigel cooking dinner. He's on call, but I don't think we'll need him. We have the list of malls, and we have this sprite. I'm not sure we'll need anything else.

But the list is endless.

Nigel included not only the high-end malls in the area, but also strip malls and outlet centers. This could take a while.

"Do you think it would let you go all necromancer on it?" I say to Malcolm. I hate to ask, but I still don't like doing that. On my own, I can generally gauge intentions, feelings, and desires, but we need something more specific if we're going to find this mall.

Malcolm holds out a hand, and the sprite slips from the coffee's steam and into his palm. "I can try."

I watch, fascinated by this. Although, truthfully, I'm fascinated by everything Malcolm does. He cups the sprite in his hands and holds it close to his lips. Then he shuts his eyes. His lashes are long and dark against his cheekbones, his mouth is slightly parted and soft. It takes every last bit of my willpower not to lean over and kiss him.

I resist. Besides, I'd only end up with a mouthful of sprite.

A minute passes, and then another. I bite my lip, waiting to hear what this ghost might tell Malcolm. The silence stretches until, at last, he exhales the sprite and slumps back in his chair. The sprite swirls around its cup, agitated again. I hop up and pour it a new one.

"Anything?" I ask.

He shakes his head as if to clear it of ghostly cobwebs. "It's weird. I kept getting flashes of things that don't make sense. Radio Shack and big hair." He holds his hands above his head.

"Radio Shack?"

"*And* big hair and grunge. It's like this sprite traveled back in time. Plus?" Now he laughs, the sound warm and soft. "I have the strangest urge for an Orange Julius."

The notion makes me laugh as well. As slim as these details are, they point to a mall, maybe an older one. It's something to go on, at least.

"Well?" I say, a notion forming in my head. "Why don't we?"

Malcolm has the uncanny ability to take the barest hints of my thoughts and turn them into action. He leans forward and shouts into the laptop's microphone.

"Hey, bro. Katy and I are heading out on a field trip."

The pounding of footfalls follows this declaration. All at once, Nigel's face looms, filling up the entire screen, his expression panicked. "The one hundred percent Kona?"

I hold a thermos between my palms. "We'll drop this off on our way out of town."

WE'VE BEEN DRIVING for hours. At each mall's entrance, I lift the sprite in its Tupperware container and let it look around. The moment it starts to sink, we move on. We don't even bother with some places. True, the Mall of America has an Orange Julius, but it's far too bustling and busy to be a good candidate.

Part of me suspects we're being led on a wild goose—or ghost —chase.

But it's early June in Minnesota. After a long and icy winter, the explosion of green and the warm air that washes over us, filled with the perfume of both lilacs and barbeques, are worth the miles we're putting on Malcolm's convertible.

At the moment, we're sitting in a strip mall parking lot, in front of a Chinese takeout place. Between us is an extra-large portion of dumplings. I hold the container steady while Malcolm alternately spears a dumpling and checks the list of malls that Nigel compiled.

My gaze drifts over the storefronts. In addition to the restaurant, there's a consignment shop, a shoe-repair store, and a karate studio. Also? One, two... five security cameras.

"If you were going to hide some ghosts in a mall," he says, "what kind of mall would it be?"

"An empty one."

I speak the words without thinking, but the moment I do, something strikes me. I shift in my seat and look at Malcolm. "If you were a necromancer with ghosts to hide, would you want to leave behind any evidence?"

Ghosts don't show up on film, but necromancers certainly do. I point to the security cameras. "Wouldn't you want to avoid those?"

He drops his fork. "You're brilliant."

Well, not really. If I were, I would've thought of that before we burned through half a tank of gas. "How do we find an empty mall?"

"It can't be too hard. A couple of guys in my frat house would go to places around the Twin Cities that were abandoned," he says, "just to see what was inside. You know, urban exploring."

"Is that legal?"

He shrugs. "Not always."

"Did you ever go with them?"

"Once," he admits. "They thought they sensed something, so they came back and got me."

"Was it a ghost?"

"Probably." He shifts again and spears another dumpling. "By the time we returned, it was gone. But there were remnants of a containment field and a ward. I didn't recognize the signature. The whole place was creepy, though, so it was just as well."

His story reminds me of the warehouse filled with Springside ghosts. That had been abandoned, too. The rooms were surrounded by containment fields and wards, all to trap the ghosts inside.

"So, this is something necromancers do?" I say. "Find abandoned places and store ghosts there?"

"Most necromancers like to keep their ghosts close. If you don't have them, you can't use them, right? But—" Here, he breaks off, considers the dumpling on his fork, and then sets it down. "There's another school of thought. About keeping ghosts in reserve, secret stashes, and all that. If you're on the run, you would always have access to some ghosts."

"Is that something the Midwest Necromancer Association might do?"

"It is."

"Orson Yates?"

"Him, too, especially."

No one—that we know of—has seen or heard from Orson since he faced retribution at the hands of the Midwest Necromancer Association last fall. Technically, he's no longer a necromancer. Technically, that means he's no longer a problem.

Most days, I believe that.

"You don't suppose these guys have been locked up since last year, do you?" I raise the sprite in its container to eye level. It bounces up and down, but that's only because I'm giving it my full attention.

"It's entirely possible. With a small enough space, a powerful necromancer could construct a containment field that could last for months, even a year."

"So," I say now, stabbing a dumpling of my own. "How do we find this empty mall?"

WITHIN MINUTES, we're ready to go, a much shorter list of malls on my phone, and only one dumpling left in the takeout container.

I hold up my phone so Malcolm can see the screen. "The Cedar Hills Mall is only five miles from here."

He pops the last dumpling into his mouth and then swings us onto the interstate. We take the first exit for Cedar Hills, which leads to an industrial park rather than the downtown area.

"I don't think I've ever been out this way before." He doesn't glance from the road, but I get the sense he's taking everything in. The woods and rolling hills that border the Minnesota River, its sandy banks, and how it twists and turns through this part of the state.

"It's a college town," I say. "Every once in a while, we'd get a call for an eradication. The historic buildings in the city center sometimes attract ghosts, and the cemetery is supposedly haunted."

He eyes me briefly before turning his attention back to the road. "Is it?"

Really? He has to ask? No matter what you've heard, ghosts rarely haunt cemeteries. Except for maybe sprites. And only then to play pranks.

"There's a memorial there, an angel carved in black stone. Legend has it if you touch it, you die within the year."

"A real tourist attraction."

"Actually? It is."

"Let me guess. Legend tripping?"

I nod. "It gets a lot of traffic on Halloween, college kids, mainly."

"I imagine there are sprites on hand to help with that."

"You imagine right."

We've been chatting for so long that it's only now that I notice the fields on either side of us. Row after row of young cornstalks, the green hopeful, the earth between each row black and rich. We've left the woods and the rolling landscape *and* Cedar Hills behind.

Before I can touch his arm or say a word, Malcolm slows the convertible and pulls to the side of the road. Traffic is nonexistent. In the quiet, birds chirp, and a rustling comes from the field to our right.

"We blew right by the industrial park," he says. "I don't even remember seeing a turnoff, do you?"

I shake my head.

"Did you see a sign for the mall?"

Again, I go with a headshake.

Malcolm swings the car around, and we head back toward Cedar Hills. I lean forward as if that will somehow help me spot the exit. We're nearly into downtown when we realize that—once again—we've missed the turnoff.

He pulls the convertible into a lot for a local park and shuts off the engine. The squeals and chatter of children playing fill the air. Laughter and splashing come from a swim area. Beyond that stretches the glimmering blue of a lake. The scent of toasted marshmallows floats in the air. The whole scene is serene and idyllic and plays counterpoint to the unease swirling in my stomach.

"That was weird," Malcolm says.

It was. It really was. "There must be a turnoff. Should we ask someone? Get a map?" I hold up my phone. "GPS?"

He surveys the crowd of parents and children. "Let's try GPS. I'm going to feel really stupid asking for directions if we missed the turnoff because we weren't paying attention."

I type in the address while he starts up the car. Since traffic is still nonexistent on the outskirts of town, we inch along at twenty miles per hour below the speed limit.

"Here!" I cry out.

"Katy, there's nothing—"

"Here," I say. "Pull over."

My phone insists our destination is six hundred feet ahead and on the right. The only thing that fills our view is a copse of trees.

Malcolm turns the wheel, the convertible bumping onto the shoulder, the tires crunching gravel. Then, with the engine off, evening rushes in, all soft air and birdsong. The road is so very quiet that I'm finding it hard to believe anyone comes out this way.

The grove of evergreens to our right is so lush that I expect pine to also lace the air. But I don't smell anything but dust and the leftover tang of ginger and soy sauce. The needles glimmer in the early evening light. The arrangement of each tree is so perfect that it looks picture-postcard-ready, like something from a calendar or inspirational poster.

In fact, I'm nearly certain I have seen this particular copse of trees somewhere before.

And that's weird.

I step from the convertible and walk toward the pines.

"Katy—"

Malcolm's voice is filled with worry and warning, but really, what's there to be afraid of? I'm a few feet away, then a few inches, and still no scent of pine, and no telltale needles beneath my feet, either.

I reach out a hand, expecting the needles to be smooth and sharp, perhaps a bit sticky with sap. My fingers pass all the way through, first the needles and then an entire branch.

"They're not real!" I spin to face Malcolm.

"What?"

"The trees. They're not real!"

To prove it, I jump straight through.

The moment I land on the other side, the illusion vanishes. The road beneath my feet is cracked, but it is a road. A few yards farther down, there's a faded sign that reads *Cedar Hills Mall*.

Malcolm's standing opposite me now. Nothing blocks my view except a few slender saplings and some weeds. I can see his convertible, the highway, and the field on the other side—all of it perfectly clear.

"Katy!" His voice and expression are panicked. He turns his head and shields his eyes, and it's only then it dawns on me.

He can't see me.

"Walk on through," I call out, but I'm not sure he can hear me.

Perhaps he can't, or maybe he's worried. Either way, he takes one step and then another, and then he's with me on the other side, his eyes wide with amazement.

"Wow," he exhales.

"I know."

For several seconds, we stand there, marveling at nothing but the saplings.

"If we go back," I say, pointing toward the highway, "do you think it will still be there?"

"One way to find out." He takes my hand, and together we head toward the highway.

When we step into the illusion, the air shifts around us. Everything is cast in a greenish hue. Then the bright red of Malcolm's convertible greets us. We turn around, and the pines are in place once again.

"Is that a necromancer thing?" I ask.

"I don't know." Malcolm is already pulling out his phone. "But I know someone who will."

Nigel picks up on the fifth ring.

"Oh," he says after we've walked him through and around the illusion. "It's a visible ward."

"A what?" Malcolm says.

"You know what a ward is, right, baby brother?"

Next to me, Malcolm stifles a growl. "Explain *visible* ward."

"Necromancers use them when they want to hide something in plain sight. You won't pick up a message or a signature with this sort of ward. Anonymity is the point of using one."

"It looks like it's from a postcard," I say, "or maybe one of those insurance calendars."

Nigel snorts. "No one ever claimed necromancers were imaginative. Show me again."

Dutifully, Malcolm holds up his cell phone and pans the copse of pines. Now that we know it isn't real, all the oddities pop out at me. No birds land on the branches. No critters scurry beneath the limbs. No deer tracks. Even though the breeze is light, the trees hold themselves far, far too still.

"Yep," Nigel says at last. "It's a visible ward. Something like this usually takes more than one necromancer, though, unless he—"

"Or she," I say.

"Or *she* is very powerful. Otherwise, it's something siblings or couples do together. Malcolm and I could make one, assuming he was any good at wards."

Malcolm's lips twitch into a smile, and he shrugs one shoulder.

"Or you and Malcolm could," Nigel says, "since you work closely together, and again assuming—"

"Yeah, yeah. We all know I'm lousy at wards."

"It's an advanced trick," Nigel continues, "but once you have one established, the upkeep is easier than a regular ward."

"How does it work?" I ask. With regular wards, you need to own—or at least claim—the property you're protecting. "Do you need an anchor?"

"Since you're hiding something rather than claiming it, no."

"And the visible part? Do you find a picture and channel it or something?"

"Yes, that part is like placing a regular ward. The picture they used fits the landscape well enough that you wouldn't even notice anything strange unless you look closely. Whoever made this probably does a drive-by now and then to reinforce it, but really, this type of ward can last for years."

"And it could keep the curious away from your stash of ghosts," I say.

"Indeed it could."

It's impossible to hide my smile, so I don't even try. I cast Malcolm a sidelong glance. "Should we go get some ghosts?"

"I think we should." Malcolm ends the call with Nigel and pockets his phone. "I really think we should."

THE ROAD to the main entrance is both quiet and disquieting. All the everyday things you expect at a mall—cars, people, strollers, and carts—are missing. Over the years, the yellow lines in the parking lot have faded, so they're barely there—ghosts lines more than anything. Weeds fill the cracks in the asphalt, and a few trees have pushed up and out of the cement sidewalk surrounding the building's four wings.

Above us, the sign remains, tarnished gilt letters proclaiming:

Cedar Hills Mall
A Dream Come True

More like where dreams go to die. Nothing about this space reassures me—nothing except the sprite's excitement as we pull up to the main entrance. It bounces inside its container as if it's urging Malcolm to drive faster. He pulls the convertible into a regular parking space and then sits there with his hands on the wheel.

"I could actually park anywhere." He casts me a look, his expression bemused. "Right?"

"You could, but—"

"It just feels weird."

It does, in more ways than one.

We step from the convertible and inspect the entryway doors from several feet away. We're far enough from the interstate that the sound of traffic doesn't reach us. I expect to hear something, at least. Evening birdsong. The buzz of insects. I scrape my foot against the cement just to break the silence that has fallen over us.

"This is kind of creepy," Malcolm murmurs.

He holds up a hand, and I know he wants me to wait while he inspects the front doors. I don't, of course. I won't let him step a millimeter closer without me at his side. He knows this as well, which is why he gives me a rueful grin when we reach the doors.

The sun glints on the glass, its touch against the back of my neck comforting—to a point. I clutch the container with one hand, the sprite ricocheting inside, and shield my eyes with the other and peer into the mall.

Shadows stretch the length of the hallway. Lumps that might be benches bisect its center. I think I see a planter and a tree, an artificial one, since it's sprouting leaves.

Malcolm shakes the doors. The chain that's looped through the handles rattles against the glass. The doors creak open, and the chain swings. From one end hangs a padlock by its shackle. The lock itself?

Not engaged.

"Oh, this is really creepy." Malcolm's words are so soft that I feel them against my cheek more than hear them. "Like horror-movie creepy."

We both take several steps back, putting space between us and the front doors.

"Do you detect anything? A regular ward, maybe?" I say, although I have no idea how you'd place one of those around an entire mall.

He holds out a hand, fingers skimming the air above the ground and then tracing a pattern around the door. "No, nothing. It's a mall, right? It's not like a single person owns this place."

"We have a ward on our business, but we don't own the property."

"But we own the right to use it. That's the difference. A necromancer couldn't claim this entire space as his—"

"Or hers."

He shoots me a grin. "Or hers. It wouldn't work." Malcolm surveys the doors again and then the parking lot behind us. "But you might hide ghosts here and use a visible ward so other necromancers don't stumble across them."

That doesn't explain why this place is so creepy. But yes, that's the most logical explanation for the sprite's incessant pinging inside the Tupperware.

Malcolm turns, studies the empty parking lot again, and the slant of the sun. "I'm not sure we should go in tonight." He nods toward the west. "There's not a lot of daylight left."

It's June, so the days stretch long. The sun won't set for a few more hours. Still, the light has that early evening quality to it and will slip away completely before we know it. I'm about to agree. The most sensible thing is to come back in the morning better prepared. Before I can suggest this, the sprite springs from my grip with supernatural force.

The Tupperware container bounces across the concrete. I lunge, but I'm not quick enough. The plastic thwacks the sidewalk. Malcolm makes a dive for it, but the sprite simply propels the container up and over him.

The gap between the two doors is just large enough that it can slip inside.

I rush forward. By the time I reach the entrance, the sprite is gone, and all we hear is the echo of Tupperware against tile.

FOR SEVERAL LONG MOMENTS, Malcolm and I stare into the abyss-like corridor.

This is just like a horror movie and just like a sprite. Leave it to them to do the most inconvenient thing at the most inopportune moment.

A hint of stale, cold air filters through the crack between the two doors. We could walk inside. It's as simple as unhooking the padlock and pulling the chain through the handles.

We stand there.

"Do you think this is a trap?" I ask at last.

It has that feel. A lonely stretch of highway, a secluded and abandoned building. An adorable sprite as bait. Sure, Nigel knows we're here, but we're also a good thirty miles from Springside.

"Yes. No. I don't know." Malcolm heaves a sigh that holds the day's weight in it. He turns to face me. "Or maybe it *was* a trap, at one time, like last year."

"You mean with Orson."

"Exactly. It would be like him to set up multiple traps."

"So, he was going to do what? Lock up some ghosts, then send a sprite for me to follow here?" I peer down the hallway. Shadows play before my eyes, almost ghostly themselves.

"This would've been an ideal spot for retribution. No witnesses, no traffic, enough room for two dozen necromancers, easily."

"What about now?" Because right now, this space is still all those things.

"He doesn't have enough allies. He's not chairman anymore, and he couldn't pull off something like this."

"Do we risk it?" I lean toward the crack between the two doors and strain my ears. Is that a light thump, thump, thump of plastic against the floor? Or am I simply indulging in a little wishful thinking?

Malcolm raises a hand, holding me in place. Then he dashes back to the convertible. From the trunk, he pulls out some of our emergency supplies. When he returns, he hands me a flashlight and drapes a whistle around my neck.

"It's not like we're headed off into the woods."

"No, but ... things can happen during urban exploring. A whistle is a lot louder than a voice."

He's right. I bring the whistle to my lips and give it the barest hint of a test blow. Oh. *Yeah.* That will work.

"Ground rules. If possible, we keep this door in sight. Anything looks sketchy, we run, hop into the car, and get the hell out of here. Deal?"

"You read my mind."

Malcolm pulls in a breath like he's about to dive off a cliff. "Okay." He takes my hand. "Let's go."

The moment we cross the threshold, cold, stale air steals everything about the quiet June evening. A chill washes over me. Even though we're both wearing sneakers, our footfalls sound loud and hollow in this space.

Again, the emptiness strikes me. I don't do a lot of shopping, it's true. The only time I've been to the Mall of America was on the way back from a class field trip to the state capitol. Still, no people, no chatter, nothing but musty air against my tongue. All of it feels wrong in so many ways.

The tile is dust-covered and grimy beneath our feet. I point. Every few squares, there's an impression from a Tupperware container.

"This might be easier than I thought," Malcolm whispers.

"It might," I agree, my words equally low. Although why we're whispering is beyond me. There's no one else here.

At least, I hope there's no one else here.

Every few yards, we halt. Malcolm turns in a tight circle, scanning high and low. I raise my chin to sample the air. Nothing. This doesn't surprise me. If the Springside ghosts are here, they're inside a containment field. Our sprite, in its Tupperware, is also in one. They'll be nearly impossible to detect.

Still, we don't want any surprises, otherworldly or otherwise.

Something else catches my eye. I point again, this time holding back a laugh. "You said you wanted an Orange Julius."

Maybe it's the power of suggestion, but I swear something sugary sweet teases my nose. Behind that smell is a brain freeze waiting to happen.

Malcolm glances toward the storefront, then at me, and back again. "I don't think I've ever seen anything quite so orange."

"How long do you think this place has been closed?" Everything about the Orange Julius looks retro—the typeface on the signage, the hard, plastic booths, all that orange.

He shakes his head, considering. "I don't know. A while, obviously, but I was expecting things to be a lot worse."

"Like what?"

"Graffiti. Black mold. Mildew. Broken glass." He points to another storefront, this one with a display of prom dresses. The mannequins' arms are spindly and seem to be reaching for us. Or maybe just for Malcolm. I place a protective—and irrationally jealous—hand on his arm. Then I blink, and the display resolves itself into a jewel-toned explosion of dusty taffeta and silk.

"The utilities are still on," he says as we make our way farther into the mall. "Some of the stores still have inventory and equipment. You'd think that would be gone, at least."

"It's like a time capsule," I say.

"It really is, like everyone left one day and never came back."

Even here in the center courtyard, the space feels that way. Above us, sunlight filters through skylights and illuminates the floor below. The fountain is dry, but a layer of copper and silver coins shine dully in the spare light. So many wishes left behind.

I wonder if any of them have come true.

I let my gaze wander. A sign urges me to visit Brett's Department Store, the anchor for the south wing. The display cases in the jewelry store, a place called Hillside Diamonds, are empty. Even so? If I squint, I swear I can catch the sparkle of gemstones.

"I mean, I don't think anyone's been cleaning on a regular basis." Malcolm turns in another circle, surveying the space. There's a calculating gleam in his eye, making him look far more like the former stockbroker he was and less like the ghost catcher he is now. "But you could repurpose this space, turn it into something useful."

"Like a home for ghosts?" I suggest.

"Sure." He gives me a sidelong glance, one that has a hint of a grin. "A home for ghosts."

I point to a sign attached to a central kiosk: Troy Season Property Management. "Maybe they plan to."

"Maybe."

The lightest tap, tap, tap comes from a long, dark hallway just off the courtyard.

I nod in its direction. "Speaking of ghosts."

Malcolm flicks on his flashlight and shines it down the corridor. Something bounces. At least, I think something does. Really, I'd have to move farther down the hall to know for sure. As it is, I've inched several feet closer.

I peer at Malcolm over my shoulder. "This is kind of breaking one of our ground rules."

"It kind of is."

"Maybe one of us could stay here—" And by one of us, I absolutely mean him.

"I don't want you going down there alone."

And he knows it.

"Well, I don't want to leave you here by yourself, either." I stare into the darkness before the obvious hits me. "You said the utilities were on. How can you tell?"

He tilts his chin toward the ceiling. "Ventilation system."

I look up as well. That cold, stale odor meets my nose, but

beyond that, I catch the telltale hint of an air current. "Then maybe there're lights, too."

Malcolm shines the flashlight up and down the walls until the beam lands on a bank of light switches. With the edge of the flashlight, he flips each of them on.

There's a crackling, a sputtering, and a fizz and pop. The overhead fluorescents are fairly put out about being pressed into service after all this time. The illumination is minimal, tinged a sickly yellow.

But we can see all the way to the end of the hallway. There, next to the restrooms and some offices, the sprite bounces in its Tupperware container.

"What do you think?" My voice is low again, as if whispering will somehow keep us safe. I point to a sign at the end of the hallway. "There's an exit."

"Which might be blocked."

There's that.

"Or will trigger an alarm," he adds.

That, too.

Down the hall, the little ghost is doing all it can to get our attention. At this rate, I'm afraid it might crack both the plastic container and the containment field holding it inside.

"We need to do something," I say.

"You're right." He holds out his hand. "Together?"

I take that hand. His skin is warm, and his grip reassuring in mine. "Together."

Before we reach the end of the hallway, the sprite scampers around the corner and out of sight. The Tupperware thuds against the tile, so following this thing isn't all that difficult.

At last, we find the sprite springing up and down in front of a bank of rental lockers. Malcolm's grip tightens on mine, and we creep forward.

The lockers tremble and shake. A muted rattle reaches my ear, like the sound must travel through molasses to reach us. One plaintive wail echoes down the hall. Then it's a full-on chorus of ghosts, each crying out, their combined efforts filling my ears, my head, the entire mall.

"Okay, guys. Okay." I hold up my hands as if that could placate them. "We're going to get you out of there."

Cheers replace the crying. The frenetic locker shaking transforms into something with a beat—something that sounds a lot like a rumba.

Malcolm manages a chuckle. "Definitely Springside ghosts."

They are. They really are. I can't suppress a grin. Despite the dank and spooky atmosphere of the mall, I feel lighter, hopeful. We'll get them out of here and take them home.

I step forward to do just that, only to collide with something very hard and very invisible. I try again, simply because I'm stubborn that way.

I turn to look at Malcolm. "What is it?"

He's crouched next to me, hands outstretched. "Containment field." His fingers trace the invisible wall up, up until he's standing on tiptoe. The barest shimmer of an outline sparkles in the dim light from the fluorescent bulbs above our heads.

The containment field surrounds the lockers—there's no going up and over, around or under. The only way to free the ghosts is to break it by force.

"Maybe together?" I suggest.

We've done that before, broken a field that was much bigger—and probably stronger—than this one is.

"Yes, together." This is what I love about working with Malcolm—and love about him in general. He connects the dots between my half-thoughts and intuition. So far, K&M the couple has not screwed up K&M Ghost Eradication Specialists.

And for that, I'm grateful.

Malcolm takes my hands, and we both close our eyes. Immediately, the containment field pops into view, its smooth surface clear now. I let my mind's eye glide along that surface, searching out a crack or flaw. Even the tiniest of fissures or a hairline fracture will work.

"Are you getting anything?" He gives my fingers a squeeze.

"Nothing." I scan again. "Do you recognize the necromancer?"

Every necromancer has a signature. It's something I can't really detect, maybe because I didn't grow up as a necromancer. But Malcolm can.

"It's weird," he says, "because it's familiar and yet ... not. Like when a word is on the tip of your tongue, but you can't say it."

I double my efforts to no avail. I don't know who this necromancer might be, except that he ... she ... they are strong.

"What if we use something physical as well?"

He opens his eyes and peers at me. "What did you have in mind?"

"There's a tire iron in your car, isn't there?"

He raises an eyebrow. "If I recall, you're pretty handy with a tire iron."

I used one once to crack open a containment field around Malcolm's convertible. I also managed to smash the window as well. But it worked. With my hands still in his, he considers my suggestion. His gaze darts down the corridor and then takes in the trembling bank of lockers next to us.

"This is an all-or-nothing deal," he says. "I'm not leaving you here alone—"

"And I'm not letting you go out to the car alone."

"Okay, we're agreed, then."

The rental lockers shake; ghosts cry and plead. They're loud, despite the containment field, although not loud enough to make a dent in it.

"Guys, please, we'll be back. I promise. We'll be back, and then we'll get you out of there." I scoop up the sprite in its container. It pings against the sides as if it's trying to escape.

"We'll be back," I say one last time.

The ghosts continue to wail as if we're abandoning them to

some terrible fate. It hurts my heart to leave them, but we have no choice.

Malcolm takes my hand, and we race through the corridors. In the center courtyard, swaths of pink and gold stream through the skylights. There's still time. We'll dash out and back in and free the ghosts all before twilight.

Really, my dear? Leaving so soon?

The sound of a voice I know so well has me staggering. Malcolm's fingers slip from my grip, and I stumble. This voice is both so very real and so very impossible.

I shake my head, strain my ears, willing myself to hear it again and hoping I won't. On reflex, my fingers go to my left cheek, where—once upon a time—I had a faded blue mark, a legacy of my encounter with a powerful entity.

My cheek feels normal, not waxy and cold. The mark and the entity are gone, long gone.

And yet ...

"Katy!"

Malcolm's voice pulls me back to the present. I inhale a deep breath and give my head one good shake. Even as I catch up and retake his hand, I can't help scanning the ceiling and then the sky above me. I can't help wondering if I truly heard what I think I heard.

My mind encounters nothing. If that voice was here, it's gone now—like a phantom cell phone ring or a baby's cry.

An echo from the past and nothing more.

At least, that's what I tell myself.

THE SECOND TIME we leave the warm spring evening behind us, Malcolm brandishes a tire iron. I clutch the Tupperware with the sprite. It pings the sides of its container, urging us to run faster. We are fierce and determined—all three of us.

We race through the mall, past the courtyard, and down the hallway. Our footfalls thunder. My breath is ragged and loud in my ears. We will free the ghosts as fast as we can. Even though the lights work, I do not want to be here after dark.

Who notices first—me, the sprite, Malcolm—I can't say.

I skid to a halt, but my momentum carries me through to the end of the hall. I wince, expecting to hit the containment field, or at the very least, the lockers.

Nothing blocks my path.

The corridor is clean, and the floor shines like it has been freshly waxed. I turn as if that will help me find the lockers that are so clearly no longer here.

"Malcolm?" His name comes out tiny and hushed.

He stands there, tire iron gripped in one hand, mouth agape. Gingerly, he uses the tire iron to poke at the space where the lockers should be.

"This isn't another version of a visible ward, is it?" I peer up at the ceiling and then take in our surroundings. "Did we go down the wrong hallway?"

That seems unlikely, but it makes more sense than the lockers simply vanishing.

Malcolm tips his head. "Do you hear that?"

Immediately, I'm on alert. I strain my ears, send my thoughts skyward. The entity? Nothing greets my search except the soft exhale of the ventilation system.

"Hear what?"

"Music, or more like Muzak." He shakes his head as if to clear it. "The stuff they piped in at malls. It sounds like 'The Girl from Ipanema'."

I'm kind of glad I can't hear it.

"I don't hear anything," I say.

But now it's like Malcolm can't hear me. He takes a step forward and then another as if he's intent on finding the source of the music. He's halfway to the courtyard when a terrible thought seizes my mind.

The notion is so wrong and so *obvious* that I'm kicking myself. I race to catch up to him, sneakers slipping on the floor. Before he can round the corner and head into the courtyard, I grab a handful of his shirt.

"Remember that thing you said?" I haul him backward. "About this being a good place for a trap?"

He stumbles, catches himself, and then snags my waist to pull me farther down the hall. He swears quietly. That Pied-Piper-like music must be gone. Now he's clear-eyed, a frown marring his brow.

"Two dozen necromancers in the courtyard?" I say.

"Yeah." He exhales a long breath. "Easily."

"Do you think that's it? That this is a trap?"

"I don't know, Katy."

He glances at me, and there's so much sorrow in his gaze that my heart lurches. We don't need a replay of last year. This much, I know.

"Emergency exit?"

He nods, folds my hand in his, and we hurry down the hall.

There's a sign, more than one, all of them pointing the way out in big red letters. What there isn't is an actual door. At the end of the hallway, all we find is the little sprite in its container, jumping and thwacking itself against the space where the lockers should be. I scoop it up, try to comfort it, but it's inconsolable.

"I guess there's only one way out." Malcolm hefts the tire iron. "This could come in handy."

But not against ghosts. Or bullets. And the last time we saw Orson Yates, he had a gun. The grim line of Malcolm's mouth tells me I don't need to remind him of that.

At the threshold to the courtyard, we pause. With the tire iron, Malcolm switches the bank of lights off, plunging the hallway into darkness. It's not much of a cover, but it's better than being under a spotlight.

"Do you hear anything?" he whispers. "Sense anything?"

I cast my thoughts upward, scanning with not only my ears and eyes but for the otherworldly as well. I search in all directions. Yes, you could hold retribution in the center of the courtyard. You could also do many other things.

"This would be an excellent spot for an ambush," I say, voice low.

"You could set up attack ghosts there." He points down the wing opposite us. "And there, behind the elevator, and there on the second floor."

The glass surrounding the second-floor balcony is frosted, but it's translucent enough to see shapes and shadows, if not actual ghosts. Even so, a necromancer—and several attack ghosts—could hide behind a kiosk or the escalator or tuck themselves inside a storefront.

Malcolm freezes, his arm with the tire iron still extended toward the balcony. "Radio Shack," is all he says.

"What?"

"That Radio Shack wasn't there before."

"You're sure?"

"Positive. I was noting landmarks in case I had to direct Nigel or someone in to find us. You know, go straight past the Orange Julius and take a left at the prom dresses."

That's more than I did, and I can't help being impressed.

"There was an empty storefront, but no Radio Shack. And there was a sunglass kiosk out in front."

"Speaking of Nigel."

"Yeah, you read my mind." Malcolm tugs out his phone. The screen lights up, but it's there and gone, and then he's shoving the phone back into his pocket.

"No signal," he says before I can ask.

"We really need to leave."

I think that's clear. Besides, since I stepped into this place, something's felt wrong, like I don't belong here. I want to say it's like being haunted. Clearly, I'm not the only one who feels that way. The little sprite is hunkered down, despondent. Its form trembles so much, it vibrates the plastic beneath my fingertips.

"We do," Malcolm agrees, but he doesn't move. He stares into the middle distance, almost like he's listening to "The Girl from Ipanema" again.

Of course, I thought I heard the entity, so maybe I shouldn't judge. But the urge to move is undeniable, almost like there's a hand at the small of my back pushing me forward.

The light in the courtyard has taken on a different quality, more deep blue than pink and gold. The benches cast long shadows. Again, I don't care if the utilities are still on. There's no way I'm staying here after dark.

"Come on." I grip Malcolm's hand even tighter. "Let's go home."

We don't stop. We don't glance around. We race through the courtyard and toward the main entrance. Again, that invisible hand presses me forward. After we clear the doors, we don't bother looping the chain through the handles.

Likewise, neither one of us bothers with the convertible's doors. It's up and over, and Malcolm peels out of the parking lot before I can buckle my seatbelt.

Before we reach the visible ward, I hazard a glance back.

For a moment, the setting sun strikes the façade in such a way that it shimmers. The gilt on the sign gleams.

Then the mall is dark, abandoned, destitute. The pavement is cracked. The glass doors are covered with a film of grime. And I'm struck, once again, by how haunted it all feels.

I'VE JUST FINISHED HELPING Malcolm heft his bike into the back of my truck. Both the bicycle and the tailgate are fastened in place, and he's halfway down the alley behind K&M Ghost Eradication Specialists when he halts.

He spins around, eyes filled with concern. "Maybe we should drive home together."

"Malcolm." I raise my hands, indicating not only the alleyway but everything around us. "This is Springside."

Granted, things can happen in Springside. But even here, in a back alley, nothing is creepy or sinister. Lamplight shines down, illuminating the space in a cozy golden glow. The Dumpster looks as if someone recently hosed it down. A few wooden pallets lean against the brick of the neighboring buildings.

There's the barest hint of refuse, but even that is benign.

Malcolm glances around, his gaze lighting on the bright blue back door of the Springside Deli and the wall art near the front of the alley. A small smile plays on his lips.

"You're right. I'm on edge, is all."

"I'm going to make sure everything's locked up," I say, "and I'll be right behind you."

He blows me a kiss and heads for the convertible parked out front.

I do a quick circuit to make sure we haven't left anything plugged in or a container of half and half out on the counter (that's not a smell you want as a morning greeting). Despite my earlier declaration, when I'm in our office like this, by myself, things are just a little bit eerie.

But the lock snicks securely behind me. My truck is waiting patiently—the mayor still doesn't like me parking it on Main Street —and I know Malcolm will have a late dinner started by the time I make it home.

I'm about to let out a contented sigh when a silhouette darkens the front of the alley. My heart jumps in my chest, but I blink, sure it's a shadow playing tricks with my eyes. The silhouette doesn't move. Or rather, it takes a step closer.

And that step has a sound, like an expensive loafer striking concrete.

I move for my truck. I'll climb in, lock all the doors, and everything will be fine. I can call Malcolm or even Chief Ramsey. I can simply rev the engine. My truck is big, the alley small, and whoever this is, they'll get out of the way.

Well, probably.

I grip the door handle. I'm about to swing it open and crawl inside when the figure speaks and stills my hand.

"Good evening, Ms. Lindstrom." The voice is smooth and assured but unfamiliar.

A few more polished steps on concrete, and a man comes into view. Despite the warm evening, he's wearing a three-piece suit. Over the past few years, I've encountered so many necromancers that I can recognize the cost of a suit, if not the brand. This one looks expensive—all narrow pinstripes and silk tie—and no doubt is. The pinstripes gleam, and I suspect they're getting a supernatural boost.

"I'm sorry." I reach for the door handle once again. "But we're closed for the day."

This is a lie. We catch ghosts, after all, and some of our best business comes after midnight.

The man chuckles as if he knows I'm lying and finds the attempt amusing. "I assure you. I can catch my own ghosts."

Well, yes. He probably can.

"But that's not why I'm here," he adds.

He wants me to ask. I can taste the anticipation in the air, almost in the same way I can taste the otherworldly. So I wait.

At last, he clears his throat, the sound weary, like he really doesn't have time for me and my shenanigans. "Let me introduce myself. I'm Roland Harrington-Hayes."

"That's a mouthful." I probably shouldn't blurt like that, but I can't help it.

I get nothing but that amused chuckle again. "Indeed. I hail from two strong necromancer families. I like to honor them both. However, I'm also the interim chair of the Midwest Necromancer Association."

Oh, this can't be good. Without Orson at their helm, I thought —or maybe just hoped—they'd leave us alone. Apparently not.

"I don't want to join your club," I say.

"And we don't want you."

Well, that's rude. Then again, so was I.

"Okay. We're agreed." I turn toward my truck, intent on climbing inside. "Have a good night."

"Not so fast, Ms. Lindstrom. We still have business to discuss." From the inside pocket of his suit coat, Roland pulls some papers. He unfurls them with a snap and then takes out a pen. "I need you to sign this." He extends both in my direction.

"I don't know what *this* is." And I'm certainly not signing something I haven't read, especially while standing in a dark alleyway with a strange necromancer.

Apparently, Roland thinks I will, because he continues. "Standard contract between necromancers—"

"I'm not a—"

"When one territory borders another."

"I don't have a territory."

"Don't you?" He raises his hands, palms skyward, indicating not just the alley but everything around us—much like I did with Malcolm. "Isn't Springside your territory? Or should I inform the association that it's open season on the ghosts that reside here?"

I feel as if I've stumbled into yet another trap. I study him. Have I seen him before? His features blur beneath the lamplight, and I wonder if this is a supernatural trick. Was he one of the many necromancers at my retribution? Was he at Orson's?

Doubt—and a hint of dread—swirls in my chest. I can't tell. I have the feeling he knows a lot more about me than I do about him.

"I never signed anything when Orson was the chair."

Roland waves away the protest. "I like to cross more t's and dot more i's than Orson did. We wouldn't want a repeat of last year, would we?"

No. No, we would not.

"Can I read what it says?" I ask.

"But of course." He offers both the contract and the pen once again.

He's far enough away that I must—against my better judgment—inch closer. The papers rattle when I snatch them. I refuse the pen—or try to. It's like the thing has a mind of its own. A supernatural force grips my wrist, and an ethereal hand presses the pen into my fingers.

It's haunted. If I don't do something—and quick—it will force me to sign.

I jump back, as much as this ghost will let me. And it *is* a ghost, possibly an attack ghost. With chagrin, I realize Malcolm was right to be on edge, and I've been foolish. I won't be able to negotiate with Roland. That much is clear. But this ghost? Maybe. So I shout.

"Stop!"

Beneath the menace, I detect discontent. It doesn't want to be an attack ghost, doesn't care much for Roland, and if it could, it would break free. I gather my thoughts and aim them at the tether Roland has on this poor thing. If I break that, then this ghost can break free.

Even with the low light, I can see Roland's features distort. His mouth is tight and angry, and his eyes blaze with outrage.

"You are in direct violation—"

"Is there a problem here?"

Another silhouette shadows the alley's entryway. Only, this voice? I know this voice and the man it belongs to.

"Leave," Roland snarls. "This is none of your business."

"I said, is there a problem here?" Footfalls echo against the brick walls. These steps are far more solid than Roland's were. "I'm Police Chief Ramsey, and what happens in Springside is always my business."

The otherworldly grip loosens, and I yank my hand free. I want to sag with relief. Instead, I fold the contract into a square and tuck it into the back pocket of my jeans. Roland jerks forward, fingers outstretched as if he plans to grab the contract. Of course, if he tries, he'll end up grabbing my butt as well.

Chief doesn't move, and I don't know how he does it, but his handcuffs jangle—ever so slightly. The sound is light, but carries with it enough intimidation that Roland takes a step back.

"I believe you're double-parked, Mr. Harrington-Hayes."

At the sound of his name, Roland flinches.

"Officer Millard is currently writing you a ticket," Chief continues, "but if you leave now, under her escort, we'll forget all about that."

And if Roland doesn't? Chief's voice is composed as ever, but beneath its even tone, I detect the promise of a night in jail.

"Very well." Roland adjusts his tie and fiddles with his cufflinks. He nods toward me. "We'll conclude our business later, Ms. Lindstrom."

"No," Chief says. "I don't think you will."

We wait until the tap of those polished dress shoes has faded, an expensive car has rumbled to life, and the rotating lights of a patrol car have passed. Then he turns his police chief glare on me.

For a moment, I almost wish I were still alone in the alley with Roland Harrington-Hayes.

CHAPTER 5

I know enough not to blurt around Chief, although truthfully, I sometimes still do. Chief lets his gaze scan the alley, taking it all in. I don't know what he sees that I don't. I suspect this is a police chief thing.

"Where's Malcolm?" he says at last.

"This isn't Malcolm's fault—"

Chief holds up a hand. "Katy, I'm just asking where he is."

"Home, by now. Probably making dinner."

Chief has an old-fashioned streak, and I'm not sure what he'll make of this. That maybe I should be the one at home, cooking dinner? So I add, "I make better coffee. Malcolm makes better grilled cheese."

Chief drops his gaze and rubs the back of his neck, and I can't tell if he's exasperated or amused. A moment later, however, he's alert.

"Are you okay?" he asks. "Mr. Harrington-Hayes didn't hurt you, did he?"

My wrist tingles from where the attack ghost gripped it, but it doesn't hurt—and it's not something Chief can help me with. I'll ask Nigel about it later.

"No, I'm fine. It's just ... I mean—" I'm not sure what I mean. Despite all he's seen, Chief is still skeptical when it comes to the supernatural. Explaining the Midwest Necromancer Association? Not something I want to do, at least not tonight. So I go with, "How did you know that he...?"

Now that I've asked it, I really do wonder. Then again, if Chief has a sixth sense, it's probably for the wellbeing of Springside.

"It was strange," he says, and his voice is oddly faraway. He's always so grounded in reality. "I was heading home when the urge to walk the block one more time hit me. That's when I saw the Mercedes parked like it owned the place."

A ghost, maybe? Or even a friendly sprite? I lift my chin, straining for a hint of the otherworldly. The air is cool and devoid of all things supernatural. Then again, Roland is a necromancer, and he did have at least one attack ghost with him. If I were a Springside ghost, I wouldn't stick around either.

"Thank you," I say, both to Chief and any ethereal helpers that might be nearby.

"You don't have to thank me." The gruff Chief Ramsey is back. "Just doing my job."

See? Here's where I think he's wrong. True, we don't always see things the same way. But he's always solid and sure, and he cares for everyone in Springside.

We *should* thank him for that.

He gestures toward my truck. This time, I make it into the cab and start the engine.

I'll give Chief this too: he's subtle when he wants to be. Even though I don't detect anything in my rearview mirror, I'm pretty sure his patrol car follows me all the way home.

OKAY, so I lied to Chief Ramsey.

Malcolm doesn't just make better grilled cheese sandwiches than I do. He makes the best grilled cheese sandwiches on the face of the planet. He uses baby Swiss and Vermont cheddar between slices of Italian bread. Then he grills them to perfection. The bread is both crispy and buttery, the cheese gooey and rich.

I catch both a whiff and a sizzle when I open the kitchen door. Before I can speak, explain, or do anything else, Malcolm leaps across the room and pulls me into a hug.

"Are you okay?" He tugs me close as if he's afraid of losing me. "Did he hurt you? Damn it. I knew I should've stayed."

How does he ...? Then it hits me. Chief Ramsey.

"Did Chief—?"

"Call us?" Nigel finishes. He's sitting at the kitchen table, although I'm still wrapped in Malcolm's embrace and can only see that shock of white hair and his eyes. "Why, yes, he did. It was all I could do to keep him"—he gestures toward Malcolm—"from running out of here."

Malcolm loosens his grip, and I ease back, a hand planted on his chest. His gaze is unfathomable, and he gives me one of his intense looks, the sort that might scar—if I let it.

"Katy." My name is barely a whisper, and he traces my cheek-bone with a fingertip.

"I'm okay. Really. Well, I mean, there's this." I hold up my right hand. The barest hint of pink circles my wrist. "From where the attack ghost grabbed me."

Malcolm's eyes go wide. "Attack ghost?"

"Let's see," is all Nigel says.

I ease from Malcolm's embrace and let his brother inspect my wrist.

"Yes." Nigel traces the mark with gentle fingertips. "This is Roland's handiwork. He likes to leave behind his calling card, so to speak."

"I think he simply lacks the control not to."

At the sound of this new voice, I glance up. In the kitchen doorway, there stands Prescott Jones, backlit by the fairy lights on the deck. He is impeccably dressed as always, his linen shirt without a single wrinkle, his dark hair smooth. The brown and white wingtips gleam as if they're new, which they probably are.

At the sight of Prescott, Malcolm bristles and eases me into the crook of his arm. As for Prescott? He's nothing but amused by this.

"Go make her some tea," Nigel says to Malcolm. "Fire spice, I think." Nigel's gaze meets mine. "Are you chilled?"

Now that he's mentioned it? Goose bumps prickle my arms, and my face is oddly cold, like I've been outside raking leaves on a brisk autumn day.

"A little," I admit.

"Definitely fire spice." Nigel nods toward the samovar on the kitchen counter. "Go."

Malcolm plants a kiss on my cheek, and his lips nearly scald. He's always so warm. But this? I rub my wrist, hoping to banish the chill. This is wrong.

Prescott pulls out a chair and then sweeps an arm in my direction. "Sit. Tell us what happened."

So I do, from the moment Roland Harrington-Hayes stepped into the alley until he pulled out the contract from his suit coat pocket.

"Wait," Nigel says. "You didn't *sign* this contract, did you?"

I refrain from rolling my eyes. "That's when he used the attack ghost. He tried to force me to sign."

Nigel slaps his hands on the kitchen table, and his gaze goes from Malcolm to Prescott. "He's stepped over the line. This has got to be an ethics violation. Right?"

Prescott shrugs. "Maybe?"

From my back pocket, I tug the contract. "I have it here if you want to look at it."

Prescott raises an eyebrow, and Nigel looks impressed. He scans it and passes it to Prescott.

"And that's a disgrace," Nigel adds, a finger aimed at the contract. He turns to me. "You would've given up all rights to Springside. The whole place would be swarming with necromancers."

Like that's never happened.

"I say we bring it to the board," Nigel continues. "Have them kick Roland to the curb before his term is even up. It would serve him right."

Prescott holds up a finger. "Maybe." He shifts and focuses his attention on me. "Katy, what did you do?"

What did I do, exactly? I pull in a breath to gather my thoughts. At that moment, Malcolm places a glass of tea in front of me. The heat from the steam and the spices clear my head. The concoction contains cinnamon and cardamom, and so many pinches of this and dashes of that. No one else could brew it the way Malcolm does.

I wrap my hands around the glass and let the tea warm my fingers. Then I take the tiniest sip (this is not a tea you gulp) and exhale. "Thank you," I say, and the words emerge with a sigh.

Both Prescott and Nigel are staring expectantly, so I continue my story.

"Okay, when it was clear the ghost was going to force me to sign, I decided to break its tether to Roland."

"You *what?*" Nigel deflates, all the righteousness draining from him. He pinches the bridge of his nose between his forefinger and thumb.

Prescott, on the other hand, throws his head back and laughs.

"What? What did I do?" I look to Malcolm, but he only shrugs.

"Katy." Prescott is still chuckling. "You can't go around stealing ghosts from necromancers."

"I wasn't trying to steal the ghost. I was trying to free it. It doesn't like Roland." I glance at Nigel, who's still pinching the bridge of his nose, and then Malcolm. "It was going to stop the attack once I freed it. I could tell."

"So much for taking this to the association," Nigel murmurs.

"What was I supposed to do?"

"In cases like this?" Prescott says. "Normally, a necromancer would deploy a ghost of his—"

"Or her."

"Or *her* own."

"I don't have ghosts to deploy because I'm not a—"

"Necromancer," Prescott finishes. "Yes, yes. We know." He gives me a look, and really, I don't think I deserve that eye roll.

"Katy?" Malcolm touches my cheek. "Are you hungry?"

I sink against the back of my chair, the weight of the day pressing down on me. I give him a slight nod.

Malcolm stands, skewering both his brother and Prescott with a glare. "We can finish talking after the grilled cheese."

WE—NIGEL, Prescott, and me—manage to remain silent until the sandwiches hit the griddle. Something about the sizzle and the steam makes us all relax. Nigel loses that pinched expression, and he has me describe Roland's reaction—more than once.

He graces me with that warm, brotherly smile. "I wish I could've seen that."

We discuss the mall and whether a necromancer could hide lockers like that or whether it was misdirection. Or could it be something more? After all, I thought I heard the entity. Malcolm thought he heard piped-in music. And our little Springside ghost was confused as well.

"So, what's going on?" I ask after I've consumed an entire grilled cheese sandwich. "Do you think it's Roland?"

His appearance—today of all days—is not exactly a fluke. This, I'm sure of.

"It's been almost a year since Orson's retribution," Nigel says. "There will be a vote in September for a permanent chair."

Prescott shakes his head in both admiration and disbelief. "If Roland had pulled off this contract thing? He would've been a shoo-in."

"Absolutely," Nigel agrees.

"Why?" I ask.

Prescott raises an eyebrow, a wry twist to his lips. "A concession from the region's strongest necromancer?"

It takes me a moment, but then I realize he means me. "I'm not a—" I begin, but then clamp my mouth shut. I try again. "I'm not the strongest in the region. There's you, and Reginald, and Malcolm and I are—"

"Katy." Nigel's voice is almost unbearably gentle. "You not only caught an entity of untold power, but you held on to it. Not even my father has managed that. That alone makes you the strongest in the region."

Something about that doesn't sound fair, doesn't take into account all factors. "And yet, I almost ended up signing a terrible contract this evening."

"Except that you didn't," Malcolm says. "Believe them." He shifts in his chair and then scoots closer. With tender fingers, he brushes a few strands of hair from my forehead. "I can see how strong you are. I've always been able to see it."

"I think we can expect more of this. It's what, June?" Prescott counts on his fingers. "July, August, September. Everyone will head back to the region, establish their residency, and either make a run for chair or at least have a say in the matter."

"Is that why you bought a house in St. Columba?" I ask.

Prescott gives me a smooth, sly smile. "In part."

I stand, collect the sandwich plates, and ease them into the porcelain sink. "Well, I don't want to be chair of the Midwest Necromancer Association. I don't even want to be part of their club."

"It's not really a club," Nigel mutters as if he, too, is tired of my shenanigans.

But Prescott laughs. "You know, it would be nice to get a little diversity into the association, not to mention a chair who isn't another Orson clone." He sighs and reaches for the tea Malcolm has set on the table. "I don't suppose that's going to happen."

That almost makes me feel guilty. Almost. But it's not what I want, not right now, and not from life in general. What I really want are my ghosts, all the Springside ones still trapped in the mall.

"Do you think the association owns the mall?" I ask.

"Possibly," Nigel says. "It's probably buried in a trail of shell organizations and paper companies, but someone owns that space. I'll start digging tonight."

"Do you think it was an old trap of Orson's?" Malcolm ventures.

"It could be." Prescott looks impressed. "That's something I can—"

Before he can finish, his phone rings. The ringtone is something soft, something approaching romantic. When his eyes light up, I know it's something exclusive to this particular caller.

"Excuse me." He pushes from his chair and heads for the back door. "I need to take this."

The screen door settles. From the backyard comes the sound of murmurings. We sit there, all three of us, wondering. At last, Malcolm clears his throat.

"I can call around to some of my college buddies, the urban explorers. I mean, this place is a gold mine. There's got to be a reason people are staying away." He turns to Nigel. "How long do you think the ward's been there?"

"Months, definitely. Possibly years. I haven't seen it in person, so it's hard to say. But it's worth checking into. Might give us an idea of when the ward was established, if nothing else."

I'm not sure what I can contribute, but the word *years* swirls in my mind. That sign:

Cedar Hills Mall
A Dream Come True

Maybe it was simply some cheesy marketing, but I get the feeling that—back in the day—this mall was a big deal. Someone here in Springside might remember just how big. I'm about to proclaim my own plans when Prescott sticks his head inside the kitchen door.

"Katy? Would you mind coming out here for a minute?"

As I push back my chair to follow Prescott, Malcolm places a gentle hand on my wrist. His fingers are warm and reassuring. For a moment, I bask in how he's so steadfast and constant, how he's always there for me.

"It's fine," I mouth, but his eyes remain worried, the crinkles deepening at the edges.

Yes, it's true. Prescott did conspire with Orson once, lured me into the dark alone, and then kidnapped me. But it's not like he's going to do it again, especially in my own back yard.

At least, I don't think he will.

PRESCOTT IS a shadowy presence beneath the willow tree. I follow the glow from the back porch lamp and let the fairy lights around the deck guide my way. Halfway across the lawn, I tip my chin toward the sky. I can't see many stars, but I greet the full moon with a quiet hello.

I'm at the curtain of the willow tree's branches when an other-worldly presence crashes down on me. I flinch. It's strong—oh, is it strong—and has the aggressive toughness of an attack ghost.

Then the air around me shimmers and sparkles. It's like standing in the middle of supernatural confetti. From beneath the willow tree comes Prescott's soft chuckle.

"Someone's excited to finally meet you." Prescott sweeps aside the branches, and I step through.

"Someone?" I turn a full circle to get a read on this ghost. I detect nothing but unrestrained delight.

"Katy Lindstrom, meet Chaucer, one of my ghosts. Chaucer, as you've already guessed, this is Katy. If you behave yourself, she might brew you some Kona blend."

"Chaucer?" I ask. "As in Geoffrey Chaucer?"

"Maybe." Prescott lets the curtain of branches swing back into place. "They simply tell me their names, or what they'd like their names to be. Sometimes I think it's aspirational."

Not unlike Unicorn.

"Well, it's nice to meet you," I say to the sparkling presence in front of me.

Chaucer manifests a human-like form and executes a stately bow.

"And there's someone else I'd like you to meet."

Just now, I notice that his phone is resting in the palm of one hand, screen tilted toward his face.

"Katy Lindstrom," Prescott says once again, "meet my ... friend, George Phan."

I've seen this man before, in a photograph on this very phone. Dark, soulful eyes meet mine. His gaze is filled with both concern and skepticism.

"You really are Katy Lindstrom," he says—or actually, demands.

"George is a lawyer," Prescott whispers, and slips his phone into my hand.

"I left my wallet back in the house," I say, "but I could go get it and show you my driver's license."

This softens him—somewhat. Despite those soulful eyes, George is unflinching. It's there in the set of his jaw, the severe line of his brow. I'm glad I'm not on the witness stand.

"Prescott's told me what happened last year," George says.

This? This surprises me. I cast a glance at Prescott. He's

standing a few feet away, hands tucked in his pockets, his gaze on the night sky, as if he doesn't care about this conversation.

Something tells me he cares a lot.

"The warehouse," George continues, "and Orson Yates, and the … the—"

"Kidnapping?" I supply.

A double sigh echoes around me, one from the phone, the other from a few feet away. The willow branches shudder as if the tree itself—or maybe just Chaucer—wishes it could sigh too.

"Yes." And George's voice is like stone. "That."

"It's not as bad as it first seems."

Because really, it's not. I've made my peace with Prescott, even if Malcolm hasn't completely come around. "If Prescott hadn't been there," I add, but then pause.

Really, there are so many *ifs* to that situation that I don't like to revisit them. What if Prescott hadn't been there and I had to face Orson alone? What if Carter Dupree hadn't turned at the last minute to cut me free? I give my head a little shake to clear it. If you think too hard about the enormity of one small decision, it could paralyze you.

So I don't let it. "Prescott was there, and it's a good thing he was."

I explain the retribution, and how he spoke up for me, how he tried—along with Reginald Weaver—to stop Orson. Clearly, this is new information. George's eyes light with discovery. He's not entirely convinced of Prescott's heroism, but some of the cynicism slips away.

And I see what it is that Prescott has done. He's let *me* tell this part of the story, unprompted. The entity once called him opportunistic and conniving. I have to wonder if Prescott is still a bit of both. Of course, the entity also mentioned that those were admirable traits for a necromancer.

But then, it would.

When I'm done with the tale, George stares at me straight on. His mouth is softer, and his eyes hold nothing but concern.

"And you're okay now," he asks.

"I am," I insist. I hold up my left hand, ring finger on display. The moonstone glimmers in the low light, the vintage setting harkening back to another era. "See? I'm even engaged."

"That you are," he says. "Congratulations."

I pass the phone back to Prescott. A few murmurs float in the air. For once, I won't give in to the urge to eavesdrop. In fact, I'm about to step through the curtain of willow branches and head back to the house when Prescott calls out to me.

"Katy, we need to talk."

His voice is devoid of the constant amusement I associate with him. His tone is like ice, and there's nothing humorous in what he's about to tell me.

CHAPTER 6

Prescott stares at the dark screen of his phone and then tucks it back into his pocket. He looks at me straight on, as if he's afraid I'll miss a single word.

"I need to apologize for what happened."

"You did already."

"Actually, I said I *should* apologize—I'm fairly certain I never did."

I search my memory, but everything's hazy. The words we spoke. Smoke from Darien's campfire. The scent of Kona blend. I raise a hand and let it drop. "Actions speaking louder than words?"

"Perhaps, but the world would be a better place if more people apologized."

He's right about that.

"So, I'm sorry. I'm especially sorry for what happened in the warehouse, with Malcolm."

Without warning, my whole body recoils. Despite the warm night, shivers wash over my skin. A wave of nausea hits me, and I'm afraid the grilled cheese will make a grand reappearance. I almost lost him that day, almost lost everything.

"I still see it in my dreams." Prescott's gaze is on the treetop and the otherworldly presence that glimmers there. "I told you once that George used to look at me the way Malcolm looks at you. I can tell you the moment my desire shattered. It was watching Malcolm, half-dead, trying to come to your rescue." He turns that gaze on me. "And it was watching you trying to save everything you love."

My mouth is numb, and my throat dry. I don't have words; I may never have words for what happened that day.

"Oh, sure," Prescott says, his tone filled with self-deprecation. "I could've held the entity. I could have ordered it to make George love me again. I could have built a life, an empire, a world all my own. Ultimately, it would've been false."

My throat is still tight, as if some invisible hand is gently—but persistently—squeezing it. "You meant to keep me safe."

This is what George and Malcolm don't understand. Prescott never meant to harm me.

"In my arrogance, I thought I could. I hadn't realized how desperate Orson had become." He stares into the middle distance and then rouses himself. "So I'd like to make amends." His tone is crisper, as if he's shaken off the melancholy and regret.

"How?" That single word comes out stronger than I expected it to.

"I know Nigel's searching, and he'll probably find what we're looking for, eventually. I'd like to add my own sort of search to this. Roland isn't acting on his own. Never has, never will. Some-one's pulling his strings. I plan to find out who that is."

I nod like I understand how he's going to do that.

"First the ghosts, your trip to the mall, and then Roland? It all has a bad feel to it."

I nod again because I absolutely agree with him there.

"Maybe it's simply a trap Orson never had the chance to spring, and now Roland's taking advantage of that. But in case it isn't—" He lifts a hand and lets it fall.

Yes. In case it isn't. Then what? "What do you need from me?"

There's just enough ambient light—from Chaucer, I think—that I see Prescott's eyebrow lift.

"I knew you'd catch on. What I need is for you not to mention this to Nigel—or Malcolm, for that matter."

Oh, a secret. I hate those. I'm a terrible liar, and really, Prescott should know that.

"Can I ask why?"

Prescott inclines his head.

Really? I sigh. "Why?"

"Because after we failed to stop your retribution, I promised Nigel that I wouldn't do certain things, deal with certain people."

"Would those be certain necromancer things and people?"

"They would. But to find out who's behind this, I may need to break that promise."

"Is that why you bought the house in St. Columba? To keep an eye on necromancer things?"

St. Columba is a small town about ten minutes away on the Minnesota River. It has a lush private college, a postcard-perfect downtown, and plenty of old buildings with ghosts. Malcolm and I have done several emergency eradications there.

Prescott gives me a hint of that sly smile. "In part."

"So, what do I tell them, then?"

He brushes off my concern. "I'll think of something. But I'm leaving Chaucer behind." He points toward the top of the willow tree.

At the sound of his name, Chaucer makes the leaves glimmer with an otherworldly sparkle. It's like standing in the center of a Christmas tree.

"Two-fold precaution," Prescott continues. "He's an excellent watch ghost. He'll keep an eye on your place, and Nigel and Sadie's as well. And if you ever need me, if something happens here, you can send him to find me."

I tip my chin skyward and call out, "Stop by the kitchen in the morning, and you can have some coffee."

Now the tree shakes so much I'm afraid it will lose all its leaves.

"Ah, the way to a ghost's heart ... I mean, if ghosts had hearts."

"I think they do," I say. "In a way."

"You could be right about that." Prescott sweeps open the curtain of branches for me.

I hesitate. I have something of my own I need to confess. I'm not sure how, so I simply rush the words all at once.

"When Malcolm and I were at the mall, I thought I heard the entity."

This earns me another eyebrow lift. "Oh, so Katy Lindstrom has a secret."

Yes. Yes, damn it, I do. I hate that I haven't told Malcolm or Nigel. But I can't. They'd only worry and fret, and it might not be anything.

"What did you hear it say?" Prescott asks.

"Something like, 'Leaving so soon?'" It wasn't that long ago, but the echo of its voice is impossibly far away.

Prescott snorts. "Mimicry, perhaps."

"So you don't think it was the entity at all?"

"It's no longer on this plane of existence."

"And you know that how, exactly?"

Prescott shrugs, all cavalier and innocent. "I may have tried to invoke it a time or two, just to see what might happen."

Yes, opportunistic and conniving.

"And I know other necromancers have tried as well. Some have even attempted to replicate the research your grandparents and Malcolm's grandfather did."

"That won't work." Really, I have no basis for saying this, except that they ended up tearing the entity from what it considered its home. Since it no longer has a home, it can't be torn from it.

As far as I know, anyway.

"So, if it wasn't the entity," I venture, "what was it?"

"There are so many beings out there that it's hard to say. An unusually strong ghost, perhaps."

"I didn't sense the otherworldly."

"A demon, then. They enjoy finding vulnerable humans and taking up residence. In which case, it could be something nearly as dangerous as the entity."

I don't know whether to be glad it wasn't the entity, or disappointed. *Nearly as dangerous* isn't something I wanted to hear.

"It likely wants you to open your mind to it." Prescott inhales a long, steadying breath as if he's steeling himself. "Let me suggest that would be a bad idea."

Yes. That would be a very bad idea.

"As I said, this whole setup has a bad feel to it, unsavory and wrong." This time when he pulls back the curtain of willow branches, I step through. "Be careful, Katy."

I stare up at the Victorian, windows aglow, with Malcolm somewhere inside.

"I plan to be," I say. "I absolutely plan to be."

WHEN I RETURN to the kitchen, the air is warm, and I hear the soft slosh and hum of the dishwasher. The table is clear of crumbs, and the sink gleams. Malcolm is straightening the tea towels on their rack. He's whistling, the sound cheerful and content, but I let out a sigh of dismay.

"I'm sorry."

He turns and graces me with one of his sweet, dark roast grins. "For what?"

"You cooked." I point toward the sink. "I clean. You know, that sort of thing."

We've never established an actual routine for these chores.

Malcolm likes to cook. He's better at it than I am (well, except for the coffee). I like the quiet rhythm of cleaning up. It helps me think.

Right now? I have a lot to think about.

"I don't mind," Malcolm says. "Besides, it looked kind of intense out there."

Oh, it kind of was.

"He wanted to apologize." I don't think Prescott will mind if I tell Malcolm this, especially if it eases things between them.

"Yeah, well, about time."

There's enough of a thin-ice edge to Malcolm's voice that I let the subject drop. Really, it's better if I don't have to relive the conversation beneath the willow tree.

Malcolm opens the cupboard where we keep our at-home supply of coffee beans and sugar and everything else we use for eradications, along with our morning coffee.

You never know when you'll need to brew a pot of Kona blend.

"Are we low on anything?" I place a hand on his shoulder and peer into the cupboard. He's warm and sturdy, and when his hand captures mine, all the tension from the evening simply melts away.

"Just checking," he says, "since we'll have a couple extras for breakfast."

In the back yard, the willow tree continues to glow with Chaucer's ghostly presence, the lights pulsing and cascading down the branches.

"It's not the most subtle attack ghost I've ever met," Malcolm says, "but maybe that's a good thing. Like having one of those alarm system signs in the front yard."

"Couple of guests?" I glance around for the sprite, but it's nowhere to be found. I raise my chin but can't even catch a telltale hint of the otherworldly.

Malcolm gestures toward the ceiling. "It found Belinda."

I follow his gaze upward. "She's opening the Pancake House with Samia tomorrow morning."

"I warned her," he says. "She's going to regret the reunion when four a.m. rolls around."

Oh, but it's been so long since Belinda's had a sprite. The new ones in town are funny and often sweet. They visit her, but they don't stick around. But this is a Springside sprite. Something tells me that makes all the difference.

I reach for the canister of beans, and I don't need to tell Malcolm that I'm brewing a thermos for Belinda. He's already filling the percolator with filtered water. This is one of those things about him, one of those things I adore.

And Malcolm in my kitchen? With the scent of Kona blend in the air?

I can't imagine a more perfect evening than this.

The aroma from the coffee is so tempting, I almost pour myself a cup. But it's too late for caffeine. Instead, I carry an extra-large mug to the back porch and set it on the rail.

"To help keep you awake," I say to the glimmer in the treetop.

Not that ghosts actually sleep. At least, I don't think they do. But no matter. Chaucer swoops down and vacuums up the contents so quickly and so thoroughly that when I retrieve the cup, the inside is completely dry.

"Doesn't Prescott give you coffee?"

A rumble, low and disgruntled, comes from the back yard. I don't talk to ghosts, not the way necromancers do, but I get the message.

Prescott makes *terrible* coffee.

This time when I return to the kitchen, I catch Malcolm whistling again. I listen for a bit. The tune is familiar, and yet not. It's like an echo of a song that I used to know.

"What is that?" I ask at last.

He stops, lips still pursed. I almost swoop in for a kiss, but he breaks into a laugh before I can.

"'The Girl from Ipanema'."

"The song you heard at the mall?"

"I can't get it out of my head."

"Try," I suggest.

"No, really, it's not a bad little song." From his back pocket, he pulls out his phone. "Seriously. Sinatra did a version with the composer. It's classic." He cues up the song, and the first strains entwine with the Kona blend still in the air.

He holds out a hand. "Come on."

"What?"

He nods toward the living room, his intent clear.

"To this?"

"Why not? It's got a beat, and you can dance to it."

I laugh. "You're crazy. I can't really dance."

"I might be crazy, but I can dance." He holds out his hand again, and I can't resist. "I'll show you how."

"It's a bossa nova," he says once we're in the living room. He plants a sturdy hand on my hip. "The basics aren't too tricky."

The basics are so too tricky. My feet are a tangle beneath me, and I feel as if I've sprouted an extra limb. But it's true: Malcolm really can dance. He did it all at Nigel's wedding—foxtrot, waltz, the Lindy Hop.

"Where did you learn to dance?"

"This dance? College. I took ballroom dancing as a Phys Ed elective."

"You can do that?"

"It was better than bowling at 7:45 in the morning. But the rest?" He twirls me. I've caught on to enough of the steps that I don't go stumbling—too badly. "My mother. She enrolled us— Nigel and me—in one of those social dance and etiquette schools. It was hideous."

Malcolm doesn't talk much about his childhood. His parents fought—constantly, from the sound of it. But I'd be lying if I said I didn't love these glimpses into his world before he came into mine.

"Did you have to wear a suit?"

"*And* a tie. But the girls had it worse. Party dresses with all those frills and white gloves."

I spent most of my childhood in shorts or jeans and coffee-stained T-shirts. Frilly party dresses? Not a chance. "I would've failed."

"We did, actually. Nigel deployed a ghost at the end-of-class party. Strawberry punch everywhere. On white linen tablecloths, at least five dresses, and all the white gloves. It looked like a crime scene." Malcolm pauses, his eyes bright with memories and mischief. "No one could really prove it was him, but we were asked to leave before they handed out the graduation certificates."

As if I've suddenly traveled back in time, I can see Nigel as a precocious necromancer, hands tucked in his pockets, waiting for the right moment to unleash a ghost, and Malcolm, adorable in a tiny suit coat and tie.

"Did all the mothers pinch your cheeks?" I ask.

"Nigel, not so much. Me?" He scrunches his face as if avoiding all those pinchy fingers. "Constantly."

I *knew* it.

He spins me again. "You know, we should have them play this at our wedding. If we get good enough, we can make it our first dance."

"I don't think it's a wedding song," I say.

"I'll rewrite the lyrics." He hums along with Sinatra and then bursts out with, "The ghost from Cedar Hills Mall goes haunting and something, something ... I'll think of the rest later."

He has me laughing again, so hard that when he twirls me this time, I land against his chest. I stay there, where it's warm and safe and perfect.

"Speaking of which." His voice is a seductive rumble against my ear. "We probably should set a date."

"For what?" The second I've said the words, I know they're the absolute wrong ones.

That rumble beneath my cheek grows ever so slightly irked. It's fairly obvious who's been stocking the lobby of K&M Ghost Eradication Specialists with bridal magazines.

It certainly hasn't been me.

"A date for the wedding," I say before he can. Maybe if I spew words into the air, he won't be so disappointed with me. "Planning takes time, so I suppose we should—"

"But?" His voice has that thin-ice edge to it.

"Well, you know," I say, hoping to make him laugh, "all I really have to wear is the skater skirt."

Now his chest rumbles with warmth laced with humor. I melt again, this time with relief.

"Here's the thing." He tilts my chin. From this angle, I can almost, but not quite, see his whole expression. "You could totally wear the skater skirt. We could get a license and get married at the courthouse. Just you and me, with Nigel and Sadie as witnesses—"

"But?" I echo.

"There was something about Nigel's wedding. I never expected it to be so"—here, he shrugs, and I inch up on tiptoes so I can glimpse his eyes—"moving. But it was."

"And it's something you might like as well?"

"I think I would."

My breath catches in my throat and lodges there. Those four words betray so much. In them, I hear hope and vulnerability and trust.

Then I think of what a monumental task it is to have a wedding, even a small one. Tulle and lace and flowing trains and flowers all compete with the thoughts in my head. I didn't even have an open house when I graduated from high school. I was raised by my eccentric, ghost-catching grandmother, after all. The closest I came to a big party was birthdays at the Springside Pancake House.

I don't even know where to start. But for Malcolm? I gaze up at him and detect that hint of vulnerability in his eyes.

"Yes." I plant a hand on his chest, above his heart. "We'll have a wedding."

Now I'm rewarded with one of those sweet, dark-roast grins of his. His hand covers mine, and the squeeze he gives my fingers is full of excitement and hope.

"You pick the date," he says. "Whenever you like, and obviously, you don't have to decide tonight."

Maybe it's my imagination, but the word *soon* floats in the air between us.

I resolve to find the perfect date—and soon. I resolve to say yes to the dress.

Just not tonight.

The best time to catch Police Chief Ramsey—and catch him unaware—is early in the morning. It's also best to go in equipped.

True, the Springside Police Department has upgraded its coffee supply. But Chief has never turned down a thermos of mine.

When I enter the lobby, the whole place already smells and sounds like the Coffee Depot. Fresh ground beans, the warm, sleepy scent of frothed milk, and the whirr and clank of a very fancy coffeemaker. It's one of those big, aggressive models, bright red. The sort that—if you don't watch yourself—might take a finger or two. The man currently running it does so with the dexterity that might impress even my grandmother.

"Oh, Katy, you're up early."

Penny Wilson is standing behind her desk, surrounded by a forest of stacked file folders—some thin as twigs, others thick as tree branches.

"So are you," I say. "And on a Saturday."

My gaze darts from Penny to Chief's broad back. He still hasn't turned around, which means he might be in a mood. I didn't expect to find Penny here, but maybe it's good that she is.

"We're digitizing all of Springside's old case files," she says now. "We had someone here from the BCA last week. She thought it might help solve cold cases."

Unless the Bureau of Criminal Apprehension has added a supernatural department, I'm not sure what they think they might find in Springside. When my grandmother was alive, she offered to help clear some of the backlog. Really, half the mischief people blame on *kids these days* can be chalked up to one cause: sprites.

Especially in Springside.

"I'm paying her overtime," Chief grumbles. He still hasn't turned from the coffeemaker, so I can't get a read on his expression. Chief Ramsey is almost always gruff, but there's gruff, and then there's *gruff*.

I need to know which Chief I'm dealing with this morning.

"And in cappuccinos," Penny adds, eyes bright, as if she's already chugged several. But then she leans closer, voice lower. "Really, I don't mind. Since Roberta retired from teaching, I'd almost rather be here. She's nonstop. Our kitchen. Complete remodel." Penny casts her gaze toward the ceiling like she can't believe the chaos in her kitchen.

It's then I notice that her frizzy hair is flecked with blue paint.

"It was a mess when we did the remodel on our kitchenette," I say. "And it's not like we had to sleep in the office or anything."

I took to brewing coffee on my truck's tailgate, using our camp stove. In fact, Chief Ramsey himself gave me a ticket for that, although I doubt there's such a thing as brewing coffee without a license.

"I suppose you've come to pay up for that," Chief says as if he's reading my mind. He turns from the coffeemaker, a patented Chief Ramsey scowl forming on his brow.

"Of course." I try to channel Penny and give him my brightest smile. "And I thought I'd drop this off as well. As a thank you for last night." I pull a thermos from the canvas sack at my side. "Although with that fancy espresso machine, you probably don't want my coffee anymore."

His expression falters, a hint of fatherly softness touching his eyes. "I will never refuse Lindstrom coffee."

"I wouldn't turn down a cappuccino." I hold out the thermos.

For a moment, he hesitates. Then the thermos slips from my hand, and he turns back to the red beast, which roars to life again.

"I already took care of it," Penny whispers under cover of the grind and whirr. Even so, she dutifully takes my credit card and pretends to process the charge.

"Chief's been kind of lonely since the divorce," she confides now, voice so low I can barely hear her.

No doubt this is the real reason Penny is here this morning.

"And I can't put my finger on it," she adds, "but even the station feels lonelier lately, like we're missing something."

Because they *are* missing something. The two sprites that used to haunt here are gone, swept up by Malcolm when he collected all the ghosts of Springside to help bring me back to this plane.

This is not something I can explain to Penny, or Chief for that matter.

Despite the free-flowing cappuccinos—and the organic raw sugar to go along with them—not a single new sprite has ventured past the front door of the police station. I'm not sure why that is, or how I might tempt a couple of the friendlier sprites to start haunting here.

Chief hands me a freshly made cappuccino. Steam rises from the foam. Really, this is sprite heaven. The station should be teeming with them. I take a sip, and the shot of espresso instantly clears my thoughts and bolsters my resolve.

"This is good," I tell Chief.

He harrumphs a response.

"Really good." I take another sip of courage. "You know, if this police chief thing doesn't work out, you could always get a job as a barista at the Coffee Depot."

That earns me a laugh. His expression softens further, and there's a gleam in his eyes I've never seen before.

"I was thinking of that, for when I retire. Or even setting up my own little pop-up shop."

"That would be amazing!"

I know better than to blurt at Chief. He takes a step back as if I might drag him from the station for an interview at the Coffee Depot. But, considering how my own went?

Hardly.

Still, while I don't know—exactly—what makes him tick, I do know my unbridled enthusiasm isn't it.

I try again.

"I mean, if you want to talk to Malcolm about setting up a small business, I'm sure he'd be glad to help."

He considers the cup of Kona blend he's poured himself and then nods. "I might do that."

"Speaking of businesses," I say, "do either of you know anything about the old Cedar Hills Mall?"

As segues go, this one's inelegant. But it's like I've uttered some magic words. The look in Penny's eyes is dreamy, her mouth a soft "o" as if she's reliving a fond memory. Even Chief has his head tilted to one side, and there's just the slightest hint of a smile on his lips.

"Some kids from the high school are trying to convince us that it's haunted," I add.

At this, Chief stiffens, shoulders and spine unerringly straight. I silently curse myself.

"Which kids?" he demands. "Ethan and his crew of delinquents?"

The last thing I need is to get a bunch of kids from the high school in trouble with Chief. Besides, Ethan's a good kid. "No, just some teens playing a prank. They wanted us to do a drive-by. Thought I'd check with you first."

"Not my jurisdiction. And the Cedar Hills police chief isn't as lenient as I am. She's strictly by the book, especially when it comes to trespassing."

Yes, because Chief's a huge softy.

"Oh, Chief, do you remember when they first opened the mall?" Penny leans forward, nearly knocking a stack of file folders to the floor. "It was a big deal. They even ran a shuttle service from Springside to Cedar Hills."

Chief glowers at his coffee as if it's offended him. "Town council wasn't too pleased about that."

"But for the kids who couldn't drive yet?" Her face glows with the memories, making her look like the teenager she once was. "They had a cineplex with six theaters and dollar matinees. We would start in one and go from theater to theater until they closed at night." Penny casts Chief a sidelong glance. "I mean, of course, *I* would always buy a new ticket for each show."

He snorts and rolls his eyes.

Penny is undeterred. "And didn't you take Katy's mom to the movies once?"

Both Chief and I freeze at the exact same moment. My throat is tight, and my heart is pounding a strange, staccato beat. This wasn't what I meant about the mall being haunted.

But now I'm wondering if it truly is.

Chief clears his throat. "It was a friendly sort of thing. I was already working full-time, night shift here at the station. Everyone else had already seen *Batman Returns*. I couldn't get anyone to go with me." He pauses, and that almost-smile makes another appearance. "Your mom, though, said she'd go with me. I'm not sure she wanted to see it again, but I was glad for the company."

I add this glimpse of my mother to all the others I've collected, many from Chief himself. Bit by bit, I'm piecing together the puzzle. I may never have the whole picture, but what I do have is bright and interesting and kind.

"Why did the mall close down?" I ask.

"Recession finally killed it," Chief says. "Not enough traffic. It limped along for a few years, but the whole place eventually shuttered."

Penny considers for a moment, chin on her fists. "But they put in that expansion. That should've saved it." She turns to me. "It was all underground—another two theaters, an arcade, a bowling alley. And in the evening, they had Cedar Hills After Dark."

"That sounds risqué."

"Nothing more than black lights and 3.2 beer at the bowling alley," Chief says, shaking his head at the innocence of it. "R-rated movies, some dance parties. It was supposed to keep the twenty-one and older crowd from going up to the Twin Cities and the Mall of America."

"We went a few times," Penny adds. "It should've been great, but it was almost like it was..." She trails off. In her sigh, I hear the start of a word, one that sounds like *haunted*.

"Recession," Chief says again. "Put a lot of places out of business. Most of the stores migrated over to River Hills Mall in Mankato, and that was that."

I wonder, though. I think of how strange the space felt, and not just because it was abandoned. I wonder if it's something more than bad business decisions and a bad economy.

I've always known the past can haunt. Usually, that's something I can take care of with freshly brewed coffee and a supply of Tupperware.

Both Chief and Penny have fallen silent, as if they're still caught in those memories. Nostalgia clouds their expressions. Penny's smile is wistful. Chief is wincing slightly, as if he's just touched a bruise.

Neither one notices when I leave. I stand on the police station's front steps and consider.

Cedar Hills Mall:
A Dream Come True.

At some point, did that dream turn into a nightmare?

CHAPTER 8

I'm still standing in front of the police station when my phone pings.

Belinda: I have what you crave.

The morning sunshine promises the first hot day of summer. I can taste the heat in the air, along with the aroma of maple syrup and bacon from the Springside Pancake House.

My stomach rumbles.

In the restaurant's big bay window, I catch the explosion of blonde curls and a wave.

Belinda's right. She absolutely does. I text Malcolm to let him know where I am, although I don't expect a response. He was up late. Apparently, contacting old college buddies involves playing video games until two in the morning.

The breakfast rush is still half an hour away, so it's seat yourself at the Pancake House. I do, picking a booth in Belinda's section. This early, I can hear the chatter from the kitchen. A few families occupy tables near the back.

Since it's Saturday, what I don't see is Carter Dupree at the counter, watching the opening numbers and paging through the *Wall Street Journal*. I'm not sure what he does with his Friday evenings, but I wouldn't be surprised if it involves video games as well.

A few minutes later, Belinda slides a plate of pancakes in front of me, along with a large orange juice. Then she dissolves into the opposite seat, a few wayward curls sticking to her cheeks.

"I don't know how Samia does it." Belinda takes a swipe at the strands, but her hand falls into her lap as if it's simply too much effort. "I'm not sure how I'm going to do it."

"You'll get the hang of it."

Honestly? She already has. This past winter, we both started taking college classes—business ones for both of us. I need to know how to run K&M Ghost Eradication Specialists beyond making the coffee. But then? I might major in history. Belinda's going for restaurant management. Jim and Samia will retire some-day, and they want to sell the restaurant to someone who loves it as much as they do.

That someone is most definitely Belinda.

"Yeah, but this whole summer intern thing kind of sucks. At least next week, I get to shadow the fry-cooks." She lifts her head and gives me that dazzling homecoming queen smile. "Thanks for the coffee—you're a lifesaver."

I spear a slice of pancake and dip it in maple syrup. "It's what I do." I then proceed to devour half the plate.

"How did you get on with the sprite?" I figure I can inhale the other half of my plate and maybe start on a second while Belinda talks. She has a sense for sprites that eludes both Malcolm and me.

"Actually? It told me about the necromancers that ... live there at the mall."

All of a sudden, my appetite vanishes. "What? The place is abandoned."

"And no one really lives at a mall, either," she says. "It's a sprite." Belinda raises a hand and lets it drop. "You know how they are."

"Necromancers," I say. "As in more than one?"

"Twins."

Twin necromancers? That's odd. That tidbit might also help Nigel narrow his search. I send him a quick text and then ponder that. Twins could most definitely create a strong visible ward. Maybe this is all starting to make sense.

"But here's the thing," Belinda adds. "One of them is old, and one of them is young."

Or not.

"Twins are the same age." It's a silly protest. Belinda knows that, and we both know how illogical sprites can be.

"According to this sprite, they're the same, but one is middle-aged, like Chief Ramsey, and the other is our age."

This is definitely nonsensical sprite talk, and I regret texting Nigel.

"Then they can't be twins."

"It insists they are. The older one is scarier and more powerful. The younger one is nicer but isn't around as much."

I shut my eyes, conjuring the mall in my memory. Obviously, one—or both—of the necromancers was there yesterday. If so, where were they? Hiding behind the prom dresses? Under the counter at the Orange Julius? Up on the second floor, tracking our every move?

A shiver washes down my spine. I almost ask for a cup of coffee, except the pancake house makes terrible coffee. That would end up being something else I'd regret.

"Men?" I venture.

Belinda nods.

"Father and son? Uncle and nephew?"

"Nope and nope. They're twins. I tried to talk it out of that theory. This is the one thing it's absolutely positive about."

"And one is evil, and one is nice?"

She shrugs, and I'm beginning to think this sprite has seen too many horror movies. Still.

"Twins," I muse. "I'm missing something here."

Belinda stands and takes my plate for a refill. "Don't think too hard on it," she says over her shoulder. "I mean, it's just a sprite."

SUNDAY MORNINGS ARE MY FAVORITE, especially in the summer, when the sky is still indigo and everything is holding its breath, waiting for the sun. Even after a long night of ghost-catching, most Sundays, I don't begrudge rising early.

This is something that the little Springside sprite must know. It plants ghostly kisses against my cheek until I—somewhat reluctantly, it's true—open my eyes.

Now that I have, I'm grateful. The breeze that sneaks in through the open windows is laced with lilacs. Something glimmers beyond the gauzy curtains—most likely someone's porch light, but I'm pretending the glow comes from stars or fireflies or maybe even Chaucer up in the willow tree.

Malcolm is warm and solid and sure next to me. He snores lightly, the rhythm reassuring.

Saturday was a long, fruitless day of searching for information and coming up empty. When Malcolm called around to his urban explorer friends, none of them had even heard of Cedar Hills Mall. Nigel was skeptical about the whole twin necromancer thing, and adding it to his search turned up nothing. I asked him to look up the property management company. Something about it or its name bugs me. According to Nigel, the company is more than legitimate, with several clients in the Twin Cities and surrounding suburbs. Not to mention zero ties to the Midwest Necromancer Association, as far as he can tell.

Again, I suspect we're missing something—possibly something obvious—and I suspect this little sprite may have some answers.

I plump my pillow and shift to sit, easing carefully so as to not wake Malcolm. Something that sounds like a grumble resonates deep in his chest. I hold my breath as he turns toward the bedroom door. Then the snoring starts again.

I hold a finger against my lips in warning to the sprite. It sparkles and skitters about, excited that we'll be chatting.

I don't talk to ghosts, not the way Malcolm and other necromancers do, and not like Belinda can. Still, I manage to communicate. I want to know more about these twin necromancers, assuming they even exist. I want to know how this little guy managed to escape when the rest of the ghosts couldn't. I don't think it's a spy, but that doesn't mean it isn't bait.

I hold out my hand. The sprite weaves between my fingers like it's running an agility course. It does a backflip for good measure before taking a second run. I can't help but laugh, just a little. I'm not gleaning much from this interaction, just flickers of images—like a scratchy home movie. An old silver percolator my grandmother retired from service years ago. A flash of cherry red that makes me think of Malcolm's convertible. Something that shimmers like gold.

These images are pieces of a story, but I'm missing a large section of the plot. The sprite is resting in the palm of my hand like this effort has completely worn it out. Since this is a sprite, I doubt that. Ghosts are such transactional beings that I suspect it's holding out for some coffee.

Malcolm grumbles once again and rolls toward me.

"Could you two keep it down?" His voice is warm with sleep and humor.

"I was trying to be quiet."

The sprite does another backflip to prove that it, too, was trying to be quiet.

A sigh rumbles in Malcolm's chest. "Katy, your thoughts are so loud, I'm surprised Chief Ramsey hasn't given you a ticket for public disturbance."

I point to the sprite. "I think it wants to tell us something."

The sprite bobs up and down as if it wants to do just that.

Malcolm plumps up his own pillows and makes a half-hearted attempt to sit. "Like whether or not it's a spy?"

At Malcolm's words, the sprite works itself into a frenzy. I knew it really wasn't tired. It buzzes around the room, doing several laps to work up speed. Then it arrows straight for us and cuffs Malcolm on the side of the head.

"Hey! Ow." He rubs his head, fingers further rumpling his hair.

The sprite takes a victory lap before settling in my palm again.

"What we need to know," I say to it, "is whether you truly escaped on your own or if the necromancers let you think that you did." I peer at it intently. "Does that make sense?"

The sprite bobs once and then sinks into my palm as if contemplating my request.

"What are you thinking, Katy?"

"If this little guy escaped, then what happened at the mall wasn't a trap."

"It could still be a trap," he counters. "Just because we don't know who these twin necromancers are doesn't mean it isn't a trap, and it could be one meant for you."

"Okay, okay. Maybe," I say. I'm still not convinced the whole twin thing is true. "But if so, it wasn't a trap ready to be sprung. How about that?"

"And?"

"And that means we can go back and get our ghosts."

Malcolm blows out a breath. "Oh, I really don't like where this is going."

"It also means these necromancers weren't expecting us."

"They will be now."

"Exactly, so why give them more time to prepare?"

I want to explain further. How strange and sometimes empty Springside feels without its original ghosts. I know I should, if not like, at least respect the new ghosts Delilah brought to town. I should be grateful we're making more money than ever before, honing our ghost-catching skills, and genuinely providing a service.

And yet, I want these Springside ghosts. I want to find two sprites to haunt the police station and perhaps one for Chief's old watering can. Maybe among their numbers is an ancient warrior ghost who can keep Mr. Carlotta company. A trio of sprites for Belinda. Some wild ones for the old barn. What I can't do is leave them there to be used or abused by some scary twin necromancers.

"What did you have in mind?" Malcolm's voice is soft and full of understanding.

"I'm not sure, exactly. I just want them back."

"We need to make absolutely certain first, though." He nods toward my palm, where the sprite still rests. "Walking into a trap is not something we're going to do."

I can't argue. I also can't tell if the sprite is faking exhaustion or not. I'm not sure it matters. Misty tendrils of a plan form in my head. I know just the thing to solidify them.

"It's nearly sunrise," I say. "How would you two like an early morning pot of Kona blend?"

The backflips are (almost) never ending.

STEAM from the coffee fortifies all three of us. Malcolm runs a thermos out to Chaucer, who makes the willow tree glimmer like it's doused in fairy lights. Even though most of my neighbors won't notice, I have to wonder if an attack ghost shouldn't be a touch more subtle.

I pour the sprite an extra-large cup, stirring in some sugar and cream. It dips and dives and then lazes on the steam. The air sparks with happiness. Then the sprite's shimmery outline shifts. Again, images flash, like an old movie.

This time, the pictures are sharper. There I am, small Katy, chasing down some sprites—including this one. I'm younger than even Tara is now, maybe no more than nine.

Malcolm chuckles, the sound indulgent and tender. "Gosh, you were cute."

My ponytail flies behind me while the sprites zig and zag, evading my grasp and my Tupperware. At last, I catch them, seal the lid, and toss them into the back of my grandmother's truck. It's only when I turn away—intent on catching a half dozen more—that a single sprite somehow slips from the container and zips off into the air.

"Aren't you the clever one," I say to it now.

Another image flashes, the cherry red that reminds me of Malcolm's convertible. Probably because it *is* Malcolm's convertible. He's stepping from it, golden samovar under one arm, his destination clear: the Coffee Depot.

And I'm blocking his path. Me, with splotches of coffee decorating my interview outfit, my hair damp, my expression defeated and dull. Malcolm's nose wrinkles, and his lip curls ever so slightly. Not that I can blame him.

Okay, at the time, I totally blamed him.

Something slips from the samovar's spigot. It's our friendly little sprite. Back then, I was too focused on Malcolm to notice, and vice versa, I'm sure.

"Hey," he says to that same sprite floating in the steam. "You shouldn't have been able to do that. I had a containment field around my samovar."

"And we all know how that turned out," I murmur.

The glower Malcolm gives me is full of eyebrows and dark eyes. But then a smile steals over his face.

"Yeah." He takes my hand, and we lace our fingers. "We do, don't we?"

The last image is darker. The space around this little sprite is empty and black. Hints of light sneak through cracks. It's at the juncture of two of these cracks that it applies all its efforts.

I swear, I hold my breath and try to make myself as small as possible. The sprite slips through and bursts into the dull light of Cedar Hills Mall.

It glides down the hallways, its moves cautious and un-sprite-like—no excitement at being free, no frenzy. It's slinking away, and it doesn't want anyone to know. It pauses for mere seconds beneath the skylights in the courtyard as if it needs to soak in the sunlight. Then it zips down the corridor and through the drafty main doors.

Truly exhausted now, the sprite sinks until it almost vanishes beneath the liquid. The steam has dissipated, and the coffee itself is too cool for drinking. I pour a fresh cup as a reward.

"There's more," I tell it. "As much as you like." I train my gaze on Malcolm. "What do you think?"

He's giving it—and me—a contemplative smile. "It's a little escape artist."

"It is, isn't it?" I wonder just how many times it has evaded my grasp. "I believe it."

"Katy—" Malcolm's tone holds a warning.

"Can ghosts lie?" I demand. "Can they lie like that?"

Granted, the sprite may have given us a variation of the truth, only the pieces we wanted to see, but I don't think it's lying.

"I don't know," Malcolm admits.

"I believe it, which means even if—and it's a big if—this is a trap, it wasn't ready. But if we wait too long, they will be ready for us. We go now, or we forget all about the ghosts."

"And you don't want to forget all about the ghosts."

I give my head one resolute shake. "No."

Yes, I know. This could be foolish, at best. But all the other ghosts are trapped. I told them we'd be back. That feels sacred, somehow.

"I promised," I add in no more than a whisper.

He considers the sprite still resting in the steam, the jut of my chin, and then the day just starting to break, all violet and pink through the kitchen windows.

"All right, then." He stands and brushes off his hands. "Let's go."

MALCOLM DRIVES my grandmother's old truck straight through the copse of pines. He doesn't slow down. He doesn't even flinch. A momentary pang of fear clogs my throat as the front bumper touches that shimmering green.

Then the pines vanish. We come roaring out on the other side, the truck's rear wheels fishtailing on some gravel.

We barrel into the parking lot, and Malcolm halts the truck across two spaces. We jump from the cab and grab all our supplies, splitting our field kit between us. Malcolm lugs the thermoses of coffee. I carry the Tupperware. His burden is heavier, mine more awkward. It's a tradeoff that works for us.

To hesitate now would give these necromancers a chance to prepare. Malcolm takes my hand, and we race inside the mall, committing fully before anyone—or perhaps anything—can stop us.

The entrance to the mall is still decrepit, still empty, still unchanged from our first visit. The padlock jangles against the glass, and the doors scrape the tile floor. This is not a stealth erad-ication.

Whoever these two necromancers are, we're taking the chance that they're not at an abandoned mall at six on a Sunday morning. We don't pause until the Orange Julius pops into view. I'm gasping for air, and even Malcolm's breath is ragged. The storefront itself is as orange as ever, and there's a hint of sugar lingering in the stale air.

"I just can't get over this." Malcolm drops my hand and shakes his head as if he's trying to clear all the sugar from it. "It's almost like we're waiting for some kid to get off his break so we can place an order."

Another wave of that fruity, overly sweet scent washes over me. The taste of citrus is sharp against the back of my throat. None of this makes sense. Even if there were sticky remains on the table-tops and inside the drink machines, it wouldn't smell like this. It wouldn't feel so real.

I lean over the counter as if I can find that wayward kid. The surface appears smooth, almost clean, although I have no plans to touch it. I wipe my palms against my jeans anyway, the sensation of residue psychic rather than physical.

"Let's go get our ghosts." I turn from the counter and confront the orange booths, the garbage containers, and the vacant corridor outside the shop. Beyond that, the shimmery hue of prom dresses and the sparkle of a jewelry store display.

What I don't see is Malcolm.

"Malcolm?" I work to keep my voice low, quiet, devoid of panic.

It isn't working.

"Malcolm?"

Maybe he stepped into the hallway, decided to do a little recon-naissance. I leave the fluorescent orange behind and do the same.

The floor rolls beneath my feet. I hold my arms out for balance, almost like I'm surfing. Around me, the display windows shift and change. The mall grows old.

Not moldering or festering. There's no mildew or decay.

No, everything is bright. The dresses in the prom display grow giant puffy sleeves, the jewel tones bright to the point of being obnoxious. The H in Hillside Diamonds is stately, almost pompous. From behind me comes the echo of a cash register and the buzz of the Orange Julius machine.

When I turn again, the space is empty. All is quiet except for the lonely hum of the ventilation system.

"Malcolm?" Now my voice is a tiny, pathetic thing. Even if he were nearby, he wouldn't be able to hear me.

A wave of queasiness strikes me, like I've taken a rough ride on a tilt-o-whirl. The urge to leave is like a solid hand against the small of my back. Everything about this is wrong, in that old-school horror movie kind of way. I should run and not look back.

My hand goes to my neck. I clutch the whistle Malcolm draped there earlier. That's an option. Then I think of a better one.

I shift the bag full of Tupperware to my other shoulder and pull out my phone only to see that I have zero reception.

That could be the mall—its construction, the thick walls, or simply terrible cell phone service. That happens, especially when we venture too far from Springside. The center courtyard with its skylights is my best bet. I might be able to pick up a signal there. I might be able to see where Malcolm went—possibly.

Maybe.

In any case, it's better than standing around here waiting for the mannequins in their prom dresses to step off their pedestals and come after me.

Not that I think they're going to.

At least, I'm pretty sure they won't.

In the courtyard—which is actually called the Crystal Court—morning sunlight spills across the floor, pink and yellow and full of promise. It's warmer here, the air musty. More like the mall has been shut for a week rather than a decade. I stand in the court-yard's center and turn in a slow circle, hoping for a hint of Malcolm. When my cell phone buzzes in my hand, my heart leaps, full of hope.

My flood of relief dries up immediately. It's not him.

It's Nigel.

But maybe Malcolm called him because he couldn't reach me, and now we're about to embark on a game of phone tag.

"Katy, could you tell my stupid brother to answer his stupid phone?"

Well, no, I can't. "You can't call Malcolm?" I hate how small my voice still sounds, but Nigel doesn't seem to notice.

"Rolls straight to voicemail. Texts go undelivered."

That's ... not good. Then again, until a few moments ago, I didn't have reception either. Maybe that's all it is. Malcolm is here, somewhere in the mall, and can't call or text because our cell phone service is lousy.

"Are you two on an eradication?" Nigel asks.

"Sort of?" I say it as a question because right now, I'm not sure what, exactly, is going on. Before I can explain, Nigel continues.

"Well, pack it in. This is more important."

I doubt that.

"Prescott sent a ghost. When it couldn't find you or Malcolm, it came over here and started shaking the foundation."

"A ghost?"

"It has news. It also has explicit instructions from Prescott not to interact with me." The frustration in Nigel's voice is thick. "I can't tell what it has to say, and all Sadie is picking up is its agitation."

Some necromancers only communicate through ghosts, it's true. But that isn't Prescott. Why wouldn't he call or send a text?

"Look," Nigel says, his tone less strident now. "I know what's going on. Prescott isn't as sneaky as he thinks he is. If he's sending a ghost, it means he's somewhere he shouldn't be, and this was his only option."

My heartbeat kicks up a notch. First Malcolm, now Prescott.

"I need you guys to come home so we can figure out what's going on."

"I don't know where Malcolm is." The words come out in a rush. Frankly, I don't have the patience to explain that I've lost his brother and my business partner and fiancé.

"Katy, where are you?"

"Cedar Hills Mall."

The disappointment in Nigel's sigh is worse than a lecture, a scolding, or anger ever could be. I want to apologize, explain, but my throat's clogged, and a spate of tears fills my eyes. All I can do is pull in a deep breath and release a sigh of my own.

"All right," he says at last. "It is what it is. What happened? You two get separated?"

"That's just it. We didn't. One moment, he was there, talking about the Orange Julius. I turn my back, and all of a sudden, he's gone."

"Without telling you where he was going?" Nigel sounds incredulous.

I want to shout: *This isn't Malcolm. He would never intentionally leave me on my own. I don't know what to do.* Instead, I say: "It's like he vanished." When Nigel doesn't respond, I add, "The way our ghosts did."

He's silent for such a long moment, I almost think we've been cut off. "Maybe you should leave."

"Malcolm would *never* leave me behind." I shake my head for emphasis, but we're not on video, so it doesn't do much good. "I can't leave without him."

"Katy—"

"What about Prescott's ghost? Maybe it could tell us something."

"You know I can't, and even if I could, it won't let me."

"There are two thermoses of Kona blend on my kitchen table, and Belinda's home. Between her and Sadie and the coffee?"

Nigel must have me on speaker, because Sadie's exclamation fills my ear.

"I'll be right back!" she says. The screen door creaks and then clatters.

A muted chuckle follows. "You have my wife running around the neighborhood in her pink slippers and nightgown."

Honestly? This isn't the first time.

"Tell me again what happened," he says.

So I do, walking through our chat with the sprite to our decision to leave to how the aroma of the Orange Julius distracted us both.

"Can necromancers do that?" I ask. "Is there such a thing as a ward that smells?"

"Not that I know of."

"It's been more than a decade." I turn slightly, trying to catch sight of that fluorescent orange. "Assuming we could smell it after all this time, it shouldn't smell good."

For a moment, my thoughts drift to Penny and Chief Ramsey. My grandmother always said nostalgia was a longing for a past that never truly was. I've done enough eradications to know that sometimes the ghosts only haunt because the humans want them to. Maybe that was why my grandmother's ghost left and never returned. Most days, I don't think to look over my shoulder to check to see if she's there.

She'd want me to look forward, not back.

What I can't imagine is someone being sentimental about a mall. Then I remember the look on Chief's face when Penny mentioned my mother—both petrified and tender.

Maybe you *can* be sentimental about a mall.

I squint as if that will help me discern what was here decades ago. I'm also on high alert for Malcolm, scary twin necromancers, and the telltale wail of trapped ghosts.

What I hear instead is Belinda's jubilant cry through the phone's speakers.

"Here I am! Let me at that ghost."

SORTING out the logistics takes a few minutes. I slip the canvas sack of Tupperware from my shoulder and ready my stance as if I'm the one who will confront this ghost.

"Do you have enough battery for video?" Nigel asks.

I do, and now I can see what's going on. We decide on Sadie's back porch. Nigel can remain in the kitchen, ready to pull Belinda and Sadie to safety if needed. From the unnatural sway of the lilac bushes, I suspect Chaucer is nearby as well.

Before Belinda steps outside, I ask her, "Are you sure?"

Hesitation flickers in her gaze, but she banishes it and gives me a brilliant smile. "I am. Really."

Still, I worry. Belinda's back to befriending sprites, but a ghost like this? One that's powerful and possibly fierce? One that Prescott won't let Nigel interact with?

This could be bad.

"Besides," she adds, "Chaucer's here on high alert. He does not like this particular ghost."

"I'm not sure that's a good thing."

"It's a rivalry," she explains. "They both want to be Prescott's top ghost."

I nod like that makes sense.

"Don't worry. They'll behave." Belinda eases through the kitchen door and places one thermos on the picnic table. The other she holds out, like a sommelier with an expensive bottle of wine. "Kona blend," she says to the air. "I bet you've never had anything quite like this."

From the resulting explosion of blossoms and leaves, I'm betting she's right.

"Pour a cup for Chaucer, too," I say.

Playing favorites with ghosts, especially when their preferred coffee is involved?

Always a bad idea.

Nigel sets up his laptop. He has a legal pad and half a dozen ballpoint pens ready as well. Prescott may have sent the message in some sort of code. Nigel will capture what the ghost tells Belinda and then take it from there.

Belinda pours two cups. She and Sadie clasp hands. They both stand still, heads slightly tilted. I hold my breath and try not to let what's happening on my screen steal all my attention. I'm still in the Crystal Court, but at the moment, the space around me feels, if not safe, then benign.

Part of me insists I should start searching for Malcolm again, but I don't dare move for fear of losing reception. So I remain frozen, my feet itching to explore, the rest of me intent on my cell phone screen.

Ghosts don't appear on video, so I can't see or hear anything otherworldly, but I notice the moment Belinda's expression shifts. Even as her eyes light up, her brows draw together in confusion.

"Prescott says that Chaucer is his favorite writer," she relays, words slow, as if she's working on repeating them just right. "But he also has a fondness for Shakespeare."

Nigel leaps up and dashes from the kitchen. He returns lugging a huge book—the complete works of Shakespeare. When he drops it on the table, the salt and pepper shakers teeter and tip over.

"It's a cipher," he says. "In case another necromancer intercepts the ghost."

From there, it's a series of letters and numbers and Nigel furiously scratching out notes on the legal pad. He flips through the Shakespeare. The pages flutter and blur. Then Nigel's image glitches. I study the air around me as if I can discern where the best reception is. With the video still frozen, I hazard a step to my left.

The display speeds up and then slows down. Nigel mouths some words, ones I can't hear, at least not entirely. Bits and pieces float from the speaker. "Demon ... factory ... Midwest Necroman ... out."

This last, I understand. It's an order. His panicked gaze meets mine. He speaks the words again. Even without sound, the message is clear.

Get out now.

"I can't leave without Malcolm."

I take another step to my left. When the screen goes black, I backtrack, hold my phone close and then at arm's length.

It's no use. The signal is gone, and I'm clutching little more than a very expensive flashlight.

The air in the Crystal Court shifts, and the floor beneath me rolls again. The sensation isn't quite as rough. I don't feel as if I've stumbled off the tilt-o-whirl. Even so, my heart is thrumming in my chest. I catch a whiff of something that smells like a combination of permanent wave solution and caramel corn.

From behind me comes the splash of the fountain. I turn, see nothing, and then turn again, only to catch droplets of water in my peripheral vision. I take quick, shallow breaths as if that will somehow keep me safe—from what, I'm not sure.

It's only when an overly peppy, Muzak version of "The Girl From Ipanema" filters through the speakers somewhere above my head that I know things are very, *very* wrong.

CHAPTER 9

The sunlight that streams from the courtyard's skylights is clear and bright. It touches my face, my eyelids. The air tastes almost clean. It's like someone unloaded an entire bottle of air freshener into the space. The staleness lingers, not completely banished, but it's muted. You could forget about it, pretend it isn't there.

From all around me comes the bustle and noise of the mall—the chi-ching of a cash register, footfalls of people rushing past, chatter and laughter that can only mean a group of teenagers. Every time I spin around, try to catch an image to match the sound, nothing but emptiness greets me.

I consider my options. Leave? Find Malcolm? Try to do both? I scan the Crystal Court. Clearly, he's not here, hiding behind the fountain or in the glass-sided elevator. So I pick a corridor and leave the sunshine of the courtyard behind.

From what I can tell, this was the wing where no one ever willingly shopped. There's an eyeglasses place. The frames in the display window are so huge that they'd swallow your entire face.

The anchor store is a Sears. Beneath the security gate is a

crushed and dingy *Going Out of Business* sign. Inside, near the entrance, someone left a tricycle. Hitched to it is a wagon where an oversized teddy bear sits and stares with dark and forlorn eyes. Something about this—these lonely toys searching for a child—makes my heart squeeze with sadness.

In the spot of glory—such as it is—sits Spencer's Gifts. Its entrance isn't barred. No security gate or doors or anything. I could step across the threshold and end up being swallowed by all the gag gifts and general tackiness.

I keep to the center of the hallway, dodging benches and trash bins and the occasional potted tree. The space feels both abandoned and yet alive, assuming a mall could live. With each step, I feel as if I'm edging deeper and deeper into someplace else.

And with each step, I feel as if I'm edging farther and farther away from Malcolm. I whirl, and the notion that someone—or something—is tracking my every move strikes me with a strength I can't deny. The vacant corridor greets me. I take a final glance at the forlorn teddy bear and head back to the Crystal Court.

Then I see him.

He's standing inside a clothing store, near the main windows. He looks bored, like he's waiting for someone to finish up their shopping. My heart turns over on itself, and I'm flooded with relief.

Malcolm.

It must be. I'd recognize that ebony hair and the set of the jaw anywhere. I don't stop to consider why he's simply standing there, unconcerned. This is Malcolm Armand, and I will always run to him. I race forward and nearly slam into the window. The glass shakes beneath my palms.

The man on the other side starts. He turns and stares straight at me. He's a bit too gaunt, a little too short. My heart plummets and then freezes.

The man on the other side of the glass is not Malcolm.

It's his father, Darien Armand.

I FEEL as if I've been whisked back in time or that I'm looking at someone who no longer exists. My fingers grip the glass as if that will steady me. But my mind cannot reconcile the image on the other side.

This is not the Darien I met last summer. He is not careworn. There's no bitterness in his eyes, no hint of disapproval in the shape of his mouth. This Darien is fresh-faced. His skin has that lovely olive cast that both his sons share. His eyes are dark but not yet flinty and disappointed. I can't look away, can't even pull my fingers from the glass. My mind scrambles for an explanation.

Because this?

This can't be real.

On the other side, Darien Armand narrows his eyes as if he's trying to place me. He tilts his chin, and something that looks like recognition washes across his features. His whole face brightens. At that moment, he really does resemble Malcolm, and my heart thumps hard in response.

One of his hands reaches for me, and our fingers meet with only the glass between them. He speaks then. I can't hear his voice, but the word he says is distinct.

Necromancer?

I shake my head. It's my go-to response, of course, and one I can't help. For a mere second, it's as if we're held in each other's thrall.

Then the air shatters. Darien vanishes in a flurry of black specks. That stale, musty odor rushes back in; the light goes from bright and lovely to dull and decrepit. The Crystal Court ages. The weight of its years, of neglect, presses down on me.

I am back where I belong, and it occurs to me to ask:

"I was gone?"

Indeed you were, my dear.

My pulse skitters through my veins. My head fills with

thoughts of demon factories (as if such a thing exists) and the Midwest Necromancer Association (which most certainly does). Is this their doing? Is it a trap? Or am I hearing the entity? *My* entity?

"And Malcolm?" I venture. If it is my entity, it will know, it will tell me.

Turn around.

The moment I do, Malcolm spots me. He appears haggard, but when his eyes meet mine, a smile blooms across his face and chases away the worry and strain. I run to him, certain that this time, I am running to Malcolm Armand.

I leap, and he catches me. He holds me close, one hand cradling the back of my head, his other arm wrapped tightly around my waist.

"Katy, Katy." His voice is soft and urgent in my ear. "What happened? I turned around, and you were gone. I've been all over the place. Tried calling, texting—"

His phone buzzes with what must be the zillion text messages Nigel and I sent him. He eases from me to pull it from his pocket.

He frowns. "This is weird."

"I know, I know," I say. "But first—"

Malcolm's phone rings then, the tone sharp and insistent. It sounds just like Nigel. It's an irrational sort of thought, but it's been an irrational sort of day. When Nigel's voice comes through the speaker, I'm vindicated.

"Are you okay?" His anger and fear echo around us. "Where the hell have you been?"

"We're both here," I say.

"Katy? I thought I told you to leave."

"I didn't hear you." Technically, that's true.

Nigel doesn't even bother with a sigh. "Belinda sent Chaucer to find Prescott, and we're heading to the mall right now, but the two of you need to get out of there."

Malcolm gives me a questioning look.

"Later," I mouth.

Nigel is right; we need to leave, and we need to do it right now, before something—or someone—can stop us, before the air shimmers and the floor rolls beneath our feet. Whether we're facing some sort of demon, twin necromancers, or the Midwest Necromancer Association, here is not the place to do it.

Malcolm doesn't question me. He simply takes my hand, and we head for the main entrance. Even so, I stumble over my feet. It's almost as if something is tugging me in the opposite direction. That's when I hear the entity again—loud and clear, and with enough force that I'm positive it is my entity.

Really, you came all this way for your ghosts, and you're going to simply leave them behind?

In the center of Crystal Courtyard sits my discarded bag of Tupperware containers. I come to a full stop, and my hand slips from Malcolm's.

"Katy?"

I think of what it is the Midwest Necromancer Association can do—and has done—to innocent ghosts. To Springside ghosts. With enough effort, I can still taste the psychic residue of the warehouse where they imprisoned and tortured ghosts under the guise of "training" them.

"Katy, what's going on?"

"The ghosts." I turn away from the main doors.

"Oh, no, no, no." Malcolm holds up his hands and gives his head a vigorous shake. "I don't know what's going on, but I'm pretty sure we leave now."

If I do leave now, I'll return to find damaged ghosts—assuming I can return. They may be damaged beyond help, beyond reason. Would they forgive me for that? For leaving them behind a second time?

"Someone is going to hurt them," I tell Malcolm.

He freezes, his expression cold with dread. "You're certain?"

"Aren't you?"

Malcolm was in that warehouse, too, imprisoned, beaten, and

damaged as well. His expression shifts, his brow set with determination. When his phone rings again, he switches it off.

He takes my hand.

"Come on. Let's go get our ghosts."

THE HALLWAY where we first found the ghosts is still empty. No lockers. No clues.

Nothing.

The fluorescent lights flicker in a way that makes my eyes ache. My temples throb. I'm trying to piece together a plan, but the only thing that comes close to clearing my head is the hint of Kona blend from the thermoses at Malcolm's side.

"I don't see how we're going to find them," I say. "But I could use a cup of coffee."

"Maybe they could, too?" Malcolm suggests.

"Coffee?"

I'm not sure how that will help, but Malcolm pulls a thermos from the field kit and uncaps it.

"Isn't it what you do best?"

The aromatic steam hits us like a tidal wave. I inhale deeply the exact moment Malcolm does. I catch his gaze, and we both manage a weary smile.

"That smells like heaven," he says.

Somewhere, from the depths of the mall, a thump, thump, thump shakes the floor. The telltale hint of that rumba beat is the happiest thing I've heard all day.

A notion lights my mind. I know what to do, how to get our ghosts back. The idea is so perfect that I don't even pause to explain it to Malcolm.

"The courtyard!" I race down the hallway, but Malcolm easily catches up to me.

Without missing a stride, he unslings the field kit and tosses me a thermos. He skids to a halt in the center of the courtyard, where the sunlight is brightest.

"Here." He plants his foot on the star-shaped mosaic directly beneath the skylight. "We set up here."

This is what I love about him, about being K&M the couple *and* K&M Ghost Eradication Specialists. His ability to take my scattered words and less-than-coherent thoughts and execute a plan.

He pulls out a thermos and starts pouring. "Three cups black."

"Three with sugar." I open a second thermos and set out the cups with care, opposite from where Malcolm placed his.

"Three with cream." He arranges these cups on a granite bench.

"And three extra sweet and extra light." I pick the spot directly across from his. After I pour, I step onto the bench and raise my arms in triumph. "Because even ghosts have a preference."

I'm not so triumphant that I don't worry, don't hold my breath. We still don't know where these ghosts actually are or whether they can reach us.

The thumping grows louder, more ominous. But the aroma of Kona blend wafting through the air feels like hope. Even better, it feels real. The scent is so strong, if I closed my eyes, I could imagine sitting in my own kitchen.

Rattling comes from all four corridors. A wrenching sound has me slamming my hands over my ears. Then, all at once, a mighty whoosh rushes into the courtyard.

I'm not fast enough to react, but Malcolm is. By the time the force of the supernatural surges from the hallways, he's at my side. When that force knocks me off my feet, I land in his arms.

Ghosts swoop and dive into the coffee, float on the steam. A group of sprites swirls around us, less intent on the coffee than getting our attention.

"Look at that." Malcolm nods toward the corridor where we first found the rental lockers filled with ghosts.

There, the bank of lockers teeters, torn clear from the wall. The sprites around us nudge and tug, pulling on strands of my hair, my sleeves, their effort slight but persistent.

"There's still some trapped inside," I say to Malcolm.

As if in confirmation, the metal creaks and quakes. Locker doors clang. The rumba beat is out of sync, weaker now that only a handful of ghosts remain trapped.

We head for the lockers. The sprites around us do backflips, overjoyed that we finally figured out what they wanted. Then they zip off to the coffee because their empathy for their compatriots extends only so far.

Malcolm yanks on the doors that are still closed. He gives one a good kick, and the bang reverberates down the hallways. "Maybe if I had a crowbar or something."

He glances around, and so do I. All we see are prom dresses and sunglasses. A fluorescent hint of the Orange Julius. And there, next to the glass elevator, the fountain.

I dash forward and kneel at its edge. The granite is smudged with grime, the coins dull with a thick layer of dust. At first, I pluck carefully, trying to snag the quarters from all the pennies, nickels, and dimes.

Then a couple of supernatural helpers insist I scoop up as much change as possible. They shove my hands, weave between my fingers, their forms icy and frantic.

They're right. We don't have the time to be picky. Plus, there's the slightest pressure on the small of my back, an ethereal urge to hurry. I choke back my disgust and sweep my hand across the bottom of the fountain, scraping up a decade of old filth along with the leftover change. Back at the lockers, I let it all rain down on the floor. Some of the coins are so thick with grime, they thunk rather than chime against the tile.

I think of what Orson Yates himself told me more than a year ago:

Every time you catch a ghost, you commit an act of necromancy.

So I do. Or rather, I reverse engineer that act. I shove quarters into their slots, willing the remaining containment fields to shatter. Malcolm adds his strength by yanking on each door. Together, we break the field one locker at a time.

The last door flies off its hinges, and we're done. Malcolm flings it across the courtyard with a triumphant whoop. The door clatters against a granite bench. Relieved of all the ghosts, the bank of lockers teeters and falls. The crash is like nothing this mall has heard in ages.

Of course, we still have the chasing and the catching left to do. At the thought, my legs wobble. My knees buckle ever so slightly, but it's enough to catch Malcolm's attention.

"Hey." His voice is warm and close in my ear, and he slides an arm around my waist. "You okay?"

"A little tired," I admit, although I feel stronger here in his embrace. "I know we need to catch them, but—"

But what's the alternative? Ask them nicely to slip inside the Tupperware while we secure the lids?

"Are you sure about the catching?" Malcolm says, his voice now laced with humor.

On the far side of the lockers, where I left my bag filled with Tupperware and lids, all the ghosts have congregated. They're so thick that the canvas tote and the plastic containers glimmer. A bevy of sprites attempts to propel a lid onto one of the larger containers without much luck.

"Wait," I say. "They *want* to leave?"

"Probably even more than we do."

Yes. They know what a scary necromancer can do to a ghost.

We sort the ghosts into containers. They jostle and slip from my grasp—and from their assigned places just as I'm securing the lids. True, they want to leave right now. Each one also wants to sit next to its special friend.

It's like herding kindergarteners.

While Malcolm collects the thermoses, I seek out the most mature ghost—maturity being one of those relative things when it comes to ghosts. I hold its container high and turn in a slow circle so it can survey the mall.

"Do we have everyone?" I turn again and even venture down each wing a few feet, just to make sure.

The ghost bounces an affirmative.

"Are we ready?" Malcolm asks.

"I think we are."

A muted cheer comes from the Tupperware containers. I can't help but grin. Malcolm takes my hand, and we run for the main doors.

We don't look back.

We burst into the late morning sunlight, Tupperware clattering at our sides. A moment later, a bright blue sedan pulls into the Cedar Hills Mall parking lot. The car has barely stopped when both Sadie and Belinda come tumbling out. Nigel follows, his pace more sedate, but when he reaches Malcolm, he pulls his brother into a tight embrace.

Then the mall itself captures Nigel's attention. He stares, a faraway look in his eyes. He reminds me of when I first met him, when he was recovering from swallowing ghosts, when he would gaze into the middle distance, sometimes for hours. Sadie takes a step closer to him and places a hand on his arm, her eyes tight with budding alarm.

He shakes himself. "I'm okay." But the smile he gives us is a shadow of itself.

I open my mouth, mentally shuffling through all the questions I want to ask. Is he *really* okay? Are there demons inside the mall, and what the heck is a demon factory? I want to confess about the entity, too, but I'm not certain I should.

Before I can ask or confess, a flashy yellow sports car speeds along the road to the mall. Prescott arrives in a flourish and out of breath. He races toward us but then staggers to a halt and stares up at the mall, much the same way Nigel is doing.

"Damn," Prescott breathes.

"Yeah." Nigel swallows hard. "I know."

I shoot Malcolm a look, but he merely shrugs.

"No wonder they're hiding it," Prescott says.

"Hiding what?" I ask. I've already guessed it's not the mall itself, not exactly. But what it is, I'm not sure.

"This"—Prescott gestures toward the front entrance—"is a demon factory."

Demon factory? Really? "Is there an assembly line?"

Nigel manages a soft chuckle. "Nothing like that. Although if the association could manufacture demons, I'm sure they would. No one really knows where demons come from, but every once in a while, a gathering of them will appear."

"And when that happens?" Prescott surveys the area and then turns his attention back to the mall. "Necromancers of a certain ilk will try to encourage and prolong the gathering."

"Like those in the Midwest Necromancer Association," I supply.

"And they just happen to own this mall—or at least own the company that owns the company that owns the mall," Prescott says. "It's one of the reasons they buy up real estate as a general rule. But abandoned properties are also good for money laundering, storing ghosts, and training both them and necromancers."

"Like the warehouse?" I cast Prescott a sidelong glance.

For a moment, his mouth is taut, but he nods. "Yes, like the warehouse."

"So, this?" Malcolm levels his gaze at both Prescott and Nigel. "This could be Orson Yates."

"Officially?" Prescott shakes his head. "No. He's no longer chairman of the Midwest Necromancer Association."

"But ...?"

"But we can't rule him out, either," Prescott says. "And there's Roland to consider. I still don't know who's pulling his strings, only that someone most definitely is."

"What do necromancers do with demons?" I have a guess, and it's the same thing they'd do with ghosts and entities as well.

"Figuring out what motivates them is harder and sometimes nonsensical," Prescott says. "I had one once that loved grass, and flowers, and nature—and nothing else. I finally drove it up north and handed it off to Reginald."

"Is that what he does up north, in the woods?" If I hadn't met Reginald Weaver myself, the whole scenario would seem kind of creepy—a lone necromancer, in the woods, doing ... things with ghosts.

"It's one of his projects," Nigel adds. "Trying to figure out the origin of demons, why some are almost like ghosts and others are so widely divergent that they're hardly ghosts at all."

We all fall silent, our attention drawn not to the mall but Nigel. His eyes have that glazed look again. He releases a sigh that cascades down his entire body.

"I never swallowed one, although I had the chance, more than once." He licks his lips as if he can taste the otherworldly. "I think I knew, even then, there'd be no coming back."

Sadie wraps her arms tight around his waist, and he pulls her close and graces her curls with a tender, grateful kiss.

Something about Nigel's confession triggers a memory. "Do you think the possession was a demon?"

That was Orson's doing, after all. If he had access to all this—whatever this demon factory actually is—then I think chances are good. The ghost—or demon—that possessed Thomas Davenport had a malevolent streak like none I've ever encountered. I wonder, too, if that's why my grandmother left me behind when she went to fight the only other possession in Springside.

"Possibly," Nigel says. "It wasn't here long enough for any of us to get a read on it."

The one person who might know—Darien Armand—isn't around to tell us. But I remember how easily he whisked it away.

"Is that what your father does? Catch ghosts *and* demons?"

Malcolm and Nigel stare at each other, mouths agape, expressions alight with both surprise and then comprehension. They both swear, the same word, at the same moment.

"Jesus, all this time." Malcolm shakes his head. He raises his hands and lets them fall. "Are we what? Stupid?"

Well, no. It's not like Darien Armand is ever forthcoming with heartfelt father-son chats, never mind providing helpful information.

"Could a demon—or demons—hide our ghosts?" I ask. "Could it ... change things about the mall, make it look different, keep me from Malcolm?"

Prescott lifts a shoulder. "Perhaps."

That he's so uncertain is not reassuring. Prescott is one of the most accomplished necromancers in the area, maybe the country. If he doesn't know, then what hope do we have of figuring this out?

"Could it show me the past?" The ghosts of Springside could, but this felt more real, more solid than that.

Prescott gives me a side-eye. "I'm sure an entity could."

Oh, no. He *didn't*.

"You heard it again, didn't you?" he adds.

Okay, so he did.

"What?" Again, Malcolm and Nigel respond in stereo. They're so loud, and they pepper me with so many questions, that I swallow the urge to slap my hands over my ears. As it is, I take a step back.

"You heard the entity? Why didn't you tell us?" There's an unbelievable amount of hurt in Malcolm's eyes. "Why didn't you tell *me*?"

Belinda steps in front of them and plants a hand on each of their chests. "Maybe this is why?"

Malcolm tries to sidestep her, but she won't let him. At last, he simply opens his arms and gives me a pleading look.

I go to him. I always will. "I'm sorry," I murmur against his chest. "And the first time, I wasn't even sure. It was more like hearing an echo. This time was different. I went somewhere, and I think the entity helped me get back."

"Where did you go?"

"The mall, only it was... new, or at least, newish. And I saw your father."

I pause, certain of that stereo response again. But both Nigel and Malcolm are oddly silent.

"Only younger," I add, and wave a hand between myself and Malcolm. "Closer to our age."

"Like when he caught the ghost that killed your parents?" The shadow that crosses Malcolm's expression reminds me of how much the past can haunt. Behind me, Nigel exhales, the sound heavy with guilt.

For a long time, all any of us can do is stare at the mall, the blank eyes of its doors staring back.

Prescott shakes himself as if shaking off tendrils of the past. "In any case, this is not a problem we're solving today." He raises his chin, his gaze scanning the area. "And here's not the place to solve it. Really, you probably shouldn't have come back for the ghosts."

The ghosts—who have been subdued up to this point, listening to the humans talk—fling themselves at Prescott. They get in a few good blows, the Tupperware ricocheting off his head, an elbow. All at once, a glow surrounds him, and the containers ping harmlessly off the supernatural shield.

Undeterred, they continue until Malcolm, Belinda, and I scoop them up and toss them into the back of my truck.

"Guys," I say, holding up the last Tupperware to eye level. It's one filled with a bevy of outraged sprites. "You're not getting through an attack ghost."

I suspect they'll wear themselves out trying if we let them.

But Prescott is right. Here is bad. Again, that strange sensation washes over me, like we're being watched. I scan the mall's façade for clues, but the space just feels wrong to me. I certainly can't detect demons the way Nigel and Prescott can.

No one says a word—not where we're going or what we'll do next. By the time Malcolm and I have secured the last container, everyone else has pulled from the parking lot.

Malcolm assesses me from across the flatbed. "No more secrets?"

"No more secrets."

When he gives me that sweet, dark-roast grin, I know everything is going to be okay.

I DRIVE ALL OF US—ME, Malcolm, the ghosts—to the nature preserve. I even find the campsite where, for the very first time, I demonstrated how to release ghosts. The area is empty and so pristine (someone even raked the fire pit), I suspect a troop of Girl Scouts last camped here.

I take it as a good omen. I take it as a sign. I promised Malcolm no more secrets. I will tell him what I'm thinking. I will. I will.

I gulp a deep breath. Yes. I will.

Maybe.

Despite the restraints, the containers clatter in the back of the truck. It's so peaceful in this part of the preserve that it's all we hear. When I open the tailgate, all the Tupperware comes tumbling out. Malcolm plucks one from the ground, moves to the edge of the campsite, and readies his stance.

He's got the technique down, it's true. Still, he's not very good at releasing ghosts. Maybe it's a necromancer thing. It's just not in their blood to let ghosts go.

"I was thinking about the day of the ghosts."

I declare these words more than say them. Unfortunately, I also declare them the moment Malcolm cracks open the lid. His hand slips. The ghosts inside can't wait to be free, and they stream from the container. Even so? The largest one doubles back to cuff Malcolm on the side of the head.

"Every. Single. Time." His tone is even, as if he's resigned to this particular fate.

"Sorry?"

He laughs, the sound both rueful and rich. "Nah, it's me. It's totally me." He spears me with that look, the one from our very first time here, the one I thought might scar—if I let it.

"Day of the ghosts?" he says, and now his tone is so expectant, so coaxing that heat flares in my cheeks.

"I was thinking," I say, and now my voice is so soft, the wind might steal all my words. "That it would make a good wedding day."

Oh, and there it is. That sweet, dark roast grin. If I could bottle it up, I wouldn't need food or water or anything else.

Malcolm drops the empty Tupperware container and steps closer.

"We'd have to wait a whole year." He smooths my hair back from my face, his fingertips so careful and gentle, it makes my heart squeeze.

"Wouldn't we have to, anyway? Isn't it hard to find a place for the ceremony and reception?"

I've only flipped through the magazines in our office, but the article headlines have made this abundantly clear. If you're not planning your wedding at least a year out, you might as well give up entirely—on it, on any other goals you might have, on your life in general.

You get the idea.

"Only if you want to book someplace really fancy." His voice is matter-of-fact, but he studies my face with cautious eyes. "You don't, do you?"

I give my head a little shake. I am so not fancy, and Malcolm knows this.

"I have it on good authority that the ballroom at the Springside Community Center is available on Halloween," he says, and now his voice is edged with hope.

"Halloween?"

"Why not? It's one of my favorite days."

"I almost lost you forever on Halloween."

"That's why it's perfect. From that day forward, you'll have me forever." He kisses me then, just a brush of his lips that leaves me breathless. "And I'll have you."

He steps back. The rush of air between us is so cold. I want to throw myself into his arms again, but the expression in his dark eyes is unfathomable. He needs something else, something more.

"You do want to do this, don't you, Katy?"

"Of course I do."

"Because if you don't want to get married, I'll understand."

I wrap my right hand around my engagement ring as if I think he'll yank it off my finger. "I want to marry you, Malcolm. I already said yes."

"But?"

Yes, there's that word hanging in the air between us. I don't know how to describe what I feel, how to articulate my fear. So I go with the simplest words I know.

"I'm scared."

He steps forward again, but I hold up my hands, halting him in place. I want nothing more than to lean in to him, but I must say these things first.

"Right now, I have everything I could possibly want. You, here with me. Springside and everyone I love safe. I'm worried that if I move too fast, do too much, want something more, I'll ruin everything."

"Oh, Katy." Sorrow laces his voice, and I know he won't tell me not to worry.

"I feel like I'm walking a tightrope. I'm afraid if we get married, we'll throw things out of balance, that we'll end up like my parents."

Comprehension lights his features, and his lips compress as if he's made a crucial discovery. "Or mine."

"And now this whole thing with demon factories and scary twin necromancers, and I—"

"Here." Malcolm leads me to the truck and lifts me onto the tailgate. I'm not sure how he knew my legs were about to give out. The ache reaches from my hips all the way to my toes.

"It's been a long couple of days." He eases onto the tailgate next to me, and it gives out a groan as if it agrees. "And, yeah, I know, I talk a big game. But I'll never be as smart or well-connected as Nigel."

I'm about to protest, but the determined look in his eyes tells me he needs to say this.

"And I'll never be the sort of necromancer Prescott is or as good with ghosts as Reginald." He shifts on the tailgate and takes my hands. "But I know this. You and me together? We have something. And together, we can work through whatever life throws at us, whether that's demons or ghosts or scary twin necromancers."

He brings my knuckles to his lips, their touch so soft, so substantial. "Think about it, Katy. Why let any of that stop us?"

Malcolm's right. Why let it?

"So, Halloween, then?" he says.

"Halloween."

"You still don't sound sure."

Malcolm hears it—doesn't he?—in my voice. And it's not doubt. It's total and complete incompetence. I draw in a deep breath and blurt the words all at once.

"I really don't know how to plan a party that size."

"Wait. What? That's it?" He blinks, lashes gracing his cheekbones for an instant. "You don't want to plan the wedding?"

Now that it's out there, this small, stupid thing, I'm so relieved that I might melt off the tailgate and into a Katy-puddle on the ground.

"No," I say, and it comes out as a cry for help.

Malcolm throws his head back and laughs, and it's full of amazement and relief. "That's it? You *really* don't want to plan the wedding."

I give my head a vigorous shake.

"Then, can I?" His eyes are bright with anticipation.

"You want to plan the wedding?"

"Katy, how many parties have I thrown at Springside Long Term Care?"

Okay, he has a point. The tea parties, the taste tests, the magic shows. Not to mention the holiday extravaganza that the residents are still raving about six months later. I beam at him—I know I must be, because I'm getting that dark roast grin in return. "You would plan our wedding?"

"I would love to." He pauses, and the grin turns sheepish. "And so would my mother."

Oh? *Oh.* "Is she the one subscribing us to all those wedding magazines?"

He makes a face. Honestly, I can't tell if that's a *yes* or a *no.* "Don't worry," he says. "I won't let her steamroller our plans."

"Oh. Sure. I'm not worried at all."

He catches my face in his hands. "Seriously, don't. I'll take care of everything, but you're on your own when it comes to the dress."

I open my mouth, but he's too fast for me.

"And no, even though it's my favorite, you can't wear the skater skirt."

"Not even with sparkly thigh-highs?"

"Not even then."

It was worth a try.

Something he mentioned earlier pings at me. I think back, searching for the exact words he said.

"The ballroom is available on Halloween, and you know this how?"

He clears his throat and glances toward the impeccably raked firepit. "Because I maybe already reserved it."

Of course he did.

"And you weren't going to tell me? What if I picked a different day?"

"I'd lose the deposit." He shrugs. "Or I'd get them to transfer it to a different day. Katy, does it matter?"

Does it? I open my mouth to speak, but again, he's too fast for me.

"Because I also had a deposit down for Valentine's Day, and one for the middle of April, and—"

"I thought we said no more secrets." I try for stern, but I'm not mad, not really. This is classic Malcolm. This is the man I love.

"The summer solstice," he manages before cringing. "I was going to tell you, but I didn't want to pressure you, then I figured you'd pick a day, and I'd be ready with a spot—"

"And then it got too complicated," I finish.

"Yeah. That."

"Halloween." I lean in to him, secure and warm in his embrace. "Let's just get married once, and let's do it on Halloween."

With my words, the quiet campsite erupts in a flurry of other-worldly activity. The newly freed Springside ghosts return, whipping up bits of grass and leaves and petals. The air is thick with the scent of early summer—rich and lush and green.

We jump from the tailgate and release all the other ghosts, not caring about technique or aim. Because for the time being? No one is going anywhere. The campsite sparkles like there's a layer of stardust on everything, including Malcolm and me. Sprites pepper my cheeks with icy kisses and ruffle Malcolm's hair.

A couple of the stronger ghosts conjure an archway with frothy streamers that billow. A bevy of sprites—the angry ones from before—transform into confetti and rose petals.

"You know what I think?" Malcolm tugs me beneath the arch-way. "I think there's a good chance we're going to have the most haunted wedding ever."

With the campsite aglow with the midday sun and any number of Springside ghosts, I think he's right.

And I couldn't be happier.

MISTY SANDBORNE AND THE VAMPIRE HUSBAND

COFFEE AND GHOSTS SEASON FOUR, EPISODE 2

While it's true my grandmother had a never-fail solution when it came to ghosts, I'm not sure it's going to work with brothers—necromancer brothers in particular. Still, I'm in the kitchen, measuring water and grinding one hundred percent Kona beans in hopes that it will.

The coffee starts to percolate. The scent is bound to catch someone's attention, ghost or human. If nothing else, the aromatic steam that touches my cheeks is making me feel better.

I peer out the kitchen door, searching for both those humans and ghosts. The morning air that filters through the screen holds a hint of fresh-cut grass and newly sawn wood. The slender branches of the willow tree sweep the ground in trembling anticipation. Chaucer can sense the coffee even if no one else can yet. I hold up his favorite mug—pink with green polka dots—to let him know a cup is on its way, and the entire tree sparkles.

Belinda wanders into the kitchen in pajama bottoms and a Springside Pancake House T-shirt. Her hair is a riot of curls in a messy bun on top of her head.

"I knew there was a reason to get up this early." She aims a yawn toward the ceiling before her gaze finds the back deck. "Not that I was actually sleeping."

At the moment, both Malcolm and Nigel are quiet, heads bent over a set of complicated blueprints. This is a truce. Both it—and the quiet—won't last.

One of the many reasons I'm brewing the one hundred percent Kona.

As if on cue, Nigel straightens. "Fine." Although his tone is almost always even, this particular word comes out clipped. "Maybe *you'd* like to build it, then."

Malcolm's shoulders tense. I imagine he's scowling in the general direction of both Nigel and the solarium that's still in pieces scattered across Sadie's lawn. Malcolm stomps toward the deck and the project he abandoned minutes before. There's a clatter loud enough to wake the neighborhood, then a determined rasp of sandpaper against wood.

"Time to deploy your weapon of mass destruction?" Belinda nods toward the cream and sugar and the cups lined up, waiting for the coffee.

"Maybe," I say, but I only pour three cups—one for me, one for Belinda, and one for Chaucer. "The problem with starting big is, there's nowhere to go later."

She takes a sip, leans back against the kitchen counter, and curls her fingers around the mug. "Or we could simply drink it all ourselves."

Before I can agree, a black blur streaks through the kitchen and lands on the windowsill that overlooks the deck. The sash is up, and through the screen comes the scent of lilacs and sawdust.

That black blur resolves into a pair of ears, whiskers, and a tail, which swishes back and forth. Malcolm is Willow's favorite. If he's back at work, then she's here to help.

"Hey there, gorgeous." Malcolm's tone is warm and indulgent. "You here to lend a hand ... paw?"

Why, yes. Yes, she is.

"You know." Belinda takes another contemplative sip of her coffee. "It's a good thing those two can't run off together and elope. You'd be out of luck."

I laugh because it's true. I put a finger to my lips and creep from the kitchen, Belinda following.

In the living room, in the far corner, tucked between my grandmother's old rocking chair and the fireplace hearth, sits a cat condo. From the bottom-most compartment, a pair of whiskers twitch. This is where the aptly named Whiskers ran to this morning when all the racket started. Then again, he runs there most mornings unless it's just me in the kitchen.

Two weeks ago, Malcolm and I walked into Cedar Springs Animal Shelter to deal with a ghost and walked out with a bonded pair. Since then, we've been going on routine calls, mostly re-catching all the Springside ghosts we freed from Cedar Hills Mall, mostly because they want to say hi. In between all the catching and the chatting, we've been learning how to be cat-parents.

Also two weeks ago? Nigel started building a solarium for all of Sadie's plants and flowers. Not to be outdone, the next day, Malcolm began work on a catio, so the cats can join us on the back deck.

It's been relentless rivalry ever since.

"Is it a brother thing, a guy thing, or a necromancer thing?" I ask Belinda on our way back to the kitchen.

She stares through the windows, taking in both Nigel's progress on the solarium and Malcolm's on the catio.

"It would go faster if they gave in and helped each other, right?" I add.

"It would," she confirms.

"Then?" I've ventured out onto the deck a few times and offered to help. All Malcolm does is give me a warm—if tired— grin. Then he'll glance toward Sadie's and say, "Nah, I've got this."

Belinda tilts her head, considering. "Necromancer thing? Maybe?" With her coffee mug, she points toward Nigel and then

Malcolm. "They both have that necromancer vibe going right now, and it's not like either one of them is trying to catch a ghost."

Unlike Belinda, I've never been able to detect the necromancer vibe that she can. Maybe it's because I grew up outside the necromancer community. I like to tell myself it's because—technically— I'm not a necromancer. But I'm not sure that's true, either.

My phone pings, and I tug it from my back pocket.

Arianna: Available for a chat?

Yes, it's phrased as a request rather than a summons. Also? I could pretend Malcolm and I are out on an early Saturday morning call—sprites are acting up again in Springside. I mean, somewhere in town, they certainly are. It wouldn't be a total lie.

And yet, Arianna would know.

I don't bother with a reply; I simply obey the summons by booting up the laptop we keep on the kitchen's built-in desk. I have the camera strategically angled so all Arianna can see is the fresh coat of paint on the cabinets, the new hanging rack with gleaming pots and pans, and the tin lampshade Malcolm found for above the table. That, and the percolator and the samovar.

We don't need her critiquing the rest of the house.

The video pops up, and my future mother-in-law appears, resplendent as always. Her hair is silver and sleek, and her makeup so flawless you can hardly tell she's wearing any at all, except for the impeccable red lipstick.

"There you are, *ma petite*."

"*Bonjour*, Arianna." That's the extent of my French, although I keep promising to take a class. She claims it will help us bond. How, exactly, I'm not sure.

She's on her balcony. Behind her, the Paris afternoon is brilliant. Sunlight glints off the Seine and strikes the buildings on the other side of the river. Yes, her camera is strategically angled as well.

I'm not sure where, exactly, Arianna and Prem (the man she refers to as her lover, much to Malcolm's chagrin) live in Paris or how much they earn. My sense is *somewhere fancy* and *a lot*.

"I have a proposition for you." She claps her hands together, and her bob sways with the movement.

I inhale a deep breath and brace myself for just about anything.

"I had the most marvelous idea this morning. How would you like to come to Paris for a wedding dress shopping trip?"

I open my mouth, but of course, Arianna is far too quick for me.

"My treat, all of it, from the airfare to the dress itself. Think of it as my wedding gift to both of you. And of course, your bridesmaids are invited as well, also my treat. We'll have a good, old-fashioned girls' weekend."

Arianna pauses, and I suspect she's waiting for a squeal or a yes, or at the very least, a nod. My mouth is still open, and now I can't close it. The taste of sawdust is heavy on my tongue. I can't think. I can't answer. I can't even move from her line of sight. Part of me yearns to say yes. Arianna is beyond generous. She only wants to help. Most of the time, she doesn't mean to steamroller everyone.

It just happens.

But the one thing I know about my wedding dress is this: I want to buy it from Marguerite at So-Sew Springside. What kind of wedding dress? That, I don't know.

As for bridesmaids? Well... Malcolm has already asked Nigel to be his best man. I want to ask both Sadie and Belinda to be my maid of honor. But I know it doesn't work that way, and that I can only ask one of them.

I haven't done that yet, either.

"It's a lot to take in, I know," Arianna says when I don't answer. "But think of how much fun it will be. Have you ever been to Paris before?"

Here, I manage to shake my head.

"We'll have to add in some sightseeing along with the shopping. We'll do all the touristy things. The Eiffel Tower, of course, and the—"

"Don't you work weekends?" It's a squeak of a protest, but I manage it. Prem and Arianna run a tour company—weekends are always busy.

"We hired a few new necromancers. Haunted Paris practically runs itself these days." Arianna swivels, and Prem comes into view.

He's tall, with dark, curly hair touched by gray. His mother was from Pakistan, his father French. His smile is full of warmth and commiseration, but the shrug he gives me is one hundred percent Gallic.

I'm on my own.

"I don't want to impose—"

"It's no imposition. In fact, I insist."

"No."

This new voice comes from the door that leads to the deck. Malcolm steps into the kitchen, his olive skin glowing with a sheen of sweat. The sawdust sprinkled in his hair makes him look prematurely gray. He's gripping a hammer—which, considering the expression on his face, he should probably set down.

"The first time Katy sees Paris, I want it to be with me." Malcolm turns to me, and that fierce expression softens. He studies the hammer and places it gently on the kitchen table. "Unless you really want to buy your dress in Paris."

"I was planning on seeing Marguerite at So-Sew Springside."

"And I was planning on surprising you with a honeymoon trip to Paris."

I gape, and again, I taste that sawdust swirling in the air. Months ago, Malcolm convinced me to submit a passport application—on the grounds that K&M Ghost Eradication Specialists might need to go international someday. A smile bubbles up from inside me. Has he been planning this trip for a year?

This is Malcolm, so yes, absolutely he has.

"I probably would've caught on by the time we reached the airport."

"It still would've been a *surprise*." This he directs toward the laptop, where Arianna, still on screen, has a fingertip pressed against her lips.

"Oh, my poor baby boy. I'm so sorry."

Malcolm grimaces.

But because she's Arianna Armand, she rallies and directs another volley at me. "How about a virtual shopping trip, then? You can't say no to a Paris original."

"I want a Springside original." I don't mean to sound rude or ungrateful, but the words stream from my mouth before I can stop them. So, yes, apparently, I can say no to a Paris original.

"For my Springside original." Malcolm gives me one of those sweet, dark roast grins of his, and he brushes his knuckles along my cheekbone.

"Very well." Arianna sighs as if I'm making a grave error. "I'll send Marguerite our mood board."

I turn toward Malcolm, voice low, mouth barely moving. "Our wedding has a mood board?"

His lips twitch. "Several."

I'm not sure what to say to this. I'm not sure there's anything *to* say. But before I can launch my own attack in the wedding dress war—by declaring I plan to buy my own dress—my phone buzzes with an incoming text.

Misty Sandborne: I'm having an issue here.

For a moment, my mind blanks on the name. Then I remember.

Harold's ghost.

Harold Lancaster was Sadie's former husband (when he was a person, not a ghost). He'd had an affair with Misty (among others—again, as a person). But when Sadie and Nigel fell in love, Harold haunted with a vengeance. After a failed eradication at Sadie's, we finally caught him at Misty's duplex.

My heart rate kicks up a notch. I'm not quite sure where Harold ended up. He wasn't among the ghosts that Malcolm collected when he brought me back to this plane.

I cast a quick look outside. Belinda, Sadie, and Nigel are lingering on the deck, trying to look as if they're not eavesdropping.

Clearly, they are.

But if Harold's ghost is back in Springside, this could be bad. Very, *very* bad.

Katy: Are you having problems with a ghost?
Misty Sandborne: Maybe? I can't tell, but I am having trouble with my vampire husband.

CHAPTER 2

I hand Malcolm my phone so he can see what I've been gaping at —yet again. Then I march to the kitchen windows. Over the flickering of Willow's tail, I call out.

"Nigel, what do you know about vampire husbands?"

He starts at the sudden question, a quick flush painting his cheeks a barely-there pink. Yes, they've absolutely been eavesdropping.

"A vampire *what*?"

"Vampire husbands. Do they exist?"

This, I think, is a fair question. Only a few weeks ago, I learned that demons actually exist. Why not vampire husbands as well?

"Do they ...?" Nigel trails off, his gaze scanning the sky as if that's where all the vampire husbands reside. "I have no idea."

"Can you do a little research?"

Now he grins at me. "Be glad to."

I turn back to Malcolm and, of course, Arianna. Wedding dresses will have to wait.

He hands me my phone. "Told her we're on our way."

This is what I love about him, what I love about us. K&M the

127

couple never gets in the way of K&M Ghost Eradication Specialists.

On the screen, Arianna is eying both of us.

"The two of you," she says, but her tone is indulgent. "You're so well-suited. Who am I to interfere?" With that, she switches off the camera.

With a fingertip, Malcolm closes the laptop. "Who is she to interfere?" he mimics before releasing a long sigh. "She'd *never* dream of interfering."

I can't help but laugh, but I hold out my hand. When he takes it, I say, "Want to go meet a vampire husband?"

"I think we should."

ON OUR WAY to Misty's, we drive past the green and white Victorian where Ghost B Gone once attempted an eviction and ended up with an entity instead. It's where I nearly lost Malcolm forever. Then again, it's also where I got him back.

Sometime last fall, the For Sale sign vanished. Since then, there's been a parade of landscapers and contractors. The house is still green and white, although now with a fresh coat of paint. Despite all the activity, I haven't seen anyone who looks like they live there.

And that's weird.

"Malcolm, remember what Prescott said about necromancers establishing residency before the next vote for association chair?" I point to the Victorian. "You don't suppose...?"

I let the question hang in the air. Malcolm slows the convertible, and we come to a halt at a stop sign. Then he puts the car in reverse and backs up until we're even with the newly landscaped lawn.

It's a riot of late-spring flowers, many of them native plants. Even from the convertible, I catch the buzz of bumblebees and hummingbirds. To one side, water tumbles down rocks into a pool. The entire property is charming and idyllic.

Malcolm's gaze goes from the top of the cupola to the expansive front porch. "Aside from the fact that they're pouring a ton of money into the place?" He casts me a look. "That's totally a necromancer thing to do. But otherwise? It doesn't feel threatening. It's too cozy. It feels like home."

I pull out my phone anyway and peck out a quick text. "We can add it to the list of things Nigel can check."

As we drive away, the barest hint of the otherworldly caresses the nape of my neck. I glance over my shoulder, but nothing lingers —human or ghost. Nothing appears out of place.

If anything, it was more like a kiss goodbye.

THE FIRST TIME we met Misty Sandborne, she was wearing only emerald silk and matching nail polish.

Today, when we arrive at her duplex, I'm relieved to see she's decked out for summer—tight capri pants in hot pink and a gauzy, billowing top in a riot of colors (not even tropical flowers are that bright). Somehow, she's managing to stride through her apartment in a pair of stiletto mules festooned with baby-blue faux fur.

Honestly? I'm impressed.

But what's captured my attention—and Malcolm's—is the inert form sprawled face-down on the carpet where the entryway meets the living area. A wave of déjà vu strikes me. I know that gleaming blond head, and I've seen it in that exact same spot, right there on the floor.

"I feel like we've done this before," Malcolm says, his tone both incredulous and amused.

"It's his own fault." Misty dismisses Carter Dupree with a wave of her hand. "He made my vampire husband jealous."

Malcolm takes a knee to check on Carter while I lift my chin and search for the otherworldly. I brace, half-expecting to find Harold's ghost glowering on the living room couch, demanding the remote control. It isn't there, but the space looks like a tornado—or possibly the supernatural—has hit it. The couch cushions are upended, magazines torn to shreds. Letters and bills litter every surface. There's even a pizza flyer stuck in the ceiling fan. The paper rattles with every slow rotation of the blades.

In the far corner, above a built-in bookshelf, a ghostly presence glimmers. It's so sweet and slight that it nearly blends in with the fairy lights that surround the perimeter of the room.

It certainly doesn't seem capable of so much destruction. I tilt my head as if that will help me gauge this ghost's intentions. The fairy lights flicker, dimming for a moment. Then the presence above the bookshelf gives me a little finger wave.

Yes, it's *enormously* pleased with itself. I glance back at Carter. Really, I can't blame it.

Also? It's the only presence I can detect. Then again, I've never encountered a vampire husband.

"What does a vampire husband look like?" I ask Misty.

"Oh, honey, you can't actually see vampire husbands. You simply feel their spirit."

So, a ghost by any other name. This is something we can deal with.

I'm about to ask what a vampire husband feels like, but I'm not sure I want the answer to that question. Before I can say anything, Carter groans and—with Malcolm's help—rolls onto his back. Carter's arm flops, and I see that he's clutching something that rolls free when his hand hits the carpet.

Misty dashes forward and scoops up what looks like a jewelry box. Her gaze darts to Carter, then to Malcolm, and then lands on me. Her eyes hold a conspiratorial gleam, and she beckons to me.

"Come on." With that, she strides down the hallway that leads to—I'm guessing here—the bedroom.

My gaze meets Malcolm's. I mouth, "Should I?"

"I guess," he mouths back.

The ghost above the bookshelf seems content. Carter appears unharmed, although he's rubbing his head. Malcolm is safe and sturdy and has things under control.

Without recourse, I follow Misty.

I'M WRONG. We end up not in a bedroom—with your standard dresser and closet and maybe a vanity—but a boudoir.

The fairy lights are doubled here, and the scent of vanilla and lavender envelops us the moment we cross the threshold. I'm expecting ornate furniture and maybe a frilly canopy over the bed.

Instead, the headboard, the nightstand, the vanity, the dressers, and the clothing trees are all blond wood. Everything is neat, with clean, straight lines. Most impressive? The built-in closet organizers that line the walls of what must have been a second bedroom. Misty's clothes are organized by season and color—I spot the emerald green robe next to one in jade and another in neon green. Her shoes go on for days.

"Like it?" she asks.

Numbly, I nod.

"I did it myself. Well, me and YouTube." She spreads her arms wide as if giving the space a hug. "It's my oasis."

"It's wonderful," I say, and absolutely mean it. True, the clothes I own wouldn't fill a quarter of the closet. But seeing all this gives me the sense that Misty Sandborne knows what she's doing with her life.

"So," I say while Misty bustles about. "When did you first start having trouble with your vampire husband?"

I think this is why she's asked me back here. She pauses, a hand resting on one of the cabinets, her gaze on the twinkling fairy lights, and I suspect I'm right.

"Everything was just fine until Carter proposed."

"Carter ... proposed?"

"Of course he did." She whirls, top billowing. "Honey, they *all* propose."

Even Harold? I want to ask but decide not to go there. "And this made your... vampire husband jealous?"

Misty sits down hard on the bed, despair washing over her. "It did, and it's not supposed to work that way."

"How is it supposed to work?"

She pulls out her phone—from where, I'm not sure—and pats the spot next to her. I take a tentative perch on the velvet duvet. Misty angles her phone so we can both see the screen.

At first, I'm not sure what I'm looking at. Whatever this site is, it's not optimized for mobile. Misty scrolls, and images and text resolve into something that makes sense—sort of.

Apparently, you can order a vampire husband online. Not only that, but he comes with his own vampire-husband engagement ring. It doesn't matter if you're already married or engaged or really anything at all. According to the website, a vampire husband is never jealous and is always there for you. A constant companion, if you will, albeit and a sexy and invisible one.

All for one hundred dollars (payment plans available).

"Do you still have the engagement ring?" I ask. "The vampire one?"

Misty strides over to the vanity and plucks something from the surface. "I took it off when he threw his fit this morning." She hands it to me and sits back down.

The ring doesn't look expensive, but then I don't know much about jewelry. The huge, square-cut stone is—appropriately enough—blood red. The setting has scrollwork and appears antique, but the ring itself looks like something you might buy at a flea market. I hold the ring between my palms, gauging whether the supernatural is attached to it.

I've really only encountered that once before, when Queenie haunted not only Mr. Carlotta but his Purple Heart as well. If it weren't for the ghost out in the living room, I'd say the husband isn't included with the vampire-husband engagement ring.

I hand Misty the ring. "I don't think this is haunted."

"It's symbolic."

I nod like I understand what that means.

She studies the ring. For a moment, her fingers hesitate, almost like they have a will of their own. But then she stands and returns the ring to the vanity.

"Can you text me that site?" I ask.

"Do you want—?"

"For our research." There are many things in this world I do not want; I'm pretty sure a vampire husband nears the top of the list.

I send the URL along to Nigel.

He sends an exclamation point as a reply.

I'm at a loss. We have what I'd normally consider a nuisance haunting, although why Carter didn't detect the ghost before it struck, I can't say. True, some ghosts can lie dormant. Not even the most experienced necromancer can detect them. But not this ghost. I peck out a quick text to Malcolm and then turn to Misty again.

"So... Carter proposed and the ghost—vampire husband—"

"Oh, that reminds me." She opens one of the cabinets to reveal a safe. With deft fingers, she punches in the code, and the door creaks open. "I'll have this appraised and then take it to the bank on Monday."

She pulls the jewelry box from her pocket and pops open the lid. She crooks a finger at me. Compelled, I'm drawn forward until I can admire the ring inside.

"Not bad." She tips the box so the facets reflect the light. "Of course, it depends on the quality of the stones."

Inside, the satin lining is embossed with an ornate letter H. Misty plucks the ring from its resting place. The large diamond in the center sparkles while darker stones—sapphires, I'm guessing —gleam.

Now, *this* is not a ring you buy at a flea market.

"That's about two carats." She gives a shrug of approval. "Pretty good for a fake engagement."

"So you're not—?" I begin.

Misty gives a half-laugh, half-sigh. "Oh, honey, I never *marry* them." She holds up the ring. "It's a game—and an investment strategy."

She returns the ring to the box, snaps the lid shut, and places it in the safe. From its depths, she pulls something else.

"Here, let me show you." She places what looks like a cross between a scrapbook and an account ledger on the bed and flips it open to a random page.

"This"—she indicates her figure with a sweep of her hand, from the artfully sloppy bun on top of her head to those baby-blue mules—"is only going to last for so long. But this?" She taps a page with a fingertip. "Well, you know what they say. A diamond is forever."

Yes, my first impression was correct. It's a scrapbook *and* a ledger. Each page details a piece of jewelry, complete with a photograph, the appraised value, number of carats, date acquired, and the name of the man who bestowed the gift—all done up with washi tape borders and calligraphy.

Again, I can't help but be impressed. Because this? If nothing else, this takes effort.

"I have actual investments too." She nods toward the living room. "Carter's steered me into a couple of really good ventures. But you know what they say—"

"Diamonds are a girl's best friend?"

Now Misty throws her head back and laughs. "Exactly."

"What does Carter get from this?" I keep my gaze locked on the scrapbook rather than let it stray to the rest of the boudoir. I mean,

I'm sure there are some things he's getting, but again, I don't want to go there.

"Oh, he wants to make that server at the Pancake House jealous."

"Belinda?"

"That's the one." Misty shakes her head, loose tendrils escaping her bun. "I told him she wasn't the type, but he insisted on trying." She flips through a few more pages. "Who am I to stop him?"

The scrapbook contains more than simply engagement rings. Necklaces and earrings fill the pages as well. I see a quick flash of names I recognize, including Harold Lancaster and a very expensive diamond tennis bracelet.

"I told Carter," Misty continues. "That girl? She's not looking for a guy, she's looking for her life. If he wants to be a guy *in* her life, he needs to do something else. I mean, I haven't been in Springside that long, but I've been here long enough to know a thing or two about the people in this town."

This doesn't surprise me. Sometimes it takes an outsider to see things clearly. I wonder at that, too. Small towns aren't always kind to strangers, especially strangers who swoop in and take things like husbands, boyfriends—and in Malcolm's case, all my customers and my ghosts.

And maybe beneath the bravado and life plans, Misty is lonely as well. From the corner of my eye, I catch the blood-red gleam of the vampire engagement ring. A companion who's also invisible, sexy, and always available? I feel the tug of temptation in that.

My phone buzzes in my back pocket. I pull it out and find a text from Malcolm.

Malcolm: Carter says he didn't detect the ghost until it hit him upside the head.

That's something ghosts do to Malcolm. Maybe it's a necromancer thing. I've been tossed about and thrown into walls by the nastier ghosts. Harold's ghost threw me into a mirror. But ghosts never cuff me on the back of the head.

Malcolm: Also? What's going on back there? I'm getting worried.

Yes, we need to do something. I turn to Misty. "Do you want us to catch your... vampire husband?"

She closes the scrapbook and then hugs it to her chest. "Is he going to keep doing what he's doing?" She nods toward the living room.

That cheeky little finger wave? Oh, definitely.

"Probably."

"Guess I'm out a hundred bucks, then." She heaves a wistful sigh. "Not all of us can grab a cutie like you did."

"I don't have a cutie," I'm compelled to say. "Plus, there was no grabbing involved."

At this, Misty raises a perfectly sculpted eyebrow. "Really? Because that sounds boring, and, honey, he don't look boring to me."

My cheeks flame so hard I'm afraid they'll ignite the pages of the scrapbook.

"I'm going to go catch your ghost now." I mean to say this professionally, but it comes out as a squeak.

I flee the bedroom before my face can set anything on fire.

CHAPTER 3

In the living room, Carter is settled on the couch, an icepack pressed against his temple. The mail sits in neat stacks on the kitchen island. Malcolm's stretching on tiptoe to dislodge the pizza flyer from the ceiling fan.

I can't meet his gaze, not even to thank him. Every time I do, my cheeks blaze hot. At last, I do the only thing I can.

"I'll brew some Kona blend." Again, I'm more squeaky than professional. I dash outside to my truck and set up the camp stove on the tailgate.

By the time the aromatic steam rises into the air and merges with the scent of grass clippings and roses, I'm back to normal, or mostly so. When I reach the door, a carafe of coffee in my hands, some Tupperware in a sack slung over one shoulder, I lose all my embarrassment. Because inside Misty's duplex, Malcolm and Carter are going head-to-head, each trying to catch the ghost.

And it's so not working.

Really, this ghost is nothing but cheek. This is the sort of ghost that—once we catch it—will manifest obscene images inside the Tupperware container.

It hovers at eye level now, in the center of the living area. The gentle breeze from the ceiling fan stretches its form before its image snaps back into place. Carter spreads his arms wide, mouth slightly open. Why he might want to swallow this thing, I have no idea. But that's how some necromancers commune with ghosts. Maybe he thinks he has a better chance of capturing it that way.

At the last moment, the ghost shoots toward the ceiling, and Carter crashes so hard, the floorboards shudder beneath my feet.

Malcolm, at least, is trying to catch the thing with an old cottage cheese container he must have dug from the recycling bin. I put the kitchen island between myself and them and then crack the lid on the carafe. Tempted, the ghost wavers ever so slightly, but it's still committed to its fun.

I can't blame it. Carter and Malcolm are all flailing arms and tangled feet. Occasional grunts and curses punctuate what is otherwise a silent battle. Really, it's like they can't help themselves. They're locked into some sort of mortal combat all over one slip of a ghost.

When Misty emerges from her bedroom, I pull two cups from a cupboard and pour. I hand her one and then ease the other as close to the far side of the kitchen island as I dare.

"I hope you don't mind it black," I say to both Misty and the ghost.

"Are you kidding me? This is great." She takes an appreciative sip. "Why didn't you... oh, that's right. Harold hated coffee."

Why, yes. Yes, he did.

With each lap of the living area, the ghost loses some of its enthusiasm for the game. And with each lap, the Kona blend captures more and more of its attention until, at last, it circles the cup with what looks like ghostly triumph and relief.

Misty studies the ghost floating in the steam, her lips slightly parted, as if she can't quite believe what she's seeing. I never considered that Misty might be a sensitive—someone who can sense ghosts, even if they can't catch them. True, Harold's presence was so overwhelming that even a die-hard skeptic couldn't help but notice him. That goes for Delilah's brief visit here as well. But this tiny thing? It's only slightly more substantial than a sprite.

"Do you know this ghost?" I ask.

Maybe it came here in the guise of her vampire husband and coincided its haunting with Carter's proposal. That's the sort of trick a mischievous ghost might play. Still, the way Misty tilts her head, her brow clouded with consideration, has me wondering.

"I... for a moment, I thought—" She shakes her head as if shaking off a sad memory. "Something felt familiar, I guess."

"Do you want me to catch it?"

She casts a glance toward the living area. Carter is spread-eagled on the floor, chest rising and falling like he's just finished a marathon. Malcolm has his hands propped on his thighs, hair rumpled and falling into his eyes.

"I think you'd better," is all Misty says.

WE'RE ALMOST to the nature preserve when Malcolm bursts out:

"Katy, I'm sorry."

"What for?" I'm holding the ghost on my lap. It refused the Tupperware, but it slid into the old cottage cheese container like it was a five-star hotel. It's been strangely serene for the entire drive, like it knows it's gotten away with something.

"I did it again, didn't I? It's like, when Carter's around, I lose half my mind."

Or when he's in a building competition with his brother. I remain silent. The ghost swirls in its container as if it's read my thoughts.

"It's like I have to prove I'm the better necromancer."

"You *are* a better necromancer."

"Yeah, but I have to *prove* it, over and over again." He taps the steering wheel in frustration. "Even I'm starting to get tired of it."

He manages a laugh, the sound of it full of self-deprecation. "I think Carter is too."

There's an upside to everything.

Malcolm slows the truck to take the treacherous curve, the one right before the road flows into the nature preserve—the one where I almost went through the guardrail one cold Valentine's Day, and one where my parents did, so many years ago. When we've passed the curve, part of me wants to look over my shoulder, to look back at it, but I keep my gaze straight ahead.

We pick a site well away from all the groups and families camping overnight. Then again, this ghost is so benign that it just might add to the midnight fun. I'm not too worried about releasing it here. When I peel back the lid and it slips off into the trees— without doubling back to cuff Malcolm upside the head—I'm sure we've made the right choice.

"Do you think that was too easy?" He rubs the back of his head as if the ghost struck him there anyway.

Now I wonder. "Should we have taken it farther out?"

It didn't seem like that sort of ghost, but then Malcolm spent more time with it than I did.

"I'm not sure." He stares into the middle distance, his gaze clouded, uncertain. "It was almost like it wanted to be caught. You know?"

Maybe? I follow his gaze but can't detect a single glimmer among the branches and leaves. I tilt my chin, but the air is free of the otherworldly. Nothing but warm earth, sharp pine, and the enticing scent of campfires.

"I know," I say at last, but unless we plan to crash through the woods, we can't do anything about it.

Malcolm's phone buzzes. He tugs it out, and his expression brightens. "It's only noon," he says, "and Sadie has lunch all ready to go."

"Because of course she does."

Sadie always has lunch, or dinner, or brunch ready to go. She's the reason the three of us—me, Malcolm, and Nigel—aren't subsisting on fast food and ramen noodles.

Malcolm holds out his hand, and I lace my fingers with his.

"Ready to head home, partner?" He gives me one of those sweet, dark roast grins, and I feel my heart stop. Right now, this day is so perfect, so lovely. I have everything I could ever want, and I'm afraid to wish for more.

So instead, I give him the biggest smile I can and say, "I am."

"Good, because I'm thinking about adding a settee to the catio. Do they make weatherproof velvet?"

I manage not to roll my eyes at that.

On the way to the truck, I glance over my shoulder. Something shakes the air. Something that sounds an awful lot like ghostly laughter.

WE ARRIVE HOME to Sadie's usual bustle. She presses cold drinks into our hands, and we devour a platter full of egg salad sandwiches. She won't let us talk business, not until we've scraped the bowl with the Waldorf salad clean.

Then, and only then, am I allowed to ask Nigel, "Did you find out anything about vampire husbands?"

I don't think we'll need to worry about this one in particular. But if someone is running a scam? We should stop it. The first step is knowing what on earth a vampire husband actually is.

"I did," he says, "but it's nothing that can't wait." He plucks Malcolm by the sleeve. "Hey, baby brother, want to help me with the solarium?"

Confusion clouds Malcolm's eyes, and he stares at Nigel like his brother has started speaking a foreign language. Then Nigel gives the barest of nods in Sadie's direction, and the brothers do this silent exchange thing. All at once, Malcolm's expression lights up.

"Oh, yeah. Sure," he says, his voice a little too loud. "I absolutely want to help you with the solarium."

They leave. Just like that.

The kitchen is quiet around us. The only sounds are the soft, soapy hum of the dishwasher and the occasional rattle of silverware. Something else is in the air, something intangible. It's not otherworldly. I'd recognize that. But it's there, and something about it makes my heart thrum with anticipation.

Belinda gives Sadie a little elbow nudge. Sadie blinks, clutches and unclutches her hands, picks lint off her slacks, and even clears her throat.

"So, earlier today, Katy, dear. We couldn't help but overhear your conversation with Arianna."

Well, yes, everyone overheard my conversation with Arianna.

"Anyway, I called Marguerite at So-Sew Springside, and she has this afternoon free. I was wondering, would you like to head over and look at some dresses?"

She just happened to? On a Saturday? In June? I don't know a lot about weddings, it's true. But either Sadie had this planned, or she pulled some serious strings to get us an appointment today.

Something wells inside my chest. Relief? Gratitude? A little of both?

I can't refuse. Also? I really don't want to. But dress shopping means picking a maid of honor, and my throat tightens at the thought. I want both Sadie and Belinda by my side. I'm shuffling through options, like having dual maids of honor, when Belinda nudges Sadie a second time.

For a moment, Sadie clasps her hands beneath her chin. Then she takes a long breath, smooths her slacks, and gives me a tremulous smile.

"Nigel and I aren't going to have children—for so many reasons. I did actually try for years, with Harold, but..." She trails off, her voice pensive. "Some things simply aren't meant to be."

I hold absolutely still. I'm unsure where Sadie is going with this, but my heart thuds like it knows it's important.

"I can't replace your parents, Katy," she continues. "I know that, but I was wondering if you'd allow me the honor of being the surrogate mother of the bride."

My chest squeezes tight. My eyes sting, my cheeks are hot pinpricks, and my throat is full of laughter and tears. I try to speak, but I don't have words. At last, I manage a nod.

Who moves first? I'm not sure. Me? Belinda? Sadie? All I know is that one moment, we're standing there, staring at each other, and the next, we've collapsed into a group hug. I'm not sure whose tears are whose. Belinda's blonde curls mix with Sadie's salt and pepper ones. Someone is shaking so hard that I think we might all crumple to the floor.

I think that someone is me.

I never realized that piece was missing, the role that my parents —my mother in particular—would play at my wedding. I never realized how empty that hole was until Sadie filled it.

I turn to Belinda now. "And will you be my maid of honor?"

"You know it."

"And you tell me," Sadie says, and her eyes blaze with fierceness. She is a lioness protecting her cub. "If there's something you don't like about the wedding plans. I know Arianna is helping Malcolm, but this is your wedding, not hers."

True, Arianna Armand is a steamroller, but the way Sadie looks right now, so righteously ferocious, Arianna doesn't stand a chance.

"Know what I think?" Belinda steps back, hands on hips, and gives me a once-over. "I think there's a bride in desperate need of a dress."

"Are you up to it?" Sadie asks. "You had a busy morning. We can always postpone."

I think back to earlier, at the nature preserve, and how I was afraid to wish for more. It wasn't fear; it was ignorance. I had no idea what was missing. Now that I do?

I'm not wasting it.

"I am," I tell Sadie. "I am."

"WHY DON'T YOU PICK A DRESS," I say to Belinda, "and I'll find something to match."

Maybe it's the bubbles from the sparkling grape juice, or the cloud-like garments covering every surface of the boutique. But this seems like a reasonable suggestion to me. Belinda, Sadie, and Marguerite all stare, silent, lips pressed together in grim lines. Belinda's the first to crack.

"That isn't how this works." She shakes her head so hard, her curls bounce. Then she rolls her eyes toward the ceiling, where her sprite is circling. It makes the air shimmer, and I'm pretty sure it's laughing at me.

I'm standing in the center of So-Sew Springside, trapped in a cream puff made of so much tulle, satin, and lace that I make rustling sounds every time I take a breath. The skirt on this thing is so huge, I'm afraid I'll knock something over simply by turning my head. I'd take a sip of sparking juice or eat another macaron, except my arms aren't long enough to reach the table with the delicately arranged refreshments.

So far, the snacks have absolutely been the best part of this shopping experience.

"I can't catch a ghost in this." I grab fistfuls of fabric and give the skirt a good shake.

"You're not going to be catching ghosts on your wedding day," Belinda says, again with an eye roll for her sprite.

"You don't know that," I counter.

All those Springside ghosts Malcolm and I released not too long ago? They could totally show up, at least for the reception. I have to be able to scold them. Trust me, not even sprites will take me seriously in this thing.

"I have the mood boards Malcolm's mother sent along," Marguerite suggests. Without rancor, I might add.

"That isn't how this works," I echo.

Problem is, I have no idea how it's supposed to work. We've paged through any number of patterns and collections. I've tried on half a dozen different types of dresses. I don't want to admit that Arianna might be right and that I should've taken her up on her offer—or at least looked at her mood boards.

Nothing has sparked my interest, never mind actual joy. Maybe some women dream of this day, have it all planned out in their heads, right down to the chair covers and table favors. But me?

I sigh. "I wish I could wear the skater skirt."

"One of these days," Belinda mutters, "I'm going to burn that thing."

Sadie tsks. I cross my arms over my chest.

"It's Malcolm's favorite."

Before Belinda can respond—and oh, she has a response—Marguerite steps forward, pinches the satin and tulle between her fingers as if she's inspecting it, and nods.

"Katy has a point. A beautiful dress is a wonderful thing, but if you want to enjoy your wedding day, it should be comfortable too. I've met far too many brides who sacrifice the one for the other." She gives her head a slow shake. "This is not the dress."

Belinda deflates. Instead of a snarky comment about the skater skirt, she says, "You look great in it, though." Then she holds out her hand. "Come on, let's try again."

Together, we walk another slow circuit around the shop. Marguerite's selection is small but chic. More and more people are probably heading to the Twin Cities to shop for formals and wedding dresses. But no one can match Marguerite when it comes to alterations—both in price and skill. Most of Springside ends up here anyway.

Sadie has already found a few contenders for a mother of the bride dress, all in various shades of pink. Belinda will look amazing in anything. Absently, I rub my ring finger with my thumb. It's a new habit, and I swear it helps me think.

Belinda's sprite buzzes around my hand and then zips to the stack of wedding magazines. It does this again, and again, and again. The air sparkles with its determination and frustration. We are all missing something crucial.

"What the—?" Belinda says.

But it hits me. My ring. Wedding magazines. *Go Vintage.*

Now, something sparks—relief, definitely. But maybe joy as well. I hold up my left hand. "Could I get a dress that matches this?"

Now I see that spark in Marguerite's expression, and she has the air of a woman on a mission.

"Let me see," she says.

I hold out my hand and let her inspect Malcolm's engagement ring.

"Hm. Something art deco, then? I have just the thing. It's form-fitting, but if you don't mind that, I think you'll look stunning." Marguerite vanishes into the shop's storeroom.

She emerges with an armful of lace and intricate beadwork. I've never even considered wearing something this sophisticated, but the patterns are lovely, and the geometric designs harken back to the art deco era.

"You really need to try it on," she says.

Belinda helps me slip on the dress. It really is form-fitting, but the lining is soft and smooth. And while it's not the sort of thing for catching ghosts, it's absolutely comfortable enough for dancing —not to mention scolding.

With the whisper of the zipper, I hear Belinda's intake of breath. I crane my neck to catch my image in the mirror, but she shoos me from the dressing room.

"You need the full effect." She clamps one hand over my eyes and steers me by the shoulder with the other. "Trust me."

Only when I'm standing on the pedestal in front of the three-way mirrors does she let me look. The transformation is startling. I'm me, and yet, not me.

"Oh, my." Sadie exhales.

"What did I tell you?" Belinda says. "You needed the full effect."

Marguerite is more businesslike. She clasps her chin, tilts her head, and studies me, her gaze not so much critical as assessing. "I'm thinking a headband rather than a veil. Belinda, go find one. There are a couple out front that might work."

Belinda dashes off while Marguerite continues to circle the pedestal. "A few adjustments, don't you think?" she says to Sadie, who nods. "But really, it's almost like I had your exact measurements in mind when I made this."

I place a palm against my stomach to calm the eruption of butterflies. "This is one of yours?"

Marguerite remains silent and inscrutable, pinching the material here and there, adjusting the hem, inspecting the beadwork. Belinda returns with a handful of headbands. Marguerite discards two immediately and then turns her attention to the other three. She and Sadie examine them, their gazes serious.

"This one," Marguerite says at last, and Sadie gives a nod of approval.

The headband's design matches Malcolm's ring, and the silver metalwork is brushed rather than shiny. Belinda pulls my hair back into a loose bun and then places the headband on my head like she's crowning the homecoming queen.

An exclamation erupts not from Sadie but from her phone. She has the camera aimed at me, and I hear what I think is evening in Paris.

"I promised her," Sadie mouths.

But I don't mind. I twirl on command for Arianna and then hold absolutely still while Marguerite and her assistant tuck and pin and do whatever it is they need to do. Although how they're going to make the dress more perfect than it already is, I don't know. Only when Belinda and Sadie are caught up in Arianna's chatter and the assistant has dashed back to the storeroom, do I speak to Marguerite.

"You made this." That amazes me. To craft something this intricate and delicate. This is the sort of dress I wanted, not just the design but also the heart that went into it, the soul.

"I did," Marguerite says.

"I can't believe it was here, waiting for me."

"Sometimes, that's the way it works." Marguerite's expression is dreamy. "You create something that doesn't seem to have a purpose or even a reason until, suddenly, it does."

"I told Malcolm that I wanted a Springside original." I press a hand against my chest and marvel at the feel of the beadwork against my palm. "I'm not sure how I can thank you."

"Believe it or not, you already have."

CHAPTER 4

With my dress tucked safely away at So-Sew Springside, under lock and key so Malcolm can't spy it until the wedding—why, I don't know, but apparently, it's a thing—I send Belinda and Sadie home.

I have one more stop to make, and this task I must do on my own.

I head down Main Street. The red, white, and blue buntings are up for next week's Fourth of July celebration. Baskets full of geraniums hang from the lamp posts and cast a rosy hue over the entire street. The gold letters of K&M Ghost Eradication Specialists gleam in the sunlight.

I pause at our storefront and trace the words. But this isn't my destination. I'm headed for the building at the end of the block. The door is closed, and the steps are empty. Despite that, and even though it's Saturday afternoon, I suspect Chief Ramsey will be inside.

I'm right. The front door is unlocked, and while Penny's desk is tidy, the scent of freshly ground coffee beans lingers in the air. The rustle of papers and the low tones of something melancholy comes from Chief's office—sad love songs without words.

My fist raised to knock, I hesitate. I don't have coffee of my own to offer up. I don't have anything at all except a request. I've asked Chief for so many things these past few years, but I have no idea how he might respond to this.

Before my knuckles graze wood, the door flies open. I yelp. Chief lets out a half-growl, half-gulp, and a few words to rival Malcolm's extensive vocabulary.

Maybe it's nerves. I can't help it. I laugh.

Chief wipes his brow and then turns that police chief glower on me. "I swear, Katy. You about gave me a heart attack."

"I hope not," I say, "because then you couldn't walk me down the aisle."

Okay, maybe I shouldn't have blurted it like that. Actually, I know better than to blurt anything around Chief.

"I mean, if you want to, that is." I rush these words so he knows it's okay to refuse.

I've considered everyone I might ask, and the list is fairly short. Nigel, of course, but he's the best man; I couldn't do that to Malcolm. Mr. Carlotta, perhaps? Maybe, but I'm afraid he'd urge me to reconsider while we walked down the aisle—all so I could marry his grandson Jack instead.

That leaves Chief, who really, in all of this, is my first choice. This is a man who's known me all my life, who knew—and maybe even loved—my mother.

Chief, as always, is inscrutable. Maybe that connection isn't enough for this sort of thing—or perhaps it's too much. He surveys me, arms folded across his chest. Then, with a few quick strides, he moves to the sideboard where the fancy red coffeemaker sits.

"I've finally figured out the trick to vanilla lattes," he says. "Want to try one?"

I nod, although, with my throat so tight, I'm not sure I'll be able to swallow, never mind drink an entire latte.

"Real vanilla." He sets a pair of clean cups on the sideboard and pulls whole milk from the mini fridge that's tucked next to it. "From Madagascar. None of that fake stuff. Makes everything taste awful."

I nod again. "Fake stuff always does."

"When is this wedding of yours?"

I almost miss his question in the whirl of the coffeemaker and the bubble and hiss of frothing milk. Warm, aromatic steam wafts upward, and I raise my chin, sample the air. Maybe there in the corner? By the file cabinets? A shy and subtle glimmer of the otherworldly? That feels promising. That gives me enough hope to answer.

"Halloween?" I say it like that, too, as a question. Because maybe Chief will be busy on Halloween.

For a moment, he shuts his eyes and presses his lips together. Part of me insists I've made him angry. Another part says he's trying not to laugh. Neither response is really what I expected.

He clears his throat. "Then there's time."

"For what?"

"For me to get my uniform dry-cleaned." He hands me a latte with lots of foam and sprinkles on top. "Got yourself a dress yet?"

"Just today." I sip the latte, and the warm flavor of vanilla soothes my nerves. I'm not sure how Chief knew I needed this particular drink at this moment, but he did. And I'm grateful. "From So-Sew Springside. It's one Marguerite made herself."

"Your mom bought her dress there, you know."

I freeze with the latte halfway to my lips. Because *no*, I didn't know that.

"Marguerite was just starting out as an assistant. I was a newly minted patrol officer, and part of my beat was walking up and down Main Street. That was old Chief Wilker's way. You need to know the people you protect and serve."

Chief still does that. At least once a week, he makes a circuit of Main Street by foot, chatting with business owners and shoppers, making sure no one jaywalks, raising a skeptical eyebrow at K&M Ghost Eradication Specialists' storefront display.

"Your mom was so excited about her dress that when she saw me through the window, she ran into the street to drag me inside."

"While wearing her wedding dress?"

"Veil and all. Good thing it wasn't raining." Chief chuckles at the memory before his expression turns contemplative. "You're like her in that."

"Running around town in a wedding dress?" Well, yes. I could see myself doing that. The only reason I didn't is that no one I knew passed by So-Sew Springside.

He laughs again. "That, and you lead with your heart."

That earlier sting of tears returns with a vengeance. For a moment, I forget how to speak. These small gifts of Chief's—these memories he doesn't have to share and yet still does—mean so much. I blow steam from my latte while I grope for words. My mouth isn't working. I can't drink, can't thank him.

All I do is fumble, and I so want to not fumble right now.

Chief raises his latte to mine. "Here's to you and Malcolm."

I touch my cup to his, and the porcelain sings out.

"I don't suppose getting married will keep you two out of trouble," he adds.

Now I have words and the presence of mind not only to speak them but to enjoy the latte warming in my hands.

"I don't suppose it will," I say.

Chief grimaces.

Not at all.

I'M SNUGGLED in the crook of Malcolm's shoulder. The heat of the day has vanished. The breeze that travels through the windows flutters the curtains and brings with it the scent of cool grass and something sweeter, like lilacs or violets. Outside, the night is quiet except for crickets and an occasional buzz and thump of insects hitting the screens.

There's something almost sacred about this time of day. Especially now that soft padding comes down the hall and across the bedroom floor. If you didn't know to listen for it, you might miss the hint of claws against hardwood or the contented purr of a bonded pair. Then, with a leap, Willow propels herself onto the comforter and settles next to Malcolm.

"Hey there, gorgeous. You ready for bed?"

Willow gives a half-meow, half-chirp.

Whiskers takes a more circuitous route, jumping up on the bench at the end of the bed, over the footboard, and then settles near my feet. If I stretch my toes, I can feel his solid weight. They won't stay here all night. This is merely a brief respite before the three a.m. shenanigans. With a sprite and two cats in the house?

There are always three a.m. shenanigans.

"You know," Malcolm says, and his chest heaves with a happy sigh. "This was pretty much the perfect day. We caught a ghost, you found a dress and rounded out the bridal party. Nigel and I didn't come to blows while putting together the solarium—"

"You cooked dinner."

His mood is contagious. I'm warm and fluttery inside, and I suspect he's right. This was a perfect day.

"And you cleaned up," he adds. "Plus? I found waterproof velvet for the settee."

That's when my phone rings.

Malcolm swears. "I jinxed it." He eyes me as I reach for the phone. "Didn't I?"

The name Misty Sandborne flashes on my screen. That warm, fluttery feeling drains away, the room going from comfortably cool to cold. Goosebumps break out all over my arms. I answer with the speaker on, and at first, we can't discern anything but garbled words and hitching sobs.

"Misty, are you okay?" Clearly, she's not, but we need her to talk, to tell us what's wrong. "Do you need us to come over? Call the police?"

Perhaps mine is the last number she dialed, and in an emergency, the first one she found.

"It's back," she says, her voice watery and thick. "My vampire husband came back, and he attacked Carter, only this time there's blood, and..." She trails off. Whether it's fear or the otherworldly that's keeping her from speaking, the outcome is the same.

"I knew it was too easy." Malcolm's already stumbling into a pair of jeans.

I grab the first thing handy—yoga pants and a T-shirt. The cats, upset by the sudden activity, go scrambling from the room in a flurry of claws and bottle-brush tails.

"Field kit's in the truck," I say to Malcolm. Then I turn my attention back to the phone. "Misty, hang on. We're on our way."

But the line is silent. A moment later, the call ends.

I KNOCK and knock on Misty's front door until my knuckles ache. I try the door handle only to jerk my hand back. It's cold.

Supernaturally cold.

"It's almost a full-on ghost infestation," I whisper to Malcolm.

He swears. Actually, he's been swearing this whole time. "Let me do a circuit. She has a patio. Maybe we can get in that way. Stay here in case she answers the door."

I nod and scan for other ways inside. A window, perhaps? It's a duplex, so maybe there's an adjoining door between homes? Or maybe not. That sounds creepy.

The ghost we caught today was energetic, but it wasn't genuinely destructive. That cheeky little finger wave? That's not a ghost bent on drawing blood.

From behind the house comes a crashing—and a lot more

swearing. I'm about to tear around the house myself when Malcolm calls out.

"Stay there. I got it."

There's nothing like waiting for someone to unlock the door during a full-on ghost infestation. The seconds tick by. With each one, I get more and more anxious. I shift from foot to foot, positive Malcolm won't make it to the door, that something will stop him, something that involves blood.

At last, the lock clicks. He yanks. I shove. When the gap is wide enough, he takes my hand and pulls me inside.

The door slams shut behind us. A thick layer of frost creeps up from the bottom, encasing the entire door, frame and all, in ice. My breath clouds in front of my face. Malcolm's eyebrows and hair are frosted. The only color in the entire space is a bright spot of red soaking a cloth Carter has pressed to his forehead.

"You okay?" I know head wounds bleed a lot. But here, with all the cold and gray, that blood is like a beacon. I can't look away.

Carter checks the cloth, returns it to his forehead, and then winces. "I'll live." His honeyed drawl sounds defeated and drained.

Malcolm has an arm around my waist, a hand anchoring me in place.

"Don't move," he whispers. In all this cold, his words are a warm, reassuring brush against my ear. "Just... taste the air."

I lift my chin, let my eyes flutter shut—briefly. The air feels heavy, and pulling in a full breath is difficult. My lungs strain under the weight. Beneath the cold come waves of malevolence and spite and revenge.

Revenge?

"We're not dealing with a ghost," Malcolm says, and now his voice is low and cautious.

No. No, we're not.

"That." He points his chin toward the ceiling fan that's covered in icicles. They appear as gray and sharp as stainless steel knives. "Is a demon."

CHAPTER 5

I reach for my phone, but Malcolm stills my hand.

"I called Nigel before I came inside." He inhales deeply and rubs fingers across his chest. "I'm hoping he can get word to Prescott."

Now that I'm here, inside, I sense what Malcolm already has. So much anger roils in the air that I'm almost afraid to breathe in the wrong way. Anything could spark supernatural outrage.

Even if we can catch this thing—a big if—containing it is another problem, possibly the bigger one. I think of that ghost Orson Yates sent to possess Nigel. The thing above our heads has that same feel. Currently, it's content to molder the ceiling. Grayish-green patches spread along the surface. It looks like a stop-motion film of an acute and deadly disease.

"We have three necromancers here," I say.

"I don't think Carter is—"

"Well, I do." That weird revenge vibe? For whatever reason, Carter's part of it. And if he's part of it?

We can use him.

"It's why it's not attacking at the moment," I add. "There's three of us." I turn then, searching for Misty. My heart rate kicks up when I don't spot her right away. Then I see her, hunkered down behind the kitchen island.

I ease from Malcolm and inch forward. "You okay?"

Her hair is a pile of tangled strands. I can't see her expression but get a tentative nod in response.

"This isn't the same ghost," I tell her.

"Then I didn't do this to him?" She nods toward the living area. The hair falls away from her face. Her eyes are wide, not so much with fear but with guilt.

I lift my chin again, sample the air, and then shake my head. "I don't think so. This is something else." I glance around the kitchen for anything I might be able to use. "Do you have any Tupperware or containers?"

She points to one of the cabinets built into the island. Inside, I find a huge plastic bowl, the sort you might use to make a gigantic fruit salad, along with a matching lid.

True, it's not Tupperware. But it could work.

I stand and offer up the bowl like a gift to Malcolm. "A container."

"Katy—"

"The first step is to contain it, right?"

He raises a hand and lets it drop. "Then what?"

Okay, he has a point. When we caught the ghost (or more likely demon) that possessed Thomas Davenport, it was all we could do to keep it contained. In the end, Darien took it off our hands. And he's certainly not around.

"If Nigel called Prescott," I say, "that will make four necromancers."

Prescott will know what to do with this demon. At least, I hope he will.

For a moment, Malcolm shuts his eyes. He takes another shuddering breath and then exhales with all his might. "It's urging me to... not help Carter." He studies Carter and then turns to me, his gaze pleading. "Do you feel it?"

Something brushes my ear, something cold and calculating. The whisper is insidious. Let this thing devour Carter, and all will be well. But I sense it for what it is: a false promise, one laced with poison. The urge isn't tempting me the way it is Malcolm.

Interesting.

"All the more reason to catch it," I say. "If nothing else, we'll be able to think clearly." Because even if I don't want it to destroy Carter, it could be urging me to do something else. And who knows what that something else is.

Malcolm swallows hard and then directs his ire at Carter. "Go put some pants on, man, and help us out."

Pants? Carter stands, and it's then I notice he's wearing nothing but a pair of boxer briefs. Misty's still hunkered down behind the kitchen island in a profusion of pink satin and silver feathers.

I open my mouth, close it, and decide the best thing to do is say nothing at all.

Carter returns from Misty's bedroom in a pair of jeans. He's secured some gauze to his forehead with duct tape. The tape is silver and crinkled and pushes his brow into a permanent glower.

Malcolm rolls his eyes. "You could've put on a shirt, too."

"You said pants," Carter replies, and his tone is nothing but belligerent.

I step between them and point to the ceiling. "We have other problems."

Carter tips his head back and swears. "I'm not getting out of here alive, or at least, not unpossessed."

"You can tell it's for you?" It's not like *Carter Dupree* is written in large letters across the ceiling. All I can detect is its malevolence.

He nods, mouth hard, jaw clenched.

"Any idea who sent it?"

"Orson. I mean, maybe?" Carter blinks rapidly. "Except this doesn't feel like him or his signature, not exactly."

"It doesn't," Malcolm says. "Like at the Pancake House. *That* felt like Orson. This?" His eyes meet Carter's. For one instant, they're unified. "I want to say it's familiar, but at the same time, it's not."

"When did it attack?" I ask.

"Maybe, what?" Carter glances about, gaze lighting on the microwave clock. "Half an hour ago. It tore in here, threw me around, and Misty called you guys."

Half an hour? The mold is already creeping down the walls. The paint is bubbling with pustules, and thick cobwebs fill each corner of the room. The place smells musty, all dirty socks and rotting wood. Oh, this thing is strong, much stronger than I first realized.

When the trembling starts, the tiny hairs on my nape freeze. It feels like someone has blown an icy breath along my skin. Vibrations shake the floorboards, run along the soles of my feet. I'm about to cry out a warning when Malcolm shouts.

"Get down!"

Malcolm launches himself across the room. I drop to the floor, and a moment later, his hands cover my head, his body shielding me from the onslaught. Books fly from the shelf. One hits the wall with so much force, it leaves a dent.

Dishes rattle in the glass-fronted cabinets. Images of needle-like splinters fill my mind, and I banish the thought, forcing myself to look anywhere but all that glass. We don't need to give this thing any more ideas.

"We need to catch this thing." My words are insubstantial, barely words at all.

"With what? We need bigger bait than coffee, and we don't have that."

"Don't we?" I squirm from beneath Malcolm and point at Carter.

"Oh, no." Carter pushes to his hands and knees. He shakes his head so hard that blond hair flops into his eyes and obscures the duct tape. "I am not going to be this thing's bait."

"You're already its target," I counter. "How's being bait any worse?"

Carter shoves the hair from his forehead and gives me a full-on duct tape glower.

"You're its target," Malcolm echoes. "And Katy and I could just sit here and watch it devour you, but that's not going to do much good."

Fighting this thing? When it has a body to command? I think of Thomas Davenport, of how the ghost that possessed him was so strong, of how its eyes burned behind Thomas's. What would Carter's ice-blue eyes look like with the gleam of the otherworldly behind them?

"Is a possession worse when the victim is a necromancer?" I ask.

When neither Malcolm nor Carter responds, I have my answer.

Yes. *Much* worse.

At last, Carter nods. "You're right. You guys didn't even have to —" He nods toward the patio door where Malcolm jimmied the lock. "I mean, when you saw it was a full-on infestation. You should've just left." In his tone, I hear the unspoken *I would have.*

"That's not what we do." I tap my thighs, scan the apartment, and try to conjure up a plan. "We have a container." I point to the bowl, a happy thing, decorated with cartoon bananas and berries, all holding hands.

"We have its target," Malcolm adds, helping me along.

So, what's missing? Why hasn't this thing gathered up its strength and attacked?

"What is it waiting for?" I ask.

From the kitchen, Misty calls out, her voice tremulous but resolute.

"It's waiting for my vampire husband to leave."

THE AIR IS SO thick and icy, it takes me a good thirty seconds to crawl around the kitchen island. I'm expecting to find Misty still hunkered down, hands over her head, but the space behind the island is empty.

"Misty?" My palms start to sweat and slip against the tile floor. If she isn't here, then I don't know where she is.

"Over here," comes a muffled reply.

I blink a couple of times, and then I see it—a thin strip of pink satin trailing from the built-in pantry. Inside, Misty is all knees and elbows encased in an otherworldly glow. I reach out a hand and touch the shimmering outline.

"I know you," I say. "You're very cheeky." I consider this second otherworldly presence and what it's doing here and add, "Not to mention brave."

This is definitely the ghost Malcolm and I released at the nature preserve yesterday.

"It's protecting you," I tell Misty.

Or trying to. There's only so much a mischievous little ghost like this one can do against the behemoth in the living room.

"Because it's my vampire husband." Despite the carnage in her apartment, her expression is tender. "I knew he was real."

Well, no. He *is* a ghost, one with more strength than a sprite, but not by much. There isn't time to contradict or explain. Still, no matter what it is—ghost or vampire husband—it *is* helping us.

"What do we need to do to get rid of that thing?" I ask it. "Do you know?"

I'm about to sweeten the deal with some Kona blend. Ghosts are such transactional creatures that they almost always want something in return for their help. Before I can, the ghost surges forward.

Misty lets out a yelp, but all this ghost wants is to talk to me. Its form brushes my lips, and a barrage of images fills my head.

Some don't relate to our current situation. I see something that is clearly high school. Crowded hallways, lockers, a cafeteria filled with lunch trays and students. Then other images flash. A bright red sports car. A wet, snowy night. A curve taken too quickly.

My heart seizes.

The pictures shift again. Dark, dank rooms remind me of the warehouse where Orson Yates kept and tortured so many ghosts, but I don't see or sense Orson in this ghost's memories. Instead, what I do glean is hints of the other ghost in the living room. This one is huge and roiling, even contained in the dark rooms of this little ghost's memory, but it wants something. All ghosts want something.

So, why does it need Carter?

That roiling changes to something natural rather than supernatural. A lake, maybe. Or the ocean. The entity once told me that all it wanted was the ability to touch a cheek, to feel, to have a physical presence, all the things humans take for granted.

The images that flash in my mind are odd, but we might be able to work with them. I cough to clear the cobwebs from my throat and the little ghost from my thoughts.

"Thank you," I say.

Jerome.

"It's nice to meet you."

Jerome retreats to Misty, encasing her in an otherworldly glow. Oh, he's so protective that I wonder at this connection, too. Later. If we survive this, then there will be time to puzzle out this relationship.

"It wants to go fishing," I call out to Malcolm and Carter.

Silence greets my declaration.

I ease the pantry door shut and crawl around the kitchen island. "Do you know anything about fishing?" I ask Carter.

I can't tell if the glower is duct-tape induced or not.

"I'll take that as a no." I glance around, wondering if there's anything we can pretend is a fishing rod. "Maybe a broom—" I begin.

"In the hallway closet," Misty shouts through the pantry door. "I have some gear."

Really? Then again, this is Minnesota, land of 10,000 lakes. Growing up, I was too busy catching ghosts with my grandmother to bother with learning how to fish, but half of Springside heads out of town for the fishing opener each year. Misty's reel is pink, and the tackle box a mix of magenta and lavender. Well, why not? I grab both and head for the living room.

Malcolm instructs Carter to sit. Then, with infinite patience, he shows him how to attach a lure to the line.

"Just do it over and over again," he says.

"It's not going to fall for this." Carter turns that scowl on the lure in his hands. "Also? Why would a fish even eat this?"

"Just do it, man," Malcolm growls.

We take up a position on either side of Carter. Malcolm clutches the Tupperware. I'm crouched by the flatscreen television, ready to add to the containment field once we catch this thing.

If we catch this thing.

Carter may be right. The ghost churns, a thick, grayish-green mist above our heads. It's like being struck by waves; salt crusts on my lips. The walls sprout barnacles and drip with what looks like seaweed. The ghost surges toward the floor, then recoils, entwining long, ethereal tentacles around the blades of the ceiling fan.

With each surge, it moves closer and closer to Carter. With each surge, I sense its longing. With each surge, it's quickly losing the last of its indecision. One tentacle takes on the shape of a hand, fingers stretching for the fishing reel—and Carter. Yes, it wants Carter—and badly—if only to stop him from knotting the line.

That's when the notion hits me.

"Carter," I whisper. "Make a mess of things."

"He already has," Malcolm mutters.

I throw him a look before adding, "Tangle up the line."

Carter coughs, studies the jumble of line and lures in his hands, and then holds it up for me to see.

"Make it even worse," I say.

I'll give Carter this—he goes all out. He upends the tackle box, scattering lures and a roll of extra line across the living room floor. He knots the fishing line so badly that it reminds me of all the ghosts sewn together at the Pancake House. Except no one's getting through this tangle without a pair of sharp scissors.

This time, when the ghost surges forward, it doesn't draw back. It keeps going, intent on possessing Carter. And while it's strong and malevolent, I sense that it wants to stop the chaos of Carter's fumbling more than it wants to destroy all of us.

My gaze meets Malcolm's. I tense, ready to spring when he does. Carter remains stoic as another tentacle becomes a second hand. I've never seen a ghost possess someone before, and I'm not about to now, not if I can help it. Once that thing goes inside Carter?

We might not be able to get it out.

Malcolm mouths a silent countdown. *Three... two... one.*

I launch forward a split second after he does. He lands with a crash against the floor. I join him, planting my palms along the sides of the fruit bowl. With all my strength, I channel everything I know about containing ghosts.

"You can help, man."

Malcolm's voice is pulled taut. His entire body shakes. I double my effort, visualizing the containment field growing thicker and thicker until it obscures the illustrations on the side of the bowl. Carter stumbles forward, lands on his knees, and presses a hand against the bowl.

That's when it starts to rain.

CHAPTER 6

We have the ghost. Or at least, I'm pretty sure we do. Despite the rain, the air has cleared. I no longer feel as if I'm gulping soggy breaths and treading water.

"Keep... building... the field." Malcolm's arms tremble, his chest anchoring the bowl to the floor. I shut my eyes and once again concentrate on the containment field the three of us have established around the bowl.

Rain drenches my back, runs down my spine, washes over my skin. The bowl rocks beneath us like a boat on rough seas. I taste salt again, but whether that's from this ghost or my own sweat, I can't tell.

"Why is it doing this?" I ask.

We've caught it, after all. It's contained. Tentacles probe the seam where the bowl meets the carpet. Maybe that's it. The seal isn't tight enough, and some of its strength is leaking through.

"It's because you've caught yourself a demon."

Prescott stands in the doorway, inserting what looks like a pointy tool into a leather case.

I stare in wonder. "How did you—?"

"Every necromancer should know how to pick a lock."

I can't actually see Malcolm's expression, but I feel him roll his eyes. "Then maybe you could help," is his grumbled reply.

Prescott walks forward, the clouds—and rain—parting for him. Chaucer is here, all bustle and pride as he shields Prescott. The air glimmers with both rainbows and the otherworldly.

Prescott takes a knee next to the bowl and adds his hand to all of ours. The rain shifts from downpour to drizzle to no more than a gentle sea mist against my cheeks.

Then it vanishes completely.

"That will hold it for a bit," he says. "Let's get the lid on and reinforce that as well."

Carter flops back on the carpet, his skin pallid and dull. Malcolm and Prescott wrestle the lid onto the container. Once they do, the three of us place our palms on the cool plastic. The storm clouds still churn. If this thing could smash through the container, it would. Its power is enough to steal my breath and make my resolve waver. It's like trying to keep your head above water; it might just be easier to let go.

My efforts feel puny next to Prescott's. His containment field is smooth—no glitches or kinks, like layer after layer of expertly applied plastic wrap. Still, it takes all three of us. Slowly, we build an impenetrable wall around the bowl.

A rumble comes from the kitchen, followed by the clattering of broom and mop handles. Chaucer floats in front of the pantry where Misty is hiding. The door shakes, the little ghost inside fierce and defensive.

"Chaucer," Prescott says. "Be nice."

Chaucer sags and then trundles into the living area, all hangdog.

Prescott sits back. He keeps one hand on the bowl and holds up a finger, signaling to Chaucer. "Be ready."

Chaucer hovers above us, swirling in a pattern that reminds me of a tornado.

Prescott pulls in a breath, readying himself as well. "Let's see if this holds."

"If it doesn't?" I venture.

He nods toward the whirling mass above us. "Chaucer should be able to contain it long enough for us to reestablish the field."

I nod, not entirely convinced.

"Malcolm first," Prescott says.

Malcolm eases one hand away and then the other. When the ghost—or demon, or whatever it is—doesn't burst forth, I think we all exhale in relief. Malcolm pushes to stand and heads for the kitchen. While Prescott instructs me to remove my hands, that clatter of mops and brooms redoubles in the background. Misty's voice rings outs, her ability to coo fully restored.

"Oh, a real gentleman."

My guess is, she doesn't mean Carter. He's still flopped on the carpet, eyes closed, lips forming silent words.

A night breeze wafts in from the patio. The air has that sweetness again, a hint of roses and lily of the valley. Prescott stands, hands sandwiching the bowl. The container rocks a bit in his grip, and he raises it to eye level.

"None of that."

The rocking halts—mostly.

I offer Carter my hand. He stares at it like it's covered in slime. Then he reluctantly takes it, and I yank him to his feet, his weight nearly taking me to the floor.

Yeah, he could've helped.

"Malcolm," Prescott is saying, "you and Carter head back in Katy's truck—"

Malcolm opens his mouth to protest, but Prescott cuts him off. "Katy's the stronger necromancer, and she's going to have to hold this"—he raises the bowl—"while I drive."

Malcolm and Carter exchange a look of distaste.

"You mean I can't drive your car?" I ask.

Prescott owns something flashy and yellow. And Italian, I think.

All I know is, whenever he cruises through Springside, he tends to stop traffic and collect appreciative stares.

"In a word?" Prescott raises an eyebrow, and I have my answer. Then he studies the bowl in his hands, the skin around his mouth tight. "Besides, you're the only one here who won't *accidentally* crack the lid."

Carter blanches, although really, how he ends up even paler is beyond me.

"My man," Prescott says to him. "You have pissed off far too many necromancers in your short life."

"So it's not just me?" Malcolm asks.

Prescott purses his lips and gives his head a quick shake. "That's the beauty, if you will, of this sort of demon. It takes advantage of other necromancers' active dislike."

He heads for the door, along with Carter and Malcolm. I turn to Misty, about to assure her that the little ghost won't hurt her—and to offer our services once we've dealt with the monster in the fruit bowl. Before I can, Chaucer whooshes between Malcolm and me. The door slams shut. Ice forms over the entire surface, and the hardware sprouts hoarfrost. Malcolm pounds on the door. At least, I'm pretty sure it's Malcolm. A moment later, he swears—loud and long.

Prescott shouts, "Chaucer, I told you to be nice!"

The walls tremble and shake. Dishes rattle in the cupboards, and the blades of the ceiling fan quiver. A wave of supernatural frustration washes over us, and there's no missing its message.

I AM being nice.

NOW THAT HE'S trapped me inside, Chaucer simply hovers in the air. His form fills the space, and while we're absolutely locked inside, nothing malicious comes from him.

Not that he's exactly patient. If he were human, there would be arm-crossing and toe-tapping. He's waiting. That much is clear. When the little ghost creeps from the built-in pantry, I think I know what Chaucer is waiting for.

But I don't know why.

An ethereal debate wages, most of which I can't follow. Still, Chaucer's insistence is too strong to miss:

Tell her, Jerome. Tell her, tell her.

Tell her... what?

Misty has her hands planted on the kitchen counter, her gaze darting back and forth between the two ghosts. Her brow furrows in concentration, but she's not gleaning any more from this conversation than I am.

Jerome's form quivers and shakes. Chaucer might be trying to help but clearly isn't making any progress. That's when I get a ghostly nudge between my shoulder blades. Chaucer might be too large and fierce to convince Jerome.

Apparently, I'm not.

I crook a finger at Jerome. He flows forward until his glimmering form grazes my lips. This time, when the images flash, all I see are the high school ones, except they're more distinct. What is clearly a friend group gathered around one of those cafeteria tables. A couple strolling down a hallway, hand in hand. A girl in a cheerleading outfit—a girl who looks like a younger version of Misty.

Oh? *Oh.*

"Did you know someone named Jerome?"

Misty's expression blanks, but in that careful way when you don't want someone to know how you feel. Then it shatters.

"Jerome?"

The little ghost floats toward her, its outline shimmering with both joy and trepidation.

"When you gave him some coffee earlier," Misty says, her voice far away, like she's been wandering those high school hallways. "I had the impression of him. He used to drink his coffee black. We'd go to Perkins on the weekends after games or parties or whatever and stay there for hours, sometimes all night."

Jerome bobs up and down in confirmation.

She reaches a hand toward him, and he weaves around her fingers. Her yelp is both startled and delighted.

"We were going to get married," she says. "I mean, we talked about it. We were both seventeen and stupid. But when you're seventeen and stupid, you think you can conquer the world. You think you're indestructible."

My throat tightens, and I take quick, shallow breaths. Clearly, Jerome wasn't indestructible.

"We fought because... you know." She raises a hand and lets it fall. "Seventeen and stupid. He wasn't even drunk, just angry. But of course, he was driving too fast." She turns to me now. "You know how the weather is around here in March. Nothing but ice and slush."

I swallow hard and give her a nod.

"There are some back roads between here and Cedar Hills. They're fine if the weather's nice and you're driving slowly."

That curve taken too quickly pops into my mind—the splatter of icy slush against the windshield, that breathless moment when the back wheels fishtail, the rush of fear when the brakes give out.

"I'm so sorry," I manage to say, although really, they seem like such inadequate words.

"I did nothing but sleepwalk through senior year. Quit the varsity cheer squad, turned down a dozen guys who asked me to prom, didn't bother to apply to any colleges. I couldn't stand to stay in Cedar Hills, but I couldn't leave the area, either. That's when I came to Springside."

Jerome sags as if he feels personally responsible for Misty's plight. He eases forward again, attentive and hopeful. The swell of emotion that flows from him has me speaking without thinking.

"He wants you to be happy. He didn't come here to scare you, but..."

Another barrage of images hits me. A necromancer with an agenda, that much is clear. Which necromancer? That's not so clear, but he—or she—has a side gig of haunted engagement rings and vampire husbands. And this particular necromancer encountered a little ghost with its own agenda as well.

"Jerome found the vampire husband website—or rather, the person who runs it." I reach for a name, but the images dissolve into little more than wisps. "And that's how he found you."

Misty hangs her head, hair tumbling from its hasty bun. The strands spread across the counter and, a moment later, sweep back and forth as if an invisible hand is comforting her.

"He really just wants you to be happy," I say again. "He didn't think Carter was going to do that."

Misty manages a half-snort, half-sob.

"That's why he let us catch him—because he thought the demon would get rid of Carter. But he was so worried about you, he came back." All the way from the nature preserve. I turn my attention to Jerome. "You are clever."

His outline expands with pride, but then he contracts, contrite.

"Also, if you don't want him hanging around, he'll leave."

With this, Misty jerks her head up. "Oh, no, you don't." She points a finger at him. "I just got you back." She examines the air in front of her and blinks a few times before her gaze meets mine. "Will I ever understand him?"

Even necromancers don't always understand the ghosts around them. "Well, you sensed him when he was your vampire husband, right?"

She gives a slow nod. "But I couldn't tell that he was Jerome."

"Because he didn't want you to." I cast the little ghost a look. "He wasn't sure you'd want him back. But between Carter and the demon, he knew he had to do something to protect you." I urge Jerome closer. "But maybe with practice?"

The little ghost flows toward Misty and swirls in a circle. When she laughs, he does a backflip.

"You were always a show-off." She holds up her hands so he can run the obstacle course of her fingers.

An indistinct knocking catches my attention. Shadows move on the patio. Malcolm, maybe? Or possibly Prescott. This chill is not as sharp against my cheeks, and the entire apartment is thawing around us. Now that Misty and Jerome are reunited, the infestation is losing its grip. As if on cue, my cell phone buzzes with incoming text messages.

Chaucer trembles like a five-year-old anticipating a scolding. Then he hangs in the air, downcast and guilty.

Yes, we're both in trouble. "You had important business," I say to him. "I won't let Prescott punish you."

Now Chaucer does a backflip, and the entire duplex rocks on its foundation.

Misty and Jerome see us to the door. Before I can step through, she takes my left hand.

"Honey, that"—she nods at Malcolm's engagement ring—"is worth more than all the ones I have in the bank. You hang on to it —and him."

"I plan to," I tell her.

Oh, I plan to.

It's been a while since K&M Ghost Eradication Specialists pulled an all-nighter. Sure, coffee can help.

But nothing beats 100% Kona when you need to stay awake.

We've gathered in my kitchen, all of us around the table, lights blazing, the space warm with the aroma of coffee and cinnamon. The rolls, of course, are fresh from Sadie's oven. I'm sitting next to Malcolm, soaking in his heat. Prescott is conferring with someone by text, his dark eyes intent on the screen. Carter stands apart from us, near the sink.

Belinda slips through the door after running a thermal mug

over to Nigel. On the laptop's screen, he takes a sip, closes his eyes, and exhales in appreciation.

"Makes losing sleep worth it," he says.

From a drawer, she digs out our first aid kit and then turns to Carter. "Sit." She points to one of the kitchen chairs.

"I'm fine."

"Stop being an idiot. You want to lose your entire forehead to a staph infection? It's either this"—she holds up a bottle of rubbing alcohol—"or urgent care. Take your pick. But no one at urgent care is going to believe your story about a demon and a ghost."

"She has a point." Malcolm leans back in his chair, enjoying Carter's distress far, far too much.

Carter lumbers in slow motion and then collapses, almost missing the chair. When Belinda yanks the duct tape from his head, Malcolm has to hide his laugh with a sip of coffee. I throw him a scowl. But honestly? I don't think Carter minds Belinda's attention.

The demon in question currently resides in my sink, still confined to the fruit bowl. As a precaution, Chaucer hovers above the lid, and every few minutes, Prescott glances up from his phone and presses a hand against the plastic, reinforcing the containment field.

"We need to do something about this." He tucks his phone away. "And soon."

"And that is?" I ask because I'm not sure what we can do.

Driving it out to the nature preserve isn't an option. Even going farther out, like we did with Harold's ghost, won't work. Releasing something this strong into the wild is not only irresponsible but dangerous. It could harm us, double back to possess Carter, or attack someone else entirely.

"Our best option—really, our only option—is returning it to its point of origin, if we can figure out where that is." Prescott runs a finger around the icy bowl as if he might glean that information from the being inside. "Demons, as far as we know, prefer their own plane of existence. From what Reginald has discovered, they don't really want to be here, which is why they're so nasty."

"Maybe they simply want to go home," I say, "but don't know how."

"Perhaps. But that doesn't stop them from being a problem."

"Our other option?" Malcolm asks.

"Reginald might have room in his sanctuary for a being this strong." Prescott taps the bowl's lid in thought. "Honestly, I'm not sure we can keep it contained on the drive up there. And once we do get up there, I'm not sure even Reginald could deal with it." He turns to Carter. "Any idea where or when you picked this thing up?"

Belinda is applying a butterfly bandage to Carter's forehead. He shifts toward Prescott and winces. "You got me."

"It was in Misty's apartment the first time we went over, because Jerome was trying to protect her." I think of how Jerome found Misty through the vampire husband engagement ring she ordered. Maybe there's a pattern.

"What about the engagement ring? Not the vampire one, but the one you had," I say to Carter. "When you proposed to Misty."

Belinda raises an eyebrow at this. Carter flushes dark pink, from the v of his T-shirt to the tips of his ears. I don't think I've ever seen him with that much color in his cheeks.

"You proposed to someone?" Belinda's voice is both incredulous and full of humor. "And they said yes?"

"Nice," Carter mutters. "Besides, I think we're kind of broken up now." Then he rallies, sitting up straighter and testing the bandage on his head with his fingertips. "That can't be it. I bought the ring a few years back. It was too good of a deal to pass up."

I open my mouth and then shut it again. Is this something guys actually do? At a loss, I give Malcolm a quizzical stare.

He leans forward, forearms on the kitchen table. "Let me get this straight. You bought an engagement ring without even knowing the woman you were going to give it to."

Carter bristles. "It's good to have one in reserve."

Malcolm makes a face. "Says who?"

For a second, Carter falters. "Orson." The name emerges with a mix of defiance and dread.

Oh. *Oh, no.* I don't have to say just how bad this is. The worry is reflected in both Malcolm's and Prescott's expressions. On the laptop's screen, Nigel rubs his temples.

"Where did you buy this ring?" Prescott asks.

"A place called Hillside Diamonds."

"Hang on," Nigel calls. "Let me start searching."

The clattering of keys comes from the computer's speakers. Strands of that pure white hair flop into Nigel's eyes. A moment later, he pushes them from his forehead and declares, "No, you didn't."

"Didn't what?" Carter asks.

"Didn't buy the ring at Hillside Diamonds, unless you went shopping while you were still in high school. It closed more than a decade ago."

The entire room goes still. Chaucer stops churning; even Prescott appears puzzled.

"Why don't you talk us through it," he says, his voice controlled like that of a hostage negotiator. "From the very beginning."

Carter sits back and contemplates the ceiling. "It was before stuff started happening in Springside."

Belinda snorts. "Like you're not part of the reason why stuff started happening."

Carter throws her a scowl. Prescott presses a finger to his lips, giving his head a quick shake. Belinda rolls her eyes and takes a perch on the kitchen counter.

"Orson was always talking about things to have in reserve, as a necromancer and"—Carter coughs—"as a man."

"Okay," Prescott says, as if this is totally reasonable. Maybe if it didn't involve haunted engagement rings purchased at out-of-business jewelry stores, it might be. "Then what?"

"He told me to go to Hillside Diamonds because no one's seen prices like that in decades."

"And this was when, exactly?" Prescott prompts.

"Summer, two years ago."

My breath catches. That was when my grandmother died, and her pact with the entity was no more. We keep coming back to that. And yet, I'm not sure how that has anything to do with Carter, this demon, and the engagement ring.

"Maybe it was their going-out-of-business sale," I suggest, although that doesn't really fit the timeline Nigel gave us. "Or maybe there's more than one store?"

Nigel starts clacking the keyboard again. Prescott stares through the kitchen windows and then turns his attention back to Carter. "Where was this store?"

"Another small town not too far from here. I had to drive down from the Cities, but it was worth it." His fingers light on the bandage now secured to his forehead. "Sort of."

"Where?" Prescott's voice has an edge to it.

"Cedar Hills?" Carter says it like a question, too, like he isn't sure where he bought the ring. "There's a mall not far from the downtown."

The silence in the room runs deep. I'm afraid to move or even exhale. When we shatter the quiet, everything changes. I feel it in the way my chest constricts and my pulse thrums in my ears.

"Are you saying you bought the ring at Cedar Hills Mall?" The words feel rough against my throat, but they emerge perfectly clear, without a hint of distress.

"Yeah, that's it." Carter grins. "Catchy name, huh?"

When no one responds, he glances around. His smile fades. "What? What did I say? What's wrong?"

Prescott shuts his eyes, his face drawn as if he's in pain. "We have a much bigger problem on our hands."

CHAPTER 7

Convincing Carter that Cedar Hills Mall has been closed for more than a decade takes longer than I think it should. At one point, Malcolm asks:

"Are you certain you didn't buy the ring at *River* Hills Mall in Mankato?"

"No," Carter says, his words slow and sarcastic. "I bought it at *Cedar* Hills Mall in Cedar Hills."

And I have to put a hand on Malcolm's arm to keep him from launching himself at Carter.

We talk in circles, show him the evidence on the internet. In the end, I suspect he still doesn't believe us. He levels a stare that suggests we're playing an elaborate practical joke on him.

None of us can explain how Carter bought that engagement ring, assuming he's telling the truth. He might be lying, but every time the demon rattles the container against the sink, the color drains from his face, and fear tightens his expression. I wouldn't put it past Carter Dupree to lie about any number of things. But this?

This isn't one of them. Then there's the question of the timing.

Carter bought the ring two years ago—or so he claims. Has the demon been attached to it this entire time? Is that even possible?

"Is this something Orson could do?" I ask Prescott.

"You mean seed an object with a powerful demon and have it lie dormant until the perfect moment?"

Yeah. That.

"Now, after his retribution? No." Prescott shakes his head, dismissing that option. "Two years ago? Absolutely. It's a failsafe. A way to keep those under him in line." He pauses and sets his sights on Carter. "Or to exact revenge in case of betrayal."

Carter's eyelids flutter, and he takes slow, shallow breaths. "So I've been carrying around that thing for two years without even realizing it?"

Prescott raises his hand and lets it drop. "Afraid so, my man."

Carter purses his lips and swallows hard. I always thought the expression *turn green* was just that—an expression. But Carter actually does. His cheeks puff out, and I point, hoping I'm not too late.

"Bathroom's that way, to the right."

He bolts from the kitchen, footfalls thundering down the hall, chair clattering against the floor. In his wake comes the screech of two outraged cats. One black streak and then another rush for the living room and the safety of the cat condo.

An otherworldly whoosh ruffles my hair. This particular presence is both familiar and friendly. Our resident sprite has joined the conversation, giving both Chaucer and the demon a wide berth.

I feel the nudge, almost like fingers on my shoulder, pushing me forward. So I ask, "Does this mean Orson is one of the twin necromancers?"

"Doubtful," Nigel says. "He doesn't have any siblings, at least not that I know of."

The little sprite swirls, agitated, refusing to give up. "But maybe a son?" I say. "Old twin and a young one?"

"He never married, so—"

I'm about to protest when Nigel holds up his hands, stopping me.

"I know, I know. He could still have a son."

"Or even a protégé," Malcolm suggests. "Not exactly out of the question, right?" He directs this at Carter, who has just stumbled back into the room.

"He ran through them," Nigel agrees, and his gaze finds Carter. "You were lucky you lasted as long as you did."

Carter crumples against the refrigerator and then to the floor. "Yeah, it's just nonstop luck for me."

Above our heads, the sprite continues to swirl, its chatter insistent and unending. Twin necromancers with no room for argument.

"Whatever the case," Prescott says. "One thing is clear: All roads lead to Cedar Hills."

THE COPSE of pines glimmers with the sunrise. The greens are brighter but more transparent. I can't tell if this is a trick of the morning light or if the ward is simply fading. Absent are the long shadows that other trees cast along the road. If anyone cared to look closely, it would be obvious something is both otherworldly and wrong.

I'm sitting in the passenger seat of Prescott's flashy yellow sports car, palms sandwiching the fruit bowl. Every few minutes, Prescott plants a hand on the lid, helping to reinforce the containment field. Despite our earlier efforts, it's starting to crack. It's like repairing a bad patch of road during an endless, frigid winter. At some point, we won't be able to keep up.

We have Malcolm and Carter on speaker. I know the moment Malcolm swerves into the visible ward because Carter's panicked voice fills our ears.

"What the hell, man! You're going to get us killed!"

He continues the litany, choosing some disparaging terms for Malcolm's parentage and general state of mind until they emerge on the other side.

Then, all is quiet.

"It's true." Prescott gives me a sidelong glance. "Silence really is golden."

I manage a laugh—barely. It's taking most of my strength to mend the cracks in the containment field. Even with strong ghosts, I've never worried they might escape once we've caught them.

This thing?

This thing is actively chipping away at the field from the inside, those tentacles probing the smallest fissures, expanding flaws that I can scarcely detect.

"Hang in there," Prescott says, and his voice is strained as if he feels it too. "I'll take over once we reach the mall."

We bump our way over the fractured asphalt and into the parking lot. Prescott swings the car around so we're facing away from the mall and toward the quickest way out. He leaves the keys in the ignition. Over the phone, he instructs Malcolm to do the same. Then he rounds the front and opens my door.

The moment Prescott takes the bowl from me, my chest expands with a full breath. I sink into the buttery-leather seat, close my eyes, and regain my equilibrium.

"I know." Now his voice is so quiet and so serious that my heart rate kicks up. "Take all the time you need."

Nothing about this is going to be easy. For the first time, though, I wonder.

Could it be deadly as well?

Before we left Springside, Prescott sent a ghost to Reginald and had Malcolm send one to Darien. Nigel called Paris to alert his mother and Prem. They booked an immediate flight to Minneapolis.

Will we need this sort of backup? The implicit answer is yes—

yes, we will. I'm trying to reconcile how something that started as little more than a nuisance haunting became this dangerous.

Prescott is always so cool, so calm, so capable around even the strongest attack ghosts. He holds the bowl steady in his grip, but his forearms tense, the muscles straining. Dots of sweat spout along his brow.

Carter turns a slow circle, his gaze darting from the road that leads to the highway to the mall's façade and back again. "I don't see how—"

"That's the problem," Prescott snaps. "None of us do." He exhales, breath suddenly ragged as if he's been running. "Sorry, sorry. It's this thing. Katy, you're going to have to take it again. Have Malcolm help you."

I rush to grab the container. The second my fingers touch the plastic bowl, despair spills over me. A moment later, Malcolm's hands join mine. The tightness in my chest eases enough so I can speak.

"Why is it so strong now? It could have—"

"Decimated Misty's apartment?" Prescott suggests.

Yes, exactly that, and us along with it.

"That little ghost. They were... confined together. This thing thought of it as a compatriot, or possibly a pet."

"Even demons have feelings?" I glance down at the bowl. The thing inside roils with malevolent glee.

"Worse. An excess of them. It also knew you and Malcolm wouldn't be able to hold it for long."

"But it wasn't expecting you," I say and then pull in a long breath. I'm waterlogged, like I've been swimming laps for hours.

Prescott tilts his head at the bowl as if listening to a response. "No, it wasn't." He closes his eyes and nods, but at what, I'm not sure. "Give me another minute," he adds.

So we do. I keep my grip locked on the bowl. The odd sensation of a boat striking whitecaps resonates in my chest. Waves roll beneath my feet. I can taste salt on my lips again, sense the speed of a boat heading away from shore.

Malcolm looks queasy, but his hand inches toward mine. We lace our fingers together. The contact helps—both me and the containment field. The demon grumbles inside the plastic bowl, clearly not happy about this development.

"Why fishing?" I ask, turning to Carter. For such a malicious being, it seems like such a benign desire.

Carter shoves his hands into his pockets. "Maybe because I can't swim."

Can't... swim? Once again, my chest constricts. Inside the container, what sounds like spiteful laughter emerges.

"I don't suppose that's something Orson might know?" Malcolm says.

"You ever try keeping a secret from him?" Carter shakes his head, chagrined. "He has a way of figuring things out."

I think of what it is Orson has done. At this point, there's no denying that it is Orson. No one else would want to hurt Carter this badly.

Well, as far as I know.

But the precise cruelty of this revenge steals my breath. Carter's worst fear—and yes, I can see it's more than not being able to swim—made manifest.

I want to comfort him, or at least say something, but all I can do is meet Carter's eyes and convey my sympathy that way. His lips compress into a thin line, and he nods, a grim sort of acknowledgment.

Prescott wanders a few feet away, phone to his ear. "Yeah, I know. It's early. Sorry about that." His expression is tender. His eyes are filled with so much love and sorrow that I know he's talking to George.

It sounds like he's saying goodbye.

The being in the bowl rumbles a low chuckle, the sound full of unsavory anticipation.

I'm starting to hate this thing.

Prescott tucks his phone away and claps his hands together. He heads for my truck and pulls out the supplies we packed—whistles, walkie-talkies, flashlights, permanent markers.

"To create a physical trail." He holds up a marker and then clips one walkie-talkie to my belt and hands Malcolm the other. "When all else fails, pull a Hansel and Gretel." He reaches for the container. "I'll take this while you two get ready."

The being in the container chortles with what can only be described as delight.

"Yeah, you only think that," Prescott tells it.

The container grumbles with what sounds like a reply.

I freeze, the whistle on its bright yellow cord dangling from my hands. "Have you been talking to it this whole time?"

"You could say that." The half-smile Prescott gives us is laced with sadness. "You could also say that I've made a deal with this thing."

CHAPTER 8

I let out a yelp, but it's no match for Nigel's outrage. His voice comes through the speaker on Malcolm's phone, the sound of it full of fury that makes my ears ring. Has Prescott been making this deal right in front of us? I think of how he placed his palm on the lid from time to time during our drive here. Those dots of sweat sprouting on his forehead, the strain of muscles, the tightness around his eyes.

Yes, he has.

Prescott raises his hands in an attempt to silence us. "The deal is this. We find the gateway between its plane of existence and ours or, failing that, I let it reside in me instead of Carter."

Carter sags, and his shoulders slump, not with relief but guilt.

"I'm stronger," Prescott continues. "I can hang on until Prem or Reginald arrives to help." He spares Carter a glance. "Carter can't. This thing will devour him in a matter of minutes, and we won't be able to stop it once it has a physical body it can fully command."

"Are you saying that it won't be able to fully command you?" I march forward and yank the bowl from his grip. "That it won't devour you?"

Prescott reaches for the container, but I hold it away from him.

"That's what I'm hoping." He reaches again, but it's a token effort.

"Don't be stupid," Nigel says. "No one can hang on that long. Not you, not Prem, not even Reginald."

"It's our only option. I can hold it. It's amenable to that. Would you have it take over Katy or maybe Malcolm?"

Nigel falls silent.

"Once this thing burns through its target, it's a free agent. There'll be no tracking it, no telling how much damage it might do. Assuming another necromancer could catch it, there's no telling what sort of damage they might do together."

That sounds harrowingly familiar. "It's not as powerful as the entity, is it?"

Prescott shakes his head. "No. It's not that kind of being. Fortunately."

The bowl quivers in my hands. It's almost like this thing knows of the entity and is afraid of it. Considering that I can't call on the entity and have it help me, I don't understand why. Still, the rumbling in the bowl is less aggressive, if only slightly.

Prescott pulls out a mall directory and map that Nigel was able to unearth during his research. He spreads it across the hood of my truck. The image is printed on computer paper and a bit fuzzy. But with sunlight creeping across the parking lot, the lines are clear and give us something to go on. I place the bowl on the hood as well, anchoring it with a hand. A moment later, Malcolm adds his own hand, and things feel more grounded.

"From what I can glean," Prescott says, eyeing the being in the container, "Hillside Diamonds is our destination. Somewhere in or around that storefront is the gateway."

Malcolm is frowning at the map. He keeps a hand anchored on the bowl while his fingers trace the path we took during our first visit to the mall.

"This isn't right," he says.

I lean forward and follow the path his fingertips take. "What isn't?"

"Maybe I'm remembering it wrong." He taps a spot on the map, one opposite Hillside Diamonds. "But I could've sworn the store was here."

Prescott curses. "Katy?"

The map blurs before my eyes. For several seconds I can't speak, because my answer is nonsensical.

"Katy?" Prescott prompts.

"I remember it in both places," I admit. "I know it doesn't make any sense, but—"

"Nothing about this makes sense." Prescott turns to Carter. "Do you remember?"

How Carter actually bought the ring here still isn't clear. The mall was definitely closed at the time, but I ask Nigel again.

"Was anything open two years ago?"

Nigel considers, the screen glitching slightly, distorting his features and slowing his reply. "From what I can tell, the last stores shuttered in late 2010 or so, and the mall closed soon after."

"What about a pop-up store or an event?" Malcolm suggests.

"Hard to track, but doubtful." Nigel frowns at his laptop screen, so all we get is his profile. "Sure, there's the space, but no traffic to speak of."

"Could Orson have faked it being open?" I ask.

Carter's shaking his head. "People were shopping and eating in the food court. I even bought a corndog. I don't see how he could have faked all that."

"Orson was powerful back then," Nigel adds, "but even he couldn't have pulled off something like that. Besides, he's too lazy. Whatever happened two years ago, it came from somewhere else."

I want to ask *where*, because I think that's a crucial piece of information we're missing. Then again, if we knew that, we'd probably know everything.

Prescott turns to Carter again. "So, what do you remember?"

Carter studies the map, glances at the mall, and then contemplates the map once again. "There's a fountain in the middle of the mall."

"The Crystal Court," I say.

"Yeah, that's it. After I bought the ring, I stood in the middle of the courtyard, in a sunbeam. I looked at the ring under natural light." An odd half-smile flits across his face. "Huh," he says, voice faraway. "It was gorgeous."

Prescott snaps his fingers in front of Carter's face. Carter blinks rapidly, as if waking from a dream.

"I can't tell you where, exactly," he continues, "except it was one of the stores near the center. I could hear the fountain the entire time I was buying the ring."

"That's a place to start, at least." Prescott folds up the map and tucks it into his back pocket. Then he holds out his hands. "I'll take that now."

I'm strangely reluctant to give up the bowl. From the way Malcolm's hand clutches the lid, I suspect he feels it too.

"Enough of that." Prescott leans forward, his mouth inches from the container, his murmur directed toward the being inside. "I know enough necromancers to keep you confined for a very long time. Granted, it won't be much fun for us, but trust me, we'll make you miserable."

All at once, the bowl springs from my grip and Malcolm's. Prescott latches on to it. He winces like he's taken a blow to the chest.

"Let's go," Prescott says, voice terse. "The sooner we get rid of this thing, the safer everyone will be."

Carter stands up straight, spine stiffening. Prescott throws his shoulders back and adjusts his hold on the bowl. Malcolm laces his fingers with mine. We stride forward, and part of me wants to steal a glance backward—at my truck, the sunrise, and the quiet beauty of this morning.

Part of me thinks we won't be back.

IT STARTS with the Orange Julius.

At first, the hallway is simply gray and dank. The door scrapes the tile like before. The benches and fake trees look despondent but perfectly benign. Everything is merely lonely and empty and nothing more.

We're halfway between the entrance and the Crystal Court when that sugary smell wafts past my nose, full of strawberry and citrus. Prescott halts near the bright orange trash cans.

"This is not right." He lifts his chin as if he can taste the air.

I do the same, only to have that stale, slightly fetid stench fill my mouth. I strain my ears but don't actually hear anything. No phantom cash register. No stroller wheels against the floor. No piped-in music. I allow myself a small sigh of relief. But I have to nudge both Prescott and Malcolm forward, and the scuffing of their shoes on the grimy tile sounds reluctant.

We're near the Crystal Court when Carter freezes. Malcolm bumps into him, but Carter doesn't budge. He's almost like a statue until he raises his arm and points.

"I've seen that before."

It's the property management sign, the one fixed unobtrusively to the kiosk.

"You mean other than here," Malcolm says.

Carter nods.

"Where?" I ask.

"It's familiar." Carter's mouth twists as if he knows the words but can't speak them. "But I can't say where."

We still have Nigel—barely—on video, so I ask, "Do you have anything new on Troy Season?"

"Nothing that jumped out, but let me double-check."

The engraved script on the plaque still bugs me. I'm sure Troy Season could be an actual person, but something about the sound of the name rings false.

"Oh."

The weight Nigel gives that single word sets my pulse racing.

"I should've noticed this before now," he says, "but Troy Season Property Management has the same PO box as the haunted engagement ring business."

Now I feel the weight of his words in my chest. I stare at the sign, the letters in the name blurring and scrambling. With dread, I realize why it looks so strange.

It's an anagram.

From my pocket, I pull out the marker. I cross out each letter as I use it. When I stand back, the name is inked in a black, wavery scrawl that looks as menacing as it feels.

Orson Yates

Carter swears, and the steel drains from his spine.

"I can't believe I didn't see it before," Nigel is saying. "This is precisely the sort of mind game Orson loves to play."

"I think we know without a doubt who's responsible," Prescott says, his tone deliberately dry. "All the more reason to finish this quickly."

He steps forward. Malcolm retakes my hand, and we follow, with me reaching back to tug Carter by the shirt sleeve. He stumbles forward, sneakers slapping the tile floor.

We reach the center of the Crystal Court and huddle in the morning light streaming through the glass above our heads. I turn and then turn again. Actually, we all do this, gazes frantic.

I swear I catch a glimpse of something sparkly, of elegant, velvet-lined displays and vibrant gemstones. When I focus my attention, everything shimmers and fades like it was nothing more than a mirage. It's like the hallway with the Springside ghosts. Hillside Diamonds should be right here, but it isn't.

The lockers should also be right here but aren't.

Prescott's eyes flutter shut. His skin is ashen. That thing in the bowl is taking a toll on him. A look of defeat washes across his face.

"Maybe we should've brought some coffee," I say.

A hint of a smile graces Prescott's lips. He's back, a determined tilt to his jaw. "A jewelry store isn't going to want coffee."

"What does it want?" I ask.

"Customers." Prescott surveys us, his eyes now calculating. "Malcolm, you take Carter—"

Malcolm's hand tightens around mine. "But—"

"I need Katy's help." Prescott hefts the bowl as if it weighs a good twenty pounds. "You and Carter take the west and south wings. Pretend you're here because Carter is shopping for an engagement ring."

Oh, of course. It makes perfect sense—or as much sense as anything in this mall does. I turn to Prescott. "And we'll pretend to be a couple and search out the other two wings."

Both Malcolm and Carter scowl at this.

"Oh, come on," I say to Carter. "You bought a ring here before, right? Pretend to do it again."

"Yeah." Malcolm elbows him. "Pretend you're here getting a ring for Belinda."

Carter's glower only deepens.

"Have your walkie-talkie ready," Prescott instructs. "If you find the store and can't get through on that or your phone, three short blasts on the whistle. If it's an emergency, one long, sustained blast."

He lifts an elbow. I weave my arm through his and place my palm on the bowl's lid.

His chest heaves, and for a moment, he squeezes his eyes shut. "Thank you," he says, his voice barely audible. Then, more forcibly, he adds, "Go on, you two. Get out of here."

We head for the north wing, my free hand resting on the walkie-talkie hooked to my belt loop. This time, the urge to look back is even stronger than before. I want one last glimpse of Malcolm, of that sweet, dark roast grin aimed in my direction.

I want to tell him that I love him.

But that feels superstitious, like I'm afraid I'll never see him again. So I keep my eyes trained forward, my hand planted on the container, and tell myself I won't regret not taking one final look.

THE NORTH WING is the one I've come to think of as the mall's sad wing. It's the one with the lonely teddy bear in the wagon. Knowing the sight that will greet us at the end of this trek makes me move my feet even slower. Or maybe this wing is longer today. It stretches endlessly before us.

"Illusion," Prescott says as if reading my mind.

"You feel it too?"

"Something is distorting our surroundings. What, exactly, that is, I can't say."

This is not reassuring.

"Necromancy is involved," he adds.

"You can tell that?"

"Between the visible ward and Orson's anagram, I think it's fairly obvious."

Okay, yes. I mean, I've figured that much out.

"Plus, I'm picking up a residual containment field, possibly the one you—or the ghosts—broke through."

Not that we have any lockers to go with that field.

"But it's more than that."

"Yes, it's a lot more than that." His sigh is tired and heavy. "I feel as if at any moment, any one of us could disappear."

Like when I lost Malcolm—or he lost me. Honestly, I'm not sure how that happened. I weave my arm closer to Prescott's. If we end up lost, at least we'll be lost together.

Static from the walkie-talkie makes us both jump. My heart thuds an unnatural beat, thick and slow. My fingers slip when I unclip my walkie-talkie from my belt loop. Prescott and I pause, stare at the speaker, braced for whatever it is Malcolm and Carter have found.

"I'm telling you, man," Malcolm is saying. "Your best bet is to be yourself."

"Yeah. Right." Carter's southern drawl is full of sarcasm. "I'm sure being yourself helped *you* get with Katy."

Prescott raises an eyebrow in my direction, his mouth forming an o of interest. A sudden flush travels up my cheeks, and my face burns hot. For once, I'm not chilled in this space.

"Katy and I weren't even friends to start with. Kind of like you and someone we know?"

Carter snorts.

"Think back to when Belinda was talking to you. It was when you were helping her with all her investments, right?"

It's true. Carter did help Belinda sort through the investments her father left her, setting up accounts for tuition and longer-term ones for the restaurant.

"Even I listen to you when it comes to investing," Malcolm adds. "I mean, sometimes. Do you like it?"

"I wanted to be a necromancer."

"So did I. Then I started catching ghosts with Katy, and that's when I knew what I was meant to do on this earth."

"So you're telling me that even if Katy ended up with someone like Jack Carlotta, you'd still be her business partner?" Carter's drawl has gone from sarcastic to skeptical.

The silence stretches. In it comes the hiss of static and what I think might be Malcolm's breathing.

"You know what?" he says at last. "If that's what made her happy, I absolutely would."

"Right. Like you wouldn't knock him into next year."

"I didn't say I'd *like* it, but if I had to trick Katy into being with me, it wouldn't work. In the long run, she wouldn't be happy, which means *I* wouldn't be happy. She loves me for who I am—"

"For some reason," Carter mutters.

"Exactly. And I can't tell you how grateful I am for that."

Another burst of static drowns out Carter's reply. Or maybe that's the roar of my pulse in my ears. My cheeks are still burning, and Prescott and I haven't moved during this entire exchange. His expression is nothing but amused. Even the being in the bowl swirls with what appears to be humor.

"As entertaining and enlightening as this is," Prescott says, "we need to focus."

He's right. We do. I hook the walkie-talkie back through a belt loop, pull out my phone, and send Malcolm a quick text.

Katy: One of you is holding down the talk button.

The walkie-talkie erupts with a final burst of swearing and static. Then the only sounds are the mall's ventilation system and the occasional drip of water. And without Malcolm's voice, the space feels hollow.

Prescott's warm chuckle breaks the quiet around us. "Ah, to be young."

"You're not that much older."

"A decade. It's more than enough. Still?" He raises that assessing eyebrow in my direction again. "I think you and Malcolm have figured out a few things that I haven't."

I want to ask about George, but Prescott nods toward the end of the wing. He's right. We need to focus, to move, to find the store and leave. From here, I can make out the metal security gate. The teddy bear and the little wagon are nowhere in sight. If their presence made me unaccountably sad, their absence is even worse.

"I don't like this," I say. "Something's different."

"In what way?"

"Things are missing from last time."

Prescott gives me a sidelong glance. "Like the jewelry store."

Well, yes, that. "I mean other things as well. Small things. Maybe it doesn't matter—"

"Small things often do." He halts again and nods at my walkie-talkie. "Comm check."

I try to raise Malcolm on the walkie-talkie but only get a crackle and a hiss of static. I try my phone. While it looks like I have a signal, my text goes undelivered, and my call rolls into voicemail. I hold up my whistle.

"Emergency only. This is merely mild panic." He says it to make me laugh, or at least not worry.

It almost works.

"Let's continue our circuit," he says. "Check the east wing, and head back to the courtyard."

We take up the trek again. Images swirl in my peripheral vision, but the floor doesn't roll beneath my feet. I don't hear phantom cash registers or smell imaginary fast food. This gives me hope. Last time, we couldn't see the lockers with the Springside ghosts, but they were here, in the mall. Hillside Diamonds must be too.

We reach the end of the wing and stand in the shadow of Sears' security gate. Still no teddy bear in its wagon. I lean forward. If I squint, I can almost detect its outline.

"There was a teddy bear. Right there." I point to a defunct display of summer fun items—beach balls and towels and crazy neon sunglasses that look like Venetian blinds. Hand still on the container, I inch closer. "I don't know why that bothers me so much."

Careful, my dear. Orson has laid any number of traps.

I leap backward so fast that my hand slips from the bowl's lid and from Prescott's arm. I stumble and land hard on a bench behind us. The walkie-talkie cracks against the surface, and my breath leaves me with a whoosh. I press a hand against my chest, hold still, and hope I haven't broken the walkie-talkie.

Prescott crouches next to me, the crinkles around his eyes deepening with concern and what looks like pain. "Katy, what is it?"

"I thought I heard the entity."

CHAPTER 9

The creases around Prescott's eyes deepen further, and the grooves around his mouth appear more pronounced. It hits me then. Even in the dim light, I can see strands of gray infiltrating his hair.

He's literally aging in front of me.

The bowl is resting on the bench, and he has both palms flat against its lid.

"It's hurting you." I reach for the bowl, but Prescott yanks it away.

"It's not that bad."

It *is* that bad. If we can't find Hillside Diamonds and the gateway, this thing will drain too much of Prescott. I'm not even sure he'll be able to hold the demon inside him without being devoured before help can arrive. It's a long drive from northern Minnesota and a long flight from Paris.

And if this thing is twisting his mind?

"Let me help." I keep my voice low and gentle. It's the tone I use for shy, scared ghosts.

A glimmer of a smile lights Prescott's expression. "Nice try, but no."

"But—"

"You just heard the entity." He taps the container. "Or thought you did."

"This thing was already with Carter when I heard the entity the first time."

"Doesn't matter."

It does matter. Or at least it should.

"It could be working with any number of beings here," Prescott adds. "This is Orson we're dealing with." He lifts his chin, taking in the entire wing, his gaze scanning the storefronts. "And he's concocted some sort of perverse funhouse."

"I'm not having a lot of fun."

Prescott's laugh comes out as a cough.

Perhaps it's the low light, but I swear his hair has more gray than when we first entered this wing. I lunge forward and plant both my hands on the container. For a moment, everything tilts. The bench lurches and then rights itself. The air shimmers. It's both light and bright. Then the hallway dims, and that stale, musty odor rushes in again.

My breath is ragged, and Prescott blinks as if waking from a dream. I think of traps and wonder if we've just fallen into one. My gaze is drawn to the Sears storefront again.

The teddy bear is back, sitting in its wagon, forlorn and lost. For the longest time, I can't divert my eyes, although I know I should. I should turn away, grab Prescott, and run.

At last, I manage to point. "Do you see that teddy bear?"

Prescott blinks again and stares, his expression neither horrified nor curious.

"What of it?"

I can't find words to explain that it wasn't there before. Honestly? I suspect if I try, he'll only think I'm crazy, or demon-influenced, or something. He won't let me help him. And I know this:

He can't do it alone.

I'm about to suggest we head back to the Crystal Court. If nothing else, the sunlight there might do us some good—clear our heads, help us think. We might be able to raise Malcolm and Carter on the walkie-talkie.

Before I can say a word, three quick blasts of a whistle punctuate the air.

They come again as I jump to my feet and drag Prescott to his.

"Do you hear that?" I'm hoping he does. I'm hoping this isn't another trick this space can play.

His grin tells me everything I need to know. We don't waste time or breath on words. We rush forward. Prescott sandwiches the bowl between his palms. I grip the sides. It's an awkward way to run. Our feet tangle, and our elbows jostle. The demon swirls in the container, and I swear it's cackling at us.

The whistle blast comes again, louder now. We will find Hillside Diamonds and the gateway and then toss this thing through.

We stumble into the Crystal Court. The sudden brightness makes me wince, but the sunshine against my cheeks is warm and hopeful. I survey the area, looking for Malcolm or Carter, straining my ears for another blast of the whistle. Then I forget all of that, because kitty-corner from us is that distinctive H with the scrollwork. The rest of the sign blurs before my eyes, but that doesn't matter.

Gemstones gleam, and those velvet-lined display cases are lush. Hillside Diamonds is a quick dash across the courtyard.

I start forward at a jog, but Prescott hauls me back.

"Katy, where are you going?"

I glance at Hillside Diamonds and then back at Prescott. "Don't you see it?"

"See what?"

"The jewelry store."

His eyes are wary, and he gives a slow shake of his head. Inside the bowl, the demon howls in delight. It, or Orson, or something, is determined to stop us. I can't let that happen. Prescott is slowly dying. Malcolm and Carter are who knows where. The one thing that's certain?

I can see Hillside Diamonds. That means I can find the gateway. To think beyond that is to hesitate, and we can't afford to hesitate. With all my strength, I wrench the container from Prescott's grip and start my run.

"Katy! No!"

I'm halfway across the courtyard when the floor rolls beneath my feet. It's a wave I'm determined to surf. I stumble forward as if I've been knocked off balance but right myself. Ahead of me, my destination sparkles. The air shimmers.

That, I think. That must be the gateway.

Footfalls slap behind me, but I have a head start. Plus, this demon hasn't been draining me like it has Prescott. Another shout echoes, but it's indistinct. All I have to do is toss this thing through the gateway. I'm sure of it. The demon itself presses forward as if anticipating that very thing.

The glass-encased display counter halts my sprint. My midsection meets the sharp edge, and I exhale hard. But I'm here, and just beyond, where a salesclerk might stand, is that shimmering patch of air that looks like nothing and everything.

I heave the bowl with all my might. It sails forward, meets that patch of nothing, and then slips through.

Everything shatters.

Shooting stars flash before my eyes. A roar drowns out all other sounds. Maybe I scream, but if I do, I can't hear myself. The floor rolls again in what feels like one enormous and violent hiccup.

Then my surroundings settle as if somehow the mall could stand, stretch, and get more comfortable. My hands are planted on the glass countertop. The velvet is a bright royal blue. Maybe it's a trick of the light, but I swear I see items artistically displayed.

Rolex watches and sparkly necklaces. Bracelets and pearl-drop earrings. Expensive silver pens that are more for show than writing.

What I don't sense is the demon. My chest feels lighter, like a sticky, psychic weight has lifted. I pull in a breath and smile to myself.

We did it.

That's when "The Girl From Ipanema" begins to filter through the overhead speakers.

CHAPTER 10

"Can I help you?"

The salesclerk behind the counter gives me a courteous, if cautious, smile.

"What?" The word emerges with more breath than substance. Noise from the mall surrounds me. The piped-in music, of course, but also chatter and laughter, the sound of water splashing. The fountain? I resist the urge to spin around to check.

Instead, I focus on the woman in front of me, the one with the patient expression.

"Are you shopping for a gift?" she asks.

"Browsing," I manage.

This can't be real, and yet it undeniably is. My mind scrambles to make sense of it all. Gateways, other planes of existence.

Other realities?

No.

And yet?

"Excuse me." I push from the counter and race for the Crystal Court.

If I retrace my steps, I can get back to where I belong. I pause under the skylights and lift my face to the sun. That, at least, feels the same—warm and reassuring. I shut my eyes against the brightness. Maybe when I open them again, everything will be back to the way it should be.

No luck.

Around me, the mall hums with activity. Crowds of teens surge past, giggling and shouting. Younger children play by the fountain, the water frothing and sparkling. A young mother sits on a bench, one hand easing a stroller back and forth, the other protecting her rounded belly.

I tug my phone from my pocket and try for a signal. Nothing, nothing at all—except for some odd looks from passersby. A few people crane their necks for a closer look. Dread simmers in my stomach, slow and steady. With as much nonchalance as possible, I tuck away my phone. Because here's the thing.

No one else has one.

I give myself a good shake. My best option is retracing my steps. I circle the courtyard until I stand kitty-corner to Hillside Diamonds once again. Nothing from here looks like the gateway. The only shimmer comes from the jewelry in the display cases. Still, it's my only option.

I start at a slow jog. It's a clumsy sort of run, and I know I can't go barging into Hillside Diamonds again. But all I need is that shimmer in the air. If that's how I landed here—and logic dictates that it is—then that's how I'll escape.

I'm halfway across the courtyard when I see him. Broad shoulders, ebony-dark hair.

Malcolm.

Even better? I know he's my Malcolm and not an illusion. He wears a whistle around his neck and has a walkie-talkie clipped to his belt. It looks like he's shouting, like his voice is hoarse from it, even though I can't hear him.

I ignore Hillside Diamonds and veer right. I race forward, ignoring all the stares I'm collecting.

I will always run to Malcolm Armand.

I slam so hard into a storefront window that the glass trembles. Malcolm stands opposite me, and I pound on the glass, not caring that it makes me look crazy. I'm praying he'll hear me, see me.

He turns. His eyes and then his entire face brighten. He rushes forward and smashes into the glass the same way I did. It shakes, but nothing more. I can't reach him; he can't reach me.

He shouts my name, but I can't hear it. He glances over his shoulder at Prescott or maybe Carter, but I can't see either of them. When he turns back, his gaze is desperate.

Then I see why. The glass between us is slowly fogging over. It reminds me of a full-on ghost infestation without the cold. My hands are oddly warm, and I match fingertips and palms to where Malcolm's are on the glass.

The fog is turning him gray and ghostly. He pounds on the window, first with his palm and then his fist, to no effect. Nothing stops this slow obliteration.

I don't know why this space is so determined to separate me from Malcolm, but it is. The thought squeezes my heart. I don't dare shut my eyes. I don't even have time to think. The only thing I can do is say the words I should have earlier today:

"I love you."

Despite the worry and fear in his gaze, he manages one of those sweet, dark roast grins. His lips move. Although I can't hear his voice, I know just how he sounds.

"I love you too."

The last bit of fog obscures my view of him. The glass shifts beneath my palms. I stand there with my hands pressed against a wall rather than a window.

How long I stay there, I can't say. I'm afraid to move, to break this final connection with Malcolm. At last, my feet grow numb, and a wave of exhaustion hits me. I press my back against the wall and sink to the floor.

I pull my legs to my chest and rest my head on my knees. I

make myself as small as possible. Maybe someone will alert mall security, but until then, I will rest here.

I have nowhere else to go.

The mall around me is loud enough that I don't notice the footfalls at first. They're more of a soft shuffle than the tap, tap, tap of dress shoes. When they reach me, I don't glance up. Instead, I peer through my arms at a pair of leather boat shoes.

"Hey, there," a voice says. "You okay?"

My gaze travels the figure before me. Stonewashed jeans. A polo shirt with the collar popped. There isn't a single strand of gray hair on his head. The look of concern on his face is nothing I've ever seen, at least, not aimed at me.

The smile he gives me reaches all the way to his eyes, and he crouches slightly, offering me his hand.

"Need a little help?"

Do I? Probably. From him? Doubtful.

Because standing there, hand outstretched, is none other than Orson Yates.

THE NECROMANCER'S NEPHEW

COFFEE AND GHOSTS SEASON FOUR, EPISODE 3

I don't want anything from Orson Yates, not even help to stand. But he gazes at me with such concern. The flesh of his palm looks tender, vulnerable, and strangely young. Then his eyes light with something else, something more. I want to call it hope, but I can't reconcile *hope* with *Orson Yates*.

"You're Katy Lindstrom, aren't you?"

The cold, hard tile makes my hips ache, and the question makes my temples throb. I don't speak. I'm positive I don't nod. Something must shift in my expression because the man before me continues, unperturbed.

"My uncle told me to expect you."

"Your... uncle?"

"Uncle Orson."

This? This I can't process. I stare at the young man towering over me. He is an exact replica of Orson Yates, or at least the version the ghosts showed Belinda and me after we freed them from the Gordian knot of Orson's own making.

"You've met him," the man adds. This is a statement, not a question.

Why, yes. I certainly have.

He is undeterred, his entire face lit with excitement. "He's told me so much about you."

This does not bode well.

"And you are?"

How I squeak out this question, I can't say. But there it is, hanging in the air between us, along with the scent of sweet citrus and caramel corn. And feet.

Everything here smells like dirty socks, although that could be because I'm still sitting on the floor. Along with all the odors, the otherworldly lingers in the air. Out of habit, I start to count ghosts but quickly lose track.

For a moment, chagrin paints his features, like my question hurt his feelings. It doesn't last. He's beaming at me again, and he has a thousand-watt smile.

"I'm William," he says. "William Yates. I'm sure my uncle's told you about me."

Well, no, he hasn't, but that's not the response the man in front of me wants. Without recourse, I give a tentative nod.

He crouches next to me. "Are you sure you're okay?"

I'm pretty sure I'm not.

"Just resting," I say, and my voice is breathless, like maybe I got winded shopping and needed to sit down. That's a reasonable explanation. Maybe if I pretend, then he'll leave me alone, and I can figure out what the hell is going on.

Or not. His gaze darts toward the courtyard, where there are any number of empty benches. The implication is clear. I should be sitting over there rather than hunched on the floor like a scared animal.

Part of me doesn't want to move at all. What happens if I lose contact with the last place I saw Malcolm? Can I find my way back? I don't even know what or where *back* is. My pulse thrums so hard that it jumps in my stomach. My limbs feel hollow, like they're not fully real.

"You look like you could use something to drink." William offers that hand again.

At the suggestion, my mouth is parched. The part of my brain that's still thinking rational thoughts knows I can't stay in this spot indefinitely. My heart, though?

My heart is begging me not to leave Malcolm.

We're collecting stares. It's only a matter of time before a security guard ambles by and asks if there's a problem, and I already have enough of those. But I need to know one thing before I move.

"Where's your uncle now?"

"Don't know." William gives a half-shrug. "He travels so much. I haven't seen him in about a week or so. Don't worry. He'll be along soon."

Actually? I am worried. But if Orson isn't here now, then I can use this time to get my bearings. The rational, reasonable part of my brain is urging me to do just that. Really, it shouldn't take all my willpower, but I have to shut my eyes and gather my strength before pushing to my knees.

Something clatters on the floor, the faint sound of plastic against tile.

"You dropped this." William scoops up the permanent marker and hands it to me.

I don't know if it's something about the pen itself or simply an echo in my mind, but Prescott's voice rings in my ears.

When all else fails, pull a Hansel and Gretel.

"Let me tie my shoe," I say.

In a flurry of laces and adjusting socks and as much subterfuge as I can manage, I uncap the marker. At first, I draw a hasty slash on the wall, down low, near where I was sitting. Then, on impulse, I ink out a quick KL + MA.

It looks commonplace, nothing more than two teens declaring their devotion. Before I stand, I pull in a deep breath and let my gaze travel the space, noting storefronts opposite and to the sides.

The sparkle of Hillside Diamonds is hard to miss.

So, yes. I can get back here. And if I can get back here, then somehow I can get back to Malcolm.

William reaches for my hand, then pulls back, a hint of pink rushing across his cheeks.

"Are you thirsty?" he asks. "Would you like an Orange Julius?"

"No!" The word comes out with more force than I intended. My insides recoil at the thought of anything sickly sweet. But that concoction in particular? I press a hand against my stomach and pull in a deep breath.

He takes a step back, hurt flashing in his eyes.

"I mean, I had one earlier today," I say, "and I think I've had too much sugar."

"You must be crashing. No wonder." Just like that, his good humor returns. He gives me that thousand-watt smile again. "I have a meeting in"—he checks the watch on his wrist—"about forty-five minutes, but can I buy you lunch?"

"Lunch?" My stomach rumbles, and that hollow feeling returns.

"You need food, not sugar," he adds. "Come on, my treat."

I think he's going to offer me his arm. The attitude is all there. He pulls himself up tall, but at the last minute, tucks his hands into his pockets. I've seen so many men pull this move so many times.

I may not know who this William Yates is, but I do know this.

He's a necromancer.

THE FOOD COURT is crowded with families and strollers and little kids running back and forth. Several clutch tiny, soft-serve ice cream cones. The seating is all hard plastic in orange and brown, with avocado trim. It's possibly the ugliest color combination I've seen in a long time.

"Yeah," William says, noting my wrinkled nose. "I'm talking to management about updating the color scheme." He holds up a hand as if to ward off the dreadful sight. "It's so 70s."

I'm about to ask if he works in the mall when he points toward one of the vendors. "I did that."

"You own the A&W?"

"No, I convinced the owners to establish a presence here. They have a place out by Cedar Lake, but it's seasonal. This way, they have business all year round."

He grins at me like this is a major accomplishment. Perhaps it is. His voice is full of confidence and the promise that everything will work out for everyone. No wonder the owners capitulated.

"Plus, the free cones for kids?" he adds. "It's a great loss leader. The owners didn't want to try it, but I convinced them that the parents would feel guilty grabbing free ice cream. Nearly everyone ends up buying something as well." He surveys the food court as if it's his domain. "They're already in the black."

"Wow." I don't know what else to say, but it's enough for William.

"What do you want?" he asks. "Anything at all. It's my treat."

Can I eat? My stomach certainly thinks so. The weight of the all-nighter presses on me. My brow throbs with the start of a caffeine hangover. Since I'm not sleeping any time soon, I'll need fuel to keep going.

But... *should* I eat?

I still don't know where—exactly—I am. The space around me looks like Cedar Hills Mall in what might have been its glory days. Is it something more? Something else? After all, when you end up somewhere you shouldn't be, there's one unalterable rule:

Never eat the food.

Hansel and Gretel and the witch's house. Persephone and Hades and the underworld.

My stomach growls again, loud enough that William hears.

"When's the last time you ate?"

I give my head a little shake. Really? I don't know anymore.

"Come on," he cajoles. "What looks good?"

The food court is crammed with options. There's the A&W, of course, but also a Sbarro and a Mrs. Fields with trays filled with cookies. Every other scent is laced with the aroma of warm chocolate. It's strangely comforting. If I shut my eyes, I can pretend I've stepped into Sadie's kitchen.

When I open my eyes, my gaze lands on 1-Potato-2. I point. "A baked potato sounds good."

I mean, a potato isn't a pomegranate.

William ticks off the options on his fingers. "They have bacon and cheddar cheese and—"

"Just butter."

"Sour cream and chives—"

"Butter's good."

His expression falters as if he was hoping to purchase the most expensive potato on the menu. But he leads me to a table, has me sit, and insists on buying lunch himself.

I let him, if only to steal a few moments to myself. My thoughts ping back and forth. Everything here is too real to be a dream. The oil and sugar in the air, the hard plastic beneath me, the slightly sticky table where my palms rest. I wipe my hands on my jeans and continue my survey.

The A&W is doing an impressive business. Kids gather around the soft-serve machine while parents exchange glances and then step up to the register and order a basket of fries or onion rings. Other than the slightly sticky tables, the space is clean.

A supernatural kiss brushes my skin, raising the tiny hairs on the back of my neck. A ghost trundles by, collecting discarded napkins, cups, and anything else on the floor. Ahead of it, two sprites work furiously to knock debris from unoccupied tables for this first ghost to gather. I watch, fascinated by this coordinated dance. Knock and scoop, knock and scoop, until, at last, the larger ghost pushes the pile of trash next to one of the bins.

A tray full of food lands in front of me and jerks my attention from the trio of ghosts.

"You've been watching the cleaning crew?" William sorts the food—my potato, some onion rings, a slice of pizza, and two root beer floats—and doesn't wait for my reply. "Best idea I've had in ages. Good job, guys!" He directs this last toward the ghosts.

The sprites twirl and preen, clearly proud of themselves. The larger ghost gives a world-weary and otherworldly nod. It's the sort of ghost that does not suffer sprites gladly, although I sense a certain affection on its part anyway.

"Of course, they can't bag the garbage. I've tried training them, but you really need a stronger ghost for that sort of manipulation." William studies the food on our tray. "And you don't want a ghost that strong in the food court."

No. No, you wouldn't. What an angry ghost might do with all that soft-serve? Hot oil from the deep-fryer? I stop my thoughts there. No sense in sending ideas out into the ether. Ghosts get enough notions on their own.

"So, you trained them to work here?" I ask.

"They're not the only ones." He tears into the pizza like he hasn't eaten all day.

How does that work? Does he pay them? Okay, with sprites, that's easy—lots of attention and a cup of Kona blend. Even now, they're toiling extra hard after that last bit of praise. But ghosts are capricious things. You really can't rely on them to punch in at nine o'clock every morning.

"What is it you do, exactly?"

His chest swells, and he sets down his half-consumed slice of pizza.

"I'm a necro-preneur." He radiates so much pride, he could power the food court for a week.

The term sounds both suggestive and slightly unsavory. I'm almost afraid to ask. "Necro-preneur?"

"It's a cross between necromancer and entrepreneur. Pretty unique, huh?"

That it is.

He gives me that thousand-watt grin. Really, he's shinier than Carter Dupree. Then his expression sobers. "Don't you like your potato?"

I'm holding my fork but haven't taken a bite. Again, I wonder if I should. If I eat, can I ever get back? Maybe I am Persephone, only with a potato instead of a pomegranate.

A squeal comes from the A&W. A teen crouches and hands a toddler an ice cream cone. The sound is happiness itself. It's both real and reassuring, and it sparks something else, something Carter said.

"Do they have corn dogs?" I ask.

William plants his hands on the table, ready to push off. "Do you want one?"

I wave him down. "No, no. Just curious. I have a... friend who likes them."

If Carter can eat a corn dog and get back, then certainly I can take a bite of this potato. It's still warm, and the first mouthful chases away the chill of the air conditioning. The entire thing might be more butter than potato. With each bite, my mind clears. My legs gain strength. I don't feel quite so hollow.

"So, what does a necro-preneur do?"

William sucks down half a root beer float and then shifts to tug his wallet from a back pocket. With a flourish, he hands me a business card.

Ghostly Solutions
O. William Yates
Owner and Necro-preneur

"I'll show you around, show you what it is I do." He checks his watch again. "I still have time."

Before I can agree—or disagree—William tugs the card from my fingers. He scribbles something on the back and pushes the card across the table at me again.

"My pager number. Trust me, I don't give that out to just anyone."

"Pager?"

He unclips a device from his belt. "You call, and it sends me a notification. Then I can call you back."

Absently, I nod before turning the card back over. "What does the O stand for?"

My stomach is warm with potato and cold with trepidation. Something tells me I already know the answer. But maybe he's an Oscar or an Orville. I stare at him hard, cataloging his every feature, comparing them to the ones in my memory, wondering— not for the first time—who this man really is.

"Apparently, I was named after my uncle." He shakes his head and rolls his eyes. "Like I want to go around calling myself Orson Yates."

CHAPTER 2

How I make the potato in front of me vanish, I'm not sure. What was buttery and warm moments before tastes like sawdust. From the corner of my eye, I steal glances at William, peering at him through my lashes, working to be as unobtrusive as possible.

I keep this up until I catch William peering back at me, that hint of pink painting his cheeks once again. My stomach drops, and a wash of dismay makes me blush as well.

Oh, *no*. He thinks I'm flirting. And I am so not flirting with Orson Yates.

"I wish I didn't have this meeting," he says. "We could... I mean..." He bites back his next words and then drowns them with the last of his root beer float. "Let me show you around, okay?"

I nod.

"You can take your drink."

I nod again. At this point, I'm as articulate as a bobblehead doll. I'm about to pick up my trash when William stops me.

"Leave it." He points behind me. "You'll disappoint them."

I glance over my shoulder. The two sprites hover, full of expectation. They positively sparkle with it.

"You guys want to clean up my mess?" I ask. It's a relief to see them there, and I cling to this bit of normality. Ghosts make sense. Ghosts are real, relatively speaking. I give them both a wave of encouragement.

One does a backflip. The other spirals like a mini-tornado, knocking the wrappers and plasticware to the floor. The larger ghost lumbers by. I give this one a small smile of sympathy. It heaves a gust that is a perfect replica of a long-suffering sigh and blows the garbage toward the bins.

"My uncle was right," William says, both words and expression full of admiration. "Ghosts really do like you."

We head toward the center of the mall. The entire Crystal Court glimmers. The stainless steel gleams. Metallic flecks in the benches and the tile reflect the light that streams through spotless windows. Even the air holds a sparkle. I lift my chin and catch hints of the otherworldly riding the air currents.

Children play along the edge of the fountain. The water bubbles and froths more than it should. Tumbling in the streams of water arc countless sprites. They dive in and out of the pool, burst through the spigots in explosions that are both damp and ethereal. The entire space echoes with high-pitched squeals of laughter. Tiny fingers strain for sprites who dart just out of reach. Supernatural and very human delight mix, and my chest feels lighter.

In fact, no one in the courtyard wears a frown. It's impossible not to smile, and I turn that expression on William.

He positively beams. "This was my first idea." He points at the fountain. "The sprites love it. The kids love it. The parents are grateful. Plus, they spend more time—and money—here this way." His gaze goes from the benches to the fountain's rim to the air above it. "Hang on."

He strides toward the fountain, his steps purposeful. Then he holds up his hands, about a foot away from the froth and foam.

Concentration carves a furrow along his brow. Then he jogs back to me.

"Had to reinforce the containment field," he says.

"Containment field?" I let my gaze canvass the space around the fountain. After a moment, I detect a shimmery outline, but not much more.

"They're spites, right? Sure, they love it, but it's not like they have much of an attention span."

"So... they can't leave?"

The fountain takes on a different interpretation, one I'm not sure I like.

"I rotate them in and out. It's not like they're prisoners or anything. Besides." He gestures again, palms outward, as if he could embrace the fountain and all the sprites it contains. "They clearly love it."

Yes, the sprites do appear happy. Waves of joy strike me, devoid of any undercurrents of sadness. And yet? I sigh, not sure I can articulate what's wrong with this situation.

"Come on," William says. "I have more to show you."

He squires me around the mall. We stop at various businesses —most of which I've never heard of before—and he shows me the various ghostly improvements he's made for the owners.

"I'm working on a personal shopper solution, but it's not going all that well." He casts me a knowing look. "You know ghosts and their sense of humor. They distort reflections in mirrors, suggest terrible outfits." He heaves a sigh, one that's a match for the world-weary spirit in the food court. "I suppose it's too much to ask a ghost to have a bit of gravitas."

"Probably. Sprites would love to help—"

"Tried that. Everyone ended up with sequins and neon-pink feather boas."

I can't help but laugh. That sounds like an outfit a sprite might pick.

By now, we've strolled to the main entrance. Something holds me back from stepping through the double doors and onto the sidewalk. The sun strikes the concrete, and the glare is almost too much. Still, I can see the parking lot and all the cars, all of them old—but old cars that look shiny and undented and like they've just rolled out of the dealership.

William places a palm against the glass. "I hate that they had to clear-cut the trees to bring in all the new equipment for the expansion. But that's one of the reasons I call my business Ghostly Solutions."

The road to the mall is in the wrong place. I swear it is. The circuitous route winds the long way around. At first glance, the landscape along the highway is bare. There isn't any scrub, never mind actual trees.

Then I see the glimmer, that familiar copse of pine. My breath catches in my throat. I know those pines; I've driven straight through them.

"Awesome, isn't it?" William says.

From the corner of my eye, I sense that thousand-watt grin.

"Visible wards are hard," he adds. "I can keep it reinforced now, mostly. But Uncle Orson helps me maintain it every few weeks when he visits."

"You... built the ward with your uncle?" Each word is a struggle, but I push the question from my throat.

"You really need two necromancers to establish a visible ward."

I'm transfixed, fingertips against the glass, eyes locked on the ward. It's the same as the other one, assuming there is another one. And while the little sprite isn't here to chime in, its insistence fills my head.

Two necromancers. *Twin* necromancers. An old one and a young one.

More than one Orson Yates?

Like one isn't already enough.

But William is so unlike Orson, or at least, the middle-aged Orson that I know. I remember what Arianna told me. How, in his youth, Orson was a much different man. Different like William? He's so full of energy and earnestness. If Orson was like William in his youth, I could almost understand why Arianna had an affair with him.

Almost.

"You okay?" William touches my sleeve, and I jump. "Sorry, sorry." He steps back, expression contrite. "Didn't mean to startle you."

I gulp a breath, raise a hand toward the outside and then let it drop. "The ward... I've never created one like that."

"You could, I'm sure. You're a strong enough necromancer."

"You can tell that?"

"Absolutely. There's a vibe, you know."

No, no, I don't, but I give him a weak smile.

"Look." William checks his watch and cringes. "I've really got to make this meeting. But would you like to go to the movies tonight?"

I open my mouth, although what I'm going to say, I'm not sure.

"Not a date," he adds, words rushed. "I'm going with some friends of mine. I'd love for you to meet them. And it would be my treat, too."

"Wouldn't *that* make it a date?"

"No, just friends."

Are we friends? After a food court lunch and a stroll around the mall? William's expression, his entire being, is filled with expectation, with conviction. He thinks we are. That much is clear.

"How about this," he says. "If you want to, we'll be at the fountain at six-thirty. If nothing else, come meet my friends?"

This last is so plaintive, I find myself nodding.

"Great! I'll see you then."

With that, he bounds away. I'm left alone with a permanent marker, a cell phone that doesn't work, and a million thoughts that spin in my head.

How long I stay near the entrance, I can't say. At some point, my legs protest, and I plant myself on a bench. The potted trees on either side look real. I even press my finger into the base of one, testing the soil. I rub the damp earth between my fingertips and consider.

Live trees, not fake ones. That's different. William—or Orson, or whoever he is—is different. My mind zooms, working overtime to concoct an explanation that makes sense.

The mall is filled with so many ghosts that the otherworldly is a background hum, much like the ventilation system. Some ghosts zip up and down the corridor on what seems like important missions. Others float lazily above strollers and baby carriages, their antics making the children laugh. So it's only when the supernatural presence at my side nudges my shoulder that I notice it.

The presence is familiar. I've met this particular spirit before. It whirls about, both excited and remorseful. The apologies come in waves, although I don't know why it's apologizing to me. It musters enough strength to extend ghostly arms as if it wants to pat my back or give me a hug. I shift, hoping to get a better read on it, and end up with a mouthful of ghost.

Another wave crashes over me, this one quite literal. The sensation of water, and lots of it. A sparkling lake. A tackle box and fishing reel and all manner of colorful lures.

"You're the demon!"

I proclaim this—loudly. A mother tugs her two children closer and keeps a wary eye on me until they vanish down the wing.

"You're the demon." This time, my words are no more than a whisper.

The ghost sags in front of me. It's so despondent that it makes a puddle of mist on the floor.

"Did you mean to hurt us?"

The puddle at my feet swirls.

"You couldn't help it?"

The swirling increases. The ghost throws off sparks. I'm onto something, although what, I can't say.

"So, in this mall, you're a ghost," I venture.

It bobs up and down.

"And in the other one, you're a demon."

It flattens itself on the floor, a surge of shame flavoring the air.

"Interesting."

The ghost pops up as if it agrees. Yes, it's all very interesting, but could I do it a favor? It swirls and then prods me between the shoulder blades so relentlessly that I have no choice but to stand. Gone is its malice. True, it's strong—quite strong—and it uses that strength to urge me toward the mall's entrance.

Once there, it slams itself against the glass, again and again, until I wince.

"Okay, okay. Stop."

I press my hands against the glass and focus my full attention on the space just beyond the outer doors.

A few people come and go, casting me odd looks, but the ghost remains at my side despite the wide-open doors. I focus again. The faintest outline of a containment field shimmers in the afternoon sunlight.

"You can't leave."

It bobs again, excited I've caught on so quickly. The ghost circles around my hand, pushing against my fingers. Once again, someone enters the mall. Once again, the ghost doesn't attempt to leave.

"You need a necromancer to break the containment field."

It shoots toward the ceiling, its entire being filled with relief. Then it prances about, puppy-like.

Do I let it go? In the here and now—wherever the here and now actually is—this ghost is more than friendly. All it wants is to go fishing. It's summer, and no doubt the nearby lake is filled with boats.

And if it's out there, it can't cross back over and attack Carter.

"Did you mean to hurt Carter?"

I get a complicated answer, full of mist and regret. Again, I think of what Arianna told me about Orson: No one trains and motivates ghosts like he does.

"Was it Orson who made you do it?"

Anger radiates from this ghost. In that complicated surge of emotion, I sense the demon that Orson unleashed.

But if it's outside the containment field?

I give the door—and the field around it—a good shove, both physically and mentally. The ghost follows, urging me forward. I push open the second set of doors as well.

It whirls around, planting a ghostly kiss on my cheek. Then it streams from the entryway, adding sparkle to the sunlight, its elation tangible. In its wake, a group of teens laughs. A few stretch their arms as if they could catch this ghost.

Then it's gone.

The icy whoosh of the otherworldly shoots past my ankles. I count three, four, maybe six other ghosts who use the crack I've made in the containment field to escape as well. I stumble backward into the mall, wondering if I've completely ruined William's business.

But I don't regret it. My chest feels lighter, even if my stomach still has that slightly sick emptiness to it. I turn and survey the corridor leading to the Crystal Court. During William's tour, I noticed a bookstore, and where there's a bookstore, there's bound to be a newspaper.

A newspaper with today's date.

I adjust my ponytail, pull in a deep breath, and decide to start there.

I FIND the Hickory Farms first. A rich, smoky scent hits me before I even cross the threshold. Everything is so very red and down-home on the faux farm. I don't think I've ever seen so much processed cheese and meat in one place.

"Would you like to try a sample?" A sales clerk gestures at a tray on a display table just inside the entrance.

Would I? I'm pretty sure I don't want to know how this particular sausage is made, but the cheese looks edible. I wait for a beat, and then another, watching two other customers pluck a sample from the tray. One doubles back for seconds.

So I try some cheese, realize I'm starving—even after the potato —and as unobtrusively as possible, eat my fill while pretending to search for a gift. I chase all that down with some chocolate mint samples from Fanny Farmer next door. I'm wondering how many other samples I can snag when it hits me.

This is dinner.

I push that thought aside and move on to the bookstore.

B. Dalton Bookseller is so bright orange, it rivals the Orange Julius (which I've been avoiding). Every few feet, a flag hangs from the ceiling, wavering slightly, reminding everyone that they're having a sale.

The space has that unmistakable smell to go along with the stacks and towers and shelves full of books. For a moment, I hold still and breathe it in. It reminds me of the Springside library, the one in the high school, and even the plane of existence where I stayed with the entity for six weeks, surrounded by endless volumes. It's the sort of scent book lovers recognize, even if they read on a tablet or their phone.

The newspapers are near the front, but I walk a slow circuit of the store, striving for casual. In the children's section, two sprites flip pages of a picture book for a toddler nestled in an older child's lap. The toddler gurgles and slaps one of the pictures with a pudgy hand.

Is this William's doing? I lift my chin but can't detect a containment field. Just the gratified glimmer of happy sprites. Of course, toddlers and sprites are compatriots. There's probably a brigade of both in the toy store. The two sprites pause long enough to wave at me. I muster a smile and wave back.

I linger in the mystery section until a line has formed at the checkout counter. In the crowd, no one notices me slip in and crouch in front of the newsstand.

It's Saturday, June 27th.

1992.

The headlines blur before my eyes—something about a sex scandal and a siege of Sarajevo. Beyond that, I can't make sense of the words. I stare for so long that my legs cramp. Someone knocks into me, and I topple over.

"Miss?" The cashier peers over the counter, concern on her face. "Are you okay?"

For one horrible moment, I can't feel my feet, and my legs refuse to work. Then I'm up, shaking my head in apology—because I don't trust my voice—and I bolt from the store.

I need to get home. Certainly, I can make that happen. After all, Carter did it. He came here—somehow, without realizing it, apparently—bought a ring, ate a corn dog, and then went home. And if Carter Dupree can do all that, then so can I.

I half-walk, half-jog back to the Crystal Court. Sudden and intense fear pushes me forward. Maybe leaving the spot where I last saw Malcolm was a mistake. I should've stayed there and waited for the mall to shift around me again. That spot, the one I marked earlier. That's the key. It must be. I'll wait there and hope I haven't irrevocably screwed up my chance of getting back.

The Crystal Court is bright and cheerful with sunshine and sprites. A crowd of children is gathered around the fountain. The ghosts there appear to be putting on a show. There's a great deal of twirling, acrobatics with flourishes and—of all things—a kick line. Even the parents look relaxed rather than harried.

I spot Hillside Diamonds gleaming in its premier position. I take this as a good omen, do an about-face, and march toward the opposite wall.

The space is blank.

I blink rapidly, blaming my eyesight, the lighting (never mind that it's so very bright in here), and my nerves. I walk right up to the wall, press my palm against it, and try not to panic.

The KL + MA is gone.

Not wiped away. Not faded. There isn't an outline or a clean spot where the letters might have been. This isn't something William's food court cleaning crew could've accomplished.

My heart pounds hard in my chest, the beat so fierce it might crack a rib. My insides churn, and I regret eating all that cheese and chocolate. Something tells me I have screwed up, utterly missed my chance.

My stomach, my head, my entire body revolts at the idea. I can't have a nervous breakdown in the middle of the mall, so I do the only thing I can do.

I run—and hope to find a restroom in time.

I SKIRT past the woman gripping a mop with a quick:

"Too many samples."

She nods sagely as if, yes, she's seen this before.

I race for the second-to-last stall, relieved she's already cleaned in here, and shut the door behind me. I sag against it, my hands fumbling with the lock. Then I wait, eyes closed, my mind whirling.

The second a thought pops into my head—about never seeing Malcolm again, of never going home—I banish it. I concentrate on my breathing and count to ten over and over and over again. After some time, I figure I need to show I'm still alive. I don't want to lose contact with the door, so I stretch my leg toward the toilet, foot straining for the handle.

An obliging ghost pops down from the ceiling and depresses the lever.

Ghosts in the restroom? Really?

That's not something you want. They love toilet humor. Plus? A little privacy might be nice. But this ghost floats toward the ceiling again, flush—if you'll pardon the pun—with a job well done.

I track the noises coming from the other side of the door. The swish of the mop. The clank and roll of the bucket. What sounds like one of those plastic caution signs settling on damp tile. Then the restroom is so quiet, I can hear the drip of the sink and the teasing melody from the mall's sound system in the corridor beyond.

Fear still bubbles inside me, but it's no longer laced with overwhelming panic. The samples rumble in my stomach, but the urge to vomit has passed. I pull in a breath filled with industrial cleanser and disinfectant, all harsh soap and astringent lemon. I don't really have a plan, but my mind insists I start making one.

Instead, I close my eyes, grateful for the stillness and the solitude. Maybe this is the extent of my plan—simply being alone until I can hold it together.

Indeed, my dear. Alone at last. And about time, too, I might add.

CHAPTER 3

My eyes fly open. Oh, no. Oh, no, no, no. This? On top of everything else? Whatever this is, I'm getting rid of it. I push against the restroom door and stand firm, hands on hips.

"Go away!" I shout the words at the ceiling, although, really, the voice is all in my head.

Is that any way to greet an old friend?

"You are not a friend. You're a demon, or my imagination, or something I don't care to deal with at the moment."

My dear, I'm here to help.

"Really? I could've used some help an hour ago."

An hour ago, this mall was crawling with Orson's spies.

"And now they've suddenly vanished?"

I believe you had something to do with that.

"Really?" I think of the supernatural rush when I opened the mall doors, a cold so sharp I felt it through my jeans. "All his spies left?"

Wouldn't you?

It has a point. That doesn't mean it's actually the entity, and even if it is, that doesn't mean it's truly here to help.

"How do I know you're my entity? Prescott said—"

Ah, yes. Prescott's been filling your head with tales of demons. You've already figured out what a demon is. I think we can agree that I'm not one.

"The ghost I set free." I pick my way through the jumble of thoughts in my head. "It was a ghost here, a nice one, too. But back... wherever, it was a demon."

Simply put, a demon is a ghost that has slipped from its own reality into a different one. Often they have no anchor in the new reality. Or something is different that angers them. Really, it could be anything.

"Ghosts are capricious."

Indeed. Perhaps here, they don't exist, or the love of their life marries someone else.

"Or they can't go fishing."

Exactly.

That makes sense, although I'm still not certain how ghosts get from one reality to another. Then again, I'm not sure how I did. But one thing at a time.

"How do I know you're you?" Although, really? The way I've fallen into conversation with it is enough to convince me.

Almost.

Prescott did warn me not to open my mind to other beings, and I've done just that.

Please. As if another being could mimic this personally tailored persona. It's rather an art form.

Maybe? Sort of? While the statement feels reassuring, it's also precisely what I want to hear. I *want* this to be my entity. Because it can do anything—or nearly so. If this is truly my entity, then it can help me get home.

"Tell me something that only I would know."

Do you remember when you first captured me, and you ran from the warehouse?

I give a tentative nod. Not that I don't remember. Of course I do. Most days, I prefer not to.

And when you finally stopped to rest? I believe you embraced a rather lovely birch.

In my mind's eye, I see it now, the image sharp, unbelievably so. The stark black and white of the trunk, the bark papery beneath my palms, the sweat rushing down my limbs from my cross-country trek. I haven't mentioned this to anyone, not even Malcolm. It's a memory locked away where even I don't visit. Even assuming another being could access my mind, I doubt it could recreate this scene in all the technicolor brilliance that the entity can.

"All right," I say at last. "You're my entity."

Finally.

That single word sounds like an eye roll.

Despite that, for the first time since I arrived here, hope wells in my chest. We can hammer out some sort of exchange. Because, yes, it will undoubtedly demand something in return. But I know, without a doubt, that it can send me home.

"So, now what?"

Now? I believe you need to get ready for your date.

I wait. Then I wait some more. A punchline lingers in the air. It must. When nothing but that soft drip, drip, drip of a faucet sounds, I'm forced to ask.

"My date?"

If you step from the stall, you'll see that your appearance could use a little maintenance.

"But I'm going home."

Silence greets this proclamation.

"I am going home, right?" I tip my head toward the ceiling. "Do I need to invoke you?"

That won't do you any good, my dear.

Oh. Understanding dawns. At least, I think it does. "We no longer have a pact?"

Maybe that's it. When all of Springside's ghosts became a

willing sacrifice, it ended my pact with the entity. That makes sense.

Oh, we most certainly have a pact.

"We do? But the ghosts—"

Merely an exchange, and I returned the favor by sending you back to earth. We never formally dissolved the pact.

"What? Is there a ceremony for that?"

The entity laughs, and the noise reverberates in my head, making my forehead ache. I clamp my hands over my ears, but it doesn't do any good.

Oh, I've missed these tête-à-têtes with you.

"I thought you were here to help."

I am helping, and right now, what you need to do is get ready for the movie. Dayton's has a lovely cosmetics counter—with samples. I believe you enjoy those. Trust me, your cheeks could use a little pink.

"I want to go home. I want to see Malcolm. Why can't you help me with that?"

This silence stretches long, and it's filled with foreboding. If I still have a pact, why can't I invoke the entity? Why is it avoiding my questions?

"You can't help me get home," I say. "Can you?"

I most certainly can, and I will, but you must have patience.

"But I can't invoke you."

No. You can't. By all means, try. But you'll find it will do you no good.

I open my mouth to say its name, a nearly unpronounceable jumble of consonants and vowels. The word lodges in my throat, and it takes all my strength to utter it.

"Momalcurkan."

Nothing. No shimmer in the air. No rumble beneath my feet. Just the constant drip from the faucet.

"Why?"

Although I don't catch a hint of that stale air, an otherworldly sigh rattles the ventilation system. Startled, the toilet ghost shoots from the vent but circles around, full of sympathy. If it could, it would pat the entity on the shoulder. It understands.

I still don't.

"Why?" This time, I let all my fear and worry and anxiety flavor that single word. "Why can't you help me?"

I can help you, my dear. Rest assured.

"But?"

But you can't invoke me, and I can't simply send you home.

The entity can do anything—or nearly so. I've watched it burn through necromancers and create swirling lava pits in concrete floors. Why is it so powerless now?

"Because?" I prompt.

The silence stretches again, and I let it. The ball is in the entity's court. It needs to tell me before I budge. Otherwise, I will simply stay here in this stall and chat with the friendly toilet ghost.

A muted supernatural chuckle reaches me, but the sound isn't entirely happy.

Very well, you win. The reason you can't invoke me is that you don't exist on this plane.

"I haven't been born yet."

That makes sense. Except. The entity hesitates. Actually, it's been doing that the entire time. This is not a being that routinely hesitates about anything.

When I say you don't exist on this plane, what I mean is, you won't ever exist.

"I won't be born?"

No, because, in fact, your mother doesn't exist, and neither does your grandmother. In this reality, the Lindstroms never emigrate from Sweden. Your parents never meet, and your grandparents never meet.

My heart squeezes so hard, it hurts. This is a scenario I never considered.

"Which means I won't meet Malcolm."

I brace for a snarky reply, but nothing but sorrow fills the entity's voice.

I'm afraid not, my dear.

"But I'm here now."

This reality simply doesn't recognize you or our pact.

With its words, that sensation of wrongness sweeps over me again. I've been ignoring the feeling—or trying to—but I can't deny it. It's more than the sense of not belonging. I'm a trespasser here. Worse, I'm violating something, like I've peeked inside a private diary.

"Is that why everything feels so wrong? Like I don't belong here?"

Indeed. It's a mark in your favor. Orson's little protégé—

"Carter Dupree?"

Yes, him. Utterly clueless. He's lucky you captured me when you did. I would've burned through him in less than five minutes.

I consider that and the fact that Carter didn't notice the obvious differences between this reality and ours.

"How did he get here and back again?"

With a great deal of intervention from Orson. Two years ago, Orson was at the peak of his powers, both as a necromancer and as a dabbler in things he shouldn't be dabbling in.

"A mark in my favor?" I venture. "Will this reality help me get home?"

See? I knew you'd catch on. It wants to neutralize your influence here. The cleanest way is to return you to where you belong.

"So, that means my reality wants me back as well."

Oh, it does.

"But?"

Well, there's the whole physics part of it we need to navigate. You had some supernatural help in getting here.

"The demon?"

Yes, it pulled you through the threshold. We need to find something that will pull you back. Trust that I'm working on it.

"So, now what do I do?"

A hint of that supernatural sigh swirls in the restroom, stirring up the disinfectant. The scent stings my nose, makes my eyes water. My mouth tastes like processed cheese and soap.

Don't you have a date?

"Not really."

That sigh again.

In any case, you most certainly need a makeover.

THE ENTITY CAJOLES me to the makeup counter inside Dayton's. How? I'm not sure. One minute, I'm slipping past the strategically placed closed-for-repairs placard outside the restroom (the entity's doing—yes, most certainly), and the next, a sales clerk is wiping my face with a rose-scented towelette.

"You're kind of grimy," she says.

I don't take it personally.

The activity draws the attention of not only other shoppers but a quartet of sprites. They bob along the glass counter, pushing bronzers and eyeshadows for the sales clerk. What starts as a chore —for both of us—turns into a three-ring circus.

She doesn't notice that I'm not interested in buying any of the items she's applying to my face. Instead, she fills a bag with even more samples. She laughs when the sprites suggest sparkly blue eyeliner but takes their advice on perfume.

"You have a date tonight, right?"

Again, how she knows this, I can only guess. That guess starts and ends with the sprites that are now nudging perfume bottles in our general direction. She grabs the closest bottle, a purple one labeled Poison that I hope actually isn't. She douses me. The sprites luxuriate in the scent like it's Kona blend.

I try not to cough.

I clutch my bag of samples, thank the sales clerk, and ease off the counter stool. The moment my back's turned and I have the sprites' full attention, I whisper.

"Help her."

By the time I reach the store's entrance, she's already rung up four purchases.

Despite my makeover, I'm still not sure about going to the movie, never mind meeting William's friends. With reluctance, I inch my way toward the Crystal Court. I stop, taking cover behind an information kiosk. A psychic shove between my shoulder blades has me stumbling forward once again.

"Ow," I say, although it really doesn't hurt.

Shh, my dear. Don't speak.

"Because?"

Even when you respond in your head, you subvocalize. You're already attracting attention. You don't need more.

The entity's right. While not everyone gives me the side-eye, enough people do that it's a problem. I'm constantly checking my sneakers for toilet paper (sure, the toilet ghost is friendly, but it's still a toilet ghost) and making sure my shirt isn't on backwards.

Even though I'm in the universal uniform of T-shirt and jeans, both have a slightly different cut. The trail sneakers on my feet are like a beacon. More than one passerby opens their mouth as if to ask me where I got them.

But if there's such a thing as a necromancer vibe, then there's probably a wrong-reality one too. I don't belong here. I'll never belong here. In which case, I shouldn't go to the movie.

Another psychic shove pushes me into the Crystal Court.

The crowd around the fountain has thinned now that the ethereal extravaganza is over. Sprites frolic in the water's froth, but the movements are discordant and unsynchronized. Chaos, essentially, which is their default setting.

Two little boys stand at the fountain's edge. They clap their hands above their heads, snagging wayward sprites. They marvel at their catch, holding the sprites between their palms for a few seconds before setting them free.

"Oh, Mama," the older one says. He's perhaps seven, the

younger one maybe four. "Look how he catches them! He's so good already!"

A woman sitting nearby gives an indulgent smile. The one next to her leans forward, face obscured by an explosion of curls.

"That's because *you're* a very good teacher, Prescott."

The voice, more than the name, freezes me in place. I can't run away—although I really want to. I refuse to step closer as well. I know that voice and the woman who owns it. If you let her, she could steamroller you.

Even here, in this reality. And if I can make it back to mine?

She'll be my mother-in-law.

Two sprites buzz about my head and tug on my T-shirt as if they could drag me over. I'm immobile, a statue, a permanent fixture in this mall. Unless some sort of portal opens to my reality, I doubt I'll move again.

The little group in front of the fountain expands. I catch sight of William, a second man with dark good looks, and yet another who—once again—I nearly mistake for Malcolm.

My heart somersaults, and I bite back the urge to cry out. But it's not Malcolm crouching next to the two boys and plucking sprites from the air with nimble fingers.

It's his father, Darien Armand.

But the smile is all Malcolm. The way he deftly captures each sprite with such precision and care reminds me of Nigel. Who is, if I'm not mistaken, the younger boy attempting to crawl into Darien's lap.

These are William's friends? I try to reconcile that, give up, and decide that, no, I absolutely cannot meet them. I won't be able to hold it together. I'm barely doing that now. My pulse thrums in my ears. All I hear is the roar of that and the splash and gurgle of the fountain. The voices have faded. Even the otherworldly hum that is constant in this space is muted. As for the entity?

Totally silent. Of course.

The two sprites buzzing about my head give up. At first, I'm relieved. I'll sneak back to the restroom and wait until the mall closes for the night. That's as far as I get with this new plan. The sprites make a beeline for William and swoop around his head.

He glances up. When his gaze finds mine, his entire face brightens. The sprites zip back to me, complete a victory lap, and fly off.

Tattletales.

William rushes forward. He raises his hands like he wants to take mine and lean in for a kiss, but he halts a few steps away. Then it's all awkward silence without even a friendly sprite to distract us.

They're never around when you need them.

"You made it," he says at last.

I lift a palm skyward. "Here I am."

"Hey, come on." He beams, his smile both excited and shy. "I really want you to meet my friends."

And I really don't want to, but I nod. When I do, inspiration strikes. "First, tell me how your meeting went."

"You really want to know?"

I nod again, and his chest swells. The odd thing is: I do want to know. I'm curious about what he's trying to accomplish here.

"I met with the mall managers and some of the business owners. They're worried about the Mall of America opening in August. I'm trying to convince them it's not the end of the world."

"Mall of America?" I've only been there once, but I can't remember a time it hasn't been open.

"Yeah, it's going to be huge, but I'm telling you, we can compete, but we have to do it in our own way."

"And what's that?"

"Look, I know everyone will go there when it opens." He gives me a guilty grin. "I mean, I plan to, but it's not something people can do every weekend."

"Too expensive." I'm not much of a shopper, but this much I know.

"Exactly. And when the end of the month rolls around, and

people can't afford gas money, never mind tickets to the amusement park? They'll remember they can get ice cream for their kids here." He gestures toward the fountain. "And come watch a show. All for free."

"And then they'll come back when they have more money to spend." As plans go, I'm sure there are worse ones. Plus, there's something more to William's schemes, something that has heart.

"My uncle says what I'm trying to build is all minor league, small-time stuff. That I need to think bigger." Competing loyalties war across his face—guilt again, mixed with pride. "Does it always have to be about money?" A plaintive note echoes in his question. His gaze goes to the fountain with its jumble of sprites. His expression is tender, like he's picking out each one and giving it special consideration.

"It can be more than that." He returns his attention to me. "Right?"

I think of all the parties Malcolm throws at the long-term care facility and Tara's Girl Scout troop selling cookies outside K&M Ghost Eradication Specialists. How what I love most about Springside is that it's Springside. That's due to the people and the ghosts.

"Building a community," I say, swallowing back a pang of homesickness, "and making something that lasts. Those things matter, too. Maybe even more than money."

Far be it from me to disagree with Orson Yates.

"I knew you'd understand." William nearly blinds me with that thousand-watt smile. "I have so many plans for the expansion here. Sure, the Mall of America will have a haunted house ride—I already scoped it out. Real cheesy, too. But we can offer a real haunted house, with real ghosts."

That sounds like a recipe for disaster. Maybe my nose wrinkles again, or doubt shows in my eyes, because William adds:

"Okay, okay. I know. They'll have to be my best-trained ghosts, and I'm going to have to figure out how to hire a few necromancers to keep them in line. But think of it!"

He continues, his voice full of optimism, his expression that of a man who knows he can scale mountains. I'm struck hard with the notion that William is not Orson Yates—or at least, not the Orson I know. Possibly Orson was like this once. Still? I can't picture his expression alight with hope, purpose, and compassion.

"William?"

The voice comes from the fountain area and freezes us in place. We stand there like statues, either dreading or anticipating what comes next. My heart is tight in my chest, and I'm not sure I'll take a full breath ever again.

"Aren't you going to introduce us to your friend?" the voice asks. "Or are we going to have to listen to the sprites gossip about her all night long?"

A flush washes across his cheeks. He takes my hand and draws me forward. Because no matter the reality or the decade, everyone obeys the summons of Arianna Armand.

CHAPTER 4

Before we step into the circle of William's friends—and the bevy of sprites that circle above their heads—he gives my hand a squeeze.

"You smell great," he whispers. "What perfume is that?"

"Poison?" I say it like a question, too, because it was chaotic in Dayton's.

"That's my favorite."

Of course it is. No wonder the sprites suggested it.

Then we're there, surrounded on all sides. William introduces me to Manuel and Edie Jones, Darien and Arianna Armand. I remain mute during the introductions. My throat is too tight for words, and holding it together is becoming a full-time job.

"Manuel and Edie choreographed the extravaganza." William points to the fountain. As if on cue, all the sprites line up and take a bow. "And Darien is the best ghost tracker the Midwest Necromancer Association has ever seen. I'm just lucky he has spare time to catch a few ghosts for me."

Darien places a hand on William's shoulder. "If you practiced more patience, my friend, you could catch them too."

"That's just it. I have no patience." William laughs. It's warm, full of humor and self-deprecation. "I want to jump straight to the training."

Darien steps forward. My heart thumps an odd, hard beat like it might take up my entire chest cavity. He extends his hand, and when I return the gesture, he brings my fingers to his lips.

"It is an honor, Miss Lindstrom, to meet a necromancer of your caliber."

My heart is in my mouth now, and I'm pretty sure it's replaced my brain since I can't find anything to say. Darien's smile is charming, and he's suave like Malcolm. His eyes, though, are perceptive and canny like Nigel's.

I'm about to protest that I'm not a necromancer, but the words wither in my throat. I want to pull away because Darien generates the same sort of heat that Malcolm does.

"We've met before, haven't we?" His voice is a match for the Darien of my reality, except the tone is lighter. He is a man content and grateful, one who counts his blessings each night.

I think of that first time I slipped through realities and ran to him, thinking he was Malcolm. Does he remember that too? From the quizzical expression—all dark brown eyes and luscious lashes —he must.

"Oh, Darien." A crisp voice cuts through the air. I blink, thankful for the interruption.

"Really, stop flirting." Arianna huffs in mock exasperation. "Can't you see we're overwhelming the poor thing?"

With a deft hand, Arianna shoos the men and boys toward the fountain. There, sprites do backflips in unadulterated joy. She tugs me toward the bench where Edie is resting, one hand gently rocking a stroller, the other on her rounded belly.

"Don't worry," she says at my stumbling approach. She points to her stomach and then the slight bump of Arianna's. "It's not contagious."

"Says you." Arianna sinks onto the bench next to her.

It takes all my willpower not to stare at Arianna's stomach. If Nigel is four or maybe five... then, yes, the math works out. I shut down that line of thought. I cannot allow myself to speculate who this baby might turn out to be, so I turn my attention to the other woman on the bench.

Edie Jones was my mother's best friend—in my reality, that is. Her thick black hair is in twin French braids that reach her waist. She wears no makeup, but then, she doesn't need to. Her skin is light brown, nearly golden, and her lashes are dark and long. There is both shrewdness and laughter in her eyes.

Arianna is her opposite. No sleek silver bob. Instead, a mass of curls adds a couple of inches to her height. Her lipstick is bright pink and perfect. Her nails, of course, match.

"I'm sorry about that." Arianna points toward the fountain. "But William's been talking about you for weeks. Then the sprites started chattering today, and you know how they are. Everyone was so excited to meet you."

Ghosts love to gossip, sprites in particular. I give a wary nod. "Weeks?" I venture, surprised I can even speak at all.

Arianna tilts her head, casts a quick look at Edie. "I think it's been at least two, maybe three?"

I'm trying to reconcile that when Edie's voice cuts through my thoughts.

"That's a pretty ring."

I meet her gaze. Yes, it's as I suspected. Shrewd. Her eyes are narrowed, lips compressed. There's a correct response to her statement—where I explain this ring is a family heirloom and no more —and an incorrect one. I'm pretty sure I'm about to pick the incorrect one.

"It's my engagement ring."

Arianna arches an eyebrow. Edie's brow furrows in judgment.

"Does William know about this?" she asks.

The question is sharp enough to stab. Maybe I deserve this—in their opinion, at least. I peer over my shoulder toward the fountain. William is telling a story, gesturing toward a troupe of sprites executing some complicated acrobatics. Maybe he feels my gaze, but for an instant, he turns my way, throws me that thousand-watt grin, and continues with his tale.

Yes, I suppose, in a way, I do deserve both their glares.

"It hasn't come up—" I begin.

"Then maybe you should let him know." Arianna is fierce, from the sway of her curls all the way down to the tapping foot in its metallic platform sandal. "He's our friend. I don't want to see him hurt."

"Because I just met him today." I blurt these words.

In the silence that falls between us, I hear the splash of the fountain, a high-pitched, yet solemn, question from Nigel and Darien's smooth, lilting reply. Arianna brings two fingers to her mouth and whistles. The men barely notice, but a trio of sprites zip from the fountain and dance at attention before her.

"Really, Arianna," Edie says. "You should be a necromancer."

Arianna waves away the suggestion. "Like I have time to chase after ghosts." She focuses on the three sprites. "All right, spill."

At her command, they do, in a cacophony of chatter and one-upmanship. They're so loud and so distinct, even I'm privy to most of their tale, from my appearance near Hillside Diamonds to my potato lunch with William, my extended restroom break, and my makeover at Dayton's.

No one asks how or why I suddenly appeared, slumped on the mall's floor. No one asks why I spent more than an hour in the bathroom. (Unless they're simply exceedingly polite. And Arianna is many things, but exceedingly polite isn't one of them.) What's clear, however, is this:

According to the sprites, I just met William today, and vice versa.

Arianna sends them away with another wave of her hand. "Sit," she says to me. Like the sprites, I'm compelled to follow her orders. She scoots, making space on the bench. I end up sandwiched between her and Edie.

Essentially, no escape.

"I like William. I don't want to hurt him." These two things are true. Perhaps it's the sprites or the tone of my voice, but both women look like they believe me. "He mentioned something about his uncle?" I hedge.

Arianna's face wrinkles in disgust. Edie rolls her eyes and sends a curse toward the skylights.

"The guys love him," Edie says, her voice full of contempt. "They think he's this world-class necromancer dispensing all this marvelous wisdom." She waves her hands in the air in a dismissive gesture.

I stifle a laugh because that's exactly how I feel about Orson Yates.

"They can't get enough of him." Edie shifts, leans in closer. She shudders and then rubs her arms to ward off the chill. "But the way he stares at you, Arianna. It's creepy."

"You know him." Arianna's statement and expression are matter-of-fact.

I'm a terrible liar, so I don't see any sense in trying. "I do, but I haven't seen him in months." Not since he tried to kill Malcolm and me, but I have no way of explaining that.

"He... I... We've never gotten along," I add. True enough. "I don't know why he's been talking to William about me or what he's been saying."

Arianna presses a fingertip against her lips in thought. "It's been all positive, at least to hear William tell it."

So I've gathered. But why? That notion has been eating away at the back of my mind. Why would Orson talk me up to... well, himself? I reach my thoughts skyward, hoping the entity might enlighten me, but it's stubbornly silent—and has been for a while. Perhaps my chat with it in the restroom was nothing more than a fever dream. A fluttery, panicky feeling in my chest suggests it was just that.

"Well, he *is* creepy," Edie says, her gaze darting to Arianna and then to me. "I wouldn't put it past him to be creepy with more than one woman half his age."

Another thought strikes—harder and more vicious than the ones before.

Is Orson here now?

What did William say? *He'll be along soon.*

Soon as in tonight, or *soon* as in sometime in the next week? I do a quick scan of the Crystal Court as if I could detect Orson lurking behind a potted tree or one of the cylindrical trashcans.

"Have you seen him lately?" To my relief, my voice comes out strong, more casual than frantic.

Mostly.

Arianna and Edie exchange a glance.

"Not for a week or so," Arianna says. "When he's here, I always see him around Hillside Diamonds. I think he owns it or something."

The sparkle and shine of the shopfront capture my attention. Whether Orson is there or not, I know this: the way back is through that store. I'm conjuring an excuse to stroll over to the display cases. What if I plant myself in the same spot as before? Maybe the entity can work some magic with quantum physics. Maybe I can simply vanish from here.

Maybe I can go home.

I'm pushing from the bench to do just that when William joins the group.

"Come on." He claps his hands together, his face glowing with anticipation of the next new adventure. "We're going to be late."

"I DID NOT MEAN to make you uncomfortable, Miss Lindstrom."

We're standing in the lobby of the movie theater. People mill about, waiting for the doors to open for the seven o'clock shows. William, Manuel, and Arianna crowd the concession stand. William already clutches the largest bucket of popcorn I've ever seen. Above the din, I can hear Arianna's sharp, crisp commands and Manuel's easygoing reply.

I'm surrounded by posters of ancient coming attractions and archaic new releases, some movies I've heard of, but many I haven't. Instead of highlighting my ignorance, I turn toward Darien Armand.

"You didn't," I say. "Not really. And call me Katy."

Darien nods, a smile lurking just beneath his solemn expression. "Short for Katrina?"

I feel as if I've had a variation of this conversation before. "It is."

"It's lovely."

Although not that reply. I'm not certain how to respond, so I ask:

"You work for the Midwest Necromancer Association?"

"I do. They sponsored us when my family emigrated from Iran —before the revolution, mind you. Still." He gives his head a slight shake. "We might not have made it without their support."

Malcolm's told me some of this—at least, the part that's the same in my reality. As with William, this Darien is different. These Armands are different. More team players and less lone wolves.

"I've lived here for years," Darien adds, "but I may never lose the accent."

"Don't," I say. "It's... lovely."

And yes, there it is. I'm flirting with my future father-in-law.

"Have you thought, Miss—I mean, Katy, about joining the association?"

"Not really."

"I'm surprised they haven't come courting. A necromancer of your ability? It's uncommon."

"What about your wife?" I ask as Arianna joins us.

"I'm a sensitive." Arianna slips into the crook of Darien's arm like she always has—and always will—belong there. "And really? Who has time to catch ghosts?" Her curls sway with the shake of her head, and her eyes dance with teasing amusement.

"Perhaps for your second act, my love." Darien bestows a kiss on her temple. Arianna's smile in response is radiant.

My heart feels as if it might splinter. I have to turn away so no one can see my expression.

William finds me like that, back turned, eyes tight with pain.

"Hey," he says. "You okay?"

I manage a nod, but there's so much concern on his face that I add, "Just a little tired."

"We're heading in now." His hands are so full of popcorn and boxes of Good & Plenty that he can't actually take mine, although the popcorn bucket teeters as if he's thinking about it.

Manuel corrals both Nigel and Prescott, who have been playing a game of tag with some sprites. "Come on, buddies. Time to see the dog movie." He is stoic and holds in what must be a resigned sigh. "Again."

The little boys cheer. They're adorable, all round cheeks and huge eyes. And yet, Prescott's confidence already shines. He holds himself tall and takes Nigel's hand. As for Nigel? Those big, dark eyes are full of wonder at all the ghosts he sees. My heart skips a beat. I want to warn someone. Darien, maybe? Or Arianna? I don't have the words to explain, and there simply isn't time, not now.

Manuel commandeers the stroller from Edie. He slips into the theater opposite ours for a kids' movie about a Saint Bernard named Beethoven.

"Thank you," Edie mouths.

Manuel blows her a kiss.

The rest of us are headed for *Batman Returns*. People crowd the entrance, and everything is humid, the air full of the scent of sugar and melted butter, the floor slightly sticky beneath my feet. A sudden thought has me glancing around. Does Chief Ramsey exist in this reality? This is the same movie. Is it the same night? Would spotting him here anchor me?

Or would I simply feel more alone?

The crowd inches us forward before I can decide. People jostle. Someone's soda splashes against my foot. We're through the doors and heading down the aisle.

That's when my cell phone buzzes.

I gasp and come to a halt. Of its own volition, my hand reaches for my back pocket. Someone knocks against my shoulder. Someone else pushes me into a row where I stay because my phone buzzes again and again.

Text messages? Voicemail? I don't know, but I'm about to find out.

Absolutely not.

The entity's voice is so loud—in my head, at least—that I wince.

"But—"

Again, absolutely not. You cannot pull out your smartphone in 1992. Do you understand? There is no way you can explain its existence. The damage that might cause this timeline? Do I need to explain further? If you damage this timeline, my ability to help you diminishes.

I try to protest, but the entity has filled my head with so much noise that I can't formulate words or thoughts, or even move my limbs.

The messages will remain there on your phone. There's no way you can respond now anyway. Later, my dear. There will be time for this later.

Maybe after the movie starts.

Especially then. I'll let you know when the coast is clear, as they say.

The entity's right. Everyone would notice that. Besides, cell phones in the movie theater? If nothing else, that's so annoying.

The others catch up to me, filing into the row as if I've been saving our spots. I scoot toward the middle and end up dead center, William on one side, a stranger on the other. Every time my fingers twitch or my hand inches toward my phone, the entity gives me a metaphorical smack inside my head.

"I thought you were here to help." I probably subvocalize this, but the lights are low, the previews have started, and I don't think anyone can see.

I am helping.

That's debatable.

Watch the movie, my dear.

I try, but my mind is zooming in so many directions that I lose the thread of the plot almost immediately. All I see is unrelenting darkness and angst. This day has been filled with enough of that already.

William nudges the popcorn closer to me. I reach into the bucket, and our fingers brush.

"What do you think?"

His words are barely a whisper in my ear. He smells of Old Spice and licorice.

"I've been waiting for this movie for weeks now," he adds. "It was so crowded last weekend, we couldn't get seats." He leans in even closer now. Our shoulders touch. "I think you're prettier than Michelle Pfeiffer."

I murmur something that might be *thank you*, although my words are more air than anything else. My pulse thrums in my ears, and I can barely hear myself think, never mind make sense of this movie.

The pressure starts hard and small and centered in my chest. I can't stay here for an hour and a half. I can't wait that long to check my phone. I can't wait, period.

Indeed, my dear. Make your excuses. The mall closes in thirty minutes.

And that means what? Where do I go then? Besides, why did the entity have me jump through a dozen hoops to get to the movie only to leave thirty minutes in? I try to pull all the pieces together, but my thoughts fracture once again.

One step at a time. Trust that I have my reasons. But unless you want to sleep on this young man's couch or in his bed—

His bed!

He's also entertaining thoughts of a Catwoman outfit.

Stop!

I wait, but the entity doesn't respond. Well, it does, but only to give me a mental shove toward the aisle.

"I'm not feeling well," I whisper to William. "I'm going to go to the restroom."

And since I'm stuck in the center of the row, I must stumble over everyone on my way out. I mumble apologies and collect any number of muffled expletives until I land in the aisle.

There, a friendly sprite is waiting to usher me out.

Aside from bored kids working the concession stand, the lobby is blissfully empty. I gulp a lungful of air and then another, the pressure easing from my chest. My scattered thoughts settle. Next step? Leave.

To your left, my dear. The restrooms are to your left.

I ignore the command and head straight for the theater's entrance.

To your left.

Again, I pay no attention. Or rather, I studiously disregard the entity's directions because my only thought is to get as far away from here as possible. I'm about to duck under the velvet rope and escape down the corridor when William's voice rings out behind me.

"Katy! Wait!"

The entity's frustration rumbles with what sounds like distant thunder. One of the kids at the concession stand glances upward, but otherwise, I'm the only one who seems to notice.

Why listen to the all-knowing being at your disposal? You could've avoided this, my dear.

I send the entity a nasty thought and turn to face William.

He pulls in a deep breath as if to steel himself. "My uncle said you're going through some tough times right now."

Oh, he has no idea.

"He mentioned you might need a place to stay?" He raises both hands as if to ward off a protest. "I don't mean it like that. Just my couch."

What did I say?

"Or you can have my bed, and I'll take the couch."

Ahem.

"Look." A quick pink flush colors William's cheeks, and he glances around at the Coming Attractions posters before focusing on me again. "My uncle said you need help. I know you're engaged." He gestures toward my left hand. "But Uncle Orson said your fiancé is kind of a deadbeat."

Orson Yates and I agree on something? How novel.

Really? This is helping? I send yet another nasty thought skyward before confronting William.

"You don't know me." I work to keep my voice gentle. None of this is his fault. "All you know is what Orson has been telling you. I may not be that girl—that person—he's created for you."

"But I *do* know you. I feel this connection." He taps his chest on the spot right above the heart. "You feel it too. I can tell."

"I just met you today." I shake my head, more out of incomprehension than denial. "It hasn't even been twenty-four hours."

And yet, the weight of decades presses down on me. It feels like I've lived here forever.

"But you're perfect."

"Oh, I am not perfect."

"But of course you are. Your ability with ghosts is amazing—they love you so much. And I can train them. What more do we need?" He takes my hands in his, and I let him. "You get me in a way no one else ever has. We could build something special here, Katy."

"I don't belong here." I pause and consider my next words carefully. "I think you know that I don't belong here."

I'm speculating. How much has Orson told his alter ego? Or at least hinted at? Something flickers in William's gaze, both desperate and hopeful.

"You could," William whispers. "You could belong here." The phrase *with me* hangs in the air between us.

"You know that won't work." I tug my fingers from his.

He lets my hands slip from his grip. His eyes are so sad, nothing but hurt reflected there. He ran home after his meeting—he must have—showered, shaved, polished a pair of loafers. For what? Me?

No, not exactly. For a fairy tale Orson's been weaving.

The cruelty of this entire situation astounds me. I have no idea if Orson wants me to hook up with William or if I'm simply here to break his heart. The latter, I suspect. But to what end? To turn him into someone ruthless and uncaring, someone like Orson himself?

"I'm sorry," I say to William. "I'm sorry I can't be the girl you want me to be."

With that, I duck beneath the velvet rope and sprint down the hall.

He doesn't follow.

MY FEET LEAD me to the Crystal Court. I run as fast as I dare, my sprint slowing to a jog. I don't want to be tackled by some security guard, but I need to get away, find a place to hide—not just from William, but for the night.

Before I can reach the fountain, a supernatural swoosh surrounds me. It's almost like an ethereal stop sign. A group of sprites latch onto my T-shirt and jerk me backward. A dozen more form a fist and punch me in the stomach.

"Hey!" The word leaves my mouth with a rush of air.

I'm about to scold them. Then I see what they already have. Standing inside Hillside Diamonds, behind the display counters, is Orson Yates.

I drop behind a stone planter bursting with greenery. I pretend to tie my shoe and peer through the foliage. The crowd of shoppers has thinned even further. A few stores are dark, with the metal security gates in place. I can still hear the whirl from the Orange Julius and taste that hint of citrus in the air.

Orson is holding a landline receiver to his ear. His face contorts. He paces as much as the cord allows him to. His words are indistinct, but the tenor is sharp, irate. He slams the receiver down, and the jangle echoes across the courtyard.

Seems someone is ignoring his pager.

"William?"

Orson prides himself on planning for every contingency, but you have a way of disrupting those plans.

I take that as a compliment.

As you should.

Orson continues to pace. His strides radiate anger. He calls again, and again slams the receiver into the cradle. The sales clerk jumps and then takes a deliberate step away from Orson and the phone.

"Now what?" I send the question skyward but get no response.

I glance around, not that I can see the entity. But there's an emptiness that wasn't here a moment ago.

The vibrations start low, barely noticeable. They flow through the stone planter and shake against my palms. The floor rolls beneath me. The world shifts. The scene around me flickers— bright and welcoming before turning dank and gloomy. My body knows what to do before my thoughts catch up. I spring to my feet even as the floor rolls again, and I surf that wave. This must be the shift in realities—or whatever is going on here. What did the entity say? It was working on the physics part of things.

Maybe this is it. The entity's fixed things so I can go home. In any case, I'd be a fool to waste the opportunity.

I send my gratitude toward the skylights and bolt for Hillside Diamonds. The few people milling around the fountain don't notice my clumsy footfalls and flailing arms. Maybe they can't even see me. I gain speed because one thing is clear.

I need to reach the display case inside the store. If that's the way *into* this reality, then it must be the way back out again. I pant, trying to draw in as much air as possible. One moment, it's warm and cheerful, the space sweet-smelling, and the next, that cold, musty taste invades my mouth.

Close. I'm so close.

I'm nearly at the entrance when Orson glances up. The phone's receiver slips from his grip, but his face lights with a smile—that smug, superior smile that's far more disturbing than his anger. He raises his hands and then lowers them with a flourish.

I flinch and then brace, expecting an attack ghost to barrel into me. Nothing happens, so I gather one last burst of speed. I crash into the containment field with so much force, I fly backward. I land hard, the shock sending a jolt up my tailbone and into my skull. My palms smack the tile, and my wrists snap backward.

For a moment, I have no leverage, no strength to push myself upright. When I do, I'm an ungainly combination of elbows and knees. Orson is standing behind the display cases, still smug.

I can't break the containment field. Now that I know where to look, it shimmers in the fading sunlight. I'm not getting home. Orson's malevolent grin tells me that. But I can do the next best thing.

I yank my phone from my back pocket—1992 be damned—and send Malcolm a text message as fast as my numb fingers can move.

Katy: I think Orson is heading your way.

If Orson notices, it doesn't show on his face. His gaze surveys me, and he gives his head a little shake as if he's supremely unimpressed. With that smug smile still in place, he brings two fingers to his brow in a mock salute.

And then, right before my eyes, Orson Yates vanishes.

CHAPTER 5

The world settles with a final roll, the damp odor of mildew fading, a rush of fresh—if recycled—air returning. I have enough presence of mind to tuck away my phone. For a long moment, that's all I can do. The containment field glimmers, a series of fissures covering its surface. A particularly energetic sprite zips toward the center. The second it makes contact, the entire field shatters.

The entity's voice comes roaring back in, a jumble of words that come so fast that I can barely understand what it's saying.

... really need to get moving. There's only so much I can do, and the mall is about to ...

Really, I don't think I've ever heard it panicked before.

"What?"

There you are. Finally.

"What happened?"

Interference, if you will. When you're on the threshold of your own reality, I can't communicate with you.

"Like having bad cell phone reception?"

Precisely. I always thought humans were so irrational about that—I'm beginning to understand the exasperation.

"So, I was almost there?"

You were, my dear.

"And let me guess, you were trying to steer me away from both William and Orson so I could get back to my own time."

Speaking of time, there isn't any for recriminations, self or otherwise.

"You could've just told me."

Actually? I can't. You possess free will, as do all the actors in this little passion play, not to mention all those in walk-on roles here—the family with the double stroller, the teenagers prowling for snacks. While I can multitask, humans cannot. There's only so much information I can feed you before your synapses overload.

"Oh, well. We can't have that." I roll my eyes. My synapses have been overloaded all day long.

Rather to my point. Besides, it isn't as if you've been listening to me.

It sounds downright petulant. I want to do the eye-roll thing again. But really, what's the use? Instead, I head to the fountain and stand in the courtyard's center, right beneath the skylights. I tip my face upward and let the last of the day's light wash over me.

The mall will close soon, and while the entity is silent, a series of psychic nudges pings the back of my mind. I should move. Before I do, I shut my eyes, inhale deeply. When I open my eyes, my gaze lands on the wall opposite Hillside Diamonds.

Something dark mars the surface, down low, near where I drew those letters hours ago. Was it only hours ago? I move toward the wall, the weight of decades, of multiple realities, a crush against my shoulders.

Time shouldn't be so heavy.

Whyever not, my dear?

At the wall, I crouch and trace a finger along the KL + MA that has magically reappeared. Only there's more now. Someone, some-where, has circled the letters with a heart.

Oh, well. Isn't that sweet?

I can't muster the strength to send it a nasty thought. This heart must be Malcolm's doing. The fact that the entity is goading me proves that much. I trace the shape once, twice, a third time before standing.

The shuddering clank of a security gate closing echoes across the courtyard and makes me jump. Through the loudspeakers comes a calm, yet ominous, voice:

"Cedar Hills Mall is closing in twenty minutes. Please make your final purchases and proceed to the parking lot. We hope you've had a lovely day."

Oh, it's been grand.

"Now what?" I say this out loud, although there's no one left to hear, just the fountain, the skylights, and the now-empty display cases of Hillside Diamonds.

Turn around, my dear.

The entity's voice is beyond gentle. Without recourse, I obey. Behind me float three sprites. Their forms are articulated just enough that they appear to be holding hands—or rather, little ethereal wisps that serve the same purpose. They're adorable, and I can't help but smile, despite everything.

They drift toward the corridor, the one with the women's restroom and the friendly toilet ghost. I follow, thinking that's where they're leading me.

It isn't. We pass both restrooms, a bank of lockers, and some offices. At the end of the hall, the sprites stop in front of a door. They bob up and down, up and down, and then swirl around the handle.

The message is clear.

When that calmly ominous voice echoes with a five-minute warning, I push open the door and step through.

AFTER NAVIGATING the mall's back hallways, I end up in what looks like an employee lounge. A long couch takes up one wall. A table and a scattering of plastic chairs crowd a corner with a refrigerator covered in magnets and stickers and a sign that reads:

Your mother doesn't work here.
Clean up after yourself.

Opposite the couch is a counter with a microwave and a toaster oven. My stomach insists that there might be food no one will miss, but my legs have other ideas. I collapse onto the couch, the cushions lumpy but soft.

This time, when I reach for my phone, the entity doesn't try to stop me.

The text messages are a jumble of one and two words, all from Malcolm. With each one, I sense his increasing frustration and worry. He sent the voicemail last, so I switch to that while my phone still has battery life.

The moment Malcolm's voice comes through the speaker, my heart catches. The sprites hover a respectful distance away as if they understand exactly what's going on. But this message, too, is mangled. I listen once, twice, a third time, piecing together words and phrases.

"Katy, hang on ... Prescott ... Nigel ... reinforcements ... necromancer association."

I'm not sure that last is a great idea, but I have no way of knowing what's happening in their reality. Maybe Orson has reinforcements there as well. For all I know, there's an all-out necromancer war going on.

"Get you back ... rescue ... myself ... love you."

I play the message as many times as I dare. Each time Malcolm says those final words, my chest constricts. Tears flirt with the corners of my eyes, but I'm too empty to cry. I tuck my phone away so I won't be tempted to drain the battery—and myself—completely.

For several minutes, all is quiet, or nearly so. The overhead lights hum, and the three sprites create a low-level, energetic buzz. But nothing else. No people. No William. No Orson. Even the entity is silent. Exhaustion rolls over me, and I give in to the urge to shut my eyes.

It doesn't last. The buzzing grows more insistent until I can't ignore it, so I open my eyes. In front of me, the sprites dance and twirl in supplication.

"What is it, guys?"

They zoom around the room, bouncing off the walls until one of them knocks over a stack of paper filters.

Coffee filters.

I push to stand. By instinct—and with a little help from the sprites—I find the coffeemaker tucked inside a cupboard. The pot has an inch of burnt sludge on the bottom, but that's an easy fix.

Harder? Finding something worth brewing. I peel back the lid on a container of Folger's. The sprites peer inside as well and then shove the can from my hands.

"I agree," I tell them, and set to rummaging through the cabinets and drawers until I locate both a grinder and a pound of Gloria Jean's coffee beans.

"It's not Kona blend," I say to the sprites, "and I can't promise miracles with an automatic drip, but would you three like some coffee?"

They clasp wispy hands and whirl about in a crazed game of Ring Around the Rosie.

I take that as a yes.

The bag of beans was sealed, so when I fill the grinder and start it whirring, the aroma bursts forth, rich and earthy. It's not Coffee Depot fresh, but it's seductive enough that I hold out hope for a decent brew.

By the time the coffee reaches the halfway mark, several more ghosts have joined us. A crew of six wait patiently at the table while others investigate the lounge, dipping in and out of the pockets of jackets that hang on the coat rack, upending the pillows on the couch, and generally making a nuisance of themselves.

"Just so you know," I say to no one in particular, "the best-behaved ghosts get the coffee first."

That settles them down—for about five minutes.

William's cleaning crew trundles in, still intent on picking up after everyone.

"You guys get a coffee break." I place several paper cups on the table before turning back to brew another pot. "Right?"

They join the otherworldly swarm that covers the entire surface of the table. With effort, they squeeze onto a chair.

Ghosts from the ethereal extravaganza slink in, manifesting leg warmers and attitude. Cliques are bad enough in real life; we don't need them here in the afterlife. I tell them to lose both or no coffee. They do, and moments later, they're teaching a gathering of tiny sprites how to do quadruple backflips.

By the time I've brewed a third pot of coffee, the entire lounge is filled with ghosts—possibly every ghost in Cedar Hills Mall. Under different circumstances, this would be a precursor to a full-on ghost infestation.

Instead, I've created some sort of ghostly happy hour.

Otherworldly complaints filter through the air, mostly about messy and picky human customers and the ghosts' limited ability to play pranks on these customers. Apparently, some customers deserve it—oh, how they deserve it. No complaints about William, although he's the one who won't let them play pranks.

In the corner, a few ghosts hover in conference. My trio of adorable sprites buzzes them and then comes zipping back to me. They do this enough times that I simply must investigate. And these ghosts?

They ice me out.

It's not an infestation, because the other ghosts aren't on board

—or simply aren't paying attention. But a chill radiates from this particular corner, flavored with resentment and disgust.

At me.

"Hey," I say to them. "What's going on?"

All five turn their backs on me—as much as ghosts have backs.

If only I had some Kona blend.

I brew a fresh pot of the Gloria Jean's and bring them the first cup. I set it on the floor between them. They inch forward and back until one can't stand the pretense and dives right in.

Then the barrage hits me. They're consumed with thoughts of William, his plans, his feelings, his every move.

"You guys must keep things running when he can't be here."

They puff up with pride. Whether they actually help or not, they certainly believe they do. That's enough for ghosts.

"And you're upset that I hurt him."

They ping around in their corner, crashing into each other, spilling the coffee. One even cuffs me upside the head.

"Hey!" I rub the spot right above my ear. "That hurt."

No remorse, not even an ounce of it, from any of them.

I grab a handful of paper towels and wipe up the mess. I think it's the sign on the fridge; it's more ominous than all these ghosts put together. Then I sit on the floor, cross-legged.

"I'm not supposed to be here," I tell them. "I didn't mean to hurt William, and I'm sorry that I did."

The ghosts hover in front of me, still with a hint of judgment seasoning the air. At my back, I sense a wall of all the others. I have everyone's attention now. I shift to include everyone in this conversation.

"You guys know that, right?" Around me, the ghosts bob in a wave of otherworldly agreement. "And Orson *really* doesn't belong here."

This sets them off. The fury starts with a low hum, but the sound and the churning grow until I'm afraid I've sparked an infestation. I hold up my hands, hoping to calm them down before the temperature drops too low.

"Have you told William how you feel?"

As a collective, they sink to the floor, despondent.

"He's not listening?"

The room erupts in a flurry. Each ghost tries to tell me a story, but I'm not following any of the threads. Anger, fear, anxiety—all of that is clear, but I'm not sure why. I tip my chin toward the ceiling. The entity has been awfully quiet, and I wonder if it's still here.

Simply watching you work, my dear. It's a pleasure to behold.

"I'm not working. I'm just talking to the ghosts—or trying to."

So you say. And you wonder why other necromancers covet your ability.

I've always maintained that my "ability" is simply not wanting to trap ghosts, or use them, or press them into service. They continue to whirl around me, frustrated by my lack of understanding.

"How is Orson getting back and forth?"

The ghostly buzzing increases, and I suspect I'm onto something here.

Do you remember your young necromancer's observation at your so-called retribution?

I think back to that, my hand reaching for my throat. At the time, I could barely breathe, and I certainly couldn't talk. But Malcolm could.

"Malcolm said Orson looked like crap."

Inelegant, but accurate.

With my eyes closed, I work to conjure up the image of Orson behind the counter at Hillside Diamonds. An otherworldly shove has me opening my eyes almost immediately. In front of me, several ghosts swirl in a mass that resolves itself into a near picture-perfect image of Orson.

His suit is expensive and well-tailored, but even that can't hide the sag of his shoulders, the slight hunch of his upper back.

Instead of sleek and self-satisfied, he's gaunt in a way that suggests illness rather than exercise. He looks no better than the last time I saw him. In fact, he looks worse.

"What has he been doing?"

Why, traveling, my dear.

What did William say? He hadn't seen Orson for about a week, that Orson traveled a lot. "Back and forth? From our reality to this one?"

And he's found a way that doesn't rely on chance.

In front of me, the otherworldly image of Orson fades, only to re-form. This time, he's standing in what looks like the back of a store, next to a safe. Methodically, he spins the dial, opens the door, and grabs hold of a ghost inside.

There are several, and each one squirms in his grip. Despite standing for retribution, Orson is still a world-class necromancer. He holds a ghost mere inches from his face as if he's taking its full measure.

Then, mouth open, eyes closed, Orson Yates gulps it down.

"He's swallowing ghosts!"

Much more than that. He is, if I'm not mistaken, swallowing demons as well.

I'm about to ask why when the answer occurs to me. "Because demons want to go back to their reality, and they pull him through with them?"

Like the fishing ghost in the bowl pulling me through to this reality. Does that mean I should try swallowing ghosts ... and demons as well? I give my head a little shake, and while I haven't said anything out loud, the ghosts glimmer in response. They think it's a bad idea, too. But as a last resort?

Maybe.

Another question pops into my head. "How close is he to addiction?"

Orson would tell you that he has everything under control. Ask Nigel for his assessment? I suspect he would see things far differently.

A sudden flare of anger has me gritting my teeth. The first time I met Orson, he taunted Nigel about his addiction to swallowing ghosts and his subsequent fall from grace.

"What a hypocrite."

The ghosts bounce in agreement.

You should know by now that rules don't apply to men like Orson.

"Until they do."

Indeed. The entity's muted chuckle rattles the ventilation system. *Until they do.*

A hush falls over the room. The ghosts simmer down. Two of the more mature ones gather up the sprites and figuratively tuck them into bed. Not that ghosts need to sleep. At least, I don't think they do. But the whole production is making me drowsy. My eyelids feel heavy, and it's all I can do to crawl across the floor and onto the couch.

You need rest.

The entity's voice is as soothing as a lullaby.

It's right. The ghosts are right.

"Someone's going to wake me up?" I toss the question out there. "Before I get caught in here?"

Maybe I could talk my way out of that, pretend I have a job at the mall and simply arrived early.

I really don't want to.

Several ghosts bob up and down. I take that as a yes. Still, I don't think I can actually sleep. But I close my eyes, feel the gentle kiss of the otherworldly against my cheek.

I dream of Malcolm.

I wake at three in the morning. The room around me is dark. The only light comes from the microwave clock and the sparkle of any number of ghosts. The ventilation system clicks, the refrigerator hums. Above that comes the soft sound of a dozen snoring sprites.

Again, ghosts don't need to sleep. But the sprites are stacked—one on top of the other—in ethereal bunk beds that reach from floor to ceiling. It's adorable, and the sight lets me pretend I don't have a dozen different thoughts swirling in my head. I shift on the couch, carefully, so I don't roll off, and pull up a ratty blanket someone—or several supernatural someones—placed over me.

"Thank you," I whisper, although it's ridiculous to do so. Other than the ghosts, I'm the only one here.

Everything is hushed, the ghosts contented. Maybe they don't need to sleep, but this crew seems to enjoy feigning it. If only I could—either for real or pretend. I shift again, give up, and scoot to sit.

"I've been thinking." I direct these words toward the ceiling.

Yes. I know.

"You do?"

It's one of the perks of having you as a necromancer. That mind of yours is always busy.

"I thought you said it was benign."

That doesn't mean boring.

It knows what I've been thinking. But *I* know this entity. It won't swoop in to answer questions I might have. I'll have to ask, and part of me would rather not. At last, the pain of it forces me to. Maybe if I speak my doubts out loud, I'll be able to go back to sleep.

"I keep thinking of what happened with you, back in Springside, with my grandparents and Malcolm's grandfather, and then with my mother, Darien, and Orson. Is it our fault? The Lindstroms? What if we had never ripped you from your home?"

In the hush, I sense a vast intake of breath, like I accidentally touched a bruise. When at last the entity speaks, its voice is subdued.

I became unmoored, if you will.

"Because of my grandparents and Malcolm's grandfather."

Perhaps. In part. I was also reckless in my youth, so to speak.

"But you're trying to get back."

The entity pauses for much longer than it usually does. The ghosts around me remain silent, although no one's pretending to sleep at the moment.

The universe is vast, even for me. By the time I find my way back, it may not feel like home anymore. That may not be a bad thing.

I don't believe it. I want nothing more than to return to Springside and Malcolm. I can't imagine the entity not wanting the omnipotent-being version of those things.

Of course you can't. Really, it's part of your charm. But to your question of whether the Lindstroms are at fault?

It's changing the subject with not only its question but a gentle

—if persistent—nudge in the back of my mind. The air sparkles around me. The ventilation system kicks in, the breeze from that chilling my arms. I pull the blanket tighter around me and give in.

"Everyone is so happy here, especially Darien and Arianna. I can't help thinking what if? What if things could've been that way in my reality?"

Let me tell you a little story, my dear. As in your reality, Darien travels a great deal, chasing down ghosts—and yes, on occasion, demons. Only here, he does so at the bidding of the Midwest Necromancer Association. This September, right after Nigel starts kindergarten, the association will send Darien on a mission to catch an elusive and powerful ghost.

I nod, although, like whispering, I don't suppose I need to.

The chase will lead him through Europe, into the Balkans, and eventually the horn of Africa.

As the entity speaks, the narrative unfolds in bursts of images and landmarks. I catch sight of the Eiffel Tower, the Parthenon, a wind-swept shore, and long stretches of desert.

At any point along this path, Darien's odds of survival are tenuous. But one thing is clear. He does not return from this trip.

The images fade, and I don't know if the entity can't—or won't—show me Darien's demise. That's not something I want to see. It must know this.

"Why would the association do that? Why risk your best necromancer?"

What's the point of having a tool if you aren't going to use it?

"That's—"

How they operate—how they've always operated.

"Well, it's stupid, if nothing else."

As you say. In any case, his death will shatter the camaraderie of this little group. Manuel and Edie will pack up their brood and head for a necromancer enclave in San Francisco. Arianna will try to raise her boys, but the shock of losing his father at such a young age will have Nigel swallowing ghosts much earlier. He will succumb, eventually.

I'm about to ask, or rather insist, that Nigel will be okay. The word *succumb* echoes in my head. And I know he won't ever give up the ghosts, or meet Sadie, or live the life he was meant to.

As for Malcolm? He will careen from one career to another, one relationship to the next—almost if he's seeking something that doesn't exist.

"Stop—"

So, you see, my dear, happy is very much a relative sort of thing. In fact—

"I get it. Just shut up."

I pull the blanket over my head, not that it hides me from the entity. Now that it has woven this tale for me, I can't banish the images from my mind. Arianna graveside, little Nigel clutching her hand. The addiction that takes him to eerie, bleak places where he lies, face down, that shock of white hair tangling with weeds. Then there's Malcolm, on a city sidewalk, one hand clutching a leather briefcase. His hair is threaded with silver, and a heavy gold watch circles his wrist. But he stares at the skyscrapers around him, his expression that of a little boy, utterly lost.

The images fade, and the room fills with a soft melody, the sound of dozens of ghosts humming a lullaby. I'm positive I won't fall back to sleep, but the song wraps around my heart and soothes the rough edges.

I murmur a *thank you* just as my eyes close.

THE NEXT TIME I WAKE, it's to the clatter and scrape of chair legs against linoleum. I bolt upright, heart pounding, my sluggish mind groping for thoughts, words, anything to explain why I'm here.

Instead of some fast-food manager glowering down at me, I spy a jumble of ghosts wrestling on the break-room floor. They tumble across the lounge, slamming into the table and knocking over all but one of the chairs. The air has that icy feel to it. Not infestation cold, not yet. It's an angry, competitive sort of chill. Even the sprites have joined in. Five or six create a larger form that takes on some of the others.

"Guys! Guys!" I toss off the blanket, push to stand, then collapse back down again. My stomach insists I need food—so do my legs. My throbbing head insists on Kona blend and lots of it.

"Guys!" I try again.

The ghosts continue to tussle. Only now that I'm fully awake do I discern what they're fighting about.

Each one wants the job of waking me up.

"Guys," I say. "I'm awake. You don't have to fight anymore."

This proclamation makes them brawl even harder, with more ghosts joining in. Honestly? I think they want an excuse to fight. William has them constantly on their best behavior—and really, that's a lot to ask of a ghost, and especially a sprite.

But I need their help. I really need some caffeine.

"If you guys don't stop, I can't brew any coffee."

The frost drains from the air. The ghosts line up, from largest to smallest, as if they've always behaved impeccably.

At last, I launch myself from the couch. There's enough Gloria Jean's coffee left for a single stout pot. Once the aroma has filled the air and I've downed half a cup, I turn to speak to them again.

"I need you to help me find William."

BEFORE I LEAVE the employee lounge, one of the larger ghosts unearths a trial-size toothbrush and some paste. Not to be outdone, a bevy of sprites floats a clean shirt my way—one with a plunging neckline, strategically placed cutouts, and neon-pink faux fur trim. The word *Available* is spelled out in silver sequins.

This is not a message I need to be sending in any reality.

"That really isn't me," I tell the sprites.

They snicker in response.

Fortified with the coffee, I slip from the lounge and down the hallway just as the first employees arrive. I gather a few groggy nods and hellos, but otherwise, I'm just like them. Here to work.

Which I am, sort of.

From what the ghosts told me, William comes to the mall every day. He reinforces the containment fields, meets with store owners and the mall management, and does a complete circuit, upstairs and down. He checks on all the ghosts—every last one. He is full of praise and cheer, and it's their favorite part of the day.

Except today I'm wondering if he'll even bother. According to the ghosts, he's late. Granted, ghosts aren't great at telling time. They *are* good at detecting routines, and William has broken his.

I haven't heard from the entity since I snapped at it. Even with my chin tipped toward the skylights, I can't sense its presence. True, it excels at hiding, and I can barely feel it here in this reality. Still, I stumbled onto something last night, something that felt almost vulnerable.

Even I have my weak spots.

The voice is so remote, I'm not sure I've heard it at all. I abandon the courtyard and head for the escalator, as if riding up to the second floor will help me hear better.

Humans are more powerful than they realize.

I glance behind me and then above. Somehow I don't think I've increased my power by riding the escalator.

What sounds like a gentle chuckle shakes the air. The teenager opening the Sunglass Hut kiosk pauses, frowns, and then continues with her work.

"I'm going to go find William."

The girl gives me a wary side-eye. I either said that out loud or subvocalized in a way that made me appear peculiar. I wait for that nudge, for any indication that this is something I should—or shouldn't—do.

Nothing. Or almost so. That friendly trio of sprites pops up, then drifts a few feet forward before doubling back, urging me to follow. The mall's sound system crackles to life. The first song of the day?

"The Girl From Ipanema."

CHAPTER 7

The sprites lead me to something called Happy Chef, a restaurant in the south wing. It has the feel of an old-fashioned diner. People sit at the counter with newspapers and coffee, and a row of booths fronts the mall's concourse. Instead of big bay windows, the space is open. You could vault over the low wall and plant yourself in a booth.

In one of those booths sits William. On the table in front of him may be the largest cinnamon roll in existence. It takes up an entire dinner plate, and the roll itself is slathered with at least a quarter-inch of icing. He reaches for the thermal carafe of coffee at the table's center and pours himself a cup.

I resist the urge to hop the wall. I don't want to get thrown out before speaking to him. I imagine they frown on wall-hopping here. When I reach his table, he doesn't glance up.

"May I?" I gesture toward the empty side of the booth.

He lifts a shoulder in barely a shrug. I take that as a yes—or, at least, an *I don't care.*

Warm cinnamon fills the space between us, and it takes all my willpower to keep my stomach from growling. The icing oozes down the side of the roll. The scent of creamy butter tells me this is no powdered sugar and water concoction.

"That smells great," I say.

He shoves the plate in my direction with so much force, I barely catch it before it slides off the table.

A waitress bustles by, an older woman with a blue rinse and cat's-eye glasses with glittery rhinestones.

"Hey, honey," she says. When she turns toward me, the rhinestones catch the light. "Can I get you a cup of coffee?"

I could use more caffeine, even in the form of restaurant coffee. But I didn't think to search the couch cushions for spare change this morning. I'm about to decline when William speaks up.

"Bring her a cup. My tab."

His voice is despondent, but at least he's talking. I wait until the waitress has placed the cup on the table before investigating the brew in the carafe. The aroma is weak but devoid of any bitterness. That's promising.

I give it a taste test. "Huh. Not bad."

I mean, it's not Kona blend, but I doubt they have that here. It's certainly better than the coffee at the Springside Pancake House. Then again, charred mud is better than the coffee at the Springside Pancake House.

"Orson said you're good with coffee, a connoisseur or something." He says this more to his cup than to me.

"It runs in the family," I say. "I learned from my grandmother. And Orson once told me that more than one man would've married my mom for her coffee alone."

William's gaze meets mine over the rim of the cup. His expression is shrouded and dull. I can't tell what he's thinking or feeling —not exactly, anyway.

"Yeah." William's voice is heavy, full of regret. "He's good at telling people stuff." He taps the plate, gently this time. "Go on. I'm not very hungry, and it would be a shame to waste it."

After my first bite, I can't help but agree. The roll is still hot in the center, and the cinnamon swirls and icing are gooey. It's something you need to eat with a knife and fork; otherwise, you risk getting covered in a sweet, sticky mess.

I'm halfway through when I pause and push an apology from my mouth.

"Don't," he says. "I'm the one who should apologize." He gives me a once-over, some of that familiar concern returning. "Where did you sleep last night?"

Yeah, I look rough. Then again, he looks no better. A day's worth of growth covers his jaw. His hair is rumpled, and not artfully, either. His clothes are clean, at least, if unpressed. But his eyes speak to a sleepless night, all red-rimmed and sore.

"The ghosts helped me," I say. Really, they haven't tattled yet? That's a surprise.

As if on cue, one swoops in and swirls about, kicking up the sugar-substitute packets and mini containers of jam before fluttering off. Judging by the self-recrimination in William's expression, he got the gist of my evening.

"It was kind of like a slumber party," I add. "I liked getting to know all your ghosts. They really admire what you're doing here at the mall."

"See? You're just too nice."

"I am?"

"That's what my stepdad told me."

"Your stepdad?"

"Yeah, I called him after I got over myself. He told me I came on way too strong." He shakes his head as if he's trying to shake some sense into himself. "It's crazy, because you were right. Orson did create this fairy-tale version of you."

He stares at me for a long moment before returning his gaze to his coffee. "It was like having a crush on a movie star."

"I am so not a movie star."

He holds up a hand, stopping my protest. "But it was *like* that. Every time I realized it was kind of ridiculous to be thinking about a woman I'd never met, Orson would feed me another story about you."

Oh, I can't imagine why Orson would have such impeccable timing. I bite back my response—along with another mouthful of cinnamon roll—because I think William needs to keep talking.

"My stepdad said I had no right to expect you to feel the same way I did. But it was hard not to." He exhales with so much force, it ripples the surface of his coffee. "Because here's the thing. You're even better in real life."

This last is so tender, so vulnerable that treading carefully is my only option.

"Your stepdad sounds pretty great."

"He is, actually."

"I never knew my parents." One confession deserves another, and I think there's more to this than a fairy tale of Orson's making. "They died not long after I was born." I hesitate and then add, "Car accident."

William's head jerks up at this. "I'm sorry, Katy."

"It's okay. I never really knew them." I place fingertips on my chest. "But sometimes I feel a hole, you know what I mean?"

"My father left when I was ten. He's this big shot in the East Coast Necromancer Association. You know all those expert financial analysts on TV? He makes and breaks them."

"Ghosts on Wall Street?"

"Exactly. He has a chokehold on all the association's necromancers and their ghosts. They call him the kingmaker."

This, I believe. The right kind of necromancer—an unscrupulous one, naturally—with the right sort of ghosts? You could make and break careers. You could make and break lives. You could hold everyone in your sway.

"My stepdad sells insurance." William's mouth twists, and he laughs, but the sound lacks humor. "He's not even a necromancer."

He picks up the carafe of coffee, flips open the lid, and peers inside. He flags down the server, who gives him a quick nod. He falls silent like he won't be able to talk until he'd downed some fresh coffee.

The icy kiss of the otherworldly whispers across the nape of my neck. I don't sense a ghost, but I tip my chin skyward.

Something to ponder, my dear. In both realities, Albert Yates left his wife and son for younger, blonder pastures, if you will.

Figures.

In this reality, William's mother attended a mixer for newly divorced singles. It's where she met Stuart Kendall, insurance salesman. In your reality? She stayed home that night.

The server eases a new pot of coffee onto the table, and William pours us each a fresh cup.

"You know I'm self-taught as a necromancer, right?"

"You are?"

"It's why I suck at catching ghosts. I started sensing them when I was three, but I missed out on all the early lessons, the ones family members are supposed to teach you."

The image of Darien plucking ghosts from the fountain's froth fills my mind. Wrapped up in all the delight of snagging sprites was a subtle lesson in technique.

"Until a couple of years ago," I confess, "I never even knew necromancy was a thing."

"It's why I was so thrilled when Uncle Orson agreed to mentor me. Obviously, my father wasn't going to. He couldn't even be bothered to help me find a mentor. In fact, he cut me off when I turned eighteen because I refused to attend Yale." William's sigh is full of sorrow and shame. "So I ignored all the other stuff about Orson—the questionable business practices, the way he treats ghosts."

"The fact he's swallowing them?"

"Yeah. That." William rubs his eyes with so much force, it makes me wince. "He's world-class, right? I figured he knew what he was doing. And I thought—at last, I can prove to my father that I'm not a loser."

"Oh, William, you're not—"

"Don't say it." He holds up both hands to silence me. "I spent all night thinking that everything I do here, everything that works, I learned from my stepdad. From talking to the management to checking in on my ghosts. He always says: 'If you take care of your people, they'll take care of you.'"

Or ghosts, as the case may be.

"Your ghosts love you." I have my doubts about keeping them confined, but last night made one thing clear: they care so much for William that they don't mind all the restrictions. "They don't like Orson at all."

For the first time since I sat down, William cracks a smile. "I know." He sobers and takes a sip of coffee. "I'm not sure I like him all that much, either."

Well, that makes two of us.

His gaze goes to the cinnamon roll. I've made a valiant go at it, but half still remains. For the first time in twenty-four hours, my stomach feels full. I'm not sure I could eat another bite.

"Need some help?" he asks, a hint of pink streaking across his cheeks.

I push the plate toward him. "Go for it."

William inhales the rest of the roll and drowns each bite with a large gulp of coffee. Now that he's quiet again, I wonder if he knows that he's Orson's alter-ego. I wonder how the same man can be so different.

In your reality, when Orson turned twelve, he went to live with his father —assuming one considers being packed off prep schools and those faux military academies a nurturing family environment.

"And William?" With all my might, I strive not to subvocalize.

He graduated from Cedar Hills High School. Instead of Yale, he chose the University of Minnesota. Instead of Wall Street, he settled here and brought his friends from the association along with him.

I ponder that. How, despite material possessions, money, and power, Orson Yates is a man chasing after something he can never have.

As for William? Deep down, I suspect he knows that he's found what he needs. And when he forgets, he has people—and possibly ghosts—to remind him.

As I said earlier, my dear, humans are more powerful than they realize.

WE SPEND a solid hour in the booth. No one gives us the side-eye or tries to rush us out the door. When our server bustles by, she casts a grandmotherly look at William. The rest of the staff treats him with all the affection of a beloved regular, which I suspect he is.

In twos and threes, sprites and ghosts swoop in. They bounce expectantly in front of William, waiting for the day's orders.

"It's going to be warmer today," he says to a pair of sprites. "Why don't you guys go keep the fry cooks cool?"

They zip off and stream through the pass-through window. From the kitchen comes a grateful cheer. William raises a friendly hand in response.

And I think to myself: this is something Orson Yates would never, ever do.

I still haven't broached the real reason I came searching for William this morning. I keep waiting for the right moment or for the entity to give me a sign. Except for the whispered refrain of: *Humans are more powerful than they realize,* I get nothing.

Does this mean I should speak to William? Or does it mean keeping my mouth shut is the best course of action? The entity said this reality would work to neutralize my influence. So maybe what I'm about to try won't even work.

Again, I send my questions skyward, and again, no answer.

"Want to come with me while I do my rounds?" he asks. "No showing off today. I promise."

From beneath the booth comes the sound of ghostly laughter.

"Okay," he says, and that thousand-watt grin makes a brief appearance. "I'll probably show off a little."

I agree because maybe it will be easier to say what I need to while we're walking.

It isn't. After the first few stops, even the ghosts know I have something on my mind. They knock into my shoulders, swirl around my head, and have William scolding them.

"Don't," I say. "It's not their fault."

We've paused by the escalator and the Sunglass Hut kiosk. The same teen is working there, and she studiously ignores us. We're both so bedraggled that I don't blame her. From below us comes the splash of the fountain. The mist sparkles from sunlight and sprites.

"They know I need to tell you something." I pull in a deep breath. "But it's going to sound crazy."

"Crazier than the last twenty-four hours?"

"Possibly."

He arches an eyebrow and raises his palms skyward. "Try me."

So I do. I blurt it out because I see no other way of getting the information from my mouth to William's ears.

"In September, the Midwest Necromancer Association is going to send Darien after a powerful ghost."

William looks at me as if I've told him something he already knows.

"It's going to be really dangerous."

Again, he looks almost... bored with what I'm telling him.

"He's not going to—"

"Katy, do you know how the association operates?"

The words I planned to say dry up in my mouth. I'm not entirely sure how the association operates in my reality, never mind this one.

"Darien works on commission," William says. "He gets paid for each ghost he catches, with bonuses for the truly powerful ones. He has a quota, too. He's been working overtime, so when the baby comes, he can take a few months off to help Arianna."

"But he's not coming back." I can barely whisper these words. They taste sharp against my lips and tongue.

William laughs at this. He *laughs*. "That's the other thing. He's *Darien Armand*. He's legendary. He always makes it back."

I'm shaking my head, trying to explain, but it's like William refuses to hear what I'm saying to him.

"Last year, he came back so wrecked with necromancer flu, Arianna had to nurse him for weeks. But he came back. He always does."

"Not this time. I can't tell you how I know this, but I do." I don't know what to say to convince him. "I'm not making this up."

Maybe it's the tone of my voice, or the fact that I really am a horrible liar, but William falters. His brow clouds with a frown.

"Can you do something?" I ask—plead, really. "Maybe you could hire him?"

"Even if I could, I don't have any ready cash on hand to pay him what he's worth." He shakes his head, his expression full of chagrin. "The damn thing is, I did. On Friday. But Orson had me drop everything I could into an IPO, some coffee company or something."

Coffee company? In 1992? "Wait. *What?*"

"I know. Stupid, stupid. Star-something-or-other. I'll probably dump the stock in a few weeks."

"Starbucks?" The word is little more than a squeak.

"Yeah. That's it."

"You might want to hang on to that." I squeak these words as well.

He gives me a quizzical look. "O-kay."

"Believe me about Darien?"

William stares at the floor. A few ghosts hover around us,

somber and respectful. When he meets my gaze again, his eyes look so old and so sad.

"I do believe you. Even Darien would believe you. He knows that every time he goes out, he might not make it back. And if I could change that—" William breaks off, his attention caught by something.

I hear it, too. The buzzing starts low and ominous. The floor trembles just enough that I feel it along the soles of my feet. A wave of irrational guilt washes over me. Strange memories pop into my head, like the first time I brewed coffee on my own—without permission. The kitchen was a soggy, sticky mess of coffee grounds and sugar. I escaped with a scalding and a scolding.

William scowls at the noise. The ghosts around us zoom off. He calls after them, but they want no part of what's about to happen. The temperature drops a good ten degrees. It's like someone cranked up the air conditioning, and the chill steals my breath.

"Do you sense it?" Right now, all I'm picking up is something icy and angry. "Is it one of yours?"

"I don't have anything that powerful here," he says. "That's on purpose. It's too dangerous."

"Orson?" Really, I hate that I have to suggest it. But an attack ghost when you least expect it? That's totally him.

William tilts his chin toward the ceiling. He's not so much tasting the air as scrutinizing it. "I don't detect his signature, but ours are so familiar, it's sometimes hard to tell them apart."

I can't imagine why that is.

Across the way, a commotion has several customers streaming from a shop. Not just any shop, but a Gloria Jean's Coffee Shop. The storefront boasts a tower made from stacked bags of beans. From top to bottom, each bag splits open. Beans rain across the floor. The clattering starts low but grows so loud that I know it's getting a supernatural boost.

"Oh, no." William is shaking his head in disbelief. "No, no, no. This could ruin me." He turns to me, panic in his eyes. "I don't have time to call Darien or Manuel, but I don't know how I'm going to stop this."

"I'll help. I know a thing or two about catching ghosts."

"You'd help? After everything?"

"Absolutely."

Another crack echoes across the mall, the exact sound of a porcelain coffee pot hitting tile.

"Come on," I say, and I take his hand. "Let's go."

We dash forward, intent on the storefront and preventing more damage. It's only when I've cleared the threshold that I realize I should have run in the opposite direction.

CHAPTER 8

This is no ordinary ghost.

The infestation is full-on inside the shop. The floor is slick with ice. Frost covers the shelves and counters. Everything is so white and bright, my eyes hurt. I squint and shield them from the glare, but it doesn't do much good. The cashier is cowering in the cabinet beneath the register, not that I blame him. But this being isn't after him, or William, or anyone else at this mall.

It's after me.

A wave of icy frustration nearly knocks me over. As it is, I stumble backward into William. I wonder if this is what the entity meant by this reality neutralizing my influence. In desperation, I reach my thoughts skyward. Between the supernatural keening and William's shouting, I have no hope of hearing my own thoughts, never mind the entity's.

Now that I've made it inside the store, this ghost intends to shove me out of it. The otherworldly force gathers strength and then rams into me. I fly backward into another clever tower of beans. I land hard on the floor, an icy spike of pain radiating through my tailbone. A bag smacks my head and splits open, showering me with coffee beans.

Slowly, the being pushes and prods me from the store. My arms flail, my feet tangle and trip on all the scattered coffee beans. When the ghost corrals me by the sunglass kiosk, I have no choice but to stumble down the up escalator.

If this thing is intent on me, then it can't do any additional damage to the mall. In the distance, I catch William's shouts, but the words are indistinct. With an unceremonious thump, I land at the bottom of the escalator. On hands and knees, I survey the Crystal Court.

Can I lead this thing away from everyone? The sprites are trembling in the center of the fountain, and the water around them quivers. The way toward Hillside Diamonds is clear. No people. No strollers. No ghosts.

Is this thing helping me—helping this reality—in its own angry, frustrated way? Is *this* my way back, clumsy and messy as it is? I decide to take that chance.

We're halfway across the courtyard when a figure approaches at full speed. His strides are long, and the distance he covers with every step is truly impressive.

"Duck!" he calls out.

So I do, hands over my head. I peer through my arms and watch Darien Armand do what he does best.

He captures this thing on his first try, with his bare hands. He tucks and rolls and then springs to his feet, cupping an otherworldly fog. The containment field crackles around the spirit. With it, the roar of the supernatural cuts off—suddenly, like the rumble and crash and destruction never happened.

A few strands of hair are out of place, and his chest rises and falls a bit faster than normal. Otherwise, Darien Armand is as cool and suave as ever. I push to stand, feeling unkempt and grubby next to him.

The being swirls between his palms. Now that I know to look

for it, I can see layer after layer of containment field. With each pass, the field grows thicker. Darien remains unruffled by its futile attempts to break free.

But his expression is nothing but concerned. "Who would send a demon after you? Do you know?"

Well, yes. I *do* have a good idea who sent the demon, but I shake my head. Explaining that? Impossible.

Around us, the mall returns to normal. Children gather at the fountain's edge, and the sprites pick up performing their show without missing too many beats. William's cleaning crew trundles by. They float contentedly up the escalator. Although, really? Do ghosts need to take the escalator? I follow their progress to the top, where William is waiting for them. He gives me a smile and a thumbs-up.

"This is very odd." Darien peers at the demon still caught between his palms. "It clearly knows you, although I can't sense how."

I lean closer to the swirling mass of frustrated demon. It sparks an angry green and yellow. Images flash through my mind—quick and unrelenting. Fire in the old barn. A particularly nasty eradication in the boys' locker room at Springside High School. The silver, industrial-sized coffee machine at the Coffee Depot erupting like a volcano.

I press my palm against the containment field, my heart thudding so hard it might bruise my ribcage. I know what it is that Orson Yates has done, and I will never forgive him for it.

The demon caught between Darien's palms is my grandmother.

FIVE MINUTES LATER, William finds us, Darien still cupping what was once my grandmother's ghost, me with a hand against the containment field.

My thoughts spin. Is this why she vanished? I'd always hoped she left to find my grandfather. But what if Orson—or more likely Carter—caught her first? She buzzes now as if trying to convey the tale, but these images are fragmented and chaotic.

"Katy?" Both William's voice and the hand he places on my shoulder are soft. "Are you okay? What is it?"

I want to explain but can't muster the words. Perhaps he sees the devastation on my face because his own expression shifts, and a hint of comprehension lights his eyes. His gaze goes from me to Darien, to the demon, and back again. He's about to speak when Arianna breaks into our little group.

"Darien?" Her expression is washed in worry and fear. "I can't find Nigel."

"Where did you last see him?" His shoulders tense, and he scans the courtyard with a sharp gaze.

"Here, with the other children." She points toward the fountain. "He was watching the show with Prescott."

Darien has the presence of mind not to unleash a demon into the mall. He tugs a baggie from his back pocket, slips my grandmother inside, and reinforces the containment field—all while conferring with Edie and Manuel.

But it's William who springs into action. He whistles, and seconds later, six ghosts line up before him. These are the composed sorts of ghosts who seldom, if ever, play pranks.

"This is not a drill," he tells them. "You know Nigel. Alert the ghosts at the doors and apprehend anyone who might try to leave with or harm him."

They stream off, full of purpose and determination. Their departure starts a chain reaction. More ghosts join the search while the sprites keep the kids around the fountain calm and entertained.

"We'll search, too," William tells Arianna. "And call security, but we'll find him. I promise."

In the confusion and commotion, I step back from the group until I'm certain no one can hear me. I tip my gaze skyward, squint against the brightness of the skylights, and whisper.

"Can you tell me who took Nigel?"

I can tell you it's the same person who unleashed your grandmother's demon.

"Would he trade? Me for Nigel?"

I believe that's his plan.

"Show me where?"

I wait for that psychic nudge. Instead, the trio of sprites drifts toward me. They beckon with those tiny wisps of hands. With a glance backward, I follow. No one notices.

That's exactly how I want it.

ONCE AGAIN, the sprites lead me down the back hallway. We pass several doorways, including the one for the employee lounge. A couple of security guards race past us, walkie-talkies buzzing, shoes clattering against the floor. I want to tell them they're headed the wrong way, except I don't think their sort of reinforcement will help.

The sprites halt outside the back entrance to Hillside Diamonds. Something tickles the back of my mind, something Arianna said about Orson owning the business.

Of course. A jewelry store has safes—and lots of them, each with compartments perfect for storing ghosts. Add in combination locks and containment fields? The ghosts aren't getting out, and other necromancers aren't getting in. It's perfectly diabolical and perfectly Orson.

I pause outside the door. I don't want to blunder inside, although that's what I've come here to do. Me for Nigel. Even if I'm hesitating, Orson knows I'll walk through this door. I reach for the knob, but before my fingertips can graze the handle, the door creaks open of its own volition.

Like I said. Orson's expecting me.

The sprites zoom off—not that I blame them. I'd zoom too if I could. Fluorescent lights hiss and buzz over my head, every other bank shut off, so the space is shrouded in semi-darkness. The hum of the otherworldly is present but suppressed. Everything from demons to attack ghosts to trembling sprites competes for my attention. The existence of so many ghosts in one place thickens the air. I feel the cold of it against my eyes and in the back of my throat.

I knew walking in that Orson had the upper hand. Now I consider whether I'll make it out alive. That was probably Orson's plan to begin with, but it doesn't mean I have to go down without a fight.

Me for Nigel. I pull in a breath. I can do this.

"Are you trying to scare me?" I call out. "Because I'm not really scared of ghosts."

"Consider, Ms. Lindstrom, that maybe you should be."

"I don't see a reason to start now."

"No." A condescending chuckle precedes Orson into the hallway. He emerges from an office, keeping the door ajar, hand on its knob. "I imagine you wouldn't."

"Where's Nigel?"

"Safe."

"Let him go. He's just a child."

"He's a child now. In a decade or two? He becomes a rival." Orson shrugs, the movement casual and cavalier. "Hindsight—or is it foresight?—being what it is, I'm not sure I see a reason for keeping him around."

"You know I won't cooperate if you hurt him."

Orson must know this. He must.

"You have much to lose," he says.

"No, I don't. Not really."

There's only so much hurt he can inflict on me. In some other reality, he's already killed me. I wonder if he senses that. I wonder if, all along, he was meant to. I think of the accident that killed my parents—that long plunge into the ravine. I was in the car, too. I should've died that day. If not for the entity, I would have.

So maybe this is how it always ends between Orson and me.

"I need you to do something for me," he says.

Yeah, like that's happening.

"I need you to break your pact with the entity."

The entity? Orson knows? He knows it's here? My breath catches in my throat. Panic churns in my stomach. I try to school my face, but it's a useless gesture. Really, I am *such* a terrible liar.

"You apparently still have a pact." He rolls his eyes toward the ceiling as if this is the most ridiculous thing he's heard in a while. "And if you could invoke the entity, you would have already. I know the rules as well as it does. It can't help you here. No one can."

Someone might. William has soured on his so-called uncle, and I'd hate to see Darien's wrath once he finds out Orson is the one who kidnapped Nigel.

But Orson's shaking his head like he knows what I'm thinking. "My dear girl, I'm the one who alerted mall security. Plus, there's video footage of you, stumbling around the mall, muttering to yourself, scaring customers."

"I haven't scared anyone."

"Let me paint a picture for you. A young homeless woman with no ID in her possession and no one to vouch for her? And then there's the mess you left in the employee lounge." Orson tsks like I'm a naughty child.

"I didn't leave a mess!"

From deep within the store comes a malicious, otherworldly laugh. The sound shakes my bones and causes my heart to tremble.

"My mistake." Orson shoots the cuffs of his dress shirt past the sleeves of his suit coat. "That must have been my attack ghosts." He raises an eyebrow. "Not that anyone will believe otherwise."

"I don't care what you do to me." Okay, that's a lie. I do care.

Orson probably knows this. "But I'm not breaking any pacts or cooperating in any way until you let go of Nigel."

Knocking and clattering come from the office. The doorknob rattles in Orson's grip, and his eyes go wide. In a burst of supernatural flurry, the door flies open and Nigel comes racing out. He kicks Orson in the shin before flying straight at me. I catch him, and his sudden weight has me stumbling backward and careening into the wall.

"The ghosts hate you!" Nigel screams at Orson. "Hate you! They're going to tell William, and so am I."

Within seconds, an otherworldly barrier blocks us from Orson—not that it will do much good. It's mostly composed of sprites and ghosts of the gentle, non-threatening variety. But they gather around us, whisk the tears from Nigel's cheeks, and give my shoulders encouraging pats.

"Would you look at that." Orson's hand goes to his suit coat pocket, and I know he's not reaching for a handkerchief or even an attack ghost, but for something else, something with bullets. "I've apprehended the kidnapper."

I open my mouth to protest, but nothing comes out. Nigel's brow crinkles in a little-boy frown.

"Set the boy down." Orson's voice is as smooth as glass. "It would be a shame if I had to shoot both of you."

Nigel clings to me tighter, his arms locking around my neck, legs around my waist. My mind scrambles. Maybe *this* was Orson's plan. Why force me to break the pact when he can just shoot me? I'm assuming that's how it works. No more necromancer, no more pact?

I can't use Nigel as a human shield. I also can't peel him off of me—literally. From the supernatural static in the air, I suspect he's getting some ghostly assistance. Orson may want to consider whether four-year-old Nigel is already a rival.

"Put. The boy. Down."

Static crackles the air. These ghosts may not be strong, but they're loyal and determined, and reinforcements continue to slip in from under the doorway and the ventilation system. The barrier between us expands until the entire hallway glimmers.

It still isn't bulletproof.

But the shimmer begins to roil, starting at my feet. These ghosts do hate Orson. The sparkle in the air vibrates with hostility. These are the ghosts Orson routinely catches (probably because they're easy to catch) and swallows. These are the ghosts forced to take him back and forth between realities.

And these ghosts? They're done.

For a moment, hope fills me. Feathery tendrils of an escape plan infiltrate my mind. The ghosts will rush Orson. I will rush Nigel out the back doorway. I hold my breath, legs braced to run.

Before I can move, William stumbles into the hallway.

CHAPTER 9

Nigel gives me a quick squeeze before throwing himself at William. Our relief and joy mix with that of the other-worldly. It's almost a party.

Except Orson is still here. Except, after William sends Nigel off with an escort of ghosts, he doesn't turn to take my hand. He doesn't lead me away from his uncle. He stands there in the hall-way, blocking the exit. His features are set, eyes dull.

I'm more boxed in than ever.

I try anyway. "William?" My voice is soft and tentative. The ghosts that remain in this space quiver as if they, too, know some-thing's wrong.

He won't meet my gaze. "I'm sorry, Katy."

"Well done, my boy." Orson claps his hands together. "Well done." He turns toward me, hand outstretched in invitation. "Shall we proceed, then? Go on. Break the pact."

"Why don't you just shoot me?"

"Because that would be messy." He raises a finger as if to hold me in place. "But still an option. So don't get any ideas."

"You said that she wouldn't be hurt, that we'd have her

committed." William focuses on me. "It will just be for a few years, and then they'll let you out, I'm sure."

Committed? As in, some sort of asylum? No doubt that would neutralize my influence on this reality.

"I'll be waiting for you," William adds. "I'll take care of you. I promise."

"But only if she breaks the pact," Orson says, his voice sharper now.

"He's not your uncle," I tell William.

Nothing. Not even an eye twitch.

Perhaps William knows. Maybe he's always known. My mind conjures up that despondent young man picking at his food in the Happy Chef. I can't reconcile that image with the William who stands across from me now.

"Do you sense all the ghosts here, Ms. Lindstrom?" Orson spreads his arms out wide. "I can swallow them all down, step through to the other side, and unleash them on everyone there. You would not believe the number of people assembled, trying to rescue you. Trust me, all your friends are there, even those who shouldn't be."

On the other side, all these ghosts will be demons. It was hard enough to catch and contain one. An entire army of them? I can't do that to the people I love. The carnage plays out before my eyes: Nigel succumbing, Belinda terrorized. Is Sadie there too? And what about Malcolm?

Well, there's always that gun in Orson's pocket.

"I'll break the pact." I don't see any other option. My only hope is that Orson can't hold the entity. What he plans to do, I'm not sure. He'll need a surrogate. I cast a quick glance at William and wonder if I have my answer.

"Go on," Orson prompts.

I manage a shrug. "I don't know how."

Orson releases a sigh filled with disdain. "How is it you call yourself a necromancer?"

"I've never called myself a necromancer."

"Hail the entity. It's been at your beck and call this whole time. I'm sure it will tell you."

I'm not. It's been awfully quiet these last several minutes. Again, I wonder if it can't interfere, or it simply won't. But I tip my chin toward the ceiling and speak.

"We have a small problem."

No, my dear. You have a problem, and it isn't small in the least.

At the sound of the entity's voice, William's eyes go huge. He braces a hand against the doorframe to steady himself. Even Orson falters, although he recovers quickly.

"You no doubt are growing bored," Orson says to the entity, his own chin tipped upward, the tendons of his neck pronounced. "What with Katy as your necromancer."

I could use a little fun.

"You won't be able to hold it," I say.

For all his confidence, Orson is far too insubstantial. The valleys beneath his cheekbones are steep, and the gap between his shirt collar and his neck makes him look as if he's shrinking in on himself.

"I don't have plans to," he says.

I turn to William. "It will burn through you. If your desire isn't pure enough, you'll be gone in minutes, maybe less."

A year ago, I watched the entity turn a necromancer into ash in less than thirty seconds. Half an hour ago, I would've sworn William had a pure desire—his ghosts, and Cedar Hills, and what he's trying to build here in the mall. Now?

Now I'm wondering if I've gotten everything wrong from the very start.

"Enough," Orson says, and his voice is like a whip. "Break the pact."

I'm about to ask how—again—when the entity intercedes.

At the moment, our exchanges are equitable. All you need to do is say my name and that you release me from our pact.

The entity's voice is clipped and businesslike, devoid of the warmth and feeling from our earlier exchanges. No indication that it even cares whether I break the pact, no ounce of regret.

I wonder if I've gotten this wrong, too.

"Momalcurkan, I release you from our pact."

My voice doesn't quaver, but the words hurt more than I think they should. They're a scrape against my throat. I shut my eyes and wait. Nothing. No fanfare. No clap of thunder.

Apparently, there isn't a ceremony.

Orson rubs his hands together, full of triumph. "Well, my boy, would you like to do the honors, or should I?"

William demurs with a slight shake of his head, eyes downcast. "I think you should."

"Very well. But be ready to catch it when it appears."

"It could be a lava monster," I warn, but no one's listening to me.

Orson spreads his arms wide as if greeting an old friend. There's nothing but elation in his features. He's won, and he knows it. "Momalcurkan."

I wait, cringing inwardly, pulse thrumming. Whatever happens next, it won't be what any of us expects. I understand the entity well enough to know that. The air is cool from the otherworldly but devoid of the stale static that so often announces the entity's presence.

The space is hushed. Not even the attack ghosts are grumbling.

"Momalcurkan," Orson tries again, an impatient edge to his voice.

Really? It's a free agent now. Pissing it off is the last thing any of us should do.

Orson turns to William. "You try, my boy."

William blanches, and his Adam's apple bobs, once, twice. He blows out a breath and then, barely audible, says, "Momalcurkan."

A few ethereal gripes come from Orson's trapped ghosts, but I detect no other supernatural manifestation. The entity's presence isn't something any of us would miss.

Orson whirls on me. "What have you done?"

Only your bidding. Under duress, I might add.

"Then show yourself!" Orson shouts the command at the ceiling.

The reverberation starts low. The vibration runs along the floor until the entire office space quakes. On the wall, pictures and certificates rattle in their frames and spindly cracks spread across the glass. The sound is long and sustained, but instead of wrath, all I taste in the air is mirth.

Oh, my. That was fun. Wasn't that fun, my dear?

My mouth is so dry, I can't squeak out an answer, not that I have one. I direct a thousand questions toward the sky, but the entity ignores them all.

"What's the meaning of this?" Orson demands.

And here I thought you knew the rules as well as I. Apparently not. Pity, that.

"Rules?" I venture, since both Orson and William are silent.

It's rude not to address someone by their name.

"But—" Orson begins.

I do not go by Momalcurkan in this reality. Really, do you think I'd make it easy on humanity? Where's the fun in that?

Oh, yes, this thing is *all* about fun.

"Your name." Orson stares at the ceiling, his expression a mask of disbelief.

Yes, of course. My name. Once you learn it, you can invoke me. Otherwise, I'll come and go as I please. I'm not a dog on a leash, after all.

A cunning expression lights Orson's eyes. He glances around and then beckons to William.

And it's not something the ghosts here know. They are wisely incurious that way.

Above our heads, the acoustic tiles bubble with a hint of lava. William stares, slack-jawed. Orson is like a blank canvas.

You might try Siberia. Lake Baikal, to be precise. There's an old crone there who holds the secret to my name. Although I warn you, she's as tough and crafty as Baba Yaga herself.

The lava simmers with delight. Now the entity is just taunting Orson—and having a great deal of fun in doing so.

Didn't I say I could use a little fun, my dear?

Well, yes. Yes, it did.

Maybe it's a premonition that has me lowering my gaze. I catch Orson's eyes, and they're devoid of everything but a deep, lingering hatred. His hand returns to his suit coat pocket. I sense the shift in his stance, but I have nowhere to run. To my back? A solid wall. To my left, William blocks the way out. In front of me?

Orson with a gun.

Yes, I think.

This *is* how it ends.

<h1 style="text-align:center">CHAPTER 10</h1>

What happens next comes with the stench of gunpowder and a burst of the supernatural.

Head down, William plows into Orson, catching him around the waist. The report of the gunshot echoes in the enclosed space. My ears ring in the aftermath. Both William and Orson are shouting, but their words are murky.

My left shoulder throbs as if I've been stung by a wasp. I clamp a hand on the spot, and it comes away red. For a too-long moment, I stand there staring at my bloody palm.

The hallway fills with ghosts. Several come to my aid, whirling around my neck, consoling me, others flattening themselves against the wound, slowing the flow of blood. Perhaps it's the chill that brings me back to myself. I inspect my shoulder—just a graze —and the hole in the wall behind me.

William rolls on the floor with Orson. They tumble my way, and I leap over their flailing arms. Orson still grips the gun. At first, I can't tell why he hasn't fired again, even accidentally. Then I see the otherworldly mass congeal around his fist. Orson's hand is in a full-on ghost infestation. His fingers sprout hoarfrost so thick they look like zombie claws.

"Katy! Run!" William's voice is ragged, full of pain and apology.

The ghosts around me poke and prod and urge me not out the back but toward the front of the store, where I saw Orson vanish yesterday. I turn—foolishly, I know—to check on William. I can't stay, but I simply can't leave him to fight Orson alone, either.

That's when Orson jerks his arm from William's grasp. Orson's hand is an icy fist, the gun itself completely frosted over. But he brings it down hard on William's temple.

Orson scrambles to his feet and runs not toward me but toward the office. He slams the door, and the lock clicks. The wood ices over immediately. I can't tell if the ghosts are keeping him in or us out. Considering the supernatural frenzy around the door, it could be both.

I rush to William's side. He's pushing to sit with one hand while the other probes the bump on his forehead.

"Are you okay?" I take a knee and try to inspect the wound.

"Am I okay?" He gives me a look. "Jesus, Katy, he *shot* you."

Well, it's not like it's the first time.

"I had to pretend," he adds, "to get close to you and Nigel—"

"I know." Or at least I know it now, here in the aftermath. I swallow back the rush of guilt that had me doubting him. "Is Nigel—?"

"Already back with Arianna and Darien."

What sounds like preternatural throat-clearing makes the floor tremble beneath us.

My dear, now would be an excellent time to return to your own reality.

Another rush of guilt floods me. I doubted the entity too. I want to speak, push an apology from my mouth, but a gentle, supernatural *shh* washes it away.

All part of the plan.

Before I can thank the entity, a rumble comes from behind the closed office door. William's eyes narrow. In that instant, he looks so canny and crafty that the resemblance to Orson is undeniable. He stumbles to his feet, wobbles a bit, and then takes my hand.

"This way." He tugs me down the hall.

Hillside Diamonds is still closed. The security gate is down, and partitions block the view to the courtyard. Sunshine from the skylights streams through the cracks, making the dust motes and the ghosts sparkle. The air around us wavers, and I feel that roll of the floor beneath my feet.

"Can you sense that?" I ask him.

"Probably not like you do, but yeah."

A cold, musty odor and the echo of footfalls compete with the splash and cheer of the fountain. With each step, William's reality recedes, and mine reaches out. The tug is like a gentle arm around my waist, a solicitous hand at my elbow.

"Have you ever been through?" I ask.

"A couple of times, mainly to establish the visible ward." His expression turns wry. "Orson tried to convince me it was the apocalypse."

"It was just abandoned." When I catch his dour expression, I add, "That doesn't mean it will happen here."

"Maybe not." His words and his mouth are grim.

I know what it's like to believe your world is one way only to discover it's far, far different than you imagined. But if a mall ever had a chance to be more than a space filled with conspicuous consumption, it's this one.

"You can still build your community," I say. "If anyone can, it will be you."

"I'm so sorry, Katy. I'm sorry Orson tried to trap you here, and I'm really sorry you have to go, even though it's the right thing." He musters a grin—not the thousand-watt one, but a smile nevertheless, one filled with tenderness. "But I'm not sorry I got to meet you."

"I'm not sorry about that either." On impulse, I rise up on tiptoes and kiss his cheek.

Despite the dim light, I catch the hint of pink as it races across his face.

William leads me to the display cases and has me step in front of him. With hands on my shoulders, he first turns me one way and then a few inches the other.

"Do you see the shimmer?" he asks. "It flickers in and out, but you should be able to see the other side."

In the space beyond the display cases, I see fuzzy outlines—an empty fountain, a defunct elevator. Figures cross the courtyard. They look more like shadows than people, and their voices are muted and distorted. My name echoes as if someone is shouting through a long tunnel.

"How do I get back?"

"How did you get here?"

"I was running straight for Hillside Diamonds." I crane my neck to peer at William. "I was trying to get rid of a demon."

"That's the trick. Run hard and fast and catch it at the right moment. The demon helped, but you don't need one. Wait until the other side looks clear, and then go for it."

William steps back to give me room.

Hands on thighs, I brace, ready to run. My gaze never leaves the flicker and waver of where one reality meets the other. Then the shadows resolve themselves—the decrepit escalators, the dry fountain, the grimy benches. That cold, musty smell invades my mouth, but I don't care, because now I can see people.

I see Malcolm.

A cry catches in my throat, and he spins as if he's heard me.

"Now!" William calls out.

I sprint forward, casting a quick burst of gratitude skyward. There's no time to thank the entity properly. I think—I hope—it understands. When I feel that psychic nudge, I believe it does. Except it's more of a tug backward.

The push knocks me off my stride. My arms windmill, and I careen forward. A wall of ghosts shoots up in front of me, but not even that can stop my momentum. I have enough time to raise my arms to protect my head.

Then I crash straight into a containment field.

I'VE WITNESSED a couple of full-on ghost infestations inside human beings. The first was Nigel's. It was at the Lasting Rest Mausoleum, right before he gave up all the ghosts for good. And, of course, last year, Malcolm swallowed all the ghosts in Springside. Together, they traveled to the plane of existence where I was with the entity as its willing sacrifice. I've even swallowed ghosts myself in yet another rescue attempt that involved both Malcolm and the entity.

I've never seen one quite like this.

Maybe it's because, along with ghosts, Orson has swallowed demons. He's encased in frost. Everything about him—his hair, his suit, his shoes—is an icy gray. Cracks run along the surface of his skin, forming a complicated, ever-branching network of lines. He looks both tremendously powerful and like he might disintegrate at any moment.

I use the counter to haul myself up, slowly, my eyes never leaving Orson. I scan the space behind him, but I don't see William. I don't dare glance away to check for Malcolm.

At first, I don't know what it is Orson plans to do. He doesn't speak. I don't think he can, not without risking a ghost slipping from his mouth. The multitude of them is reflected in his eyes. I've never been afraid of ghosts, but the sight of so many trapped souls sends a chill through me. It's eerie and disturbing, and the urge to help them nearly overwhelms me. The demons are giving him strength, but the garden-variety ghosts and sprites are fighting for a way out.

Then I remember Orson's threat.

The jolt that gives my heart has me peering over my shoulder, risking a look.

Nearly everyone I love is on the other side. Once Orson steps through, every single ghost inside him becomes a demon. How many are there? Fifty? A hundred? Does it matter?

The containment field to my back is solid, but it's of Orson's own making. He can demolish it, but I certainly can't. I ease around the display case anyway, putting distance between myself and Orson. The demonic light in his eyes tells me it's a useless gesture.

Then his expression shifts, into something that's not so much fear, but amazement. He stares just past my shoulder, and his gaze is so intense, I find myself turning and looking as well.

There, in the other reality, his legs stretching, his arms pumping, is Malcolm. I think to myself: I will always run to Malcolm Armand. But when I can't?

He'll run to me.

I shout, trying to warn him about the containment field. Certainly, he'll crash into it the way I did. Either he can't hear me or he simply doesn't care. His stride never falters. Malcolm once told me he ran both cross-country and track in high school, that he was co-captain of the varsity team during his senior year.

Some instinct must tell him he's close. He hits the mark and then leaps. I don't know if he ever competed in the long jump, but he knows how. The momentum pushes him through the air, straight for me, straight for the containment field.

At the last second, he covers his head with his arms.

Then Malcolm Armand, my business partner, my friend, my fiancé, destroys Orson's containment field. No fissures. No cracks. One moment, the shield is in place. The next, it evaporates.

With a thud, Malcolm lands next to me. He brings with him the odor of must and sweat. Beneath that, I catch his Ivory soap and nutmeg scent. My heart lurches. His arms wrap around mine, his breath ragged and warm. For the first time in what seems like forever, everything feels right. Everything feels like home.

"Katy."

And my name sounds like a prayer.

A muted cheer comes from inside Orson. How he maintains his grip on all the ghosts and demons, I'm not sure. It's possible that all this time, I've underestimated his ability as a necromancer. No one else could hold on like he is, even now, with half the beings inside him fighting to get out.

Malcolm adjusts his grip, securing his arms tighter around me, as if he's afraid this reality will pull me away once again. After a quick brush of his lips against my cheek, he lifts his chin and stares down Orson.

"Do you know how many people—how many necromancers—hate you? Can you count the number of people you've screwed over as chairman of the Midwest Necromancer Association?"

Orson remains silent. Again, I'm pretty sure he can't speak. And really? I don't miss the sound of his voice.

"Care to take a guess?" Malcolm says. "Care to guess how many people hate you but love and respect Katy? Because they're all there on the other side."

"I don't know that many necromancers," I say.

"Sure you do." And now, Malcolm sounds almost jocular, like he's enjoying this immensely. "Why, there's Reginald Weaver. And of course you know my father. Prem flew all the way from Paris. True, you haven't met Prescott's brothers and sisters or his father, but they're all here. I invited them to the wedding. Hope you don't mind."

I give a numb sort of nod because I simply don't have words.

"And then there's that contingent from the east coast."

Orson hasn't faltered during this, but now he plants a hand on the doorframe as if he needs strength to stand.

"Something about a kingmaker and revenge," Malcolm adds. "I didn't get the whole story, but apparently, no one liked your father that much, either."

Orson takes one step back and then another. All at once, he halts as if something is blocking his way.

That's when I see the iridescent outline of a second containment field.

Behind it stands William, arms crossed over his chest, bathed in an ethereal glow from more ghosts than I can count. They're so thick, I can't see the hallway behind him. Nothing but ghost after ghost after ghost. Orson palms the barrier as if he can find a fracture to exploit.

"I'm sorry," William says, sounding anything but. "There's only room for one Orson Yates in this reality." His gaze locks on not his so-called uncle but on Malcolm. "Take care of her," he adds, his voice softer now.

Malcolm gives a single terse nod.

Orson turns again, surveying first one reality and then another. Behind all the trapped souls is the crafty, cunning look I know so well. He's weighing his options. That much is clear. I see the moment he decides on ours. Really, he doesn't have much of a choice.

He shoots the cuffs of his dress shirt past the sleeves of his jacket and then brushes away some imaginary lint. I want to roll my eyes, but I don't dare look away.

"Will we be able to stop him?" I whisper to Malcolm.

"With everyone on the other side? Absolutely."

"The demons will want to pull him through," I say, "But here's the thing. All the ghosts inside him now? They'll become demons on our side."

"Oh." The word emerges with a long breath. In it, I hear Malcolm's comprehension. He shifts his stance and clenches his jaw. His fingers tighten on my forearms.

Decided, determined, Orson musters that creepy, triumphant smile and releases his hold on the doorframe. He takes a step forward and then another, his pace as easy and graceful as if he were merely strolling from the back of the store to serve a customer.

"If we can delay him, would that give the others a chance?" I ask.

"Yeah. Possibly." Malcolm clutches me close, and I'm flush against his chest. "I hate the idea of losing you again."

"You've never lost me. No matter where I am, I'll always be yours."

"Then let's do this." He brushes my cheek with another kiss before positioning us in the opening between the display counters.

Orson remains unperturbed by all of this. Between the force of the demons who want to return to our reality and the ones that will become demons once he arrives, his chances are more than good. None of the necromancers on the other side are expecting to fight demons in addition to Orson. I think of how quickly that one demon drained Prescott—and it was contained. I think of how well Orson motivates and trains ghosts.

He could win this. Maybe he already has.

Before Orson can take another step, an angry buzzing fills the space. The noise is odd and out of place. Every last ghost is either inside Orson or behind William's containment field. The sound is filled with admonishment and reminds me of when my grandmother would chastise sprites—not that it ever did any good.

My grandmother.

My breath catches in my throat, and I work to track the persistent and irritated hum.

It's her. It must be. I don't know how she escaped Darien's containment field, but if any demon could, it would be hers. Then she zips by, lightning quick. She ruffles Malcolm's hair and plants a cold, stinging kiss on my cheek.

She whirls about, gathering speed, and her fury is like a tornado. Then she launches herself straight for Orson, aiming not for his mouth, but his eye. She strikes him so hard, a spray of blood splatters his face, the red stark against his frozen skin.

Orson cries out. The moment he opens his mouth, my grandmother dives inside.

DURING HER LIFE—AND afterlife—my grandmother has tipped the balance more than once. She always knew when to pour a fresh cup or what blend from the Coffee Depot a particular ghost might like. She helped Nigel release all the ghosts inside him. She helped me rescue Malcolm.

Can she make a difference now?

Orson staggers, but he hangs on. It's a tenuous grasp—this is clear. Despite the full-on infestation, sweat sprouts along his brow. The drops freeze within seconds, sharp and unforgiving. In moments, his entire forehead is bathed in a watery pink.

The cracks along his skin grow deeper and wider. Instead of blood, something else oozes from the fractures, something that looks like tar.

Malcolm swears softly, and he sounds as spellbound as I feel. I can't look away. I owe my grandmother that. I will witness her final battle with Orson Yates, the man responsible for her daughter's—my mother's—death.

The room around us creaks and groans. The glass in the display cases trembles, and I'm afraid it might splinter. The air swirls, bringing with it a cacophony of sights and sounds. I catch a whiff of Orange Julius and strains of "The Girl From Ipanema." Lights flash from bright and unrelenting to gray and dim. One instant, the courtyard gleams. The next, it languishes under a decade's worth of grime.

In all of this, Malcolm holds on to me. Orson lifts a foot to take another step, but he's unable to set it back down. He remains there, immobile, like a grotesque statue from a house of horrors. The floor rolls beneath us before the shaking starts in earnest.

Malcolm stumbles, and I shoot out a hand to steady us against the display case. The trembling continues. But instead of spreading across the space, the shaking concentrates on Orson. His entire body quivers, slowly at first, then faster and faster until his features are nothing but a blur.

The air is viscous. Color leaches from everything until the world is ashen. Malcolm raises his chin, his entire being on high alert. Then he drops to the floor, taking me with him. He cocoons me in his arms, his body covering mine, shielding me from any fallout.

Then, before our eyes, Orson Yates shatters.

He is glass. He is crystal. He is ice. No blood, no body parts, nothing but slivers of the thinnest icicles. En masse, the tiny shards arrow into the air, peppering the ceiling, dislodging acoustic tiles, blasting the cabinets.

The storefront quakes. Glass in the display cases cracks before cabinets teeter and fall. Support beams moan with so much force, they sound alive and in pain. Malcolm scoots us to the only shelter he can find.

It isn't much, but we hunker down behind the cash register. He whispers my name—just once—and again, it sounds like a prayer.

Then the world caves in. Malcolm cries out and is suddenly, awfully, silent.

My heart must stop. After all of that, it simply must. Instead, it races in time with a single thought searing my mind.

No, no, no, no, no.

My throat aches, as if I'm shouting the words rather than merely thinking them. I try to call Malcolm's name, but I can't. I try to gauge his breathing, but I can't do that, either. The space is too dark, too clouded with debris and dust. It coats the back of my throat, chokes me. My lungs feel heavy and clogged.

Be alive. Please. Be alive.

I chant this over and over. All the while, dust settles heavy and thick against my face, weighs down my eyelashes. All I want is for Malcolm to be alive.

But he doesn't move. His chest doesn't rise and fall. He doesn't whisper my name. I don't know where I'm sending this prayer, only that I'm sending it outward, into the universe, with all my might. I'm sending it in hopes someone might hear.

Please let him live. Please.

It's my last thought before the darkness takes me as well.

CHAPTER 11

My limbs ache, and my temples throb, but the pain is more psychic than physical. Stabs along my left shoulder remind me that, yes, Orson Yates did shoot me. The sensations wash over me, harsh and quick and unrelenting. Then what feels like a soothing balm coats everything—my limbs, my face, even the roaring ache inside my head. I can't tell if I've opened my eyes or not. It's the same either way.

The air is stuffy. Despite the dark, the space feels enclosed. I reach out a hand, let it travel along a series of what feels like splintered lumber and jagged rocks. Then I encounter something else.

The warm, solid form of Malcolm.

A cry catches on the dust in my throat. With careful fingertips, I skim his shoulders, his head, find the pulse in his throat and the gentle rise and fall of his chest. Then I cry for real. I sob long and hard until I'm gasping for breath. He's alive, and that's all that matters.

He's alive.

"Don't... don't cry." His voice is rough, barely a murmur.

"Malcolm?"

"I'm here. Maybe a little broken, but here."

"Where are you hurt?"

"Everywhere? But my legs, mostly." He tries to move, and a groan echoes in the dark. "I think something fell on them."

I imagine it's more than his legs, and when he speaks again, I'm positive.

"I can't move them."

I try not to read too much into that—try and fail. He's here. He's alive. For the moment, that's enough.

"Are you—" He breaks off, a cough racking him. "Are you okay?"

"I think so. Nothing's broken, at least."

I shift ever so slightly, and a burst of pain catches me off guard. This time, sensation wraps around my ribcage. I yelp, which has Malcolm scrambling, although he doesn't get very far. He swears.

"Katy—"

"Shh." I hush him and then shift so I can reach his forehead and stroke the grime and worry from his brow. "Don't try to move. I'm here. We're together."

"I thought I'd lost you. When you vanished, we had no idea what had happened. I think we all went a little crazy. Both Prescott and Nigel contacted every necromancer they know and called in every last favor."

The information makes my head swim. "For me?"

"Of course for you, Katy. Don't you—?" He breaks off and coughs again. "Don't you know how much you mean to all of us?"

My throat tightens from more than the dust in the air. I want to take a deep breath but can't.

"That was pretty clever," Malcolm continues. "Sending us that bit of graffiti."

"I did it for me, so I could find where I landed. I totally freaked when it vanished."

"Yeah. We kind of freaked when the heart I drew disappeared."

He shifts ever so slightly. "That's when I knew we could get you back."

"What happened?"

Slowly, Malcolm relates the tale of how necromancers started arriving. Friends and allies first—Reginald Weaver, Prescott's brothers and sisters and his father, then Prem from Paris, and Darien from Marrakesh.

"It was a good thing he was there and not somewhere in the middle of the Sahara or the Falklands."

I'm about to say: *Your father doesn't like me.* Then I think of the other reality, the other Darien, and wonder how true that is.

"Then, random necromancers started showing up," Malcolm continues.

"How did they—?"

"Ghosts. I mean, we sent plenty, but I'm telling you, all the ghosts in Springside wanted you back too, so they went off on their own and found every last necromancer they could."

"Did my message make it through? About Orson?"

"Yeah, it did. We all went crazy trying to find him. Chaucer had a lead on him, but then it was like he simply vanished."

Probably because he slipped back through to the other side. A shiver of a thought chases along my spine. Was Orson in the mall with me? All night long? No. The ghosts—not to mention the entity—would've alerted me. The ghosts, and the entity, kept me safe. But where Orson went?

We'll probably never know.

"And then, like magic," Malcolm says, "the east coast necromancers started showing up."

"How'd they get here so fast?"

"Katy, these are necromancers. If they don't already own a private jet, they can charter one." Malcolm half-chuckles, half-coughs. "One guy even landed his Cessna in the parking lot."

Well, that can't be legal.

"But this is good, right?" Hope builds in my chest, and I take that deep breath I couldn't manage before. "They can dig us out of here?"

"I don't think—"

"What?"

"I don't think we're getting out of here." He shifts again. Loose debris clatters, the sound like rainfall. "Actually, I'm not sure we're still here."

"Here?"

"Alive."

I touch my arms, my nose, press a palm against my chest, and then Malcolm's. I feel alive, and so does he. "Then where are we?"

"I don't know. Limbo. Purgatory."

"This isn't purgatory."

"And you know this how?"

"If this was purgatory, I'd be here with Carter Dupree."

Malcolm chokes out a laugh, but it's one laced with pain and exhaustion. My fingertips find his forehead again, and I work the tension from his brow.

"Rest," I say. "You've been talking too much."

He doesn't argue. Instead, he merely takes my hand and tucks it against his chest. Without his voice, this space feels hollow, more ominous.

And I can't help wondering if Malcolm is right.

"I DON'T SUPPOSE you have your phone?"

It's later when Malcolm asks this. How much later, I'm not sure. I've been counting his breaths and straining my ears, hoping to hear sounds of rescue.

But my phone! I twist and turn and then panic for a second when I can't find it. I paw the space around me until my hands meet something smooth and plastic.

The screen is cracked, but the phone lights the small space.

Shattered display cases surround us, their sides splintered and adorned with odd bits of torn velvet. Above our heads, two support beams are keeping debris from caving in on us. It's flimsy, at best. I try to slow my ragged breathing so it won't disturb this precarious arrangement.

I'm about to dial for help only to see there's no reception.

"I can't call," I tell Malcolm. "I can't get a signal."

"That's not why I want your phone."

"But—"

"Katy, the entire second floor caved in on us. It's a miracle we're still alive. I mean, I'm assuming we are." His voice trails off, and I will him to change the subject—for his sake, not mine. "I just wanted to see you in your wedding dress."

"My... wedding dress?" That's a change in subject, but not one I was expecting.

"It would be nice if, before I die, I could see you in your wedding dress."

"Malcolm, you're not—"

"Did you take any pictures?"

"They wouldn't let me." I'm filled with regret, and I sigh. "They were afraid I'd break down and show you before the wedding." Really, I should've taken some in the changing room mirror.

Malcolm manages a laugh before a quick intake of breath cuts it off. "Figured as much."

He continues to talk, asking me questions about the shopping trip and the fitting. When I interrupt, insisting he should save his strength, he only responds with:

"Katy, what for?"

And I can't answer, because my optimism is draining as fast as my phone battery. He's right. We *are* trapped. As much as I strain my ears, I can't hear anything to the sides or above us. No light filters through. I'm not even sure how sufficient the air supply is. I run my phone's flashlight over the crushed drywall and framework and consider that maybe we only have hours.

So I let Malcolm talk. When he tires, I tell him about the other reality, which is almost, but not quite, like our own. About William, who was Orson, but not. About a world where nearly everyone embraces sprites, and they'll even help you shop.

I don't mention his parents.

"So Orson set you up with himself?" Despite the pain in his voice, Malcolm sounds both amused and incredulous.

"I'm not even sure why he went to all the trouble. I mean, he wanted the entity, obviously. But why involve William? Why build me up like some perfect girlfriend?"

Malcolm is quiet for a moment. In the light from my phone, I can tell he's pondering something.

"Remember what the entity told you about Orson's desire?"

In my mind, I hear the echo of the entity's voice:

He wants that which he can never have.

"He wanted youth," I say.

"His *own* youth," Malcolm adds. "And, oh, look. He found a way to actually get it."

I wonder how many regrets Orson lived with, what he planned to do differently in that version of reality. From what I could tell, he was urging William to make the same mistakes, only faster. Still, something isn't adding up for me.

"I wasn't around when Orson was young."

"No." Malcolm sounds almost like himself, voice full of humor and just a bit sly. "But your mother was."

Oh? *Oh.* "Really? That's kind of creepy."

"That's one word for it. It's a guy thing. Trust me. For some men, the one who got away holds way too much power."

"Women, too," I counter. "Actually, everyone. Look at how many ghosts won't let go."

"I suspect you're right." Malcolm lifts a hand to touch my cheek. "I wouldn't be able to let go of you."

He falls silent, and I think we've been chatting far too much. I shift again and hold the phone so he can see the screen. Then I scroll through all the photos of Whiskers and Willow. I follow that with the shots from our engagement dinner at A Taste of Persia.

"You know I got them to cater the wedding," he says.

"You didn't! They have to come all the way from Minneapolis."

"Plus? I talked Springside Bakery into baking a wedding cake for us."

"The white chocolate raspberry?"

"You know it."

"But..." I trail off.

Springside Bakery has a *No Wedding Cakes* policy; there's even a sign in the window. Too much drama, the owner has always told me.

Except when it comes to Malcolm, apparently.

"You're incorrigible."

"I am," he says, his voice heavy with both humor and exhaustion. "I really am."

His eyes flutter closed. I tuck my phone away and rest my hand on his chest, counting its rise and fall until I'm breathing in tandem with him.

"I wanted to make it the perfect day for you." And now his voice is sleepy and faraway.

"You already have. I can see it all in my head, from Chief Ramsey walking me down the aisle to dancing in the community center ballroom."

"You know he called me in for a man-to-man chat after we got engaged."

"No. He didn't!"

"Sure did."

"And you're telling me this now?"

"I promised Chief I wouldn't say anything. I didn't want to embarrass him, and you're—"

"A terrible liar." I am. I really am, and when it comes to reading facial expressions, Chief Ramsey is better than most. "And where did this cozy little chat take place?"

"Over a few beers at the Last Ditch Bar and Grill."

"Did they ever fix their sign?"

"Nope. It's still the Last Itch."

Something about that is strangely reassuring.

"Chief's worried that I'm"—and here I sense Malcolm raising his hand, and I know he's drawing air quotes—"too smooth with the ladies."

"No. Tell me he didn't actually say 'smooth with the ladies.'"

"Word for word."

Malcolm's always been a flirt—but it's an equal opportunity sort of flirtation. He makes people comfortable in a way I never can. He sets them at ease, plucks the right kind of small talk from the air. I've never been jealous. Well, except for that one time with a certain so-called ghost whisperer, but that was before we were K&M the couple.

"Your flirting is good for business."

"Your coffee is better."

He pauses for so long that I suspect that he's fallen asleep. But again, he fools me. His voice is even softer now—weaker, if I'm honest with myself—and I barely catch his words.

"I love you, Katy."

My heart feels as if it's cracked wide open. "I love you, too."

Something about those words sounds so final that I keep my hand on his chest, counting each breath. He's still with me, but part of me worries that he's given up, that he's accepted what I refuse to.

We're not getting out of this alive.

WHAT I NOTICE FIRST, I can't say. Is it the icy kiss against my cheek? The slight, if persistent, buzzing in my ears? No light filters into the space, but an ethereal glow bounces before my eyes.

It's a sprite.

"How did you get in here?"

I raise my hand, and it twines between my fingers. When it does, I realize this isn't an ordinary sprite. It's the one that's attached itself to Belinda. Which means...

"Can you go tell her we're here and that we're alive?"

It circles my head, leaving sparkles in its wake. After another kiss on my cheek, it zooms upward and vanishes into the dark.

I tug out my phone, hoping for a signal. Or music. I could play music or maybe shout, assuming my throat will cooperate. I cough and hack what feels like a pound of dust from my lungs. In all of this, I've kept a hand on Malcolm's chest, gauging his breathing. Merely asleep, or has he slipped into unconsciousness? It's a question I haven't let myself ponder—too much.

Before I can shout or unlock my phone, scrabbling comes from the other side. Voices echo loud at first, but then they fade. It's as if whoever is on the other side is walking away.

"Here! We're here!" The words come out choked and clogged, and I doubt they reach beyond the darkness of our cave.

The voices return, along with creaks and groans and a clattering of something heavy hitting a tile floor.

"Belinda, no." The strained southern drawl makes me think it's Carter. "Don't. That's not something you should see."

"I'm telling you, they're alive." Her voice is sharp and no-nonsense. By the sound of it, I think she might be digging us out with her bare hands.

Somebody else says something. And while I can't make out the words, this voice contains more authority and what might be an order to halt.

Belinda lets loose a string of obscenities so fierce and so creative, I'm certain everyone on the other side is shell-shocked. Then the scrabbling and scratching pick up again, and now I'm sure she'll tear this place apart by herself.

"Katy!" Belinda's voice cracks with anguish. "Malcolm!"

"Here!" I try again, but a cough racks my chest, and no one responds.

I opt for my phone. The battery's at nine percent, but that's enough. I hit the alarm, the one that sounds like a zombie klaxon. I wince, nervous the sound might disturb the delicate balance of support beams and rubble. I'm worried that the noise will wake Malcolm, then frantic when it doesn't.

Above the din from my phone comes more voices, more scrabbling, and something that sounds—for lack of a better word—organized. All of it ferocious and determined. Heavy dust rains down, and I shield Malcolm's face so he doesn't inhale the worst of it.

My phone turns itself off, but that doesn't matter. A rush of air hits me a second before the light does. I squint, can barely hold my eyes open against the glare. Something that sounds like a half-sob, half-laugh comes from Belinda.

"Oh my God, oh my God." Belinda is full-on sobbing now. "They're alive!"

The cheer that goes up is like nothing I've ever heard—humans and ghosts celebrating together. Belinda's sprite zips in, caresses my cheek and then Malcolm's.

It's still gathering my tears when I manage a soft and heartfelt "Thank you."

I'm passed from Nigel and Prescott to Belinda—who gives me a soggy and fierce hug—to an EMT. She checks my shoulder, inspects my ribcage, asks about head wounds, and drapes a reflective blanket around me. Then I'm gripped tight, and Sadie's embrace is so ferocious it pushes the air from my lungs. It feels like a mother's embrace, like I'm her lost child, and she'll never let me go again.

It's only when Arianna joins us that the tears start.

"Oh, *ma petite*," she croons. "It's okay. You're okay."

"But Malcolm—"

"They're getting him out. I promise you."

"But—"

"I promise you."

And as if on cue, as if she commanded it herself, I hear one of the EMTs shout.

"We need a backboard over here!"

I can't help but whimper. Before she can hush me again, I blurt out, "I'm sorry, I'm so sorry. He shielded me. That's why he's so hurt. That's why he—"

"I would expect nothing less from my son." A new voice joins us, this one with a familiar lilt.

"See?" Arianna says. "If you won't listen to me, listen to Darien. Malcolm wouldn't be Malcolm if he didn't try to save you."

And now I'm shielded again, this time from the achingly slow progress of extracting Malcolm. Debris scatters across the tile. Muted voices come from the pile of rubble that somehow housed both me and Malcolm. Then, at last, the clatter of stretcher wheels against the gritty floor echoes through the mall. I step back and let Arianna rush to his side. She places a careful hand on his chest.

"Oh, my baby boy." She leans in and kisses his forehead. "You will be just fine."

I don't know how she can sound so confident. My heart pounds, but whether that's from hope that Arianna is right or fear that she's wrong, I can't say.

"Katy?"

Malcolm's voice is scratchy but steady. I slip from Sadie's embrace and the blanket and rush to his side.

"I'm here." I touch his cheek, and his skin is warm beneath my fingertips. "I'm here because of you."

He shuts his eyes for a moment. So much relief and gratitude wash across his features that it steals my breath. His hair appears prematurely gray from all the plaster dust. His jaw sports both a few days' growth and grime. But he's here. He's my Malcolm.

"See?" I tell him, my voice shaky with a repressed sob. "Not purgatory."

He can't throw his head back, and he's in too much pain for that sweet, dark-roast grin, but he manages a small laugh. "Right now, it looks like heaven to me."

One of the EMTs touches my arm. "We need to leave." Her gaze flickers toward Malcolm. "We're taking him straight to Mayo, in Rochester."

Numbly, I nod.

"You need to go to the ED as well," she says. "If you go to urgent care, they'll just send you over there."

This, I know. My legs are wobbly. While I'm no longer bleeding, my shoulder aches. The band of pain around my ribs vies for my attention. The full force of my injuries will hit soon—and hard. So I lean in and kiss Malcolm.

"I'll be right behind you," I whisper.

He closes his eyes again, the smallest of smiles on his lips. "I know," is all he says.

I watch the EMTs roll Malcolm away, both Sadie and Arianna flanking my sides. Sadie covers my shoulders again with the reflective blanket.

"Perhaps, *ma petite*," Arianna says, "you should be on that ambulance as well?"

Probably. But I have something here I must do first, no matter how much it hurts to part from Malcolm. I must do it quickly, too. The moment the adrenaline wears off, I'll be a Katy puddle on the mall floor.

Before I can do or say anything, a man steps forward. Unlike the other necromancers milling about the mall, he wears a suit, the pale linen impeccably clean. His shoes sport the thinnest layer of dust. And—unlike everyone else—he appears well-rested, showered, and smug.

He is also someone I absolutely do not want to talk to.

"Before you leave, Ms. Lindstrom," Roland Harrington-Hayes says, "can I ask what you were doing in territory belonging to the Midwest Necromancer Association?"

He's asking me this now? We all stare at him. Even the other necromancers, who have been casting their gazes toward the mall's ceiling—where a thick layer of ghosts floats—turn to follow this unexpected development.

Darien raises an eyebrow. I've been on the receiving end of that look. I know the full force of its disdain, only now it's entirely focused on Roland.

"As interim chairman of the—" Roland begins.

Prescott clears his throat—dramatically. "You're no longer interim chair. We voted earlier today."

Roland sputters. "But you can't cast a vote without the chair being present."

"You might want to review the bylaws. You received the ghost, did you not?"

"Yes, but—"

"According to the bylaws, if the chair declines to attend a gathering, the members may vote to proceed, especially if there's pressing necromancer business." Prescott sweeps an arm toward the rubble of Hillside Diamonds and then indicates the other necromancers.

Only now do I realize just how many strange necromancers are wandering around the mall. Some I recognize, but many I don't, and I assume those are from the east coast. Reginald is working to contain them, urging them away from the wings and off the escalator. But these are necromancers, after all, and it's a lot like corralling cats.

"You proceeded without me?" Outrage paints Roland's face a strange, delicate pink.

Prescott raises his hands, palms skyward. "We had a quorum."

Arianna steps forward. "And the first order of business was to investigate the inadequate performance of Troy Season Property Management in maintaining the mall, which is why I asked K&M Ghost Eradication Specialists to investigate."

She did? I open my mouth but close it again when Prescott throws me a wink.

Arianna casts a glance toward the rubble. "It's no surprise that this particular concern was connected to Orson Yates. No doubt a mere oversight on your part?"

No doubt it wasn't.

Roland peers down his nose at Arianna. "And you are?"

Really, who on earth looks down their nose at Arianna

Armand? Several nearby necromancers take a step back, eyes wide, expressions wary. Prescott's lips twitch in amusement. Darien looks almost serene, like he knows what comes next and can't wait to see it.

"I'm the chair of the Midwest Necromancer Association," Arianna says. "Perhaps you've heard of it?"

FOR THE NEXT SEVERAL MINUTES, there's a flurry of activity —human and otherworldly. The ghosts churn above our heads. They love drama, and we're giving them plenty. They dart downward only to scurry skyward whenever a necromancer tries to catch them. The ghosts remain tantalizingly out of reach. It's a prank that has the entire collection of them highly amused.

Roland canvasses group after group. Some necromancers duck and hide when he heads their way. Others remain implacable, arms folded across their chests, gazes stony, Roland's entreaties bouncing off them.

When it's clear he can't raise a quorum, Roland rounds on Arianna.

"You're nothing but a sensitive." He steps all the way into her personal space, finger inches from her nose.

Both Prem and Darien ease closer to Arianna. We have everyone's attention now; even the ghosts stop their teasing.

"Only a necromancer can chair the association," Roland adds.

"Who says I'm not?"

Roland looks as if he's about to speak—or really, shout—but then thinks better of it. His gaze roves over the assembled necromancers, but none of them contradict Arianna.

Prem steps forward. He hip-checks Roland, who stumbles backward.

"In the six years we have run Haunted Paris, Arianna's skill as a necromancer has been instrumental in the business." Prem's words are soft, with a hint of a French accent, and it's like he's telling us a bedtime story. "She can coax the most reclusive ghost from the catacombs. There are few here who could do the same." He nods toward Darien. "Present company excepted."

I hold my breath, uncertain what Darien will do or say. He doesn't smile. But then, Darien Armand isn't the sort of man who smiles at a rival—romantic or otherwise. He does incline his head in gracious acknowledgment.

"Not even I," Darien says, "have much luck coaxing ghosts from the catacombs." He pauses, and I think he's expecting us to laugh, that this is the Darien Armand version of a joke. We're all too transfixed to even breathe, so he continues, his gaze finding Arianna.

"In all the years I have known"—another pause, and for the barest second, I think he'll say *my wife*—"Arianna Armand, it's been evident that her skill could rival even my own. The only reason she did not practice necromancy is that she chose, deliberately, to raise our sons. But she is a necromancer with a great deal of business acumen. I see no reason she cannot chair the association."

"I can think of one," Roland says. "She lives in Paris. She has no connection to the region."

"Oh, nonsense. I own a house in Springside, have for nine months now."

She does? I glance around, but no one else seems surprised by this.

"It's a lovely place, green and white, in the Victorian style. Of course, I am having the interior completely redone." She touches her collarbone, her hands—and her French manicure—protected by work gloves. "You don't expect me to live in a construction zone, do you?"

The green and white Victorian? The ghost house? *Arianna* is the one who bought it? I dart a look at Nigel, but he deliberately avoids my gaze.

"After all, both my sons live in Springside. And there's always a chance for grandchildren." She beams at me, and in true Arianna style, knocks all the thoughts from my head. "Hope springs eternal."

"Nine months meets the bylaws," Prescott says, his tone wry, "if anyone is curious."

I'm not sure what I expect to happen next. Maybe for Roland to stamp his foot and vanish into the ground like Rumpelstiltskin. Or to call in a reserve of ghosts or necromancers. But he doesn't seem to have either. Still, he surveys the mall as if the cavalry is about to ride in.

I know who he's searching for, so I step forward.

"If you're looking for Orson, he's in there." I clutch the blanket with one hand and point to what's left of Hillside Diamonds. "And he's in so many pieces that no one can put him back together again."

Roland stares, his eyes brimming with horror and comprehension.

"He was filled with so many ghosts and demons and so much greed, there wasn't room for anything else." I say this not only to Roland but all the other necromancers here—as a warning. Not that any of them will listen.

They are necromancers, after all.

At last, Roland exhales. He looks smaller, somehow, and paler. He nods first to me and then to Arianna.

"I concede."

He turns then, with precision, almost a military about-face. He heads down the wing toward the main entrance. His footfalls echo, and it's a sad, lonely sound.

But when the doors scrape closed behind him, the ghosts let out a cheer.

Honestly? So do most of the necromancers.

Prem scoops up Arianna in an embrace, one so joyous her feet leave the floor. He spins her around before setting her back down. He takes her face in his hands.

"You were wonderful," he says right before he kisses her.

And that kiss is so tender, so heartfelt, that my entire being aches for Malcolm. Part of me wishes I'd left in the ambulance with him.

Arianna slips from Prem's embrace to face Darien. She places a gentle hand on his arm. "Thank you."

Her words are warm, her smile radiant. She looks decades younger. In my mind's eye, I can see them in the other reality. Again, Darien inclines his head, but there's a tenderness in his eyes I don't remember seeing before—at least, not here. He takes her hand and folds it between both of his. When he speaks, his words are soft.

"I suspect you will be magnificent in your second act."

Perhaps it's the shift in the ventilation. Something like a sigh from far away lingers in the air, two words that are as delicate as a caress:

My love.

After that, things blur, and we're standing in what might be the strangest receiving line ever. Each necromancer congratulates Arianna. No actual ring kissing, but there is much conferring, whispered suggestions, sly asides, and winks.

As they pass me—because, somehow, I'm included in all this— the necromancers nod. Most are circumspect; a few are polite, if reserved; and a couple slip me their business cards.

"They are necromancers, after all," Prescott murmurs in my ear. "Hope and avarice spring eternal."

I hand him the cards, which he takes with an inappropriate amount of glee.

Then, at last, it's just us, the Springside group, the people I love most in the world. And I need to send them all away, at least for a few minutes. I still must do that one thing before I completely collapse.

I have the horrible feeling they won't let me, that it will result in hand-wringing and objections. That band of pain around my ribcage pulses, each throb sharper than the last. I don't have the fight in me. But I can't leave Cedar Hills Mall.

Not yet.

I take a step toward the rubble that was once Hillside Diamonds, and then another. No matter how quietly I move, my sneakers crunch debris. Sadie notices first, and she's on it.

"Katy, dear, it's past time we got you to the hospital." She swallows me in a gentle hug, inching me away from the rubble and toward the mall's entrance.

With each step, my ribs sing out. A burst of agony radiates along my skull. I choke back the gasp, afraid that if I show any pain, I'll lose my chance. But part of me wants to remain in Sadie's embrace, warm and safe. So I do the only thing I can: I stand absolutely still.

"Nigel," Sadie says, her voice rising ever so slightly. "Tell her." When he remains silent, she surveys the group. "What are we waiting for? The police? I'm surprised they haven't shown up yet, but Katy's our first priority."

Oh, I suspect there's a necromancer reason for why the police haven't come roaring in. Considering how many necromancers were—and are—here, the mall may be encased in multiple containment fields. After all, the association managed not one but two retributions on my front lawn without anyone in the neighborhood noticing. When Prescott and Nigel exchange a glance, I'm positive this is the reason.

"One of us can stay to explain." Sadie's lips compress in disapproval, and I can tell she's choosing to ignore those exchanged glances. "I'll take Katy over to the hospital here in Cedar Hills. Arianna, I'm sure you'll want to drive straight through to Rochester."

The mention of Rochester galvanizes Arianna. She shakes herself, blows out a breath, and says, "Yes, of course. Of course. And perhaps Katy should come too. After all, the association's insurance will cover everything."

She falls into a discussion with Sadie about whether I'd be better off at the Mayo Clinic, or if the shorter drive to Cedar Hills would be best. Really, it's a good thing I've stopped bleeding.

But the discussion is not enough of a distraction. I'm still encased in Sadie's embrace. I need help, an ally, and no one here is listening. They're all talking around me and about me, but not actually to me. At last, my gaze lands on Darien. Of everyone here, he's the last person who might assist me. And yet, something flickers in his expression. Recognition? Comprehension? He can't possibly know about our brief connection in the other reality.

And yet.

"Help?" I mouth.

He inclines his head before striding into the center of the group. He claps his hands, once, and the sound ricochets throughout the mall. The entire group falls silent.

"Ms. Lindstrom needs a moment alone," he announces.

The group erupts, everyone protesting. Belinda's shaking her head, curls escaping her ponytail. Sadie grips me tighter, as if I'll bolt at any moment. I can't hear Arianna, but her lips form the phrase: *Absolutely not*.

"Please," I say, although my voice is lost in the cacophony of all the others. "I need to do something."

Darien clears his throat and claps his hands once again. "The ghosts will watch over her." He points, indicating the misty forms fogging the skylights. "The sooner you allow her to do this, the sooner we all can leave."

As if on command, two ghosts zip from the ceiling. They stretch themselves tall and stand at my side as if keeping a vigil. Maybe it's this, but more likely, it's Darien's insistence that everyone head for the parking lot.

It takes a moment, once I'm alone with Darien, to find my voice.

"Thank you. I know, I mean, I'm the reason Malcolm is so injured—"

Darien raises a finger. "Perhaps, Ms. Lindstrom, you are the reason he's still alive."

Maybe? Partially? I'm not sure. But I'm in no condition to argue.

"You can call me Katy," I say instead.

He arches an eyebrow. "Short for Katrina, correct?"

"Yes. Like the hurricane."

The smallest of smiles flirts on Darien's lips. His gaze travels from me to the heap that was once Hillside Diamonds.

"Something Orson Yates should have considered."

With that, he leaves, and I'm alone with nothing but the ghosts.

CHAPTER 13

The mall is far less spooky now that it's filled with any number of ghosts. The two at my side keep the curious and the mischief-makers at bay but allow a few sprites to nestle at my side. They unerringly find all the bumps and bruises and the series of what I suspect are fractures along my ribs. Their cold steals the pain and clears my head.

The storefront looks as if it has folded in on itself. It reminds me of those collapsible boxes Malcolm uses in his magic show. A fine layer of plaster reaches all the way to the courtyard and the fountain. Footprints crisscross the tile, and I wonder how long they'll last. In twenty years, will someone else come exploring and wonder what happened here?

In fact, I wonder now. How did we survive? How—and why— did the EMTs dig us out without asking any questions? How did the sprite find us in all that rubble? Part of me insists we didn't survive; we couldn't.

Not without intervention.

With caution, I step toward the remains of the main display

case and cash register. I scan the area, not with my eyes or ears, but with my mind. The air wavers ever so slightly. The threshold to the other side still exists. Even if the smallest of sprites can't slip through, I'm certain my thoughts can.

"Are you there?" I add my voice to the effort. I don't know if it will help. But I'm alone, so I might as well speak since I subvocalize anyway.

Yes, indeed you do.

I shut my eyes and let both relief and gratitude flood me. I don't know how the entity saved us, only that it did. I don't know how it's still here, only that it is.

Why wouldn't I save you? After all, you are my necromancer.

"But I broke the pact."

Let's review, shall we?

Do I have a choice?

A faraway rumble shakes the air, the sound full of humor.

Consider that you cannot break a pact that doesn't exist. Do you know my name in the other reality?

"No—"

And did we have a pact there?

"But—"

Then you merely spoke some nonsense words, which isn't all that unusual for humans.

I ignore the dig and concentrate on what the entity said about the pact. Something doesn't add up.

"If we didn't have a pact, then why did you save me?"

We have one in this reality.

It sounds smooth and assured, but something's off.

"But not *there*. You said so yourself. I couldn't invoke you. You could barely help me."

Please. I believe I put in more than a minimal effort.

"That's my point." I huff, exasperated. "You did something."

Whatever do you mean?

"You hurt yourself. You... no, we tore you again. Malcolm and I, like before with our grandparents."

You did no such thing.

"But you're injured. I can tell."

Despite the soothing chill from the sprites, my ribcage aches. It's hard to draw a full breath, and all my other bumps and bruises are competing for my attention. My heart is tender and sore in my chest, and it's all I can do not to rush out of here and insist that someone drive me to the Mayo Clinic and Malcolm.

But something else lingers beneath all that. Something ethereal and yet severe, something that—if I felt the true weight of it— would crush me.

It's what the entity is feeling right now.

Oh, my dear. If you can feel that, then there is no doubt that you are still my necromancer.

"Because we're connected?"

Indeed.

"Then I'm sorry."

There's no need to be. I will heal. In a millennium or two, it's true. But that's no time at all from my perspective.

"But you hurt yourself to save us."

Why wouldn't I? You'd do the same for any one of your friends.

"So... are we friends?"

We're much more than that. No matter what rules govern our interactions, in some ways, you will always be my necromancer.

"I will?"

I thought you would've figured it out by now.

"Figure what out?"

In the stillness, I hear a sigh that sounds both wistful and amused.

Shut your eyes for a moment.

I comply, although I'm not sure what compels me to do so.

Now, think of Springside.

The images come unbidden. The gilt letters of K&M Ghost Eradication Specialists. The scent of pancakes and maple syrup from the Pancake House mixing with freshly roasted beans from the Coffee Depot. I catch a glimpse of my house and Sadie's, her new solarium and our catio. How Malcolm and I danced at Nigel and Sadie's wedding, and then later with the ghosts in the old barn. Parties at the long-term care facility and releasing ghosts at the nature preserve.

All of it coming so fast, I can barely keep up. All of it like a soothing balm for my injuries and my soul.

"I'm thinking," I say, and my voice is soft and reverent. In its own way, the status quo in Springside is a miraculous thing.

Now understand this: You are my Springside.

I can't muster a response, never mind actually speak. I mouth some words, but at this point, I'm not even subvocalizing. A spate of tears stings my eyes. I'm filled with love and gratitude for this thing that has both tormented me and rescued me, been my nemesis and my savior.

"Thank you," I say, finally speaking the words I've been meaning to since everyone left the mall. "Thank you for saving Malcolm and me."

No, my dear, thank you. You've done far more than you can ever know.

While we've been speaking, the threshold between us has grown smaller and smaller, and I sense the entity's presence fading.

"Will we meet again?" A sob swells in my throat. I barely manage to whisper the question. Part of me doesn't want to know, and I'm filled with regret for the times I wished the entity away.

Truly, I cannot say. Still, you found me not once but twice, against all possible odds. Chances are you will again.

"Maybe when I least expect it?"

An unearthly chuckle shakes the floor beneath me.

Undoubtedly. Now, go marry your young necromancer and capture everything wondrous about being human. Until we meet again, fare thee well, my dear.

Fare ... thee ... well.

For several moments, the entity's promise and the sound of its voice reverberate through the courtyard. One last time, that soothing balm touches my lips and coats my heart.

I'm still sitting there, replaying the entity's words in my mind, when Darien Armand comes to lead me from the mall.

Only after Orson shattered into a million pieces and the threshold collapsed in on itself did William let his containment field dissolve. It evaporated like mist, its momentary sparkle like diamonds.

The rush of ghosts knocked him flat. William collapsed spread-eagle on the floor, breath leaving him with a whoosh. He stared up at the ceiling while sprites peppered him with kisses. The more mature ghosts floated around his head, muttering a litany of grievances against Orson.

They had a point. Several, actually.

"I'm sorry, guys," he said once the air had returned to his lungs. "I'm so, so sorry."

The sprites, ever-forgiving, continued to nuzzle and kiss. The other ghosts swirled about, patient and attentive. Most had been with him these past four years, even before Orson stumbled through the threshold and promised William the world.

They'd been so loyal. Him? Not so much. So perhaps they needed to hear his confession as much as he needed to speak it. Maybe even more so.

"I just wanted it all." The words had a substance of their own. He could taste their promise in the air because it was true. He *had* wanted it all: Money. Power. Respect.

The girl.

Was that the pure desire Katy had spoken of? William stared at the ceiling as if the answers were written there. Something told him there was a fundamental difference between aspiration and desire. What that was, exactly, he couldn't say.

But chasing it had led to this, to losing everything. His friends, obviously. Once little Nigel had told Darien and Arianna who had kidnapped him, well, there was no returning from that. And once the mall's security and management got involved?

He might as well start packing now.

What did he have left? Nothing? Well, nothing but his ghosts.

William pushed to his knees and braced to stand.

"Okay. Line up for a headcount."

The ghosts complied, rearranging and shuffling themselves from smallest to largest with a minimum of shenanigans. They were subdued. Then again, in the back hallway, Katy's blood was splattered across the wall, and a small pool of it had congealed on the carpet. Never mind the distinct hole in the drywall that could only have come from a bullet.

That was going to be difficult to explain—assuming he got the chance.

Focus. He took a breath. *Count your ghosts.* The thoughts steadied him. No matter what, he still had his ghosts. It was the one crucial difference between himself and Orson. He should've listened to them from the start.

"You guys were right."

They loved being right. The resulting glimmer was nothing but pleased. No hint of *we told you so*—except for the grumpy ghost who managed the cleaning crew.

The ghosts pulled themselves up straight and tall, and William mustered a smile. They always tried so hard to please him, and never cared when he failed so utterly. He ran through the count three times, going as far as pulling out the paper inventory, even though he didn't really need it.

"I'm not missing anyone, am I?"

He didn't think so, but sometimes the sprites covered for each other when one—or more—ended up distracted by something shiny. Some of them were so slight, telling them apart was nearly impossible.

"I don't want to lose any of you." He pointed toward the threshold. "I need to close that, permanently. There's no coming back if someone's on the wrong side."

The rift between this reality and Katy's would resolve eventually. He'd tended to enough of them to know that. Before Orson, William had sealed them off, worried he was losing ghosts to the other side. And after Orson?

There were ghosts to lure into traps and demons to cultivate and all the journeys back and forth. Creating a single, larger portal was the simplest way to accommodate that.

Confident he had all his ghosts, William stepped toward the threshold. But before he could raise his hands and create the first of many layers, an otherworldly voice locked him in place.

Would you allow me a moment or two, young necro-preneur?

A preternatural hush filled the space. Every last ghost sank to the floor, quivering in fear and reverence. William's heart rate tripled, and he pressed a hand against his chest. He was much too young for a heart attack, but certainly, this was what one felt like. The sweat sprouting along his brow. The pain radiating through his entire being. He tried to draw a full breath, but the air was too thick for his lungs.

I should like to say goodbye.

The request sparked something, a single thought—a hope, really. How he found the words, William couldn't say, but he managed them nevertheless.

"Is Katy—"

Alive and relatively unscathed? Why, yes, she is.

The relief that coursed through his limbs took him by surprise. Worth it, he thought. If Katy was alive, it was worth it, worth losing everything.

I'm delighted you think so. I'm rather fond of her myself. Now, if you'll allow me my privacy?

What compelled him to step back, he couldn't quite pinpoint. Granted, there was a supernatural grip on his shoulder, and an encouraging—if invisible—hand at the small of his back. The ghosts followed as if they, too, were honoring the request.

William found himself outside Hillside Diamonds, in the mall's back hallway. He stared at the closed door and then tried the knob, only to find it merely rattled in his hand.

What now?

Then he turned and caught sight of Dan McBride, director of security, heading his way.

OF ALL THE mall's upper management, William liked Dan the best, even if the director was his worst detractor. Tall and lithe, the Black man held himself with military precision—two wars, William had learned, Vietnam and Desert Storm.

No police, so perhaps Dan was here to escort him from the premises and nothing more. Around him, the ghosts faded into the walls and ceiling, most of them heading for their various tasks as if this were a perfectly normal Sunday. The few remaining sprites gathered around William's ankles until it looked like his feet were encased in fog.

"We haven't caught the perpetrator," Dan was saying. "The police have an APB out, but I'm not holding out much hope. Still, I wanted to personally congratulate you on a job well done."

Dan halted—again, with those precise steps—gripped William's shoulder and shook his hand.

"I know I doubted you, son. You and Ghostly Solutions." Dan shook his head like he still couldn't quite believe in ghosts, despite the ones misting the floor around them. "But they—and you—may have saved a boy's life today."

"I'm sorry," William began. He wasn't sure what Dan was talking about, but if he couldn't explain about Orson, at least he could apologize. "I didn't know—"

"How could you? According to the parents, the boy was lured away because the man said you were in trouble and needed help." Dan gave another shake of his head. "We tell kids to look out for stranger danger and not take candy, but pretending to be a friend or relative, in this case, your uncle, is far more common."

"My uncle?"

"Unless he's five foot five, weighs about one fifty, and is close to seventy years old, then he's not your uncle."

"No." William gave a quick shake of his head. "He's not."

"Let's talk later this week. I know I blew you off the first time you gave me your pitch." The smile on Dan's face was both friendly and self-deprecating. "I like to think I'm big enough to admit when I was wrong." He took William's hand again like they were sealing a deal. "What do you say? Let's make Cedar Hills the safest mall in America."

"Let's," William echoed, the word emerging with more strength than he felt.

After Dan had left, William sank against the wall. For a while, he merely stared at the door to Hillside Diamonds, the signage blurring before his eyes. Then he tried the knob again.

The handle still rattled beneath his fingers. Without recourse or destination, William headed down the hallway.

His feet led him to the Crystal Court. He stood in the shadows, much as Katy had done a day ago. Was that all it had been? A mere day, and nothing more? How could that be when it felt like she'd blazed a hole through his life—and his heart?

By the fountain, several children were gathered, waiting for the

Sunday Follies to start. This was a low-key performance, mostly silly antics that kept kids distracted while their parents nursed hangovers. Little Prescott had his arm around Nigel's shoulders as if to keep him close. Otherwise?

Otherwise, everything appeared as it should.

Arianna spotted him first. She raced across the courtyard and launched herself into his arms. William barely had a chance to catch her. She was all curls and tears and a cloud of Obsession.

"Thank you," she choked out between sobs. "Thank you, thank your ghosts." She tipped her chin skyward and blew several kisses to the ghosts floating there before planting one on his cheek.

Darien's steady hand landed on William's shoulder. "My friend, there are no words."

William squeezed his eyes shut. How had it come to this? His best friends in the whole world, and he'd let Orson nearly destroy that, destroy them.

"I'll make it up to you." His whispered words were low, meant only for the ghosts—and himself. "I swear I will." His gaze found Nigel again, at the fountain, hands reaching for a sprite. "Is he—?"

"Fine, just fine." Arianna gulped, swallowing back what sounded like more tears, but graced him with a watery smile. "The ghosts caught up to him before anything could happen." Arianna heaved a soggy sigh, and Darien slipped an arm around her waist. "We're going to have to have a safety talk—or ten. But no ... trauma."

"Except for you," William said.

Arianna dashed away a second round of tears. "We were think-ing." She darted a quick look toward Darien. "When the baby's born, would you be its godfather?"

William's chest constricted, and his throat seized. "Would I...?"

Darien placed his hand on William's shoulder once again. "It would be a great honor for us if you would."

William shook his head, but he wasn't declining. "No. The honor is all mine."

Arianna and Darien returned to the bench by the fountain. Only then did William draw in a sustained breath and release it with a long, shuddering exhale. One of his righthand ghosts floated a few inches above his shoulder, its presence reassuring. It was busy keeping tabs on everything, and other than the demon in Gloria Jean's and a near-abduction, this Sunday was not unlike any other.

"I still don't know what happened," he said, more to himself than the ghost.

Don't you, young necro-preneur?

A shift in the air caught William's attention. There was substance to it, the sound like a cash register, or pennies slipping into a child's porcelain bank. He glanced around the courtyard. Everyone was either watching the show or watching the children's delighted response to the sprites. Most storefronts were open or were lifting their security gates. No one was paying attention to him—or the preternatural presence that was clearly here in the mall.

Not even Darien.

Yes, well, when I want Darien Armand's attention, I know how to get it.

At that, William managed a laugh. A being this powerful? It had its choice of necromancers. Although why it had chosen him, William couldn't say.

"So, Orson?" he ventured.

Wasn't here today, didn't appear on any security footage, never interacted with little Nigel. As to why he suddenly stops visiting Cedar Hills? I leave that to you. No doubt you can conjure up an excuse.

No doubt he could.

"How do I repay you?"

You already have. And I'm meticulous when it comes to recompense.

Really? He had? How?

Not only were you instrumental in Katy's survival, but you extended the courtesy of leaving the threshold open. You'll find the rift has repaired itself, although you may wish to reinforce it from time to time. Unless you want more uninvited guests tumbling through.

No. No, he did not.

And now, I bid you adieu, young necro-preneur. As you kids might say, it's been real.

"No one actually says that anymore."

But the entity's presence had already evaporated.

William let his gaze travel the mall until it came to rest on Hillside Diamonds. The realization struck him all at once, less of a blow and more like cold water against his face. The store was his now. As were all the investments, and the wagers Orson had him place in Vegas. The mansion on Cedar Lake.

All of it.

His.

There was only one Orson Yates in this reality, after all.

Oh, sure, there was hinky stuff going on with paper companies and money laundering, and there were some back taxes to pay. But he could straighten all that out. No more haunted jewelry. No more vampire husband engagement rings—no matter how lucrative that sideline was. He'd dump everything and start anew.

Then he thought of the Starbucks IPO—and Katy's expression when he mentioned it. Okay, maybe he wouldn't dump *everything*. He'd let it ride.

For now.

The ghost at his shoulder knew to fetch Darien before William asked.

"I want you to come work for me," William said before Darien had the chance to open his mouth. "I'll match what the association is paying you plus health insurance, and you can take as much time as you need when the baby comes."

"My friend, that *is* generous, but we've spoken of this before. You simply can't afford—"

"*Couldn't* afford," William corrected. He let his gaze stray to Hillside Diamonds for the briefest of moments. "You might say I've had a windfall. I can hire on Manuel too." He clasped his hands together, the excitement building inside him. "Think of it. The three of us. We could certainly make a go of it, couldn't we?"

"You're serious."

"I am."

Relief washed across Darien's features, a heartfelt smile erasing years from his face. "I'll speak with Arianna, but I already suspect she will agree."

So did William.

"Oh, and Darien?" he said before his friend could return to the bench where Arianna was sitting. "Have you ever been to Siberia?"

"Many times."

"Lake Baikal?"

"Is a region filled with any number of powerful ghosts." Darien gave him a quizzical look. "Is there a reason, my friend, you are asking this?"

"I might have a line on something, something big. But it can wait until after the babies are born."

Darien nodded, that necromancer spark clear in his expression.

Yes, William thought, it could wait. Because now? Well, now it was time to go on rounds, reinforce the containment fields, and make sure all his ghosts were happy.

After all, he had a community to build.

EPILOGUE

Three hours ago, I was racing around the Springside Community Center gymnasium, playing tag with a group of children and sprites as part of the annual Springside Halloween party. Hours before that, at sunrise, I drove my grandmother's truck all through Springside, a jangle of thermoses at my side.

I imagine there are many things brides might do on their wedding day: a visit to a spa, the hairdresser, a makeup artist. Mani-and pedicures. Then again, most brides don't have to bribe the ghosts of Springside into behaving on their wedding day. I pulled out the one hundred percent Kona to do so.

I can only hope it works.

True, Belinda had to bodily remove me from the gym. In my defense, I was having fun. But Malcolm was due to perform a magic show. Apparently, there are rules about the groom seeing the bride before the wedding. Then, she didn't even trust me to drive, but instead frog-marched me to Arianna's.

"Ladies," she said to both Arianna and Sadie, who were hovering by the door, ready for an ambush. "I give you Bridezilla."

Now, I'm standing in a tiny side room near the community

center's ballroom. What this space was originally used for, I don't know. It certainly wasn't meant for someone as substantial as Chief Ramsey.

He braces a hand on the doorframe and ducks his head to enter. He's resplendent and terribly official in his dress uniform, but he simply stands there, immobile, more statue than police chief.

Chief doesn't emote; I seldom know what he's thinking. But now, his eyes are tender, and a genuine smile lights his face.

"You look just like your mother," he says at last.

I take that as the ultimate compliment.

Soft strains of music float in from the ballroom. Prescott and Reginald must be seating everyone by now. Our guest list expanded after the events at Cedar Hills Mall. With so many necromancers in one place?

It takes someone like Reginald or Prescott to keep them in line.

Belinda slips in with Tara and her little brother, Thomas. After much debate over whether twelve is too old for a flower girl, we discovered there was such a thing as a junior bridesmaid.

Here Tara stands, in a pink tuxedo jacket and poofy tulle skirt with pink and white cat clips secured to her braids. She's adorable, as is Thomas, in a matching pink clip-on tie. He's our quasi-ring bearer. Because really? Handing wedding bands to a three-year-old? That's like giving them to a sprite.

Belinda, of course, is stunning. Her dress is a replica of a 1920s formal gown with a slit that runs well past mid-thigh. The necromancers not here for the ghosts are definitely here for Belinda.

"You're glowing," she says to me.

I lift the bouquet, an intricate concoction of white roses and forget-me-nots. "It's the sprites."

Malcolm's prediction came true: we are having the most haunted wedding ever. So many ghosts and sprites wanted to participate that we had to give them jobs—or suffer the consequences.

Half a dozen sprites are swirling among the petals of my bouquet. The roses glimmer like ice, and the forget-me-nots are so blue, it makes my eyes sting. The sprites' plans are mist in the air that I can just taste. Who will end up with the bouquet once I toss it over my shoulder, I can't say. I only know this: Someone most certainly will.

And it's probably going to hurt.

"No." Belinda sweeps a wayward strand of hair from my forehead. "*You're* glowing. And Malcolm's beside himself. He's all fidgety, and Nigel keeps slapping him on the head."

"So... everything's normal?"

Belinda laughs, but then her face crumples. She throws her arms around me, and her hug is a fierce thing, full of memories and ghosts and hope.

"Sorry, sorry." She eases back and takes a careful swipe beneath each eye with her ring finger. "Sometimes it just hits me, how close we came to losing you both. But you're here, and you're getting married to Malcolm, and—"

I swallow a sob past the lump in my throat. "I know, I know. I feel it too."

At times, I'm back there, in the rubble of Hillside Diamonds, trapped with Malcolm with no way out. Lately, the flashes aren't as intense, and they don't come as often. But they never fail to remind me just how tenuous life sometimes is.

Chief coughs and then pulls a handkerchief from his pocket and passes it to Belinda.

The music shifts, and so does Belinda. All business now, she lines up Tara and Thomas and then hands them each a basket. Inside, rose petals churn. How the sprites residing in there have managed to behave for so long, I don't know. I suspect Arianna had something to do with it.

Chatter from the guests waiting for the ceremony cuts off. Belinda peers through the crack in the doorway.

"Darien," she whispers. "He's just walked in with Arianna.

They are *badass*. Half the necromancers look like they want to run away. Oh, and now Prescott is escorting Sadie to her seat."

My heart crashes against my rib cage, the pain of it sharp, like it's punching a hole in my chest. I clutch the bouquet tighter. The flowers tremble, and not just from the sprites.

"It's only Malcolm waiting for you," Chief says, his voice low and soothing.

Yes, of course. I nod, but the thought is both comforting and terrifying.

Belinda straightens, smooths her dress, gives Tara one last word of instruction, and then she's out the door—Springside High School's most ferocious homecoming queen. I feel sorry for the necromancers.

Almost.

Tara and Thomas start down the aisle. Halfway, Thomas decides his mother's lap is the better option. I don't blame him. If I could sit on someone's lap right now, I would.

Then it's me and Chief and the music I can barely hear because my pulse is roaring in my ears. I take his arm, and he secures my hand with his.

"Slowly," he says, and he's patient and fatherly. There's no one else in the entire world I'd rather have walk me down the aisle than this steady man at my side. "No one's starting this wedding without you."

That's both reassuring and not. In a moment, we'll step through the doorway and begin the long walk to the front of the banquet hall. With everyone staring.

At me.

Despite the noise and my panicked thoughts, an other-worldly buzzing catches my attention. It zips about my head, plants an icy kiss on my cheek. With it comes the sensation of a warm hug on a cold day. I feel as if I *am* snuggling on someone's lap.

My grandmother's.

She's here! I can't hide my delight, especially when she zooms around Chief Ramsey as well.

A frown forms on his brow. He tracks my grandmother—just barely. But he does, and his eyes light with recognition.

"Is that—? I mean, it can't be."

I shrug. When it comes to ghosts, I've learned it's best to let Chief draw his own conclusions.

My smile is still wide as we take our first steps down the aisle. I'm safe and secure with Chief next to me, my grandmother making the air around our heads glimmer, and Malcolm waiting for us—none too patiently, it seems.

His fingers drum the side of his leg—his injured one. It's a gentle tap, tap, tap, but nervous energy rolls off him. He and Nigel are wearing vintage-inspired tuxedos, complete with top hats and walking sticks.

Like the memories of that day, the ache in his leg comes fast and hard. For the moment, the walking stick leans against a chair, a contingency I hope he won't need.

Still, in the past four months, Malcolm has pushed himself so hard in physical therapy. He told me—and only me—that he regained feeling in his toes on the drive to the Mayo Clinic. I think of that last rush of soothing balm the entity sent into this reality, and I wish I could thank it all over again.

All week long, Malcolm and I have been practicing our first dance. We decided against "The Girl From Ipanema" (although now and then, I catch Malcolm whistling it). Instead, we picked a dreamy, almost haunting, rendition of "Can't Help Falling in Love." Our dance is a slow, easy thing. It's simple enough for me (so I won't mess up the steps) and gentle enough for Malcolm. He won't be pulling a Patrick Swayze and lifting me above his head.

Even so? Malcolm still has plenty of moves.

I predict that he will be "smooth with the ladies" at the reception. Also? I have it on good authority that there will be a magic show, complete with a top hat.

I wouldn't want it any other way.

My grandmother reaches Malcolm first. He lifts his chin, intent on the iridescent sparkle in front of him. After a moment, he nods, and my grandmother graces his forehead with a kiss.

It feels like a benediction.

Malcolm turns then, and when his eyes meet mine, he wavers. I'm about to break from Chief Ramsey and grab the walking stick, but Malcolm steadies himself. His smile is a slow, seductive thing that blooms into that sweet, dark-roast grin I know so well.

And then I'm there, next to him. For a second, Chief shuts his eyes, and the lines around his eyes and mouth are tight, almost like he's in pain. Then he gives Malcolm's shoulder a squeeze and kisses me on the cheek.

"Go be young," he says before linking my arm with Malcolm's.

And then we're there, standing before the judge who married Nigel and Sadie.

"I don't know why I forget," Malcolm whispers.

"Forget?" The word emerges with more air than sound. I can barely form thoughts, never mind actual sentences. Malcolm is devastating in his tuxedo. His ebony hair gleams, and the crinkles around his eyes deepen as he surveys me in my dress.

"That real life with you is always better than my imagination."

The judge clears her throat—lightly, so only we can hear. "I'm assuming you two would like to get married," she says, her tone nothing but amused.

Why, yes. Yes, we would.

My knees are wobbly, my stomach jumps, and I'm not sure how I remain upright. Except Malcolm's at my side, his hand in mine, and I can do anything when he's next to me.

The judge pronounces us husband and wife.

She instructs Malcolm to kiss the bride.

I'm only slightly shocked that she means me.

But then he does kiss me.

The cheer—human and otherworldly—tells me we've been

kissing for quite a while. The sprites release the rose petals and confetti too soon. A ghost knocks over the walking sticks, the chair they were leaning against, and one of the flower arrangements. Malcolm slips a hand around my waist and pulls me from the spray of water and damp petals just in time.

Then he spins me, and I laugh. Hand in hand, we race up the aisle. I blow kisses to all our friends, including the supernatural ones. When we reach the lobby, the ghosts—led by my grandmother—slam the doors behind us.

It's just us here in the lobby. Well, us and all the ghosts. They gather about us, nudging Malcolm even closer to me—not that he needs much encouragement. He takes me into his arms, and he is all Ivory soap and nutmeg and home.

His lips meet mine in a second, much longer kiss.

In it, I taste the promise of things to come—all the adventures we'll have, all the ghosts we'll catch, all the memories we'll make. It is both sweet and bitter but full and sustaining—because coffee and life are like that. I could live on this kiss for the rest of my days.

I'll have Malcolm for the rest of my days.

At any moment, the doors will burst open, and everyone I love will spill out. We'll stand in the receiving line, eat cake at our reception, and dance our first dance. We'll drive up to Minneapolis and make the last flight to Paris for our honeymoon.

But right now, it's just me and Malcolm, and all the ghosts of Springside. They sparkle and dance around us, and Malcolm spins me in their midst.

Right now, I have everything I could have ever wanted.

And it's more than enough.

ABOUT THE AUTHOR

Charity Tahmaseb has slung corn on the cob for Green Giant and jumped out of airplanes (but not at the same time). She spent twelve years as a Girl Scout and six in the Army; that she wore a green uniform for both may not be a coincidence. These days, she writes fiction (long and short) and works as a technical writer for a software company in St. Paul.

Her short speculative fiction has appeared in *Flash Fiction Online, Deep Magic,* and *Cicada.*

ALSO BY CHARITY TAHMASEB

YOUNG ADULT FICTION (WITH DARCY VANCE)

The Geek Girl's Guide to Cheerleading

Dating on the Dork Side

YOUNG ADULT FICTION

The Fine Art of Keeping Quiet

The Fine Art of Holding Your Breath

Now and Later: Eight Young Adult Short Stories

PARANORMAL

Coffee and Ghosts, Season 1: Must Love Ghosts

Coffee and Ghosts, Season 2: The Ghost That Got Away

Coffee and Ghosts, Season 3: Nothing but the Ghosts

Coffee and Ghosts, Season 4: The Ghosts You Left Behind

FANTASY AND FAIRY TALES

Straying from the Path, Stories from the Sour Magic Series of Fairy Tales